THE GREEN LEAVES OF SUMMER

by the same author

DEATH MAY SURPRISE US
THE LEFT-HANDED SLEEPER
MAN-EATER
THE CHURCHILL COMMANDO
THE BUCKINGHAM PALACE CONNECTION
THE LIONS OF JUDAH
THE NAKED SUN
THE MOST BEAUTIFUL GIRL IN THE WORLD
WOMAN IN A DRESSING GOWN AND OTHER PLAYS
WHATEVER HAPPENED TO TOM MIX? (Autobiography)
SPRING AT THE WINGED HORSE
A PROBLEM FOR MOTHER CHRISTMAS (for children)

THE GREEN LEAVES OF SUMMER

The Second Season of Rosie Carr

Ted Willis

MACMILLAN
LONDON

First published 1988 by
MACMILLAN LONDON LIMITED
4 Little Essex Street London WC2R 3LF
and Basingstoke

Associated companies in Auckland, Delhi, Dublin, Gaborone, Hamburg, Harare, Hong Kong, Johannesburg, Kuala Lumpur, Lagos, Manzini, Melbourne, Mexico City, Nairobi, New York, Singapore and Tokyo.

British Library Cataloguing in Publication Data

Willis, Ted
    The green leaves of summer: the second season of Rosie Carr.
    I. Title
    823'.912 [F]   PR6045.I567

    ISBN 0-333-35941-0

Typeset in Perpetua by Bookworm Typesetting, Manchester, England.
Printed in Hong Kong.

For Mike Noonan

PROLOGUE

Summer, 1918

She walked down the street in a silence that was broken only by the echoing sound of her shoes on the slabbed pavement.

All the normal voices of evening were mute now and her neighbours, standing by their doors, averted their faces as she passed, acknowledging that her grief was a solitary and private thing. The time for words and gestures would come later.

They had seen the telegraph boy ride his red Post Office bicycle into the street, watching his progress with a chill of fear. Wives and mothers with husbands and sons at the Front had waited, rigid with tension, until he had passed them by. When he swung his leg nonchalantly over the saddle and, standing on one pedal, glided to a halt at Rosie's door, they had felt the now familiar surge of relief and guilt that always came to the lucky ones at such times. There had been six other telegrams delivered to Shakespeare Street since the outbreak of the war: six telegrams in almost four years, six men killed out of the twenty-four who had marched away. This one was the seventh. Who, they wondered, will be next? When will it end?

Leaving the street and the watchful sympathetic eyes, Rosie came presently to Woodlands Park. There was sound here, the shrill happy sound of children frolicking on the grass, but she hardly heard it as she made her way towards the wooded area in the far corner and sat down on a green bench in the shadow of a plane tree.

This was her special place: it was here that she came when she needed relief from the pains of the day, when she wanted to think things through, or simply to feel the cool air, cleansed of its poisons by the friendly trees, surge into her lungs. She came to this place even in winter, when the plane trees were bare, moving through in the mornings on her way to work, and she loved its cold austerity then almost as much as the green flourish that would come later.

She looked down at the telegram from the War Office and smoothed it with her fingers. A small oblong of paper, with a few words on it. Not much to show for a man's life, to mark his passing. Not much to hand on to his children. It would not feed them or fill the empty space in her bed.

Private Thomas Thompson. Killed in action . . .

A young man went past, his arm around the waist of a pretty girl. His light happy laughter came back to her as they moved away towards the ornamental gardens. Why aren't you in uniform, thought Rosie fiercely, why should you be alive and laughing and Tommo dead!

The anger passed as quickly as it had come and her mind went back to the old days in the market in Fortune Street, when Tommo had been like that young man, only infinitely more spry and colourful. She could see him clearly in her mind, perched on a wooden box beside his market stall, wearing his wine-coloured waistcoat with the imitation gold watch-chain stretching from pocket to pocket, the purple drainpipe trousers and the shining top-hat, coaxing and cajoling the customers into buying his dubious goods.

Oh, he had been alive then, a card, a character, who could bring a chuckle to your heart with his impudence. And how the girls had loved him! Rosie smiled a little at the remembrance of the time when, quite by accident, she had discovered that Tommo kept a record of his female conquests on the wooden shafts of his barrow, cutting a notch to mark each successful seduction.

How different he had been on his last home leave! The old jauntiness had almost gone, he had aged beyond his years, and the impudence in his brown eyes had been replaced by a look of bewilderment. It was as if the trenches had sucked the juice from his nature, leaving him dry, without drive or certainty. They had grown closer together on that leave than ever before

before as she sensed his need of her and her heart opened in love and pity to this new, hesitant and sometimes child-like Tommo.

She wept now, at last, and with a strange feeling of relief, as the tears spilled down her cheeks. She let them flow unhindered, sobbing quietly.

A woman wearing the uniform of a bus conductor stopped and asked in a gentle, kindly voice: 'Are you all right, dear?'

Rosie nodded her head, unable to speak. The woman saw the telegram in her hand and recognised it immediately.

'Ah,' she said, with quiet sympathy, 'I know how it is. I had one of those. So I know how it is, dear.'

Rosie looked at the plump, generous face through a blur of tears. She tried to say something but the words were overwhelmed by a sob.

'Have you any kids?' asked the woman and as Rosie nodded again, she added: 'Well, it's them you have to think of now. Right? It's the kids you have to think of, dear. They're a comfort. You'll find that out, believe me. Here, take this. And good luck.'

The woman thrust a clean handkerchief into Rosie's hand and moved briskly away. She had disappeared from view before Rosie could call after her. She unfolded the handkerchief, which turned out to be a square of spotlessly clean rag, and dried her eyes.

The children. Eddie and Van. Thank God, they were accustomed to the absence of a man in the house, for on his two periods of home leave Tommo had appeared as a curious stranger, briefly to be enjoyed and then forgotten. In any case, Eddie at five and Van at three were too young as yet to be introduced to grief, too young to understand. Later. Later.

Now, somehow, she had to care for them alone, to make a place for them in this terrifying world. Well, she would do it! Tommo could sleep easily in his alien soil. The children would not go hungry, not so long as she had a breath in her body. And they would have their chance to make something of themselves also.

'I promise you that, Tommo. I make a sacred promise,' she whispered, hoping at first that he might hear her, then smiling wanly at this foolishness.

CHAPTER ONE

1

When Rosie opened her eyes that Monday morning she had a feeling that there was something special about this particular day but, for the moment at least, its significance eluded her.

She switched off the battered old alarm clock and waited for a few moments, trying to focus her thoughts. From the street outside there came the normal sounds of early morning: Mr Thomas's horse-drawn milk-float clip-clopping along, the distant rattle of a train, two men exchanging a greeting as they passed each other, the high-pitched yapping of a young dog.

It was going to be hot again. There was no movement of air, the thin curtain drooped before the open window like the banner of a defeated army. Already she could feel the sticky pressure of the heat on her skin provoking a listlessness which was near to exhaustion. I've got a day's work ahead of me, she thought ruefully, and I feel tired before it has started. Another day, no different from all the others, nothing special about it after all.

She sighed, indulging herself in a moment of self-pity. She had started as a drudge in a public house at the age of thirteen and now, seventeen years later, she was a drudge still. Nothing had changed, except that she had grown older. She was trapped, caught in a web of poverty, of small everyday obligations and complications, in a routine in which survival was everything and in which there was no room for anything exciting or magnificent to happen: the days long and wearisome, the nights heavy with loneliness. The dream of escape to something better, of a good life for the children, now seemed to be only a mockery.

She glanced at the clock. It was now well past five-thirty, and telling herself briskly that this was no time to be lying there feeling sorry for herself she slid quickly out of bed. Eddie had a newspaper delivery round and her first task each morning was to get him off to his work. Rosie padded down the passage in her nightgown to the back bedroom, her bare feet flapping on the worn linoleum.

She shook the boy gently by the shoulder and whispered his name so as not to wake Van, who was asleep in an adjoining bed. Always at this moment, as she stood waiting for him to respond, she felt a pang that was an odd mixture of guilt and pride. Eddie, at ten, with his corn-coloured hair, dreamy blue eyes and handsome good looks, seemed to have been pressed from the same mould as his father. His real father. There were times, as Eddie entered a room or laughed or made a sudden graceful movement of his hands, when the boy reminded her so vividly of Russell Whitby, her first lover, that she wondered if the man had come back in miniature to haunt her.

Tommo, dear Tommo, had known the truth from the beginning. But he had wanted Rosie, wanted her desperately, and marriage, giving his name to the boy, was the price he had to pay for her. And it had to be admitted that he had kept the bargain faithfully: not even in his wildest moments had he betrayed her or been less than a true father to Eddie. So the boy had grown up in the belief that the dead soldier, whose fading sepia photograph stood on the kitchen dresser, was his father and Rosie had never found the strength or, indeed, a good reason to tell him otherwise.

The blue eyes were open now and a slow smile spread across his face as he left his dreams behind and looked up at Rosie.

'Come on, son,' she said, 'time to make a move.'

It was a few minutes later, in the kitchen, when she placed a mug of hot sweet tea and two thick slices of toast spread with beef dripping before him, that she realised why this day was special. He produced a penny bar of Fry's milk chocolate and gave it to her with a shy smile.

'Happy birthday, Mum,' he said.

Rosie thumped her forehead with the palm of her hand in mock anguish. 'My birthday! I knew there was something. I shall forget my head next!' Moving round the table, she gave him a quick little hug; she was careful not to overdo it for Eddie had reached the stage when kissing and outward displays of affection embarrassed him.

When Rosie had settled to her own tea and toast, Eddie asked: 'How old are you, Mum?'

'As old as my tongue and a little older than my teeth,' said Rosie lightly.

'No, seriously.'

'Work it out for yourself. It is nineteen twenty-three now and I was born in eighteen ninety-three.'

'Thirty,' he said, after a pause for calculation.

'Thirty,' she acknowledged.

And once again the thought came to her that her life was trickling away. The years slipped by and she was no further ahead. Each day was a struggle, a struggle from which there seemed to be no respite, and no improvement. Would it still be the same when she was forty?

And then the old indomitable Rosie took hold again and she chided herself for this flow of hobbling, one-legged thoughts. She wasn't old, a woman couldn't be considered old at thirty. Eddie looked at her face and asked:

'What are you smiling for, Mum?'

'Well, son,' she said, 'it's a lot better than crying. Isn't that right?'

2

When she had seen Eddie off, Rosie took a kettle of hot water to the sink in the scullery and began to wash herself. It was a moment in the day which she always enjoyed: the freshness of the soap and water on her skin rarely failed to revive her spirits and to put her in a better mood for the day ahead.

As she reached for the towel, she saw Mr Bennett in the doorway. The Bennetts occupied the upper part of the house (with the exception of one small back room) and shared the use of the scullery and the lavatory with Rosie's family. Sharing the scullery presented few problems since Mrs Bennett only used it once a week, on Mondays, to do her washing, but the joint use of the lavatory was a constant source of irritation. The house had never been designed for two families and its original builder had seen fit to put in one lavatory only. Indeed, put *out* would have been a more accurate description, for he had built it in the back-yard and the only access was through Rosie's kitchen and out through the scullery.

There were four Bennetts, father, mother, a son and a daughter, and it often occurred to Rosie that they had been born with the loosest bowels and the weakest bladders of any family she had ever known. It seemed sometimes as if a constant stream of Bennetts was moving through her kitchen to barricade themselves one by one in the little back-yard shed. The routine had become so familiar that they never bothered to knock, simply trampling through as if of right and usually doing so at the most inconvenient times.

At any rate, here was the first of the morning's invaders, Mr Bennett, his gut bulging under the vest and moleskin trousers, a thin, home-made cigarette dangling from his lips, a copy of yesterday's *Daily Sketch* under his arm and a faintly lascivious look on his flabby unshaven face. Rosie was aware that she was still in her nightgown and that Mr Bennett's eyes were sliding over the shape of her body with keen interest. She had untied the blue ribbon which fastened the gown at her throat and tucked the ends down, the better to wash, with the result that the upper part of her firm white breasts lay open to view, and it was here that Mr Bennett's wandering eyes came to rest.

'Morning, Mrs Thompson,' he said.

'Morning, Mr Bennett,' she replied, holding the towel higher.

'Going to be another scorcher.'

'Yes.'

'Hot enough to fry an egg on the pavement.'

'Yes.'

'If only we had an egg, eh?'

His throaty chuckle was stopped in its track by a rasping cough and Rosie turned away more in disgust than pity. The coughing faded, and with a little wheezy sigh he moved past, contriving as he did so to brush lightly against her. As he reached out a hand to open the back door she checked him.

'Mr Bennett.'

'Yes?' he said, turning.

'I'd be grateful if you'd tell Mrs Bennett that it's her week to clean the lavatory and the front-door step.'

'Is it?'

'She missed last week.'

'She wasn't up to the mark,' he said.

'Well, she was up to the mark on Monday,' said Rosie sharply. 'She spent all day in the scullery doing her wash. The lavatory doesn't clean itself, you know, neither does the step. I've done them both the past two weeks.'

'I'll tell her,' said Mr Bennett. 'I'll have a word with her when I go back up.'

'I'd be obliged,' Rosie said.

3

She spent the next hour cleaning and tidying the kitchen, scullery and passage; she heated an iron on the gas-stove, dealt with a pile of clothes and then mended the hem of Van's dress. She worked briskly and cheerfully, and when all the outstanding jobs were done, she felt a sense of relief and satisfaction. She hated to fall behind with her daily tasks, it was not in her nature to leave things until the morrow. Some inner instinct told her that this was the only safe course, the only way to retain some modicum of dignity. She had seen too many people who had allowed poverty to overwhelm them, seen them lose heart and hope and allow themselves and their homes to slip into dirt and squalor.

Her next task was to raise Van, supervise her as she took a

reluctant wash in the scullery and prepare the sugared bread soaked in hot milk which made up her regular breakfast.

Watching the girl, Rosie recalled a remark that Tommo had made on his last leave. 'That's a bit of luck, Rosie,' he had said, chuckling. 'She's got your looks. Bloody good job she doesn't take after me, eh?'

But she does take after you, Tommo, thought Rosie. Not in looks, maybe, but in her nature. She has the same cheeky scallywag attitude to life, the same natural confidence. And she is forever playing a part, inventing characters for herself, writing short childish stories in which she appears as a tragic nurse, a gallant woman explorer, an actress, a duchess and in a dozen other roles. She was only eight but Miss Rowbotham, her teacher at West Green Road Primary School, had told Rosie that her daughter had a definite talent for self-expression.

Rosie smiled wryly to herself, remembering that she had not learned to read and write until she was eighteen. And, oh, what a struggle it had been to master the letters! She had been driven along, often reluctantly, by the indomitable Miss Jones of the Workers' Educational Association who refused stubbornly to allow Rosie to relax or give up. Rosie could still see the bright enthusiasm in the eyes of her teacher, still hear the sharp, dry voice:

'The letter V. Look at it, Rosie. So simple, just two strokes. Down – up! But what a beautiful sound it makes when you say it. Vee! Vee! And all the lovely words that begin with V. Violin. Violets. Vermilion. Velvet. Verdant. Vine. Vision. Oh, I think that V is the most beautiful letter in the alphabet, the loveliest letter of all!'

Her children apart, reading was now almost her only pleasure, her one escape. At night, when the house was still, she stayed up to read her library books; all the accumulated tiredness of the day seemed to vanish as she sat fingering the pages, living in her imagination, and with an incredible delight, the stories they spread before her. She was on to Dickens now and she felt a little thrill at the thought that Pip and Magwitch and Miss Havisham were waiting in the bedroom between the covers of *Great Expectations*.

And when the time came, Rosie, remembering Miss Jones's words, had called her daughter Vanessa. She had come across the name in a library book and thought it beautiful and different. Her friend, Big Bess, and the midwife, had expressed the view that Vanessa was altogether too fanciful a name for a little working-class girl but Rosie had stuck to her guns. In an odd way, it expressed her hope for the girl, the hope that her life would be beautiful and different also.

'Now, listen to me, Van,' Rosie said, opening her purse. 'Here's sixpence. When you've had your breakfast I want you to nip along to Williams's and buy a pound of sausages.' She paused. 'Van, are you listening?'

'What?'

'Don't "what" me! Listen when I'm talking to you.'

'I was listening.'

'What did I say?'

'I forget.'

Rosie sighed and repeated the instruction, adding that there would be twopence change. Van's eyes brightened at this.

'Can I buy a pennorth of cakes at Hamilton's?' she pleaded. 'Please, Mum, please.'

It was the custom of the local baker to sell his stale weekend stock off cheaply and there was always a queue of people waiting on Monday mornings to buy a pennyworth of crumbling cakes or broken biscuits.

'The twopence change is for potatoes,' said Rosie firmly. 'We're having sausage and mash for tea tonight. Take a bag with you and get the potatoes at Reilly's. Don't go to Spellman's, do you hear? His spuds are rotten.' She looked into the girl's face. 'Are you listening?'

'Yes, Mum,' said Van, looking disappointed.

'I don't know,' Rosie said, with a little smile. 'You must think I'm made of money.' She opened the purse once more and took out a penny. 'Here. Get some cakes. But listen. You get the sausages and potatoes first, do you hear?'

'Yes, Mum,' said Van, grabbing the coin.

'And bring some of the cakes home for your brother, do you understand?' Van nodded carelessly and Rosie went on: 'When you come back, put the sausages in the cupboard and the potatoes in the box by the sink. Then off to school. And after school, come straight home, don't hang about the streets. I'll be back from work by five and if you're not in the house when I get in I'll tan your backside until your nose bleeds buttermilk! Do you hear me?'

Van nodded again. This speech, with minor variations, was part of the regular morning ritual and she was used to it. Rosie shook her head. 'I don't believe you listen to a thing I say,' she said. 'It's in one ear and out the other half the time.'

Rosie leaned down and kissed the girl. 'I'll wake your gran and then I'll be off to work. Be good, love.'

Van, her chin stained with milk, reached up impulsively and hugged her mother. 'I love you, Mum,' she whispered.

'Yes, yes. I'm sure you do,' Rosie said, with a teasing smile. 'You love me so much that you don't even remember what day it is.'

'Today?' Van looked puzzled.

'Today.'

'What's today?'

'Never mind. If you don't know, I'm certainly not going to tell you.'

Van sat deep in thought as Rosie added hot water to the teapot, shook it round a little, and poured a cup of tea.

'It's your birthday!' Van shouted suddenly.

'She remembered, she remembered!' Rosie said mockingly.

'Oh, Mum, I'm sorry. I did remember yesterday, honest. But I forgot about it today.'

Van looked so crestfallen that Rosie relented. 'It's all right, darling. To tell you the truth, I forgot it myself.'

'I'll make you a present tonight. I'll write you a special story.'

'That will be nice,' said Rosie. She ruffled Van's hair in a little affectionate gesture. 'Now don't forget what I said. Be good.'

She picked up the cup of tea and went up the creaking stairs to the back room which, for the past four years, had been occupied by the only legacy Tommo had left her.

His mother.

4

The air in the little room, thick with heat and fetid with the smell of urine and sweat, almost stopped Rosie in her tracks. Wrinkling her nose, she put the tea down on a chair beside the bed, and forced the windows open. The corded sashes squealed a protest which was echoed from the bed.

'What are you doing!' rasped Gran. It was an accusation, not a question. Her voice, as harsh as a foghorn, was almost always belligerent, as though she were at war with the world.

'It stinks in here,' Rosie said crisply. Averting her eyes, she pushed the cracked chamberpot under the bed, out of sight.

'I don't want the windows open!'

'You need some air. This room is like an oven.'

'I'll catch my death!'

'You?' Rosie smiled. 'That'll be the day!'

Indeed, there were times when Rosie felt – although she was always a little ashamed of the thought – that Tommo's mother would live for ever, that even Death himself would hardly dare to challenge so formidable a figure. Gran, as she was known to family and neighbours alike, had grown more subdued as the years took their toll, but the aggression was still there in good measure. Utterly self-centred, concerned only with herself, Rosie had never known her offer more than a grudging word or sign of affection, never known her perform an act of genuine kindness. The sharp eyes, as black and hard as anthracite, glared at life with all the hostility of a caged animal.

Rosie had taken her in, partly out of desperation and partly because she was Tommo's mother and that imposed an obligation which had to be honoured. For years Gran had lived alone, moving from room to room as her landladies grew tired of her roistering, drunken ways and fierce tongue, until one winter evening she was arrested for assaulting a policeman outside The Fox, a public house in West Green Road.

She had used an empty beer bottle in the attack but fortunately, more by accident than design, the policeman had escaped with little more than a headache. However, since this was merely the latest in a long series of offences stretching back over the years, the magistrates took a serious view. It must be said that her chances were not improved by her contemptuous attitude towards the law or by her sturdy assertion that she had no personal grudge against the policeman. It was simply, she said, that she had an abiding hatred for uniforms.

They sent her to prison for twenty-eight days, adding the comment that, but for her age, she would have gone down for three months. Since Gran felt that she had been unjustly treated, and since Good Conduct was a legal and social concept which lay beyond her understanding, she made her presence felt in Holloway Prison and served the full term, without any remission. On the day of her release she was roaring drunk by noon and attempted to repeat the assault. On this occasion some neighbours restrained her just in time and Rosie was sent for.

She moved Van downstairs to share with Eddie and put the old lady into the upstairs back room. Her presence had not made Rosie's life any easier. Gran had, for example, a strong prejudice against soap and water and from time to time Rosie had to force her to the sink and stand over her while she washed.

Her capacity for drink was almost matched by an appetite so voracious that it made alarming inroads into Rosie's meagre stores. Worst of all, perhaps, she revealed a strong dislike for children in general and for Eddie and Van in particular. Whenever Rosie was absent she assumed control of the household, a role which she interpreted as a licence to nag and bully the children.

On the last occasion, when Rosie found blue pinch-marks on Van's arms, she had been forced to tell the old lady that, if it happened again, her next stop would be the workhouse. This threat effectively put an end to the physical bullying but the hatred remained, manifesting itself in more subtle ways.

The only positive contribution that Gran made, with some reluctance, was to the family budget. Her total income consisted of an old-age pension of ten shillings a week and, in her first weeks with Rosie, she had blithely spent every penny of this on drink, often running through it in a single evening to return home roaring drunk. After one violent clash with an innocent postman who had made the mistake of going to the pub in uniform, Rosie put her foot down and took possession of Gran's pension book.

She drew the money at the Post Office each Thursday, fed two shillings into Gran's gas meter, and put six shillings into her own purse as a contribution towards rent and food. The last two shillings went to the old lady, to do with as she wished. Gran resented this arrangement with typical bitterness but she had met her match in Rosie and there was nothing she could do about it. Moreover, she had come grudgingly to realise that her limbs were not as spry as in earlier days and that without Rosie's help she would be utterly lost. Few things frightened her, but one of them was the thought of ending up 'over the hill', in the workhouse. Another was Rosie's wrath.

She sipped her tea and made a grimace. 'Ugh. This tea tastes like gnat's piss.'

'Sorry about that,' Rosie said cheerfully. 'How did you sleep?'

'Sleep! With my aches and pains? What do you think? It was toss and turn, toss and turn all night.'

'I'm not surprised,' said Rosie. 'It's a wonder you didn't suffocate in here.' She fanned the air with her hands to illustrate the point.

'Much sympathy I get from you!' retorted Gran. 'You ought to have my stomach!'

'No thank you,' said Rosie.

Gran winced as though in pain and closed her eyes. Rosie, who was well used to this performance, surveyed her calmly.

'Like a rat,' muttered Gran, 'like a rat gnawing at my innards.'

'I've got to go,' said Rosie.

'No, wait!' The old woman opened her eyes in alarm and her voice crackled like burning wood. 'I got to talk to you.'

'Make it quick then.' Rosie sat on the edge of the bed.

'I want you to do something for me, gal.'

'What?'

'Will you promise?'

'I can't promise what I don't know.'

'I mean, I want you to do something for me after I've gone.'

'I don't want to hear talk like that!' said Rosie sharply.

Gran clutched Rosie's hand, her bony fingers pressing into the flesh, as if she were afraid that the younger woman would leave.

'Rosie, listen.' The dark eyes searched Rosie's face. 'I want a proper funeral, and I want you to see to it.'

'Time enough to talk about that—' Rosie began but Gran cut in fiercely:

'It'll be too bloody late when I'm dead!'

'All right,' said Rosie. 'I'll see to it.' She had never seen the old woman in this mood before; it was the first time she had spoken of death, and Rosie felt a sudden twinge of guilt. How often in the past years, in moments of desperation, had she thought how much more simple life would be if Gran were dead, if she were free of this additional burden? She touched the thin brown hand gently as if to reassure her.

'A proper funeral?' asked Gran.

'You'll have a proper funeral,' said Rosie.

'You promise?'

'I promise.'

'You swear a solemn oath?'

'Yes, yes.'

'Say it!'

'I swear a solemn oath. Now, I must get to my work. Can't afford to be sacked.' Rosie tried to rise but the old woman held her with surprising strength.

'Wait,' she said. 'I haven't told you what I want. First off, I want a private grave. I don't want to be shoved in with a load of others, like a bloody pauper. I want a place of my own to lie in. I mean, I'm going to be there a bloody long time!'

'A private grave,' said Rosie patiently. 'Anything else you want, your ladyship?'

'A nice polished oak coffin with proper handles. Old Mrs Woodward was took off in an oak coffin and it looked like a Christmas treat. I want one like that.'

'An oak coffin,' said Rosie.

'And I want to go to the cemetery in a real hearse, with two horses. Black plumes on the horses, of course. A hearse and two carriages to follow. Now, you got all that?'

'Yes, I've got it.' A private grave, an oak coffin, a hearse and two carriages, she thought. Where in the world did the old woman think the money would come from to pay for all that?

'Don't forget the black plumes on the horses,' Gran said. 'They give it a bit of class. And two carriages.'

'Two carriages? Who's going to ride in them, for heaven's sake?'

'Don't you fret yourself about that!' Gran chuckled hoarsely. 'Always find plenty of folk ready to go to a slap-up funeral.' She paused. 'Now, Rosie, there's the matter of the headstone.'

'Headstone!'

'You don't expect me to rest in an unmarked grave, do you?' said the old woman indignantly. 'I want a proper stone – a cross – with my name on it and some nice words. Think up some nice words.'

Rosie smiled and shook her head. 'Now, are you quite sure that's all you want?'

'Don't mock me, Rosie,' said Gran. 'I been thinking about it a lot lately.' She cackled at her own thoughts. 'I never made much of a show in my life, always been as poor as a three-legged pig. But I made up my mind a long time ago. When the time comes, I'm going to ride out of this street like a bleeding duchess. Horses and black plumes. Horses and black plumes!'

The old woman lay back, her mouth widening into something that was almost a smile of satisfaction. Her breathing was uneven and laboured, the skin over her cheekbones seemed to be almost transparent. Rosie tucked in the sheet and the blanket and moved quietly to the door. As she turned the handle Gran spoke again. 'You going?'

'I have to.'

'Shut the bleeding window before you go then! Just because I've made my funeral arrangements that don't mean I intend to lie here in a draught and perish of pneumonia!'

'You'll never die,' said Rosie, relieved to hear this flash of the old spirit. 'You're as tough as a copper's boot. You'll see us all out.'

'I'll have a bloody good try, gal,' said Gran. 'I'll have a bloody good try.'

Rosie could still hear the harsh, crackling laugh as she opened the front door.

CHAPTER TWO

1

It often occurred to Rosie that her life was an island surrounded by other people's laundry. As a child she had helped with the piles of washing that her Aunt May took in to supplement the family income; at The Winged Horse it had been part of her duties to wash and iron for the landlord and his lady; and now, years later, here she was working five and a half days a week in the ironing room of the Goldie Superior Hand and Steam Laundry.

Mr Morton Goldie, whose enterprise it was, catered for the middle-class folk who lived to the south of the neighbourhood. He made a speciality of the stiff white collars and cuffs (much in favour with clerks and their employers), which were steam-cleaned in a special machine he had installed for this purpose. He was excessively proud of this contraption, citing its purchase as an example of his progressive, up-to-date approach to industry.

The laundry was not exactly an industry but it was a thriving little business. Mr Goldie employed a man whose job it was to stoke the boilers and maintain the equipment: five women and girls in the washroom and five in the ironing room: a needlewoman who was charged with the task of sewing on buttons and carrying out small repairs: and two boys, who collected the soiled laundry from the customers and took it back in pristine condition on specified days.

Mr Goldie liked to boast, though not too ostentatiously, that he had never failed a customer. If pressed, he would modestly refer to a letter he had once received from Sir William Roberts, the local Member of Parliament, complimenting him on the quality and promptness of his service. Urged on by his wife, and despite his own protestations – for he liked to think of himself as a humble man – he had framed the letter and allowed it to hang on the wall of his office at the works.

Mr Goldie often remarked that his mission in life was to bring cleanliness to the world. He always said it with a smile, so that people would know he was making a joke and that he was being neither vain nor improper. He believed fervently that cleanliness was next to godliness and he busied himself not only with the cleaning of clothes but with the cleansing of minds and souls also. One of his favourite sayings was that the mind was like a room which had to be swept and scrubbed regularly so as to keep it worthy of habitation.

He was, indeed, a man of many sayings. The laundry and the ironing room were lined with hand-painted mottoes, all of his own creation, which were designed to influence his workers towards cleanliness both in thought and deed. Scarcely a week went by without a new message taking its place on the walls. Only that morning, for instance, he had tacked up his latest inspiration:

Humility is the First Rung on the Ladder of Happiness
– M. Goldie

This had joined earlier gems like:

Industry is the Mother of Fortune – M. Goldie
Wilful Waste makes Woeful Want – M. Goldie
Providence Provides for the Provident – M. Goldie
An Unclean Mind is the Devil's Workshop – M. Goldie

From time to time, Mrs Goldie urged her husband to bring these reflections before a wider public by putting them in a book, but, while admitting that the suggestion had merit, his innate modesty had kept him from taking this road to fame.

'I like to think of myself,' he had told his wife, 'I like to think of myself as a very small candle shining in the darkness of a very small corner.' He had been proud of this more or less spontaneous remark and had noted it down for future reference in the little black-covered notebook which he always carried in his waistcoat pocket.

2

At a quarter to eight on this Monday morning, refreshed by his Sabbath rest, Mr Goldie arrived at the laundry in Ernest Street and, after checking that the boilers were in full working order, took up a position just by the main gates.

It was his long-standing custom – indeed, he looked upon it as his Christian duty – to welcome the workers to their daily tasks in person. He liked to think that they were in his care, that they were all one happy family. Apart from the greeting, this practice also served to point up a useful lesson in discipline, for although the official starting-time was eight o'clock, Mr Goldie expected his employees to arrive well before this so that they could don their overalls or aprons and be ready for duty on the tick of the hour. There was, in his view, a moral principle involved, and he had once admonished Rosie when she arrived five minutes late with the words: 'You are an honest young woman, Rosie, I know that. You would not dream of stealing my money – yet you quite happily steal my time. Time is money, Rosie, time is money. You must see that.'

Rosie did not see it. It was on the tip of her tongue to remind him of the unpaid overtime the women put in but she knew that to argue with Mr Goldie was like cycling blindfold up a dead-end street and so held her peace. At the end of that particular week she discovered that Mr Goldie had pressed home his point by deducting threepence from her wages. Since she was paid fivepence-halfpenny an hour, this meant that he had more than compensated himself for the lost five minutes and she thought wryly of his little homily on the subject of theft. Still she said nothing, for jobs were hard to come by and the pound note plus a few pence that she took home each week spelled the difference between respectable poverty and utter destitution.

At the laundry Mr Goldie always wore a long, starched white coat, partly to protect the immaculate suit underneath and partly to indicate to his employees that he, too, was a worker. He was a small, rounded, springy man with a bounce that reminded Rosie of a rubber ball: he was not stout but he had just enough stomach to suggest importance and wellbeing, while his shining pink dome fringed with grey hair and his broad, constant smile added a touch of genial distinction. He had all the outward appearance of a good, benevolent man: only the sharp darting eyes, watchful as a crow's, hinted at another concealed Mr Goldie whose thoughts were some distance removed from that beaming surface.

He checked in the early arrivals, giving them a cheerful good morning, occasionally asking after the health and welfare of their families. Then, promptly at five minutes to eight o'clock, the gold hunter watch which he wore under the white overall appeared in his hand and his greetings, although accompanied invariably by a smile, took on a sharper edge.

'Morning, Mr Goldie.'

'Good morning, Amy. We shall have to hurry, won't we?'

'Sorry, sir. Clock was slow.'

He tapped the watch with his finger. 'This is never wrong. We must look to it, Amy, we must look to it.'

Amy, a mild, tired-looking woman with greying hair and a face that had been steamed pink by her years in the laundry, gave a little frightened bob in Mr Goldie's direction and hurried inside.

Dora, a young girl still in her teens, was the next to receive his critical attention. Mr Goldie was not quite certain of Dora for she wore her hair in a fashionable bob cut and her skirt barely covered her knees. The legs that were thus revealed were shapely enough to arouse thoughts of a distracting nature in his mind. There had been a time when he had contemplated dismissing Dora on the grounds that she was rather flighty and tended to lower the tone of what was essentially a respectable establishment, but he had turned away from the idea as being un-Christian. It was, he argued, his duty to reach young people like Dora and do his utmost to improve their moral outlook.

'Good morning, Dora.'

'Morning, Mr Goldie,' she said cheerily and would have moved on but that he checked her.

'Dora!'

'What's up? Not late, am I?' She smiled easily at him, with none of the fear that had shown itself in Amy's eyes.

She was wearing a thin, low-cut dress and it took an effort of will on Mr Goldie's part to lift his eyes away from the inviting channel that separated her firm young breasts. Sternly he said:

'It is two minutes before eight, Dora.'

'Is it now? I'd better get a wiggle on then, eh?'

And before he could say more, she smiled again, and went in. He watched the flashing legs and the neat, rounded bottom disappear with pursed lips. Dora really was becoming too familiar, he would have to check her impudence. He decided to speak to her later, in private.

As it happened, he was able to vent a little of his irritation on Rosie, who arrived at three minutes past the hour, her face reddened by the effort of running. She pulled up short when she saw Mr Goldie.

'Good *afternoon*, Rosie,' he said with a frosty smile.

'Sorry, Mr Goldie,' she said breathlessly. 'I'm sorry.'

'What is the excuse this time?'

'It's Gran. My husband's mother. She's poorly.'

He shook his head. 'My wife is in poor health. She is not well, not well at all. I have to do a great deal for her. Yet, as you see, I manage to get here. I am not late.'

'No, Mr Goldie.' Rosie was tempted to point out that Mrs Goldie had a maid-of-all-work to look after her and the house, that there was no basis on which it was possible to compare the circumstances of the two women; as usual, she held the words back and stood silent before him.

'Nothing more to say?' he asked.

'I am sorry.'

'Apologies, apologies. Apologies come cheap,' he tutted. 'I

look to you to set an example to the others, you know that.' He took out his notebook and she knew that he was going to dock her wages again. He made a careful note, put the book away, and sighed. 'I know you have problems, Rosie, I am quite aware of that. We all have problems. But bad timekeeping is a bad habit and bad habits are catching. They spread, like disease. If I allow you to get away with it, the other women will see it as a sign of weakness. Do you get my drift?'

'Yes, Mr Goldie.' She lowered her eyes, twisting the plain gold ring on her finger. A fine start to my birthday, she thought wryly.

'You are a good worker, I have never denied that and never will. But we are none of us indispensable, Rosie. Remember that. I have a dozen women come here every week, strong able women, seeking employment. Do you get my drift?'

'Yes, Mr Goldie.'

'Capital. Then we understand one another. Now, off you go to your work.'

Fear prickled Rosie's skin as she hurried to the ironing room. It was the first time that the threat of dismissal had been put so explicitly: to lose her job now would be disastrous. Hard on the heels of fear came shame – shame that circumstances had forced her to stand in silence like a frightened schoolgirl and listen to his hypocritical admonitions. And then came anger. She felt a surging sense of injustice that some people should have so much power over the lives of others.

3

As the morning wore on, the heat in the ironing room grew to tropical proportions. There was no movement of air, for Mr Goldie forbade the opening of doors or windows on the grounds that this would waste the heat generated by the six gas-rings on which the irons were warmed.

Heat surged upwards from these flaming rings: steam hissed into sweating faces as the hot irons slid across the dampened clothes, and gushed into the atmosphere from between the long pads of the press that was used for heavier garments, like suits or skirts. And all the time the sun hammered at the windows, mocking them with more and more heat, so that as the women worked the patches of sweat on their clothes joined together to form a single uniform greasy clamminess. The heavy air lay on their skins like a coarse blanket, gritting their throats, making breathing an effort, and halting the usual flow of gossip and conversation.

Rosie began to feel as if the midday break would never come, as if time itself had abandoned them. She was concerned about Amy in particular, who seemed to be on the point of collapse, and watched her anxiously. They were all exhausted, but Amy looked as if the heat had sucked all the energy from her body. Her eyes were dull and lifeless, wisps of lank hair hung over her neck and forehead, and even the normally pink face had assumed a greyish pallor.

'Why don't you sit down for a few minutes, girl?' asked Rosie. Every woman in the laundry, no matter what her age, was referred to as 'girl'.

'I can't,' said Amy. 'I'm behindhand as it is.'

'We'll all do a bit for you,' said Rosie. 'Help you catch up.'

'No, ta. I'll be all right. I'll manage.'

A tin basin, filled with the water they used to dampen down the clothes before ironing, stood beside each woman. Rosie noticed that Amy's basin was almost empty and picked it up. 'I'll get you a fill-up at any rate,' she said.

She crossed to the old chipped sink in the far corner, filled the basin, and soaked a piece of clean rag in the lukewarm water. Sighing with relief she ran the wet rag over her face and neck; then she squeezed the rag dry, soaked it once more and turned to go back to the bench.

It was as she turned that she heard the crash of an iron on the stone floor and a scream of pain. She ran forward, the water slapping in the basin, to find Amy on her knees by the gas-rings, clutching her left arm. Work stopped at once and they half-carried the sobbing, frightened woman to a chair by the sink, soothing her with words, bathing her skin with water.

Burns were a common occurrence in the laundry. It was all too easy in the rush of work to brush a hand or an arm against a hot iron or momentarily to forget to use the padded iron-holder. It seemed that Amy had staggered as she went to the gas-ring to change her irons and had half-fallen on to the flame. A livid burn marked the thin arm, stretching almost from wrist to elbow. Rosie was binding it with strips of wet cloth when Mr Goldie came in. He made sympathetic clucking noises and shook his head as Rosie explained what had happened.

'She ought to see a doctor,' Rosie added.

'No, no,' said Amy. 'I don't want a doctor. I'll be all right.'

What you really mean is that you can't afford a doctor, thought Rosie. Aloud, she said: 'At least, you ought to go home and rest, Amy. You've had a nasty shock.' For Mr Goldie's benefit she went on: 'I'm not surprised. It's a wonder we haven't all keeled over with the heat.'

He answered this boldness with a bleak smile. 'Well,' he said, 'it's almost time for your luncheon break now. I suggest that you take Amy out in the yard. The fresh air will do her good and we can see how she feels when it's time to start up again. How does that strike you, Amy?'

'Thank you, sir,' she said.

He nodded and looked at his watch, 'It's only twelve twenty-five,' he said. 'Still, we won't worry about that today, eh?' He put a silver whistle to his lips, blew on it three times to signal the end of the morning shift, and moved out.

'Don't forget to close the door behind you, ladies,' he said.

4

Mr Goldie always referred to the period between twelve-thirty and one-fifteen p.m. as the luncheon break or as the lunch hour but to Rosie and the others it was, quite simply, their dinner time. Breakfast, dinner and tea was the daily order of their meals with a bite for supper if they were lucky.

Rosie was relieved that she had left bloater-paste sandwiches and some apples at home for Gran and the children and that on this day, at least, she would not have to go home and look to their needs. The sandwiches and the stale cakes would keep them going until teatime when they would have their high tea of sausage and mashed potatoes.

She took the tin in which she had brought a sandwich and an apple for herself and went out into the yard to join the others. As she eased herself down beside Amy on one of the laundry baskets she kicked off her shoes. 'Swelp me Bob, that's a treat! First time I've been off my feet since early this morning.' She turned to Amy. 'How do you feel, love?'

'Not so bad,' Amy replied.

'You ought to go home.'

'No, Rosie. Lucky it was my left arm. I can still work. I'll stick it out.'

Rosie did not press the point for she knew that Amy could not afford to lose a half-day's pay and that she was afraid to show any sign of weakness lest Mr Goldie should pronounce her unfit and put her off. We're all caught in it, she thought ruefully, we're all caught in the same bloody trap!

They were sitting in the shade of a side wall and, after the heat of the ironing room, the air seemed fresh and cool. By degrees, their spirits revived, their tongues fell into the old familiar rhythms. Her meal finished, Rosie sat back and allowed a sweet drowsiness to pervade her body: she closed her eyes and only half-listened to the banter of the others.

Nell, a sturdy, big-breasted woman with muscles that would have done credit to a coal-heaver, gave Dora a nudge that almost knocked her off the basket and said: 'Who was that young fella I saw you with on Saturday?'

'Careful, you silly cow,' said Dora, easing herself back on to the basket, 'careful. You nearly made me drop my sandwiches!'

'Never mind about dropping your sandwiches,' Nell said, with a cackling laugh. 'Did you drop your drawers on Saturday, that's what we want to know.'

'We're not all like you,' said Dora primly.

'Give over, Nell,' murmured Rosie, 'give over.'

'I was only asking.'

'If you must know,' said Dora, 'that young fella, as you call him, was a friend. He took me to the pictures. We saw *The Four Horsemen of the Apocalypse*.'

Talk of Rudolph Valentino and John Barrymore, of Douglas Fairbanks and Mary Pickford and of their respective merits drifted towards Rosie in a murmur of voices which gradually sounded more distant as she leaned her head against the wall and gave herself up to sleep. She had worked such long hours all her life that this habit of catnapping came naturally to her: two or three minutes of sleep, of complete relaxation, snatched at odd intervals, hardly ever failed to refresh her.

She was aroused by the sound of singing. Nell was leading the girls in a parody of 'After the Ball', her lusty mannish voice rising above the others. Rosie smiled and wondered vaguely what Mr Rudolph Valentino would think of the irreverent words:

> After the film was over
> Rudolph took out his glass eye
> He put his false teeth in water
> And wrapped up his bottle of dye.
> He put his cork leg in the corner
> His wig in his walnut bur-eau,
> And all that was left went to bye-byes
> After the show.

A patter of clapping followed and they swung round to see Mr Goldie beaming at them. Beside him stood Nick, one of the delivery boys, holding a tin tray on which there were about a dozen ice-cream cornets.

'First rate, ladies. A1 at Lloyd's,' said Mr Goldie, advancing upon them. 'You should take that voice to Italy, Nell, and have it trained. At all events, she should take it somewhere, eh, ladies?'

They laughed dutifully. 'Now, let's see what we have here,'

he continued. 'Hand them round, boy. A little cooling refreshment, compliments of the management. They are melting in the heat, ladies, melting fast – so eat them quickly, eh?'

He smiled benevolently as the cornets were handed round to a chorus of thanks. Not for the first time, Rosie thought what an odd mixture this man was: he would make them work in stifling conditions behind closed doors and windows to conserve heat, he would dock them a half-hour's pay if they were a few minutes late, and yet he was continually springing these little surprises upon them. Sometimes it would take the form of cakes, sometimes – in the winter – he would bring them an offering of little bags filled with humbugs or brandy balls. The gesture clearly gave him pleasure for there he stood, smiling paternally upon them as a father might when he had brought gifts to his delighted family.

The interlude lasted as long as the ice-cream cornets. Rosie had scarcely swallowed the last tiny piece of cone when Mr Goldie said: 'Come along, ladies. All good things must come to an end. Back to work, back to work!'

And, to emphasise the point, he blew three blasts on his silver whistle.

5

Although the sun, moving westwards, relaxed its grip on the windows, it seemed to Rosie that the atmosphere in the ironing room was more oppressive than ever. The irons grew heavier by the minute, the piles of clothes before her seemed to grow rather than diminish and, what was unusual for her, an odd listlessness took possession of her limbs. It was a condition that affected all the women: once again, except for the odd word or two, and the occasional flash of irritation, they lapsed into a weary silence.

Amy, her face tight and grey with pain, struggled to carry on but she came near to fainting and Rosie intervened firmly.

'That's enough, Amy. Enough's enough. Off you go. It's home for you.'

'I can't, Rosie, I can't.'

'Yes, you can. I'll explain to old Goldilocks. And don't worry about your money. Leave that to me.'

She led Amy to the gates and watched her on her way, then as she turned to go back to the ironing room she saw Mr Goldie coming towards her.

'What's going on, Rosie?' he asked.

'It's Amy. She almost passed out just now. I've sent her home.'

'You sent her home?'

'I told you. She almost passed out.'

'Hmph. I'm not saying you did wrong, Rosie, I'm not saying you did wrong. But I like to be asked about these things.'

'I was going to tell you.' Rosie paused and, surprised at her own boldness, she went on: 'And I was going to ask you about Amy's money.'

'Money?' The eyebrows went up a little.

'I mean – well – you know how she's fixed. She can't afford to lose a half-day's pay.'

'I see. And you think I should pay her for work that isn't done, you believe that I should be penalised for her carelessness?'

'She wasn't careless!' said Rosie sharply. 'She was worn out like everyone else. It's worse than an oven in there. They're all about ready to drop.' And then, seeing the cold glitter in his eyes, she dropped her tone and continued: 'Honestly, Mr Goldie. I've never known it so bad.'

'I see,' he said, 'I see. It is too much for you, is it?'

'I didn't say that,' she said hastily.

'Perhaps you'd like to follow Amy and go home?'

'No. Really. I only meant—'

'In that case, perhaps you'd be so good as to go back to your bench.'

'Yes, Mr Goldie.'

As she moved off, he checked her. 'One further thing, Rosie. I shall see to it that Amy doesn't go short. If she turns up for work in the morning she will receive her full money at the end of the week, including payment for this afternoon's absence.'

'I'm sure she'll be very grateful.'

'I do not seek gratitude. But I would add that I do not need you or anyone else to tell me my duty in these matters. Do you get my drift?'

'Yes, Mr Goldie. I'm sorry.'

At that moment the door to the ramshackle women's lavatory opened and Dora came out, a half-smoked cigarette between her lips. She flushed at the sight of Mr Goldie, dropped the cigarette behind her and made a clumsy effort to stamp it out.

'Dora!' said Mr Goldie.

'Yes?' she answered guiltily.

'Kindly go to my office and wait there for me. As for you, Rosie, back to work. And be so kind as to tell the others that I shall expect Amy's work to be done before they leave this evening. You can share it out among yourselves.'

'Amy's work?' said Rosie in shocked surprise.

'Of course. I have a business to run. I have customers to serve. We all depend on their goodwill, Rosie. Remember that. Now, off you go.'

6

Mr Goldie closed the office door carefully, glanced at Dora, and went to his chair behind the desk, then, without saying a word, started to check some papers.

'Please, sir—' Dora began.

'One moment.' He made a mental note of the fact that she had called him 'sir', that her tone was less impudent than it had been earlier in the day, and allowed himself a little satisfied smile. At the same time he was conscious of her standing there before him, the flimsy dress moulding her young body, and felt an absurd quiver of excitement stir in his blood.

When he put his pen down and looked up, his face was stern.

'Well, Dora, what are we to do with you, eh?'

'Sir?'

'Let us just run through the catalogue, shall we? The catalogue of your shortcomings. First, your lack of punctuality.'

'Sir?' She looked at him blankly.

'You were late again this morning.'

'I was here just before eight.'

'Dora, Dora,' he said sadly. His eyes caught the thrust of her nipples and he looked quickly up into her face. 'You know the rule. I expect everyone to be here by five minutes to eight at least. Others manage it, I manage it. Why can't you?'

'It won't happen again, I promise.'

'We shall see, we shall see. Perhaps you may not have the opportunity.'

'Please, Mr Goldie—' she began fearfully.

'Wait.' He held up his hand. 'Let us continue. There is then the matter of the quality of your work. I checked some of it this morning, Dora, and I am sorry to say that it is not good. It does not come up to our usual standards. *Slipshod* is the word that comes to mind. Slipshod. Do you get my drift?'

'Yes, Mr Goldie. I'm sorry. I will try to do better.' Tears trembled in the wide china-blue eyes.

'Again, we shall have to see, won't we? I am not a bad employer, am I, Dora? Would you say I was a bad employer?'

'No, sir. You are very kind.'

'Well, I am glad you think so. But it can hardly be said that you repay like with like.'

'Sir?'

The afternoon sun reached through the tiny window at this moment and in its brightness the girl's dress appeared to be translucent: he could see the outline of her body beneath the material, the clear shape of her knickers under the skirt. He felt a trembling in his leg, a hardening in his loins, and gripped a ruler with both hands as if it were a lifeline. His voice was husky as he continued:

'You know how I feel about smoking. It is an evil habit. I have made the point often enough. What you do in your own time is no concern of mine. But you have deliberately flouted one of our cardinal rules.'

She stood in silence, her lips quivering.

'Well, there is the catalogue. Unpunctuality, shoddy workmanship, smoking on the premises.' He paused and ran the tip of his tongue over his upper lip. 'So. I have been forced to a certain unhappy conclusion.'

'Sir?'

'I have been forced – by your conduct – I have been forced to conclude that you no longer wish to work here.'

'Oh, but I do, sir, I do.' The tears came freely now. 'Please. I will do better. Please. My mum will murder me if I go home and say I've been sacked.'

'Now, now. No tears, if you please. Tears will not impress me, Dora.' He started to rise, to go round to her, but checked the impulse. An inner voice warned him sternly that he should dismiss the girl at once, get her out of the office.

Instead, he heard himself saying: 'How old are you, Dora?'

'Eighteen, sir,' she said tearfully.

'I have a daughter of seventeen,' he said. 'Did you know that?'

'Yes, sir.'

'I discovered that she had been smoking in secret. Do you know what I did, Dora?'

'No, sir.'

'I punished her. Old as she is, I put her across my knee and gave her a good spanking.'

The girl looked at him as if she did not understand but the intensity of his stare and the faint edge of excitement in his voice alerted her own senses and she edged away. He plunged on recklessly, caught up in his fantasy. 'Does your father spank you when you misbehave, Dora?'

'No.'

'Perhaps that is what's wrong. You lack discipline.' He tapped the palm of his left hand with the ruler and her eyes followed the movement with a sort of bewildered fascination. He continued: 'My father always maintained that the best way to drive bad thoughts out of a child's head was to start at the bottom. He spanked us regularly until we were well into our teens. It did us no harm. I believe it did us good.' He paused and almost whispered his next words. 'Do you think a spanking might help you, Dora?'

The question hung in the air between them for a full ten seconds.

'Well?' he asked.

'I don't know, sir.' Her voice was almost inaudible, her eyes were fixed on the swing of the ruler.

'It does present an alternative, you see. I wish to help you. I like you, Dora, I look upon you as a daughter. I could dismiss you and that would be the end of the matter. But that really wouldn't do you any good, would it?'

'No, sir. Please, sir.'

'On the other hand, we could try what – what a little fatherly discipline would do. It would have to be with your full consent of course.'

'I don't understand, sir,' she said, more to gain time than anything, for in truth she had now grasped the direction in which this extraordinary interview was leading her.

'Let me put it this way, then. I cannot forget your various misdemeanours, nor can I allow them to continue. On the other hand, you do not wish to lose your position here. So – we have a dilemma. There seems to be only one way in which we can resolve the situation to the satisfaction of both parties. Do you get my drift?'

'I think so.'

'Capital. So if you will agree – freely and of your own free will – to accept a proper punishment – a punishment that is for your own good, let me emphasise that – then we shall see an end to the matter.'

'You want to – to give me a hiding?' She could not bring herself to use his words.

'Not a hiding, Dora. No, no. Nothing so strong as that. And I don't want to. It's the last thing on my mind. I feel simply that it would help you to understand the need for greater self-discipline.'

'I don't know,' she said, shifting nervously.

'No one need know, Dora,' he said urgently. 'It will be better for your sake if they do not.' He dropped the ruler, stood up and moved to the door, where he slid home the bolt. He took off the white coat and hung it on a hook beside the door and as he did so she saw that his hand was trembling, that he was breathing quickly, nervously.

'You see?' he said. 'We shall not be disturbed. And it will only take a few moments.' He closed in on her and she felt a strangely cold hand on her arm. 'Come, Dora!' he continued more sternly. 'It is for your own good. If you will accept your punishment in the right spirit, then we shall be able to wipe the slate clean of your misdemeanours.'

Still she stood there in silence, bewilderment and fear in her eyes, and when he attempted to draw her forward to the desk she stood her ground. His voice took on a more persuasive tone.

'Just imagine that I am your father. You have been a naughty girl and like any reasonable father I must teach you the error of your ways. I shall put you across my knee and give you a spanking. Not severe – just sufficient to persuade you to behave better in future.'

Releasing her arm, he went back to his chair and swung it round away from the desk; then he sat down and patted his knee.

'I am ready, Dora.'

The girl took a step towards him, moving as though in a trance. At that moment, a hand rattled the handle of the door, to be followed immediately by a knock. Mr Goldie jumped up and, for the first time since she had known him, Dora saw fear in his eyes.

'Who is it?' he called.

'It's me – Rosie.'

'One moment.' He lowered his voice and sent a hissed whisper in the direction of the girl. 'Not a word of our conversation! You understand? It is a private matter between us. You get my drift?'

She nodded dumbly. He studied her face for a second as if

looking for reassurance, pulled at the lapels of his coat and opened the door. 'That will be all, Dora,' he said in a loud deliberate voice. 'Just remember what I have told you.'

Rosie stepped aside as Dora brushed past, surprised by the quick, half-ashamed, half-frightened look that the girl threw in her direction, and, as she moved into the office, she noted the film of perspiration on Mr Goldie's forehead and an unusual gleam – was it apprehension? – in his eyes.

'What is it?' he asked sharply.

'It's about the work, Mr Goldie.'

'Well?'

'They've just sent six more baskets over from the laundry room. Sheets, towels, nightshirts and other stuff for the Oakwood Hospital. We were told that it had to be done for today – before we finish.'

'That is correct. I promised the hospital that it would be delivered first thing tomorrow morning.'

'You expect us to do Amy's work and all that extra before we go home? It will take two hours at least.'

'Two hours?' Mr Goldie seemed to have recovered some of his confidence as the familiar note of deprecation entered his voice. 'Surely you exaggerate, Rosie? I do not wish to be unreasonable but I am sure that if you ladies put your backs into it you will be able to clear that little lot in no time. An hour at the most, an hour should see you clear.'

'They're all dead beat, Mr Goldie. The conditions in there are terrible.'

'I realise that things are not all they might be. But it is hardly my fault that we have been afflicted by a heatwave.'

'It can't be done, Mr Goldie. You're asking too much. I don't think you realise—'

'I realise only too well,' he interrupted sharply. 'This is the second time today that you have taken it upon yourself to intervene in my affairs. First you send Amy home without consulting me. And now you try to tell me what can and can't be done in my own business. I am a patient man, Rosie – too patient, perhaps – but you are beginning to try me. Now, let us have an end of this. Go back to your work. And tell the others that I want the hospital order finished before they leave.'

Rosie took a deep breath. 'The girls feel—' she began.

He interrupted her again. 'The girls?'

'Yes.'

'Am I to understand that you have talked this matter over?'

'Yes. And we all feel—'

'I see. So. I have a revolt on my hands, is that it?'

'No, Mr Goldie. But we don't think it's fair. Last week we did six hours' overtime without pay. And now—'

'Ah,' he said coldly. 'Now we are getting to the bone of it. It's money, is it? You are not satisfied with the wages I pay.'

The tiredness, the suppressed anger, the sheer injustice of it all, now combined to lend Rosie a new boldness. Instinctively she realised that she had gone too far already, but she knew also that retreat would be too shameful to bear, and she pressed on, her voice rising a little. 'You're quick enough to dock our wages if we're late. But you keep us late and we get nothing for it. Do you think that's fair – do you?'

There was a long, heavy silence. Mr Goldie looked as shocked and as sorrowful as if he had just been accused of taking money from the offertory box in church. When he responded at last it was in a hushed, hurt voice.

'I never thought, I never thought that I should live to see the day when one of my employees addressed me in that fashion. I could say that I am shocked. But that is nothing compared to my disappointment. I give you employment, I struggle and work to keep the business going only because of my sense of responsibility to you all. I strive to treat you fairly, I look upon you as a family – and all this is thrown in my face. It is heart-breaking, heart-breaking.'

'I'm sorry,' said Rosie firmly, 'but that's how it is. The girls can't put in any more time today; it's beyond them.' She felt her mind clench like a fist as she continued with greater boldness: 'And in future they will want paying for overtime.'

A vein began to throb in Mr Goldie's forehead. Defiance of this sort, from any quarter, was beyond his experience, and his emotional equilibrium had already been shattered once that afternoon. He felt a scream of anger surging to his throat and it took an effort of will to translate it into a long sigh which was expressive of ingratitude.

He opened a drawer, took out a tin cash-box, meticulously counted out three shillings and ninepence and banged the coins down on the desk in front of Rosie.

'One day's pay. Rather more, in fact, since you were late this morning and will be leaving earlier this afternoon. Take it, if you please, and remove yourself from these premises immediately.'

'It will be a pleasure!' said Rosie, scooping up the money. She threw a penny back at him. 'There. That's for the bloody ice-cream you bought me. I wouldn't want to be beholden to you for anything.'

It wasn't until Rosie was halfway to Shakespeare Street that the full realisation of what she had done came home to her. The other women in the laundry room as well as the ironing room had wanted to walk out with her but she had persuaded them otherwise.

'Jobs don't grow on trees, girls,' she had told them. 'No sense in you all getting the sack – old Goldilocks can pick up fifty new hands tomorrow.'

And it was true. She would not find it easy to get other work. Yet, oddly enough, along with the apprehension she felt a sense of release. She had been telling herself to make a change and now circumstances had combined to force her to do just that. Maybe this year would be better after all! And now, in spite of everything, there grew and swelled inside her the excited feeling that her life was about to bound forward, that the days of waiting were over.

With this thought in mind, and remembering again that it was her birthday, she stopped at Pender's sweetshop on the corner of Susan Road and, with reckless abandon, treated herself to a glass of their home-made lemonade and a pennyworth of home-made treacle toffee.

She would have been surprised to know that, as she sipped the lemonade, Mr Goldie was on his knees in the bolted office, murmuring an urgent prayer. Rosie's name was not mentioned in the supplication, for he had dismissed her from his mind; but he had now realised, with a sense of fear and guilt that made him sweat and tremble, the enormity of the danger in which he had placed himself with Dora, and he was begging the Almighty to forgive him and to purge his errant flesh of these sinful manifestations.

CHAPTER THREE

1

'Is The Missus around?' asked Rosie and then corrected herself hastily. 'Mrs Quorn, I mean.'

The barman, a small man with a wispy moustache and watery blue eyes, was a stranger to her, which was not surprising, for it was ten years since she had worked at The Winged Horse and in that interval her visits to the pub and to her old haunts in the Fortune Street market had become much less frequent. The barman removed the drooping stub of a hand-rolled cigarette from between his lips and looked at her without interest.

'Who wants to see her?'

'Tell her Rosie. Rosie Thompson. Rosie Carr as was.'

'What do you want?'

'To see The Missus.'

'What about?'

'Look——' Rosie began, but he interrupted her.

'If it's work you're looking for, there's none here, I can tell you that.' The barman struck a match and held the flame so close to the cigarette that it burned the tip of his beaky nose and he shook it out in irritation. When he looked up, he seemed surprised to find that Rosie was still there.

'I told you, no use hanging around here,' he said sharply.

'If it's all the same to you, I've come to see Mrs Quorn,' said Rosie with equal asperity. 'Tell her it's an old friend.' To describe her relationship with The Missus as one of friendship was rather gilding the lily but in the circumstances she felt the exaggeration to be justified. At any rate, it did the trick, for the barman's attitude changed in some slight degree and with a surly, complaining note in his voice he said: 'I'll see if she's in.'

He shuffled off, moving through a glass-panelled door at the side. Rosie relaxed now and looked around at the saloon bar, her mind echoing with memories. It was here, at the age of thirteen, that she had first met the formidable Mrs Quorn, known to her customers and staff as The Missus; it was here that she had cleaned and polished and, as she grew older, served behind the bar; it was here that the late Mr Softley had encouraged her to play the piano and here, when The Missus had rebuked her for wasting time and reminded her that she was just a skivvy, that Mr Softley had consoled her with words she had never forgotten.

'Listen to me, little Rosie,' he had said. 'You may be a skivvy, but you are also a human being. A person. You won't always be a skivvy, that will pass, but you will always be a person. You have intelligence and wit and a big, big heart. And beauty too – soon you will be a beautiful woman. With that sort of equipment, you can make yourself a good life, a fine life. Have faith in yourself, Rosie, believe in yourself.'

She had wept as he spoke and she was near to tears now as she remembered. God, she thought, how disappointed he would be if he could see me now, years older, and still no better than a skivvy! But Mr Softley was dead: it was to this room that the police had come, making terrible and unbelievable charges against him, and Mr Softley, fleeing to the cellar, had hanged himself from a beer-hook.

The pub was not yet open and in the yellow light that filtered in through the thick tinted windows it looked tired and shabby. Rosie remembered it most of all as a glittering palace of a room, especially on Saturday nights when the red-shaded lights were on and it was packed with people and the air seemed to throb and dance with life and excitement. Now, like everything else, it appeared to be suffering from the depression which the newspapers kept talking about: the paint on the ceiling and walls had gone brown with age and neglect, the linoleum which she had once scrubbed and polished daily was cracked and worn, wisps of horsehair peeped through the covers of the benches.

Rosie smiled as she saw that the piano was still there, standing as always on the little platform in an alcove near the bar. It was years since she had played a piano and, as she moved towards it and looked down at the yellowing keys, she wondered if she had lost the touch which had once enabled her to roll out the popular numbers of the day almost without effort. At first she had been ashamed that she could not read music and could never learn to play like Mr Softley, but he, as usual, had lifted her spirits: 'Never mind, Rosie. We can't all be like Paderewski or Rubinstein. God has given you a gift – a natural ear for music. Perhaps it is only a small gift, but even a small gift is not to be sneered at. So use it, Rosie. Play. Enjoy yourself.'

She had not revealed her ignorance of Paderewski or Rubinstein but she had taken Mr Softley's advice to heart, so much so that after his sad death The Missus had promoted her to the position of pub pianist.

Rosie's fingers began to stray over the keyboard: that she had lost some of her dexterity was only to be expected, but she was pleasantly surprised to find that she could still pick out the notes and still remember the chords Mr Softley had taught her. Caught up in the pleasure of the moment, she drew up the stool and sat down. The tune of 'The Lost Chord', the very first piece that she had learned to play right through, began to sound in her mind and, with quick obedience and scarcely a mistake, her hands translated her thoughts into sound.

'Well, I never! Rosie Carr! Rosie Carr at the piano! That takes us back a bit, eh?'

Rosie turned guiltily to see the hovering bulk of The Missus standing just behind her. She rose from the stool, jumped down from the platform and stammered an apology.

'I'm sorry, ma'am,' she said.

Ma'am? She heard herself say the word with a surprise that bordered on astonishment. It was extraordinary that after all these years she should still feel in awe of this woman, still feel herself fluttering with nerves when she faced her.

'Sorry!' said The Missus. 'No need to be sorry, Rosie. It was a treat to hear you. That old piano hasn't had an outing for donkey's years.' She turned to the barman who was lounging by the bar, watching them, and said, in the acid tones so familiar to Rosie in the old days, 'Is there anything wrong with the bar, Albert? Is it about to fall down, do you think?'

'No, ma'am.' He looked puzzled.

'In that case, there is absolutely no need for you to hold it up, is there? Don't stand there like a tit in a trance, man. Get those front windows washed. If I've told you once, I've told you a dozen times, there is no room for idlers in this establishment!'

'Yes, ma'am.'

As he scurried out of the door, The Missus lifted her huge bosom in a sigh. 'They're all the same these days, Rosie. Bone idle, bone idle. If I didn't keep after them every minute that God gives, there'd be nothing done, nothing. I'm not a hard woman, you know that, and there's many would vouch for it. On the contrary, I'm too soft with them, too soft by half, and they take advantage of my good nature.' She paused to draw breath, then continued: 'No, they don't make them like they used to, Rosie. Take you, for instance. You knew what work was, you were one of the best workers I ever had. Oh, you had your faults, I won't deny that, but you were a fair worker. Whereas nowadays—'

She expressed her opinion of the current crop of workers in a derisive snort, dismissed the subject from her mind and went on: 'And how are you, Rosie?'

'Oh, up and down like Tower Bridge,' answered Rosie.

'Kids all right?'

'Oh, yes. They're no problem.'

'Are you working?'

'No.' And Rosie added defensively, 'Not at the moment.'

The Missus gave her a sharp look, taking in the situation immediately. 'I see.' She paused, then continued: 'Would you like something to wet your whistle?'

'A lemonade would be nice,' said Rosie, surprised not only by the offer but by the revelation that, over the years, The Missus had lost some of her genteel manner and that her language had taken on a coarser edge.

'A lemonade be buggered!' said The Missus contemptuously. 'We'll have something better than that, for old time's sake. A port and lemon, eh? Yes, that'll go down very well.'

As she moved to the bar, an elderly man came through from the back room. He checked when he saw Rosie and The Missus and blinked nervously, as though uncertain whether to proceed.

'What do you want?' demanded The Missus roughly.

'Nothing,' he muttered, 'nothing.'

'That's a bloody lie for a start!' she retorted. 'I wasn't born yesterday.' Turning to Rosie she added: 'If I didn't watch him like a hawk, Rosie, he'd drink the pub dry.'

'Rosie?'

The man turned and shambled a few paces forward, peering shortsightedly at her, and suddenly, with a sense of shock which was tinged with pity, Rosie recognised The Guv'nor.

The Guv'nor, Mr Quorn himself, the man who once had strutted from bar to bar of The Winged Horse in dandified splendour, an exotic waistcoat and gold watch-chain embracing his round belly, the sheen of his patent-leather boots matching the gleam of his dark pomaded hair and spiky waxed moustache.

Everything about him seemed to have dwindled. Patches of grey skull showed through the thinning hair: the moustache drooped sadly over the corners of his mouth; the waistcoat over the shrunken belly was shabby and stained; the patent-leather boots had been replaced by worn carpet-slippers. Above all, the jauntiness had gone from him; he walked like an old man and in his pale eyes there was the flickering uncertainty of age.

Rosie looked from The Guv'nor to The Missus and back again. The Missus seemed scarcely to have changed at all: a touch of grey at the roots of her hair, a few lines beneath the eyes, a certain coarsening of the skin, an unmistakable thickening at the waist, that was all. Rosie had the odd feeling that the bloom and spirit which had deserted The Guv'nor had somehow entered his wife, making her more formidable than ever.

'Rosie? Rosie Carr?' he said again.

'Of course it's Rosie Carr, you daft ha'porth!' said The Missus.

'How are you, Guv'nor?' asked Rosie.

'What?'

'You'll have to speak up, Rosie,' said The Missus. 'The poor old sod is going Mutt and Jeff.'

Rosie repeated the question in a louder voice, but he only smiled and nodded in response. The Missus drew a small tankard of ale from one of the pumps and took it to him.

'Here,' she said, not unkindly. 'Take this into the back room. Go on, hop it, hop it!'

Shaking his head and muttering Rosie's name, he set off towards the front door, but The Missus, with a heaving sigh of resignation, turned him as one would an errant child and headed him back to the door behind the bar.

'The silly bugger doesn't know where he is half the time,' she said, with a shake of the head. 'Went down with pneumonia two winters ago. It was touch and go and he's never been the same since. Like having a kid around the place.' She poured two ports, added a drop of lemonade to each, and handed one to Rosie. 'Here, put that where the buses can't run over it.'

'Cheers,' said Rosie.

'I thought you were working at Goldie's laundry,' said The Missus.

'I was,' said Rosie.

'Ah,' said The Missus.

'I was wondering,' Rosie began hesitantly, 'I was wondering if you knew of anything.'

'Work, you mean?'

'Yes.'

'Here, at the pub?'

'I wondered.'

'Rosie, you can stand there and wonder till a sparrow builds a nest up your backside and then you can wonder how he got the straw there,' said The Missus. 'I mean, look at the place. I can hardly afford to pay the staff I've got. Trade's fallen off something shocking in the last couple of years. All this unemployment, you see; there's no money around.'

'I thought I'd ask,' said Rosie despondently.

'No harm in asking,' said The Missus.

Rosie drained her glass. 'Well, thanks for the drink. If you should hear of anything—'

'I'll let you know.' Rosie was halfway to the door when The Missus spoke again. 'Wait a minute, girl.'

'Yes?'

'I tell you what you could do. You could come in on Friday and Saturday nights and play the old joanna. Like you used to in the old days. Couldn't pay you, mind, couldn't afford to pay. Had to let my last pianist go because I couldn't pay. But if you like to come in and do it just for the tips – well, you might make yourself a few bob. And I'll throw in a free supper. What do you say?'

Rosie hesitated only a moment. Years before there had been times in which she had earned as much as five shillings in tips in a single evening. Even if she did not do as well as that, at least she would be earning something and still have time to look for work during the day. And the best part of all was that she would be doing a job she liked, she would be back on familiar ground, among friends.

'I'm a bit rusty,' she said.

'We're all a bit rusty,' replied The Missus with a smile. 'When I bend over I can hear my bones squeak. See you Friday, then? At half-seven?'

'Friday. Half-seven,' said Rosie happily.

2

The port-and-lemon and her cheering talk with The Missus had combined to induce in Rosie a feeling of wellbeing, and in this relaxed mood she decided to take a stroll through the Fortune Street market to look up her old friends.

It was still early and many of the marketeers were setting out their stock, dressing their stalls and barrows in preparation for the day's trading. Rosie was relieved to see how little it had

changed: there was the same litter of boxes and crates, the same
cheery exchange of greetings and curses, the same tangy
fruit-and-vegetable smell hovered in the air. Only the faces were
different.

Big Bess's jellied-eel stand, with its prime pitch outside The
Winged Horse, was still there, but the name above it had been
changed and it now carried the title:

JACK'S JELLIED EELS

SHRIMPS, WINKLES

AND

FRESH FISH DAILY

Jack, a pleasant, fresh-faced young man, smiled as he saw
Rosie examining his wares. 'Got some lovely kippers and
bloaters, lady. Fresh in from Billingsgate this morning. Or I can
do you some nice mussels? No? Cockles? A lovely dish of
cockles?'

'No, thanks,' said Rosie. She returned his smile and moved
on.

It was much the same further along the street: even where
the stalls had retained their familiar names they were manned by
people who were strangers to Rosie. The pitch from which Mr
Crooks had once sold his neat little skewers of cat's-meat and
tended the minor ailments of sick pets was now occupied by a
sprauncy young man wearing a curly-brimmed bowler hat and a
fancy waistcoat, who in style and manner put Rosie in mind of
the young Tommo. His stock, which seemed to consist only of
tins of pink salmon, was piled haphazardly on a barrow and,
considering that there were few customers around, he was
doing a fairly brisk trade. A board above the barrow was
inscribed with the words: MARK MOSS – THE PEOPLE'S FRIEND.
Rosie paused, amused to hear the young man produce a spiel
which, once again, reminded her of Tommo.

'I challenge you, ladies and gents, I challenge you. Go up the
High Road – go to Sainsbury's or Liptons – and ask them the
price of the best Canadian pink salmon. No, I'll save you the

journey. In Sainsbury's or Liptons or the Home and Colonial you will not get a tin of salmon under ninepence. That's right, my friends, they will ask ninepence a tin. I have here the identical tin containing the identical goods – the finest Canadian salmon. Do I ask ninepence? Do I ask eightpence? Sevenpence – even sixpence? I do not! You know me – you all know me – Mark Moss, The People's Friend. And Mark's price to you, my friends – don't faint, lady, here it comes! – is fourpence. That's correct. Four pennies for each tin of the best Canadian pink salmon. Two tins for sevenpence-ha'penny!'

He maintained this constant flow of sales talk while handing out the tins to eager customers and pocketing their money. After a moment's hesitation, Rosie decided that a tin of salmon would not only make a nice treat for the family tea but that it would also be a way of celebrating the resumption of her career as a pub pianist. She fumbled in her purse, brought out sixpence, and handed it over.

'There we are, darling,' said the people's friend, giving her a wink and twopence change. 'And remember, remember Mark Moss's golden guarantee. Money back if you are not satisfied.'

When she was clear of the stall, Rosie examined the tin more closely. It seemed in all respects, even down to the brand name, to be no different from the salmon on sale in the shops for more than double the price. What, then, was the catch? How could Mark Moss afford to sell so cheaply? Had the salmon been stolen? In the vernacular of the streets, had it fallen off the back of a lorry? And she remembered how Tommo had once bought a stock of frying pans and saucepans to sell in the market and had been sent to prison for twelve months for receiving stolen goods.

At any rate, she thought, it was none of her business, and she moved on to Hoddle's greengrocery stall with the intention of buying half a cucumber to go with the salmon. The name was still there above the stall, but it took Rosie a good twenty seconds to identify the plump young woman who was setting out a box of fresh lettuces.

'Lily?' she said cautiously.

The young woman swung round, stared at Rosie for a moment and then her eyes brightened and the broad face creased in a smile.

'Rosie! Rosie Carr! Well, I'll be blessed!'

They took each other's hands and stood there, shaking their heads in wonderment at this unexpected reunion.

'Look at you!' said Lily. 'Look at you! You haven't changed a bit!'

'Wish that was true,' said Rosie.

'You've still got your looks, your figure. Blimey, look at me! I've come out like a bloody airship!'

And, indeed, it was hard for Rosie to believe that this was the Lily Hoddle who had been the leader of fashion among the girls of the district, the girl who had once lent Rosie a hat and a handbag so that she could look smart on her first date, the girl who had seemed to be so wise in the ways of men and had passed this wisdom on to Rosie and countless others. Time, fifteen years of relentless time, had transformed the pretty, self-confident girl into a bulging matron.

'Are you running the stall now?' asked Rosie.

'Have to,' said Lily. 'Dad's well past it. Me and George run it between us.'

'George?'

'My old man.'

'I didn't know you were married.'

'Got spliced about a year after you and Tommo. Lived up north, in Manchester, until Dad took sick, then we moved back here to take over.'

'Everything's all right then?'

'As right as it will ever be, I suppose. George is not so bad; there's a lot worse. But what with the stall and four kids, I've got my hands full.'

'I remember the time,' said Rosie, 'I remember the time you swore you'd never work in the market.'

'Ah, well, we say a lot of things when we are young and daft,' said Lily, with just a touch of bitterness. 'I was going to open a posh dress shop in the West End, I was going to get away from the market, I was going to be different – rich and all that – pictures in the magazines.' She laughed and shook her head. 'What a load of old swosh! I've learned one thing, Rosie, I've learned one thing if I've learned nothing else. You are what you are. You can't escape that. When you're young you can fill your head with fancy dreams but that's all they are – dreams. Life soon knocks them out of you. I was born in the market and I dare say I'll finish here. And it's no use pining about it.'

The young man who had been selling the salmon came over at this moment. 'Hey, Lily,' he said, 'keep an eye on my barrow while I go and have a cuppa, will you?'

'Right, Mossie,' replied Lily.

The young man looked at the tin of salmon in Rosie's hand and grinned. He had keen, dark, impudent eyes that seemed to be teasing her. 'Got yourself a bargain there, missus,' he said.

'Is it really good stuff?' asked Rosie. 'You haven't done me, have you?'

'Done you? That's the genuine article, girl, on my life!'

'How come you can sell it so cheap?'

'Ah,' he said cheekily, 'that's a trade secret. Back in ten minutes, Lily.'

They watched him walk jauntily away. 'Now,' said Lily, 'there's a bloke who will go a long way. Smart as a ten-pound note, that one. Works all the hours that God sends. Does a different market every day. The Caledonian, Well Street, Bermondsey, Surrey Street – you name it, he's there.'

'How can he sell so cheap?'

'Quick turnover,' Lily said. She took the tin of salmon from Rosie's hand and pointed to a mark stamped on the label. Below the mark were the letters STR. 'See that? These are army goods. Those letters mean Surplus to Requirements. So the army sell them off cheap. Mossie's got a contact inside. He tips him off when there's something good going. And Mossie buys seconds and damaged goods from the big firms. You know the form, Rosie – your Tommo used to do the same thing. Mossie buys in big quantities – and sells cheap to make a quick sale. He bought five thousand tins of that salmon, told me so himself. And he'll sell that lot in a week. I reckon he's making a penny on every tin. Work it out for yourself – he'll clear twenty pounds profit for a week's work. Not bad, eh?'

Not bad at all, thought Rosie. Twenty pounds in a week! She felt a twinge of envy for young Mark Moss, a feeling of jealousy that he had taken over the place and position that had once belonged to Tommo. But her spirits, which had been seesawing up and down all the morning, suddenly lifted and as she walked home, an idea formed in her mind.

Why shouldn't she go into the market? There were sites available, she had seen that, and she had learned enough from Tommo's operations to know where to get supplies and how to price them. If that young man could do it, so could she!

There was only one problem. The same, ever-present problem. Where could she lay her hands on the capital sum necessary to begin such an enterprise? She would be hard put to raise twenty shillings, let alone the twenty or thirty pounds that would be needed.

By the time she reached Shakespeare Street, Rosie had dismissed the idea as a fanciful and impractical dream and, in any case, her thoughts were diverted elsewhere by a scene that had become a regular feature of the London streets in the past two or three years.

Five men were making their way slowly along the crown of the road, singing 'Roses of Picardy' to the accompaniment of a concertina. They were mostly young – Rosie judged that the oldest among them could not be more than forty – and the one in the centre of the file had the face of a schoolboy. He walked with a hand on the shoulder of the man in front and, with a sense of shock, Rosie realised that he was blind. Two one-legged men on crutches hopped along the pavements on either side of their comrades collecting, with surprising agility, the odd coin which was tossed towards them. All the men had war medals pinned to their ragged clothes and two of them were wearing old regimental caps. The man in front carried a placard on which were inscribed the words:

UNEMPLOYED EX-SOLDIERS
You Cheered Us Once –
Help Us Now

The singing was not particularly good but the sight of the shuffling, pathetic line of hungry men and the sentimental words of the song stirred Rosie's heart. She had a vivid remembrance of a day in 1916 when Tommo had come home from France on leave. The ruddy face that had marched away was now the colour of margarine and in his quick nervous eyes she had seen the look of a man who had seen unspeakable horrors. During those seven days he had said nothing about the war or what it was like in the trenches but his silence had been more expressive than words.

She took out a penny and slipped it into the outstretched cap of one of the collectors. As he thanked her she said: 'There's no money down this street, mate. Why don't you try somewhere else?'

'We have, lady,' he replied. 'We have. They don't like us in the posh streets, they set the police on us. No, it's the poor that helps the poor, isn't that right?'

3

As one day followed another and the money dried up, Rosie grew more and more desperate. She hid her feelings from the children and from Gran as best she could but she was aware of a growing tension inside which revealed itself in sudden short bursts of irritation and anger. The children watched her warily, vaguely frightened by the change and by the uncertainty which was nibbling at their sense of security.

The evenings at The Winged Horse had proved to be a disappointment financially: Rosie had managed to attract more people into the Saloon Bar and The Missus was well satisfied with her bargain, but the tips had not come up to expectations. She could, it is true, have drunk herself stupid on Friday and Saturday nights for, more often than not, a satisfied customer would choose to buy her a drink rather than put its equivalent in cash into the saucer which Rosie had placed strategically on top of the piano. However, she arranged with The Missus that these free drinks should be collected discreetly and resold; the resultant profit was split equally between them, an arrangement which pleased The Missus but hardly worked to Rosie's advantage, since she found it difficult to keep check on the number of drinks.

At any rate, she found that she was making an average of two shillings on Fridays and three on Saturdays, an income which, though better than nothing, fell far short of her needs. She had tramped the streets in search of work without the slightest success: there were no vacancies for barmaids and for every humble charring job there seemed to be a hundred eager women. For the first time in years, Rosie was in arrears with the rent and, worse still, there were days when she was at her wit's end to feed the children. She had seen, with a feeling of shame, the same plaintive look of hunger in their eyes as she had seen years ago in the eyes of the urchins who had queued each morning at the backdoor of The Winged Horse begging for scraps.

Against all her instincts, she dismissed her pride and applied for Parish Relief, the first time in her life that she had asked for charity. In due course, and after waiting in line for two hours, she found herself standing before the two committee members, Mr Parr and Mrs Stringer, whose delicate task it was to question and assess all applicants.

They sat side by side at a table covered in green baize, and to one side, at a desk, a small, mild-mannered, elderly clerk kept a record of the proceedings. The walls were painted in the colour which was known locally as workhouse brown, as if to remind suppliants of the sterner fate that lay in store if their situation grew worse. The only adornment was a framed photograph of the King and Queen, and there was no chair for the applicants.

It was a setting, thought Rosie, that Dickens had described to perfection a dozen times. And the two assessors not only matched the room but might have stepped whole out of one of his books.

Mrs Stringer was as plump as Mr Parr was thin. Her ripe body was constrained by a whalebone corset which had the effect of forcing her breasts upwards and outwards, so that they pushed against the thin silken blouse like two rabbits trapped in a net. She wore a large hat decorated with artificial flowers over piled-up hair, and beneath this a round pink face with two rippling folds of flesh under the chin surveyed this nether world of poor relief with a suspicion that she made no effort to restrain. She examined Rosie through pale, almost colourless eyes for a full twenty seconds and then, in a fluting voice edged with resignation, she spoke.

'Your name?'

Rosie gave it and the clerk's pen began to scratch across his Application Book.

'Where do you live?'

This time it was Mr Parr who addressed her, polishing some rimless spectacles on a white handkerchief as he spoke. He had on a heavy clerical-grey suit and there was a slight film of sweat above his upper lip. Rosie found her eyes moving from this to his almost bald head where a blue vein, standing out from the putty-coloured skin, throbbed ever so slightly. Fascinated by this, Rosie forgot to answer Mr Parr's question and he repeated it in a sharper tone.

This time she replied at once. Watch it, Rosie, she told herself. A neighbour, an expert in these matters, had warned her that the important thing at such interviews was to be respectful.

'You have got to be respectful to them, Rosie,' she had said. 'They expect it. They don't understand, you see. They think we're all bone-idle buggers who wouldn't do a day's work if it was offered. They are the sort who think the poor like soup. So keep your eyes down, be respectful and for God's sake don't answer back!'

So Rosie put her eyes down and stood there with what she hoped was the appropriate expression of humility in her bearing.

They listened in silence and with no hint of sympathy as she told them of her desperate need. Their faces seemed to be telling her that they had heard it all before, but she ploughed on nevertheless. When she had finished, there followed a long, icy pause during which Mr Parr polished his glasses once more and Mrs Stringer tapped the table with a pencil.

'You look like a strong, healthy young woman, Thompson,' said Mrs Stringer at last. 'Are you sure that you have tried to find work?'

Inwardly, Rosie flared. The condescension implied by the use of her surname angered her. She was Rosie, she was Mrs Thompson. I don't have much, she thought, but at least I have a name, a proper name. What right had they to strip her of this small dignity?

But outwardly she maintained her calm as she replied meekly: 'I have tried, ma'am. Truly I have. But there isn't the work about.'

Mr Parr peered at her, owl-like, over the rim of his spectacles. 'You had work, I understand. At Mr Goldie's laundry. Why did you leave?'

'I was sacked,' Rosie said. She had been dreading this question, and now it had come she felt her cause to be hopeless.

'Dismissed,' said Mrs Stringer, the disapproval clicking in her voice like castanets, and she exchanged a 'these people are hopeless' look with Mr Parr. Raising her eyes momentarily, Rosie saw that the blue vein on his skull was moving in and out like the gills of a fish.

'I think I may say that I have known Mr Goldie long enough to know that he would not dismiss an employee without due cause,' said Mrs Stringer, adding for emphasis: 'Yes, I think I may say that Mr Goldie is a fair and considerate man. So, why were you dismissed, Thompson? Tell me that.'

'We had a bit of an argument,' replied Rosie, trying to keep her voice down. 'It was a boiling-hot day, you see, just like this, and—'

Mrs Stringer interrupted her coldly. 'Thank you. I don't think we need the details. The fact that you had an argument with your employer is enough.'

'Quite so,' said Mr Parr.

'It wasn't my fault,' Rosie protested.

'It never is,' said Mrs Stringer with a sigh, 'it never is. But because of your wilfulness, you are now without work and have become a burden on the community. Do you see that, Thompson?'

'Yes, ma'am,' said Rosie, controlling herself with an effort of will that took all her mental strength.

'If you had conducted yourself in a reasonable manner when you had employment you would not be here now,' said Mr Parr gravely.

'No, sir,' said Rosie in a whisper.

'You should have given thought to your children,' said Mrs Stringer.

God give me strength, thought Rosie. But she said nothing.

'If we do decide that we can help, it will be out of consideration for your children,' said Mr Parr. There was a hint of promise in the remark that sent Rosie's hopes soaring.

'Now, Thompson, you are quite positive that you have no other source of income – nothing more than you have already told us?' asked Mrs Stringer.

'Nothing,' said Rosie, 'nothing apart from the five or six shillings I pick up in tips at the pub.' As soon as the words were out and she saw their faces, she realised her mistake.

'The pub!' said Mrs Stringer.

'The pub?' echoed Mr Parr. 'What exactly do you do at this public house?'

Rosie explained, trying desperately to retrieve the situation.

'I see,' said Mrs Stringer. 'So when you told us that you were without work, that wasn't the truth, was it, Thompson?'

'It's not a proper job. You can't call it work,' Rosie protested.

'But you earn money from it.'

'Five or six shillings at the most. How far does that go?'

'With prudent management it should go quite a long way,' said Mr Parr. He looked at Mrs Stringer, who nodded briefly, and then continued: 'I'm sorry, Thompson. But the parish does not have unlimited means. We have to reserve our help for those who are in real need. Application dismissed.'

Rosie stood there, hearing the scratching of the clerk's pen, her mind a whirligig of warring thoughts, her heart as heavy as a stone. Part of her wanted to scream at them in anger; a smaller part urged her to plead, to humble herself still more.

Mrs Stringer looked up and seemed surprised that Rosie was still there. 'That will be all, Thompson,' she said.

Rosie walked to the door in a daze of hopelessness. Then a little of her natural fire flared into life and, turning, she said: 'I'm *Mrs* Thompson. That's my proper name, thank you very much. *Mrs* Thompson.'

But as she pushed her way through the crowded waiting room, she knew that the retort had been feeble and inadequate.

4

There was a queue of women outside the door of Secker and Sons, pawnbrokers, waiting by a faded sign which read PLEDGES and beneath the three familiar glinting brass balls. They stood in the hot sunshine with their bundles and bags in virtual silence, scarcely exchanging a word, their faces etched with the kind of resignation which borders on hopelessness. Rosie took her place with some nervousness: she was no stranger to Mr Secker but she still felt a sense of shame at being there, in the open, as if in parading her poverty to the public gaze she had been robbed of her privacy.

Rosie clutched the brown-paper parcel under her arm and shuffled forward as the queue began to move. Inside the brown paper there were three threadbare blankets: they had been pledged to Mr Secker before and she knew that there was little chance of getting a loan of more than a shilling or two for them. But with a shilling she could buy four pennyworth of scrag end of lamb, a loaf and a few vegetables, and conjure up enough succulent stew and bread-and-dripping to satisfy the family for a couple of days.

The Pledge Office itself was divided into three cubicles, the idea being that the customers would enjoy on the premises the privacy they were denied outside. This arrangement led to some jostling by the more experienced women, since it was generally reckoned that the left-hand cubicle, manned by old Mr Secker himself, offered the most hopeful opportunities while the one on the right, where his stern-faced wife operated, was likely to be less favourable. The booth in the middle provided more of a gamble and could be good or bad, depending on which assistant was in charge and to what extent Mrs Secker interfered with his judgements.

As Rosie edged towards the front of the queue one of her neighbours, a Mrs Bushell, came out of the Pledge Office. She had clearly been unsuccessful for she was still carrying the two unwrapped blankets with which she had gone in, and there was a glint of tears in her eyes as she glanced at Rosie.

'They're not taking in any more blankets.'

'Why? Why is that?' Rosie felt herself tremble.

'He says he's got a room full of them already. No more blankets.' She spoke quietly, with an edge of desperation in her voice and then she moved away, shaking her head from side to side as if she still could not believe what had happened. Rosie felt the urge to call her back, to say something – anything – to her, but no words came. What could she say? They were all in the same boat, after all. She shifted uneasily, unhappily, conscious that the parcel under her arm seemed to be growing heavier by the minute.

Another woman emerged from the office clutching a shabby suit. In contrast to Mrs Bushell, this woman was red-faced and angry and she turned in the doorway to give expression to her feelings:

'You miserable old cow! I hope your perishing pawnshop gets burnt to the bloody ground!' She gave Rosie a half-hostile, half-pitying look and added, for her benefit: 'I've had this suit in and out of this place twenty times. They've made a bleeding fortune in interest. Now they won't give me a penny on it, the stingy bastards!'

'Why don't you try Walpoles, the pawnshop in the High Street?' suggested one of the women in the queue.

'That's just where I'm going!' said the woman with the suit and, raising her voice again she roared at the unseen Mrs Secker: 'Bugger you lot for a game of Sundays! That's the last you'll see of me, you mean old bitch! I'm taking my custom elsewhere!' Muted laughter and the odd giggle came from the queue as she marched off with a defiant stride.

A few minutes later, Rosie found herself in the left-hand cubicle facing Mr Secker himself. The tall, thin, yellowish old man gave Rosie a weary look from behind the high counter.

'What have you got?'

'Three blankets.' Rosie blushed as she put the parcel on the counter. 'They're good blankets, Mr Secker.'

He laid a long bony hand on the parcel to stop her opening it. He had discarded his jacket, and the celluloid cuffs on which he did his calculations had slipped down to the tops of his hands. Rosie stared blankly at the figures pencilled on the cuffs and heard his bleak voice: 'Blankets. Everybody brings in blankets. Sorry. I'm already full up with blankets. Blankets I don't need.'

Rosie lifted her head. 'I don't want much, Mr Secker. A couple of shillings, that's all, a shilling even.'

'Sorry.'

'I'll redeem them in a couple of weeks. You won't have them on your hands long.'

'No, I'm sorry, my dear. If I do it for you, I'll have to do it for everyone else. And then I won't be able to move for blankets.' His was not an ungenerous spirit and he spoke with the patience of a man who had some understanding of the desperate need of these women. On his shelves, in the shape of ornaments, rings, watches, bed-linen, suits, boots and a dozen other items, he had stored away, against sale or redemption, the evidence of their poverty, the story of their lives.

Rosie put up a hand to take the parcel and, as she did so, she said suddenly: 'How about this?'

'How about what?'

She twisted the wedding-ring from her finger. 'Here. This. It's eighteen-carat. What will you give me on it?'

He fixed her with his sad, dark eyes. 'Are you sure you want to do this, my dear?'

Rosie nodded. 'It's a good ring. Cost over five pound new.'

She remembered that she had wanted to buy a cheaper ring but Tommo, in his flamboyant way, had insisted on something better. 'I don't want people to think I'm marrying you on the cheap, girl,' he had told her.

Mr Secker took the ring with a little shake of his head, screwed a glass into one eye, and scrutinised the thick gold band. The examination seemed to take a long time and Rosie watched anxiously, her heart hammering with hope. He put the ring down at last and gave a little nod.

'Ten shillings?'

'Yes, yes. That will do. Thank you very much.'

He took up a strip of three pawn tickets and inserted it into the pen machine which stood beside him. This contraption, which was Mr Secker's sole concession to modern technology, consisted of three pens and three inkwells mounted on a wooden base: the pens were connected to each other by metal struts, so that by using the pen on the right the other two pens were brought into play and three tickets could be written at once. Mr Secker wrote carefully, in a small neat hand. With equal care he blotted the wet ink and tore the completed strip into three separate but identical tickets. He took some coins from a wooden till and counted them out.

'There you are, my dear. Sixpence deducted for the first month's interest. Nine shillings and sixpence.'

Rosie hurried from the shop as though fearful that he might change his mind and she did not stop hurrying until she reached The Common, a small stretch of green about a quarter of a mile from Shakespeare Street, and sat down for a few moments of rest on one of the green benches.

She was sweating, yet at the same time she felt an odd inner chill. In all her married life, she had never removed her wedding-ring, never taken it off even for a moment, and the sight of the thin band of white skin standing out against the pinkish-brown of her hand gave her a sensation of nakedness, of public shame. She rubbed the white skin but this only seemed to make it stand out the more.

An idea came to her then, or rather the remembrance of something that she had heard from one of the girls at the laundry.

Thus it was that when Eddie came in from school he found his mother on her knees, rubbing her wedding-ring against the stone floor. As he appeared, she slipped the ring on her finger and stood up quickly.

'What are you doing, Mum?' he asked.

'Nothing,' she said guiltily. 'I just dropped my ring, that's all.' She reached for her purse and gave him sixpence. 'Here, son, take a basin and go up to Coltman's. Get six pennyworth of pease pudding and faggots for our tea.'

When he had gone she looked at the ring. It was a brass curtain-ring and it had cost fourpence in Woolworths. At first it had seemed to be far too shiny and new but now, after much rubbing and scratching, it looked suitably worn and not too much unlike the real thing. She was sure that it would pass muster, that neither the neighbours nor anyone else would be able, at a glance, to tell the difference.

All the same, the brass ring had a strange and alien feel to it, and Rosie, who was not normally a superstitious person, could not escape the thought that she had done something black and terrible, something that would bring ill-luck to her and the family. She heard Van come in and, unable to face her for the moment, she went out into the yard, locked herself in the lavatory and gave herself up to tears.

Rosie never forgot this incident and, in later years, she looked back upon it as the low point in her life, as the day on which her fortunes had touched rock bottom.

And then, on the following Saturday when the money raised on the wedding-ring had almost gone, a small miracle occurred.

CHAPTER FOUR

1

Rosie thought it strange that Mark Moss, The People's Friend, should make a habit of popping into The Winged Horse on Saturday evenings, for he was an abstemious young man who drank nothing stronger than shandy and never touched cigarettes. Moreover, he seemed to leave his extrovert market manner outside with his barrow: his usual practice was to sit quietly in a corner, sipping his drink and making calculations on scraps of paper produced in profusion from his pockets. He scarcely ever joined in the singing although he never left without putting sixpence in Rosie's saucer – a sum which was by far her largest tip.

Small wonder, then, that he had aroused in her a feeling which had begun as nothing more than simple curiosity but which had now gone beyond that – although she would not have admitted this even to herself.

They seldom spoke except to murmur a brief greeting, but she was keenly aware of his presence: when she raised her head from the piano, she would find herself looking in his direction and, as if sensing this, he would answer her look with a smile and lift his glass in a silent toast.

He was not handsome in the conventional way, he did not possess the smooth good looks of a Rudolph Valentino or a John Barrymore. His face was broad and rugged, the face of a street-fighter, and he had the small, stocky body of a worker. It was the eyes which illuminated his personality, eyes as black as boot polish that shone with intelligence and good humour.

Rosie had met a lot of what the locals called 'wide boys' in her time, flamboyant figures who had the wit to turn a quick pound or two and were not too particular about how they did it. The wide boys seldom lasted: like dragonflies they buzzed and blazed for a little space and then faded from view. But some instinct told her that Mark Moss was not like those others, that he had more depth and stamina, and this only served to increase her interest in the young man.

So his entry on Saturday evenings always lifted her spirits: she liked the way he greeted her, with a thumb jerked upwards, as if to assert that all was well, and the impudent grin that began in his eyes and then spread teasingly across his face. Once, when he failed to appear, she had felt an unaccountable sense of loss, a stupidity for which she chided herself. She meant nothing to him or he to her, she told herself sternly.

On this Saturday evening he surprised her by coming to the piano. She continued to play as he bent down and whispered in her ear: 'When you get a break, darling, come over and have a drink. Right?'

She looked up, conscious that she was blushing slightly, and nodded. He grinned, patted her shoulder, and went back to his place. What was that all about? she wondered. Since Tommo's death she had collected her fair share of propositions from men but she knew only too well that for most of them, married or single, the attraction lay in her status as a young widow. Widows, especially those with youth on their side, were considered fair game. A drunken bookmaker had once told her as much, in a speech of unflattering and brutal frankness. He had said:

'The point, Rosie, the point is this. You're not like a lot of these young fillies. You know what it is all about. You've been broken in. And don't tell me that you don't miss it. Once had, never forgotten, eh? I'll lay all Lombard Street to a china orange that you are dying for a good old-fashioned poke.'

That gentleman had finished up with the contents of a tankard of ale over his head and since then Rosie had been doubly wary of any advances. All the same, there were moments when she had to admit the truth, in part at least, of what the bookmaker had said. Her mind did not dwell on sex but sometimes, waking from an untroubled sleep, or seeing a young couple walking hand in hand, she felt the sharp edge of her own loneliness and the familiar quickening in her blood. Lately she had been too tired, physically and emotionally, to give the matter much thought but she knew that the need was still there, lying in ambush in her flesh.

She prolonged her session at the piano deliberately, just to show Mr Moss that she danced to no man's tune, and then, mustering up what she hoped was a casual, disinterested manner, she crossed to his table.

'Well, I'm here,' she said.

He looked up from the envelopes and scraps of paper which were spread on the table before him and grinned a welcome.

'Oh, hello, darling. Sit down. What will you have?'

'What are you drinking?'

'A shandy.' And, as if this needed explanation, he added: 'Half beer, half lemonade.'

'I know what a shandy is,' she said, with more sharpness than she had intended. 'I haven't worked in pubs for nothing.'

'Sorry,' he smiled, but there was mild surprise in the look he gave her.

'I'll have the same, please,' she said in a more conciliatory tone.

'Right you are. Hold on a minute, darling.'

He returned from the bar a few moments later with two foaming glasses, one of which he set before her.

'There you are, darling. Put that where the buses can't run over it. Cheers.'

'Cheers,' said Rosie, taking a small sip. She lifted a hand in the direction of the papers and envelopes. 'What's all this for?'

'What does it look like? These are my accounts. On Saturdays I work out what I've spent out and what I've taken in. That way I can reckon my profit.'

'I see,' she said. 'And have you had a good week?'

He consulted the back of an envelope. 'A good week? Not so dusty. Better than some, worse than others. Eight pounds, two shillings and threepence clear.'

'Very good.' Rosie was impressed and tried not to show it. At the same time she was conscious of a twinge of jealousy. Eight pounds, two shillings and threepence sounded like a fortune. What would she not give for half that sum!

Perhaps he caught something in her tone or read the thought in her eye for he looked at her and said quietly: 'You all right, darling?'

'My name is Rosie,' she said tartly.

'I know,' he said.

'Then use it. I'm not your darling.' It's all going wrong, she thought. He had said or done nothing to deserve the rough edge of her tongue.

'Look, Rosie,' he said quietly. 'No harm meant. I wasn't trying to poke my nose in. I'm sorry.'

She could see bewilderment in the bright black eyes and felt even more guilty.

'Did you want to see me about anything special?' she asked, trying to get a little more warmth into her tone.

He fiddled with his glass for a moment, twisting it in his hands. 'Your old man. Tommo. I remember him.'

'You and a lot of others,' she said defensively, wondering what was coming next.

'I used to go to the market and watch him in action. I tell you frankly, he was the best. The best.'

'There was no one to touch him,' said Rosie.

There was a pause and, as she watched him making circles with his finger in a little spillage of drink, it suddenly occurred to her that this so-confident young man was nervous, actually nervous. She smiled inwardly at the thought and said, more gently than before: 'Is that why you asked me over? To talk about Tommo?'

He lifted his head and met her eyes. 'No. Not about him. Something else.'

'Oh? Well, spit it out then. I haven't got all night.'

'I'll tell you the truth. No lies. And what is the truth? I'm doing well – better than some, not so good as others. Is this enough, I ask myself. And what is the answer? The answer is no.

To build a bigger fire a man needs more wood. So – I have decided to expand. But this also presents a problem. Can I do it alone? No. Four pairs of hands I have not got. The conclusion to all this is that I need help.'

'What are you worried about?' She smiled. 'Nowadays you can take your pick. Just say the word and you'll have a hundred men queuing up for the chance.'

'Oh, yes. An idiot I can get tomorrow. And what do you get from an idiot? Trouble! But what I'm looking for is someone who understands the markets. The selling? No problem. The selling I can take care of. A salesman I don't need. I want someone who can deal with the suppliers, keep check on the stock, handle all this stuff.'

He shuffled the litter of paper before him, then looked her straight in the eyes and said softly:

'Is this an idea that would appeal to you, Rosie?'

'Me?' Her eyes widened in astonishment.

'Who else am I talking to? You, of course, you. You could do such a job standing on your head. You know the markets, you get on with people. How about it? Two quid a week for starters. What do you think?'

'Think?' She still could not believe what she had heard and looked at him with uncomprehending eyes. From a far corner of the bar a man called:

'Hey, Rosie, how about a tune on the joanna?'

'In a minute, in a minute,' she replied sharply, without taking her eyes from Mark.

But at that moment Mrs Quorn loomed up and frowned down at Rosie. 'Would it be too much trouble for you to get to the piano, young lady?'

'Just coming,' said Rosie, her eyes still on Mark.

'Hmph,' said Mrs Quorn, giving them a full and formidable glare of disapproval before she moved away.

'Look,' said Mark, collecting up his bits of paper. 'I have to go now anyway. Got to see a man about a dog. You think it over, eh? I've got a little lock-up at the back of Culross Road where I keep the old barrow and bits and pieces of stock. I'll be there tomorrow morning. Come round and give me the verdict then. All right?'

'All right,' she murmured mechanically, still too stunned fully to take in what had happened, and went back to the piano. On his way to the door Mark dropped his usual sixpence into the saucer, favoured her with a broad wink and then was gone.

Rosie played in a daze at first, the thoughts churning in her mind. There were so many questions that she had wanted to ask, questions that would have to wait tantalisingly until tomorrow. But she began to play with more verve and spirit as the full reality of the change in her fortunes came home to her. A job! A job! Two pounds a week, two pounds a week! Twice what she had earned at the laundry!

But her optimism dimmed a little at the end of the evening when Mrs Quorn asked her why she had been talking to Mark.

'He's offered me a job,' Rosie said.

'A job! I hope you told him what he could do with his job!'

'What do you mean?'

'He's an Ikey. You don't want to work for the likes of him. Well, you've seen him. Tight as a duck's arse – like all Jew-boys. Sits here for hours with one bloody shandy.'

'I like him,' said Rosie quietly.

'Hmph,' said Mrs Quorn, with immense scorn. 'I wouldn't trust him or his sort as far as I could throw that piano! Steer clear of him, Rosie, steer clear!'

2

It was near midnight when she pulled the string on the latch of the front door and let herself into the house. She saw a strip of light under the door of the children's bedroom and, sliding her shoes off, she went inside. Van was asleep but a candle was burning beside Eddie's bed and his head was bent over a library book. He looked up guiltily as Rosie padded towards him.

'What do you think you're up to, eh?' she whispered. 'Do you know the time?'

'I didn't realise,' he said.

She took the book and glanced at the title: *Wireless for the Beginner: How to Build Your Own Wireless Set.*

'Is this your latest fad, then?' she asked.

'It isn't a fad, Mum. I'm going to save up to buy the parts. I know a boy who has built his own set. It's terrific!'

'Well,' Rosie said, 'you won't be able to build anything if you don't get your sleep. You have to be up in the morning for your round.'

'Sunday tomorrow,' he said, with a sigh of pleasure. 'I don't have to start so early.' And, as she put the book down on the rickety table by the bed, he added: 'I earned one-and-six today, Mum. And fivepence in tips. And Mr Hamilton gave me a loaf and a bag of broken biscuits.'

'That's good, son, that's very good!' she said.

As always she felt a surge of pride and affection as she looked into his young eager eyes. Perhaps because he had known nothing else, their poverty seemed not to touch him: he was always active with some project or another, always looking towards a new horizon. He did not wait for life to come to him, he ran eagerly towards it, arms outstretched to embrace every minute of the day.

And he worked hard, sometimes too hard, she feared, for in addition to school and the paper-round he had a Saturday job, helping Mr Hamilton, the baker, with his deliveries. From the paper-round and Mr Hamilton he earned a total of four shillings weekly apart from tips, and from the beginning, without hesitation, he had given the money to his mother. He kept the tips and Rosie always returned sixpence to him, but she was conscious of a certain guilt about it all. She had sworn to herself that her children would not have to work as she had done, that they would enjoy a better life, and she felt as if she had let them down.

On the other hand, she knew that Eddie was as proud of the contribution he made to the household finances as she was of him, and that to turn away his money would be to hurt him deeply. It made him feel as though he were a man already and his few shillings were crucial in her present circumstances. So she had come gradually to accept the situation.

But don't, she pleaded silently, don't be in too much of a hurry to grow up, son. Plenty of time for that. The world outside is dark and full of menace and it has a way of strangling your dreams. Stay young, enjoy yourself while you can; above all, don't leave me. Not yet, not yet.

She surprised him with a quick little hug, and seeing the glint of tears in her eyes he asked: 'Is anything wrong, Mum?'

'No, son,' she assured him. 'As a matter of fact, I had a bit of good news tonight. Things might be looking up. Not before time.'

'What? What has happened?'

'I'll tell you when it's definite. Now, off you go to sleep, before you are another minute older.'

She tucked in the bedclothes, snuffed out the candle and went quietly up the stairs to make her nightly check on Gran. As she eased open the door she heard the querulous old voice.

'Who's that?'

'Me. Rosie. Who do you think it is?'

She felt her way to the fireplace, took a box of matches from the shelf and held a lighted match to the gas-mantle. It was broken again, she noticed, as she adjusted the gas level: the delicate white mantles cost threepence each and Gran was forever breaking them.

Turning to the bed, she said: 'You all right?'

'As right as I'll ever be,' said the old lady, as Rosie began to straighten the blankets around her. The room smelt, as always, of stale beer, stale air, and the indefinable scent of old age.

Despite her tiredness, Rosie sat by the bed and described the events of her day, omitting only Mark's offer of a job. The old lady looked forward to this regular recital: she seldom went out these days and Rosie's encounters and activities were, for her, a small window on the world.

At last, when she had answered all the questions, Rosie rose to go, yawning, to her own bed.

'Wait a minute, girl,' Gran said.

'What is it now?'

'Remember what I asked you – about the funeral?'

'Don't let us go into that again,' said Rosie sharply.

'Wait. Don't bite my head off, girl. I've got something for you.'

'Can't it wait until the morning?'

'It won't take a minute. Here. Reach under the pillow.' The old lady lifted her thin shoulders as she spoke.

From beneath the pillow Rosie drew out a small bag, its grey cloth stained with grime.

'Open it, open it!' Gran commanded.

The bag clinked as Rosie loosened the draw string at the top and shook out the contents. A little stream of coins, mainly half-crowns, poured on to the blanket before her astonished eyes.

'Well, what do you think of that, then?' asked Gran proudly. For the moment, Rosie could find no words and the old lady continued: 'There should be twenty-one pounds there. For my funeral expenses.'

Rosie found her voice at last. 'Where did you get this?'

'Ah, no, that would be telling,' said Gran, screwing up her eyes.

'Where did you get it?' Rosie demanded, more sternly.

'I saved it,' whined Gran. 'A few coppers at a time. Took me years.'

'You are a bloody liar!' said Rosie. 'You've never saved a penny in your entire life. Where did you get it?' Then, suddenly, she remembered a piece of gossip which had been relayed to her by a neighbour. Some three weeks earlier a commercial traveller had reported the loss of a purse containing his week's takings: a notice had appeared on the board at the local newsagent's shop offering £1 reward for its return. The gossip indicated that he thought, although he could not be certain, that he had lost the purse while enjoying a drink or two at a public house called The Duke of Cambridge.

'You stole this!' Rosie shouted, and then, realising that the Bennetts might overhear, she lowered her voice to a hiss: 'You thieving old cow! You pinched the money – you pinched it from that bloke up at the Duke!'

Gran cringed away, fearful that Rosie would strike out at her. 'It was his own fault,' she protested. 'He was half-drunk and he didn't know how to look after his money. It dropped out of his pocket on to the seat when he got up to go to the men's lav. No one saw it but me. So I whipped it up and hopped off. When I got outside I went into the yard and slipped it down my bloomers.'

'You're a bloody thief – a rotten bloody tea-leaf!' said Rosie, as she began to gather up the coins and replace them in the bag. 'What did you do with the purse?'

'I chucked it away, didn't I?' said Gran, with a cunning little smirk. 'Pushed it down a drain. I mean, the purse was evidence, right?'

'Right?' said Rosie scornfully. 'There's nothing right about any of it. Did you ever stop to think what would have happened if you'd been caught?'

Gran cackled. 'Well, I wasn't caught, was I?' More fearfully she added: 'What are you going to do?'

'I don't know,' said Rosie. 'I'd give the money back if I knew where to find the bloke.'

'No! No!' moaned Gran. 'That's for my funeral! He was a toff, Rosie! He won't miss it. I don't want to be buried on the parish, Rosie – please. Please!'

'You don't deserve to be buried at all!' said Rosie sharply. 'You should be dumped in the river!'

She had never known the old lady give way to tears but she began to weep now, the tears dripping uncertainly down the dried-up old face as though surprised to be released.

'All right, all right,' said Rosie, softening. 'You can turn off the waterworks.'

'What are you going to do with my money?'

'It's not your bloody money! I don't know what I shall do. It wants thinking about.'

With the bag in her hand, she crossed to the gas-bracket and turned it off. Out of the darkness came Gran's voice. 'I only took it for my funeral, Rosie. I don't want to be buried on the parish.'

'Go to sleep,' Rosie said quietly. 'You'll have a proper funeral, don't fret. I'll see to it.'

'Horses with black plumes?'

'Horses with black plumes,' said Rosie, closing the door.

As she went downstairs, the bag clutched in her hand, she began to smile. The smile became a chuckle as she pictured the old lady walking home with the purse tucked down her drawers.

It was wrong, all wrong, but you had to admire the wicked old devil.

She knew also there was no way that she could return the money without implicating Gran and causing endless complications. Perhaps the old lady deserved her slap-up funeral, her last defiant gesture to a world that had given her so little.

She decided to hide the money and think it out when she was not so tired.

3

When Rosie found Mark in his lock-up store in Culross Road the next morning, he was cutting long slabs of hard yellow soap into small oblong bars with a long wire, one end of which was fixed to the bench. It reminded Rosie of the cheese-cutter that Mr Davies used in his dairy. The size and cleanliness of the store surprised her: it was wide and light and neatly stacked with boxes and cartons of various sizes.

He looked up with a cheerful grin when she appeared in the doorway. 'Now, there's a pretty thing,' he said, 'there's a sight for sore eyes.' He pulled an empty box forward and dusted it with an elaborate flourish of his hand. 'Take a seat, darling.'

'What are you doing?' she asked.

'This, darling, is the bargain of the century! I buy a slab of soap direct from the factory. It costs me a Scotchman – two shillings. I cut it up like so, and if I'm careful I can get twenty-one bars of soap out of it. Now, tell me, what would you pay for a bar like this?'

'Threepence or fourpence,' she replied.

'Ah!' he said. 'I hoped you'd say that. I can sell it at three bars for a tanner – a cost per bar of twopence only. The identical all-purpose soap that you buy for threepence or fourpence. The People's Friend strikes again! I do my customers a favour—'

'And make one shilling and sixpence profit on every slab,' she interrupted.

'You're quick-silver, darling. And you're right. One slab equals twenty-one bars. I buy for two bob and sell for three-and-a-kick. Simple arithmetic. Good business.'

She looked at the slabs of soap that were stacked to one side. 'How many of those have you bought?'

'A hundred, to start with. I want to see how they go. I'm aiming to shift this lot in three days.'

Rosie did another quick mental calculation. If Mark sold out, it would mean a profit of over seven pounds! For little more than three days' work! But, as if he were reading her thoughts, he said: 'It's not all profit, you know. I have to live, and I've got my overheads to consider.'

'Still it isn't bad,' she said.

'No. Bad it is not. But this is only the beginning, darling, small stuff. You wait until I really get going – they won't see my backside for dust!'

'They'll see your head, though,' said Rosie. 'It's getting bigger every minute.'

He grinned. 'Confidence, Rosie. A human being can either climb up or slip down. And what am I? I'll tell you – I'm a climber.'

'That's one way of putting it,' she said.

'Look,' he said, 'do ya fancy a cuppa tea?'

'I wouldn't say no,' she said.

'So, let's have tea. Will you make it while I get on with this? You'll find everything you need behind that curtain.'

The curtain he indicated stretched from wall to wall at the far end of the shed. When she pulled it across, Rosie had yet another surprise, for she found the area equipped as living quarters, even down to a low truckle bed. There was a worn armchair, a table and a wooden chair, a sink, a small gas-stove and a cupboard. All the furnishings were obviously secondhand but the place was scrupulously clean and tidy.

'You don't live here, do you?' she asked.

'A lot of the time,' he replied. 'My proper home is in Flower and Dean Street, up the East End, but when I've had a long day I don't bother to go home. I just kip down here. That way I can make an early start in the morning.'

'Have you got a family?'

'My dad was killed in the war. Besides Mum, I've got a sister and a brother.'

While the kettle was boiling, Rosie took a surreptitious peep at Mark. Really, she could not see that being Jewish made him look different from dozens of other men. In any case, what did it matter what he was? As far as she could see, he was hard-working and generous: he could teach a lot of people a thing or two in that respect. On the other hand, did he have some deeper, unspoken motive for offering her a job? The bed, for instance. Was all this leading in that direction, was he simply trying to buy her?

When she took the tea out to Mark he asked: 'Well, did you think over what I said?'

'Of course,' said Rosie.

'And?'

She felt herself blushing as she replied: 'I'm not sure.'

'What's the problem?'

'I don't know,' she said hesitantly. 'I mean, it's good of you to offer . . .'

'Listen,' he interrupted. 'Do me a favour and listen for a moment.' He took her by the shoulders and set her down on the empty box. 'Sit there and listen. I meant what I said last night. I need someone who is bright and quick, who knows the markets and who is not afraid of hard work.'

'But—' she began.

'Listen!' he insisted. 'I'm growing fast. I'm going to grow even faster.' He pointed to the pile of envelopes and scrap paper. 'Look at that. My books, my records. That's no good, is it? I've got to open a proper bank account, keep proper books, all that. And I haven't got the time and patience myself. You could do that, you could help buy the stock, you could help me sell. Come on, darling. You'll be doing me a favour.'

'You haven't looked,' she said, her head whirling.

'I have, you know. I've tried half a dozen people – they were useless. A donkey to pull the cart, this I can get. Do I need a donkey? No. I need someone like you. You are just the ticket!'

'I don't think I could do it, Mark,' she said.

'Standing on your head,' he said. 'You could do it standing on your head.'

'I don't know,' she said, surprised at her own stubbornness, yet still unable to frame the question that loomed in her mind.

Their eyes met and there was a long pause. Then, as if he had suddenly understood the reason for her hesitation, he leaned forward and took her hand.

'Rosie. I like you. I'd be a liar if I said anything else. But that's not why I want you to work for me. You've got to believe me. I need help, that's all there is to it. I've asked around and I can't find anyone to say a bad word about you. I know you could do the job and I know I can trust you. That's all I need to know and that's all there is to it, straight up.'

'I didn't mean . . .,' she began apologetically.

'Look,' he said, 'I tell you what. Try it for a week or two. If it doesn't work out – well, too bad. No bones broken, no harm done. What do you say?'

'People might talk,' she said defensively.

'People always talk. Tongues have no bones – so they can't help being loose. Do you care about that? I don't. What we're making is a business arrangement, nothing else. All square and above board.'

Why not, she thought, why not? God knows, I need the job, I need the money. What did it matter what people said?

He interrupted her thoughts: 'Do it, Rosie,' he said, 'do it for your own sake. Team up with me and we'll really go places. I know I'm working on the right lines, and I don't intend to stay in a back alley all my life. I'm going to make money, Rosie, because that's the way to be free, know what I mean? Don't get me wrong, I'm not saying that money is everything, the be-all and end-all. But without it, what are you? You work for somebody else, your life belongs to other people. Money is the thing that can spring you free, open the door, make you independent. You understand me?'

Oh, yes, she thought, I understand you. All her life she had been a kind of prisoner, she knew the restraints of poverty as well as or better than he. Aloud, she said:

'All right. We'll give it a go.'

CHAPTER FIVE

1

In the late summer of that year, the newspapers occupied their
space with several stories of varying interest. They made
headlines out of the death of the President of the United States
and the swearing in, as his successor, of someone called Calvin
Coolidge. The perpetual problem of Ireland flared again with
the arrest of Eamon de Valera and there was a big earthquake in
Japan. In Germany something called wheelbarrow inflation
aroused considerable interest but little sympathy.

Much was made of the possibility of an autumn general
election and of the almost unthinkable suggestion that the
Labour Party, under Ramsay MacDonald, might come to power
for the first time. The general thrust of most articles on this
theme was that MacDonald and his colleagues were dangerous
agitators, in the pay and the pocket of the Soviets.

Apart from these heavyweight stories, the newspapers
entertained their readers with features about Bernard Shaw's
mammoth new play, *Back to Methuselah*; about the tango, a new
dance which was said to be sweeping Britain; about the length
or rather the brevity of women's skirts, a subject addressed with
passion by a group calling itself 'The League for the Defence of
Public Morals'; and – a recurring theme, this – the development
of wireless broadcasting and the danger to family life and
culture if the British became a nation of addictive wireless
listeners.

It has to be said, however, that much of all this went way
over the heads of the residents of Shakespeare Street. Few, if
any of them, had heard of Calvin Coolidge, Ramsay MacDonald
or Bernard Shaw; not one resident had tried to tango; and there

was not a single wireless set in the street, although rumour had it that Rosie's son, Eddie, was in the process of building one.

The people in Shakespeare Street, in addition to the persistent and apparently insoluble question of simply making enough to eat and pay the rent, were concerned about another major problem.

Rats.

2

There had always been the odd rat in the street; rats and mice and cockroaches were seen as part of the penalty of living in near-slum conditions. But, quite suddenly, an army of rats, so formidable that it would have challenged the talents of a Pied Piper, descended on the district. Huge rats they were and bold, so bold that they raided dustbins, entered kitchens and bedrooms, gnawed their way into cupboards and through floorboards, and often stood their ground when challenged.

It was not difficult to locate the source of this plague. The local Council was clearing a huge rubbish dump, about a mile or so away, to make way for a property development and so driving the rats from a place that had been their home for generations.

Rosie first became aware of the problem when she entered the kitchen one morning and found two large brown rats on the kitchen table. They were so busy with a half-loaf of bread that her entrance was scarcely noticed and when they did deign to recognise her presence it was only to stare at her with bright eyes and twitch their tails. She stepped warily past the table, opened the back door and then, seizing the frying pan, chased them out into the yard. Shuddering, for she loathed the creatures, Rosie boiled up some water and scrubbed the kitchen floor and the table until she was satisfied that no trace of the intruders remained.

Later that morning, neighbours spoke of similar experiences.

Old Mrs Budd's cupboard had almost been cleared out; dustbins had been looted; a cornered rat had flown at Mrs Bushell and bitten her on the arm; Mrs Miller's daughter, aged ten, had woken to find a rat on her bed and gone into hysterics. Almost every household had its story to tell. Mrs Bushell had to be taken to the Cottage Hospital for an injection and Mrs Miller's daughter, still shaken, was kept off school for the day.

When the pattern was repeated in the following days, Rosie decided that something had to be done and she took herself to the Town Hall to register a complaint with the official Rat-Catcher. She was kept waiting for an hour in a bleak corridor and then informed by a haughty girl that the post of Rat-Catcher had been abolished.

'You mean we don't have a Rat-Catcher now?' demanded Rosie.

'That is correct,' said the girl.

'Then who is responsible for catching the rats?'

'That comes under the Pest Control Officer.'

'All right,' said Rosie. 'Whatever he's called, I want to see him.'

'I am afraid he is not available at the moment.'

'When will he be available, as you put it?'

'I'm afraid that he is under considerable pressure at this time.'

'So are we,' Rosie said. 'We're being overrun by rats.'

'Yes,' said the girl. 'Indeed. We've had several similar complaints in the past few days. The Pest Control Officer and his team are doing their best to cope. If you will leave your name and address, I will see that your complaint is dealt with ASAP.'

'ASAP?' asked Rosie.

'As soon as possible,' said the girl with a touch of impatience. She noted the name and address and dismissed Rosie with a curt 'good morning'.

'Tell him it's urgent,' Rosie said.

'I will see that he gets the message,' said the girl.

Two days went by without any sign of the so-called Pest

Control Officer or his team and without any diminution of the rat invasion. Home-made traps were devised and put in place, bits of food which could ill be spared were impregnated with poison, but the total haul was pitifully small. The rats, contemptuous of these amateur efforts, attacked the street in greater numbers. Night was disturbed by their relentless gnawing and scurrying, and during the day it was scarcely possible to move outside without seeing the creatures.

A telephone call to the Town Hall met with a dusty answer and a half-hearted promise that some action would be taken the next day. But that day passed also and no one came. Mrs Perryman, who worked as a charwoman for one of the local councillors, did report that she had actually seen the Pest Control Officer and his team. Apparently the councillor's wife had spotted a rat in her garden that morning and had informed the Town Hall in terms of some hysteria. The Pest Control Officer, ever conscious of his duty to the elected representatives of the people, arrived hot-foot within an hour of receiving the call. This report outraged Rosie and fuelled her growing anger.

3

'Rosie! Rosie!'

She heard the cry and the insistent hammering on the door as she prepared breakfast and hurried along the passage. Mollie Ryan, the Irish girl who lived three doors away, was standing on the step in a state of near-hysterics. Blood stained the shawl she had thrown on over her nightgown and there was more blood on her hands. She seized Rosie's arm and pulled her forward.

'Rosie – please. Come quick! Come quick!'

'What is it?'

'The baby. The rats.'

Rosie felt her heart contract with terror. Together they raced down the street and into the Ryan house. In the kitchen they found Donal, Mollie's husband, holding a bloodstained bundle to his breast. He was rocking to and fro, crooning as he did so, and when he looked up at Rosie she saw huge tears glittering in his eyes. Gently she took the bundle from him.

Michael, the baby, lay silent, his eyes closed as if in death. There was a bloody gash at his throat, and in three places on his arms and legs the flesh had been ripped open. The wounds gaped at Rosie like raw meat on a butcher's slab and she felt the nausea writhe in her stomach.

'Hot water!' she commanded. 'And some clean rags. Quick now!'

Mollie brought water and tore a sheet to make clean strips of rag. Donal sat silent, locked in his grief.

'Will he die?' whispered Mollie.

'He's breathing, that's something,' Rosie said as she bathed the ugly wounds. 'How the hell did you come to let this happen?'

'We were asleep. I woke when I heard the baby crying but I took no notice at first. I mean, he cries a lot, you see. That's why we put him in the back bedroom, so that Donal could get his rest. I must have dropped off again, then I heard Michael scream. I rushed in to him and – Holy God – the rats were at him! Four great rats – it was like they were feeding on him! I could see the blood on their jaws, I tell you. I drove them off. One of them wouldn't go at first, he defied me. I snatched the baby away and ran in to Donal.'

Rosie turned to Mollie's husband and said sharply; 'Don't sit there feeling sorry for yourself, man. Get your clothes on, quick, sharp. We must get this baby to hospital!'

She left the Ryans in the waiting room at St Anne's Hospital half an hour later and walked slowly home. A numbing sense of shock pervaded her body, and her mind was haunted by the image of a mutilated baby and of four rats crawling over the home-made crib . . .

Word of the incident had spread down the street and a group of men and women waited outside Rosie's house, quietly talking. They turned as Rosie approached, eager for news.

'How is he? How's the baby?' asked Mrs Miller.

'I don't know. The doctors haven't said yet.'

'Is it bad?'

'What do you think!' said Rosie scathingly.

'They should have known better than to leave a young baby to sleep alone at a time like this,' said Mrs Gibson.

'That's the Ryans for you,' said Mrs Archibald. 'Feckless. Always have been.'

'Never mind the Ryans!' said Rosie, anger taking over from shock. 'What about the bloody Town Hall! They're responsible. They're the ones responsible! Bloody murderers! They're quick enough to act when it's some bloody councillor but they ignore us. Well, I'll tell you something, I'm not putting up with their old slop any longer. I'm going up there to give them a mouthful of my mind and I don't intend to leave until they do something! And if you've got any guts you'll come with me!'

4

Thus it was that, later in the morning, a procession of some sixteen women descended upon the Town Hall. Young, old, middle-aged, they walked with bitter determination printed on their faces, and the very fact of marching together, of acting in unison, seemed to each woman to add strength to their purpose. Rosie led the way and Mrs Miller brought up the rear, pushing Mollie Ryan's old perambulator in which, instead of a baby, there was an old wicker basket.

The attendant at the Town Hall, a former sergeant-major with the Coldstream Guards who had lost an arm at the Battle of the Somme in 1916, eyed the deputation with a certain doubt, sensing that the anger on the faces of these women was the preface to trouble.

'What's this all about, then?' he demanded, in his best regimental manner.

'We want to see the what's-his-name – the Pest Control Officer,' said Rosie.

'Have you got an appointment?'

'No.'

'Ah,' he said. 'Then you have a problem, ladies. Mr Hargreaves is a very busy man.'

'So are we,' said Rosie, 'we're all busy. Just tell him we're here, will you? Mrs Thompson and friends. We want five minutes of his time.' She gave him her most beguiling smile. 'Go on. See what you can do, eh?'

He did not return the smile although the frosty glint in his military eyes melted momentarily. After a brief hesitation he said: 'Wait here. I will see if Mr Hargreaves is available. What shall I say is the nature of your business?'

'Rats,' Rosie said shortly.

He nodded gravely, not at all surprised by her reply, and began to climb the wide stairway to the first floor. Rosie watched until he disappeared around a bend in the stairs then turned to Lily Miller and Maisie Pembroke.

'Lil, nip out to the pram and bring that basket in. Look sharp. And you, Maisie, get over the road to the offices of the *Tottenham Herald* and tell them there's trouble at the Town Hall.'

'Trouble?' said Maisie.

'There's going to be, you silly moo,' said Rosie. 'Now, scoot. Tell them to send a reporter.'

The attendant returned a few minutes later, his thin lips pursed beneath the waxed moustache. 'Sorry, ladies, it is as I thought, Mr Hargreaves is in conference at this moment in time.' He turned to Rosie. 'However, if you will leave your name and address with me, he will contact you regarding an appointment.'

'We'll wait,' Rosie said.

'Ah,' he said. 'Ah. I don't think that will help you. You see, after his meeting, Mr Hargreaves has several other appointments.' He was clearly puzzled by the determination of these women: his usual experience was that most people of their type deferred to authority.

'We'll wait,' Rosie repeated. 'We'll wait all day if necessary.' And suiting action to the words she sat down on the floor.

'We'll wait,' echoed the other women and, one by one, they

joined Rosie on the floor. The attendant looked down at them in astonishment.

'Ladies, please. You can't wait here. Be reasonable. Shove off home like good girls.' When this produced no response he added sternly: 'You are trespassing, you know, trespassing. Committing an offence.'

'This is the Town Hall, right?' asked Rosie.

'Yes.'

'Our Town Hall. Built and paid for by the people of Tottenham. We've as much right to be here as anyone.'

He looked from one to the other, shaking his head. 'I shall see someone in authority about this,' he said feebly and hurried up the stairs.

'Will he bring the police, Rosie?' asked Mrs Gibson.

'He can bring the bloody army as far as I'm concerned,' Rosie replied.

'Blimey,' said Mrs Archibald. 'In the rush, I forgot to put my drawers on. This floor is a bit cold on the old arse.'

By this time, news of the invasion had begun to filter through the building: clerks and officials peeped down over the landings at the ragged group of women. People entering and leaving threaded their way through with muttered apologies and astonished looks.

The attendant came down to them once more, his face composed in a look of grim authority.

'Well?' asked Rosie.

'I am instructed by His Worship the Mayor to inform you that he will not countenance this irregular behaviour. Further, to add that if you do not vacate these premises within ten minutes, the police will be summoned and instructed to eject you.'

'Oh,' said Rosie, 'you spoke to the Mayor, did you?'

'I did. I spoke to His Worship in person.'

'We'll see him, then,' said Rosie blithely. 'He'll do. After all, why speak to the oil-rag when you can talk to the engine-driver?'

'I must warn you—' he began. But Rosie, pushing herself to

her feet, interrupted him. He was a foot taller, slim and straight as a ramrod, but she looked up at him with complete composure.

'Don't warn me, mate. I've been warned by bigger and better men than you.' She turned to the others. 'Come on, girls, on your feet.' As they rose, Rosie moved towards the stairs.

'Where are you going?' blustered the attendant.

'Haven't you heard the saying?' replied Rosie. 'If Mahomet won't come to the mountain, the mountain must come to Mahomet. Or words to that effect. We're going to see His Worship.'

He tried to bar the way but again Rosie confronted him without fear. 'Don't make trouble for yourself, mate. If you try to stop us, we'll put you on your arse. And don't run away with the idea that we couldn't do it!'

'You'll be sorry!' he threatened, but it was the last shot in his locker and, acknowledging defeat, he stood aside as the women surged past him.

At the top of the stairs a gaggle of clerks and secretaries, torn between incredulity and amusement, watched Rosie lead her troops upwards.

'Where does the Mayor hang out?' she asked.

'Along the corridor. Second door on the left,' replied one of the group and he added, for good measure: 'Best of British luck, ladies!'

The second door along was plainly marked MAYOR'S PARLOUR and Rosie opened it without ceremony. Half a dozen sober-faced and sober-suited men looked up in astonishment as the women crowded into the room.

'What on earth is going on here?' asked the man in the centre chair at the table. He was small and precise, with thin gold hair plastered over his balding head and thin gold-rimmed spectacles to match.

'Which one of you is the Mayor?'

'I am he,' said the man in gold spectacles, rising from his chair. 'What is the meaning of this intrusion?'

'Good,' said Rosie, advancing into the room. 'We're from

Shakespeare Street. We want to know when you intend to do something about the rats.'

'Wilkins!' said the Mayor coldly. 'Call the police and have these persons ejected.'

One of the men made a hesitant move towards the door but Rosie and Mrs Archibald blocked his path.

'You try it and we'll have your trousers down, sonny.' As he backed off, Rosie said: 'Maisie, Nancy. Watch that other door.' Two of the women moved across to a side door which linked with an adjoining office and stood with their arms folded.

'This is preposterous!' said the Mayor.

'Not half as preposterous as the bloody rats you've let loose on us,' said Rosie.

'Now, listen to me, my good woman,' the Mayor began angrily, but he was interrupted.

'Perhaps, if you will allow me, Mr Mayor?' A tall thin man in a black jacket and striped trousers stepped forward. 'I am the Town Clerk. Now, what seems to be the problem?' His tone, honed by years of experience, was deep, mellifluous and utterly reasonable, his face sternly polite although Rosie fancied she could see a twinkle in his blue eyes.

'You're not going to treat with these people, Town Clerk!' demanded the Mayor.

'Since they're here, Your Worship,' said the Town Clerk diplomatically.

Rosie, prompted by some of her companions, told the story of the rat invasion and, in particular, what had happened to the Ryans' baby. The Town Clerk nodded in sympathy and murmurs of horror and disbelief came from the men at the table.

'All right, ladies,' said the Town Clerk. 'I can well understand your anxiety.'

'Understanding is one thing,' replied Rosie. 'Doing something is another.'

'We will send some men first thing tomorrow.'

'I've heard that one before.'

'I give you my word,' said the Town Clerk.

'What's wrong with this afternoon?' asked Rosie. 'Why wait till tomorrow?'

He looked down at her and smiled. 'You are a persistent young woman. Very well, someone will call this afternoon and see what needs to be done.'

'You'd better not let us down,' she said and then, astonished by both her own temerity and growing confidence, she added: 'If you do, I promise that the story will be on the front page of the *Tottenham Herald*! The reporter is outside now.'

'This is blackmail!' stuttered the Mayor, but the apprehension on his face told Rosie that she had registered a bull's-eye.

'Call it what you like,' she said. 'We want something done, that's all. And if that baby dies, God help the lot of you!'

'We will get the officer there immediately,' said the Town Clerk quickly.

'Good,' said Rosie. 'Thank you. Come on, girls.'

As they moved to the door, the Town Clerk said: 'You've forgotten your basket.'

'Oh, no,' said Rosie, 'that's yours. A little present from Shakespeare Street. Just as a reminder, just so you don't forget us.'

When the women had gone, the man called Wilkins opened the lid of the basket gingerly. He closed it with a shudder just in time, just before one of the big grey rats inside could leap out at him.

5

On the way back to Shakespeare Street, Rosie felt an extraordinary sense of triumph and wellbeing. She marched along with the other women, chattering and laughing, mocking and imitating the Mayor and his minions, savouring every moment of this famous victory.

What on earth happened, she wondered, what took hold of

me? It was almost as if the events of the morning had thrown up another kind of Rosie, a woman who could not only lead and organise others but who enjoyed doing so. There had been moments in the Mayor's Parlour when she had scarcely believed that it was Rosie Carr saying those things, when she had been astonished by her own boldness. What voice, for instance, had prompted her to take along the basket of rats, to sit down on the floor of the Town Hall, to call in the local newspaper?

She had no experience in such matters, and certainly nothing had been planned or premeditated. No, it had all come naturally, each step leading to another, and it had worked, that was the wonder and miracle of it all. They had stood up to the bureaucrats and won. Was this then the way to change things, she wondered, was this the way to check injustice and make life better for her own kind?

And then the old practical Rosie began to assert herself, warning her to come down out of the clouds. All right, all right, she had not done badly. But she had not been alone, without the support of her friends nothing would have been achieved. It was a small victory after all, it would not really change the way they lived. It would not change things for the Ryans' baby, that was certain. And at the thought of the child, lying in a hospital cot with those terrifying wounds, she felt ashamed.

The other women sensed her altered mood and responded to it. They fell silent except for an occasional word and were silent when they arrived in the street. They waited while Rosie went to the Ryans' house, acknowledging her new role as their spokeswoman without argument.

'Mollie's at the hospital now,' said Donal. The sturdy young Irishman seemed to have shrunk, haunted eyes looked out from a haggard face. ' The doctor reckons the baby will be all right.'

'Thank God for that,' Rosie said.

'The next twenty-four hours will tell.'

'Anything I can do?'

'No. You've done enough. Thanks and God bless you. We'll be fine.'

She did not tell him that the Council had promised to deal

with the rats. What was the point? What consolation would that bring him?

When she got home, Eddie, his eyes bright with excitement, told her that Donal had gone berserk during her absence. Wielding the shovel that he used for navvying he had gone from yard to yard, alley to alley, overturning bins and searching rubbish dumps and sheds for rats.

'He must have killed twenty or more, Mum,' he said. 'And he was cursing and crying, cursing and crying all the time.'

6

The Council did come that afternoon. A small army of men, many of them recruited from the ranks of the unemployed, descended on Shakespeare Street and the surrounding area with traps and poisoned bait and declared war on the rats.

Within a week the worst of the nightmare was over and it was possible to sleep without fear. Within a month, the rats had been destroyed or driven out and life went back to normal, more or less. It was reported that packs of rats had been sighted, heading for the marshes at Hackney, but the inhabitants of Shakespeare Street were hardly concerned. Someone else could deal with that problem.

The Ryans' baby, discharged from hospital after five weeks, seemed little the worse for the experience. But the scars were there at his throat and on his legs and arms and would remain there for a long time, if not for the rest of his life.

The incident passed into the folklore of the street and became a sort of mark in its mental calendar. People began to date events by saying that such and such a thing had happened 'before the rats' or 'after the rats'. And the street was never quite the same again. The action at the Town Hall had brought the residents together, broken down their old antagonisms, even given them a certain pride.

Rosie did not fully realise it, but her life was never quite the same either. Word of the way she had stood up to the Council, fanned by a report in the *Tottenham Herald*, spread throughout the district. People began to come to her for help with their problems, women stopped her in the street to ask advice.

Over the next few months, this new involvement and her growing interest in Mark Moss's developing business produced a subtle change in Rosie. It was as if events were edging her towards maturity: her life seemed to have some purpose and direction at last and with this was born a new confidence. More important still, she was happy, she actually looked forward to the days ahead.

It was at this time, some six months after the invasion of the rats, that Rosie found herself, figuratively speaking, up to her neck in tea.

CHAPTER SIX

1

It began with a statement which, on the surface at least, had no great claim to significance. Mrs Archibald, taking a cup of tea with Rosie one evening, remarked as she refilled the cups: 'I wish I had a pound for every cup of you-and-me I've drunk in my life. I'd be a bloody millionaire!'

Had it not been for her association with Mark Moss, Rosie would not have given this old cliché a second thought, but now it occurred to her that Mrs Archibald might have expressed a truth of some business significance. She felt a sudden inner excitement as if a light had flashed on in her mind, and the more she thought about it the more excited she became.

The plain fact was that the average person's daily intake of tea was enormous. Indeed, if anyone had taken the trouble to conduct a poll into the drinking habits of the people in Shakespeare Street they would have discovered, probably to their surprise, that the consumption of tea exceeded that of beer or any other beverage by a very large margin.

Of course, no one ever referred to tea by its proper name. It was variously known as 'Rosie Lee', or 'you-and-me', or 'char', and in at least one household it was called simply a 'cup of sailors', this being an obscure contraction of 'sailors of the sea'.

Tea was seen as a sort of universal panacea. There was nothing like it as a pick-me-up after an exhausting day; it had the power to soothe and relax tortured nerves, to settle the spirit after an emotional upheaval, to repair fractured friendships. The received wisdom was that on a hot summer day nothing cooled the blood more effectively than a cup of hot tea; while, in winter, tea with lemon or a dash of whisky made the finest remedy for a cold. Hospitality and good manners demanded that, no matter the time of day or night, visitors should be told that the kettle was on and invited to take a cuppa. The men who were fortunate enough to have jobs invariably took to work a gooey mixture of fresh tea-leaves and condensed milk so that they would have an instant brew-up during their break.

Tea. Tea. Tea. The word rang in Rosie's head and with it came a half-formed idea which she resolved to mention to Mark Moss at the earliest opportunity.

She had now been working for Mark for some six months and their association had proved to be a good one for them both. For Rosie, the real breakthrough had come when, finding herself faced with what she knew to be a bargain and unable to contact Mark, she had taken a deep breath and bought two hundred cases of jam. Each case contained forty-eight jars of strawberry jam and each jar bore the label and trademark of a famous firm: the only snag was that the parchment tops on most of the jars were damaged. But Rosie got the consignment at a throw-away price and set to work to repair the damage with squares of grease-proof paper and elastic bands.

Mark was doubtful about the success of this operation and, indeed, as they worked into the night, there did seem to be an awful lot of jam. Rosie began to have her reservations also, but the deal had been agreed and there was no going back. In the event, her first instinct proved to be right. Mark offered the jam in the market at half the normal shop price and the housewives queued to buy it. The entire consignment was sold in five days, yielding a net profit of over one hundred pounds.

The delighted Mark pressed a bonus of ten pounds on a somewhat reluctant Rosie and from then on gave her a free hand to purchase anything which she considered to be a bargain. Much of the buying was now concentrated in her hands, while he specialised in the selling. He also conceded the need to keep better records and allowed her to open a bank account in his name. Few people could refuse Rosie anything and she persuaded one of the younger cashiers, a Mr Lightblow, to teach her how to keep simple books. Mark's scraps of paper became almost a thing of the past and, in cashbooks purchased from Woolworths, Rosie kept a neat record of the stock in hand and of all their transactions.

A month or so before the sale of the jam Mark had experienced one of his rare failures. A large batch of cheap alarm clocks, bought at a bargain price, did not sell as well as he had expected and many of the clocks turned out to be defective. Angry customers queued to take him up on the sign that was painted above his stall: MY PROMISE — MONEY BACK IN FULL IF YOU ARE NOT SATISFIED. He honoured the promise but the result was a heavy loss and a warehouse stacked with clocks which nobody wanted.

After this experience, and under Rosie's influence, Mark decided to concentrate on foodstuffs. She knew from experience that housewives who had to make every penny count could not only smell out a bargain for themselves but would also spread the word to others. All you had to do, in Rosie's view, was to take Mark's philosophy of pile it high and sell it cheap, apply it to a basic and essential commodity like food, and you had a sure recipe for success.

So, the morning after Mrs Archibald's chance remark, the raised the subject of tea with Mark.

2

It was raining heavily outside and Mark had decided to give the market a miss until the weather cleared up. He was filling in the time by checking through the accursed alarm clocks to see which were in working order and could be sold with confidence. The ticking of dozens of clocks and the regular eruption of their alarms, combined with the noisy drumming of rain on the corrugated-iron roof made communication difficult and Rosie assumed from Mark's blank look that he had not heard her question. She raised her voice above the din: 'I said – what do you think about tea?'

'Tea? Am I mistaken or didn't we just have a cup? You feel the need for more already?'

'Not to drink, you daft ha'porth. To sell. Like we did the jam.'

He lifted his dark eyebrows in a question mark, pursed his lips and generally did his best to look doubtful. Undeterred, she pressed on. 'I was thinking yesterday. Everybody drinks tea. Well, almost everybody. If we could get a supply at the right price I'm sure it would sell.'

'It might,' he said, 'it might.' But there was no conviction in his tone.

'You don't like the idea?'

'A snag,' he said, lifting a warning finger. 'I see a snag. I don't think we could get the merchandise.'

'Why not?'

'How do people buy their tea? In sealed packets with brand names on them. Liptons, Mazawattee and so forth. Such firms are not going to sell cheap to us and then stand by while we undercut them. They should be so stupid!'

'Where do they get their supplies?'

'That is also a question. And the answer? I think Liptons have their own tea plantations in India and Ceylon.'

'There must be some independent tea wholesalers.'

'Tea wholesalers there are. Undoubtedly. But here's another problem. Tea comes in bloody great chests, Rosie. How am I supposed to sell that? I should ask the customers to bring buckets and dish it out by the shovelful?'

Three alarm clocks went off simultaneously and this interruption gave Rosie an opportunity to ponder the problem. When the noise subsided she said: 'Why couldn't we package the tea ourselves?'

'It would be one hell of a job,' he said.

'Needn't be anything elaborate. Weigh it up and sell it in ordinary paper bags – a quarter- or half-pound at a time. I mean, you can't drink the packet, it's the tea that's important. If we could sell a decent tea at a lower price than the shops, the customers wouldn't care if it came wrapped in old newspapers.'

Mark was beginning to show some interest now. 'No,' he said. 'No. That is where you are wrong for once. It won't sell if it's wrapped up any-old-how. People are used to having a name with their tea, a name they can trust.'

'Right,' said Rosie. 'So let's think up our own name.'

'A name?' he said, smiling. 'A name I have already. Why should I want a new one?'

'Not that sort of name! A brand name. A sort of trademark.'

He looked at her in silence for a moment or two, then nodded slowly. There was a gleam of real excitement in his eyes.

'Maybe this is a good idea, Rosie. Our own name. We could get old Milton, the printer, to do us some special bags – with the name printed on them!'

They sparred eagerly with several possible names, rejecting them one by one as unsuitable. Mark suggested Rosie Lee, arguing that this was not only the Cockney name for tea but that it had a very proper connection with Rosie herself. Rosie had her doubts about this one and came up with the idea that they use Mark's initials and call it Double-M Tea.

'No,' said Mark. 'It's your idea. If anyone's name goes on the packet, it's got to be yours.'

This spurred Rosie to another thought. 'Why not both our names? Put them together like. How about that?'

'Too long,' said Mark.

'Cut them down,' answered Rosie. 'Use my maiden name, Carr. Call it Carmoss Tea.'

'Carmoss?' Mark shook his head. 'Wait. Carmo. What do you think?'

'Carmo?' said Rosie. 'Carmo Tea.' She repeated the name. 'Carmo Tea! Yes! And underneath that we'll put your slogan. I can see it now: CARMO TEA – THE PEOPLE'S FRIEND.'

'The People's Friend!' said Mark and put out a hand. 'Carmo. Yes, I like the idea. In some respects, Rosie, you are a genius. Let me shake your hand.'

They shook hands with some solemnity as if they were

congratulating each other on a new birth. Each sensed, without knowing why, that this moment held a special significance. Hitherto, they had been anonymous street traders, buying and selling other people's products: now by adopting a name they had given themselves an identity and invested their enterprise with a kind of status.

'We still have one problem,' said Mark.

'What's that?'

'Where to lay our hands on some tea?'

'Leave that to me,' Rosie said, with a confidence that she did not entirely feel. And, as if to emphasise the point, half a dozen clocks chose that moment to sound a shrill alarm.

3

It was Mr Lightblow, the friendly bank cashier, who pointed Rosie in the right direction.

'Mincing Lane. That's the place. That's where the tea merchants have their offices.'

'Where's that?' asked Rosie.

'I'm not exactly sure. In the City somewhere. Yes, wait. It's not far from the Tower. If you got yourself to the Tower of London and asked a policeman, he'd direct you.'

Mr Lightblow's geography proved to be more or less accurate. Rosie took a tramcar to Liverpool Street and found her way from there to the Tower where a City policeman directed her to Great Tower Street and thence to Mincing Lane. But what had appeared to be so simple and straightforward when talking to Mark now took on a different and more complicated aspect.

For a start, she now found herself in a strange and almost alien world. She was used to seeing crowds in the market, but this was all so different. Clerks in stiff collars and dark suits, smartly dressed secretaries, uniformed messengers, important-looking gentlemen in top-hats or bowlers whose view on the weather outlook was seemingly so pessimistic that they all carried furled umbrellas, jostled purposefully with each other for elbow room. A mixture of motor-cars, vans and horsedrawn vehicles cluttered the roadway and, from time to time, street urchins no older than her own Eddie darted into the jam of traffic armed with brushes and pans to sweep up the horse-droppings.

Rosie felt dwarfed by the magnificent buildings and overawed by these City folk: with each step her resolve weakened and, when she reached Mincing Lane at last, it was in her mind to turn back and abandon an expedition which now seemed less and less plausible. At that moment a hand grasped her arm and a stern voice boomed in her ear: 'And what do you think you are doing here, my girl!'

She turned in sudden fright to find herself looking into the gruff, smiling face of Mr Waterlow. Rosie only knew him as a regular Friday- and Saturday-night customer at The Winged Horse and she had never seen him as he appeared now, clad in a long frock-coat which was held together by gleaming brass buttons, braided trousers, and a brimmed hat shaped like a gentleman's top-hat except that it was half the size and boasted a feather at one side. It took Rosie a full ten seconds to realise that this was some kind of uniform.

'Mr Waterlow!' she said, smiling with relief. 'Fancy meeting you, of all people!'

'It's a comical old world,' he said. 'What brings you up this way, Rosie?'

'I've sort of come shopping,' she stammered, realising that this must sound strange and foolish almost before the words were out. He confirmed her doubts with a grunt: 'Funny place for shopping! Look, would you like a cup of you-and-me?'

Tea, she thought, I can't get away from the blessed stuff. Aloud she said: 'I don't want to take up your time.'

'I was just going to get one. Come on.'

Without further argument he took her arm and led her down a cobbled alley to a coffee-shop which bore the odd name of Pearce and Plenty. Two equally odd-looking mirrors framed the doorway and Mr Waterlow, with a smile, invited Rosie to examine herself in each in turn.

The first one reflected a thin and skeleton-like Rosie above which there appeared the legend: BEFORE EATING AT PEARCE AND PLENTY. The second reversed the distortion so that she appeared grotesquely large and rounded under the words: AFTER EATING AT PEARCE AND PLENTY. Rosie smiled, thinking that Mr Pearce must be a very clever man to think up such a way to attract customers.

Further proof of the man's enterprise was provided by the trays of sausages, saveloys, onions, mashed potatoes and small individual beefsteak puddings which sizzled and steamed in full view behind the windows. The appetising mixture of smells floated out of the doorway and into the street, tormenting the nostrils of the innocent passers-by, tempting them inside to investigate further. On the window itself a careful hand had painted the words: TODAY'S SPECIAL: HARRY CHAMPION. Rosie had once seen the music-hall comedian at the Wood Green Empire and heard him sing his famous song so she understood at once that the astute Mr Pearce was simply indicating that boiled beef and carrots was on the menu that day.

'Hungry?' asked Mr Waterlow when they were seated.

'No. No, thanks,' Rosie said, not wishing to impose on his generosity. 'Just tea.'

'Come on,' he said masterfully. 'I'm going to have a ham roll. Join me.'

She agreed with only a small show of reluctance for it was some time since she had eaten and the fragrant smells from the trays had whetted her appetite. The roll, hot and crusty, spread with real butter and packed with mild lean ham, was delicious, and the tea, living up to its reputation, soothed away Rosie's earlier fears and she began to relax.

'Fancy bashing into you,' she said. 'I mean, it's a chance in a million. Do you work near here?'

'In the Lane,' he replied. 'Mincing Lane. I'm a doorkeeper at one of the big offices. He brushed some crumbs from his uniform. 'That's why I wear this clobber.'

'Doorkeeper? What's that?'

'What it says. I open up in the morning and lock up at night. I check that the cleaners do their work. During the day I have to greet visitors, direct them to the right office, keep out beggars and suchlike, take messages round the City, find cabs for the tenants when they want them, keep an eye on their cars – all that.' His face creased in a wry smile. 'I was only a corporal during the war. Now I'm a general. A general dogsbody, that's me.'

'Aren't we all?' said Rosie sympathetically.

'Oh, it's not so bad,' he replied. 'It's a job. I'm lucky to have it. Half my mates are out of work.'

'It's bad all round,' Rosie said.

'It's a comical old world,' he said reflectively. 'Had my own business before the war. Me and the missus ran a little boarding-house on the south coast. Nice place. Bit of a struggle to get by but we managed. The bloody war put paid to that, of course. I mean, who wants a holiday in war time? I went into the army and the place went to rack and ruin. We tried to get it going again but it was hopeless. We just had to sell up and get out. Breaks my heart when I think of it. Still, as I say, at least I've got a job.'

The war, thought Rosie. Nothing comical about that! In their innocence, they had thought that it would be all finished with the end of the killings but now, years later, the war was still with them, shading their lives like the wings of some huge threatening bird.

'What are you thinking?' Mr Waterlow asked gently.

'What? Oh, sorry,' she said. 'I was miles away.'

'What have you come shopping for?' he asked. 'You said you'd come here to do some shopping.'

'I was looking for tea,' she said hesitantly.

'All this way for tea!' he said, his face crinkling with amusement. Then he added more seriously: 'Mind you, you've come to the right place. Mincing Lane. You can't spit in Mincing Lane without hitting a bloody tea-merchant.'

'Do you know any?' she asked quickly.

'Know any? There are four firms in my building! I can't get away from them! Why?'

'I want to talk to someone in the tea business,' she said and, seeing the bewilderment in his eyes, she explained the nature of her errand. The bewilderment changed to admiration as he listened.

'Well, well,' he said. 'It is a comical old world. I mean, I never guessed you were in a line of business, Rosie. Imagine that! You're a dark horse, you know that?' He rose from the table and looked down on her with a smile. 'Come on, then. Don't sit there like an empty glass, girl. Our Mr Prout is the man for you – he's a very decent old gent, as gents go.'

4

Mr Waterlow paused outside the door marked SMETHWICK, HOWARD AND PROUT, TEA IMPORTERS, straightened his shoulders, winked at Rosie and whispered: 'Here we go, girl. Over the top and the best of luck!'

Rosie took a deep nervous breath and waited as he knocked. The door opened on a spotty-faced boy with ink-stained fingers who blinked uncertainly at Mr Waterlow and then turned the same uncertain look on Rosie.

'Ah, Mr Melrose,' said Mr Waterlow, 'this young lady has called to see Mr Prout on a matter of business.'

'Oh, yes.' The boy shuffled uncertainly, still blocking the doorway.

'A matter of business, Mr Melrose,' said Mr Waterlow firmly. 'I'll leave her in your hands then.'

Before the boy could react, Mr Waterlow turned to Rosie and touched the brim of his hat respectfully. A mischievous twinkle danced in his kindly eyes as he said: 'Mr Melrose will look after you, ma'am. Good day to you.'

He was halfway down the corridor before Rosie remembered that she had not thanked him and by then it was too late, for instinct told her that it would be inappropriate to shout in these chaste surroundings.

'This way, madam,' said the young Mr Melrose, and ushered her into a large, musty-smelling office, in which the central space was almost entirely occupied by a long high desk. Eight male clerks, of varying ages and sizes sat on stools around the desk, four to each side, checking ledgers and documents. At the end of the desk, facing the clerks and with his back to the crinkled-glass window, there sat a ninth man. Unlike the clerks, who were without jackets and wore long coverings over their shirtsleeves, this man was fully clothed in a black suit with a stiff collar and cravat, and his chair, mounted on a small platform, possessed both a back and arms. He was clearly a person of some importance for, as Rosie entered, the clerks lifted their eyes in unison towards her and then, with the same accord looked at him.

Mr Melrose advanced respectfully to the important person, leaving Rosie waiting uncertainly near the door, and whispered something to him. The important person glanced curiously at Rosie, adjusted his rimless spectacles, waved Mr Melrose aside and, sliding from the chair, moved ponderously towards her, a frown on his pink face.

'What can I do for you?' he said coldly. His manner indicated that she was not in the usual run of visitors or customers, that he had placed her immediately as someone from an inferior class. To emphasise the point, he took out a gold hunter watch, snapped it open and, after a quick glance, snapped it shut again, as though to indicate that his time was precious. He sniffed and the spiky black hairs in his wide nostrils quivered in response.

If this conduct was intended to overawe or subdue Rosie it had the opposite effect. She had learned a thing or two about bureaucrats and pomposity in the past year or so and she felt a surge of indignation that, at the same time, served to stiffen her courage.

'Are you Mr Prout?' she demanded.

He chose not to answer her directly. 'Mr Prout is not

available at this time. Perhaps you would be good enough to state the nature of your business.'

'I want to lay my hands on some tea,' she said.

'Tea?'

'Tea,' she reiterated and added in a sharper tone: 'You know what that is, don't you?'

'You wish to purchase some tea?'

'That's the ticket,' she said. 'Now you're catching on.'

'I have to tell you,' he said pompously, 'I have to tell you that we deal only with accredited traders.'

'How do you know that I am not — what-you-call-it — accredited?'

'I assume you have a business card?'

She did not fully understand what he meant by this. 'No,' she said, 'I don't have a business card. But I have something better.'

'Oh, yes?'

'Cash. If I like your tea and if my boss likes it also, we pay cash down, no argument.'

'That is not the way we do business here, madam.'

'I wonder you do any business at all,' she said cheerfully. 'Still, not to worry, I don't like the look of this place anyway. I'll take my trade somewhere else, thank you very much.'

A titter, rising from the clerks, was silenced by a fierce look from the very important person. By the time he turned his eyes back to Rosie she had her hand on the door-handle. She left him with a parting shot: 'Don't smile, will you, mate? You might crack the enamel on your face!'

It pleased her to see his cheeks redden in anger but before he could gather himself to reply she was gone.

5

In the corridor outside, Rosie shook her head in disgust. What on earth had possessed Mr Waterlow to send her to see such a toffee-nosed git! Then, cooling a little, she began to direct the blame to herself. After all, he had said that she should talk to Mr

Prout and to no one else. Mr Waterlow had described Mr Prout
as a kindly, decent old gentleman but she had allowed her anger
and quick tongue to destroy any chance of dealing with him.
She would have to learn to control herself, to realise that, in
business, it was necessary to deal with all kinds of people, even
those whom you might not like.

As she moved towards the stairs Rosie began to wish that she
had never involved herself in the business of tea and, once again,
she wondered if she should give up the pursuit. But a certain
pride was at stake now: she had persuaded Mark to go along
with the idea and she did not relish the thought of going back to
him to report failure.

Pausing outside the door of another suite of offices which
was inscribed with the name: CAMERON AND SON – TEA
IMPORTERS AND BLENDERS, she knocked timidly, uncertainly,
half-hoping that there would be no response. As her knuckles
tapped the polished woodwork she became aware of a confusion
of sound from within, a noisy mixture of bangs and shouts and
laughter which was reminiscent of a children's playground,
except that the voices were deeper. It seemed, at the least, to be
an advance on the graveyard atmosphere of Messrs Smethwick,
Howard and Prout and, when her knock remained unanswered,
she pushed the door open cautiously.

She stood on the threshold for a few moments wondering
whether she had entered a madhouse. Half a dozen clerks were
crouched around the room in various positions, so engrossed in
a game of indoor cricket that they either ignored or did not
notice Rosie's presence. A waste-paper basket had been
up-ended as a wicket, the ball was a roll of paper tightly bound
with string and the bat a round ebony ruler.

The batsman, a young man in shirtsleeves, with untidy sandy
hair, swiped at the incoming ball, hit it fair and square and sent
it soaring towards Rosie who, without thinking, put up her
hands and made a perfect catch.

A roar came from the crouching clerks. 'Out! Well caught!'

'Hold on!' said the sandy-haired young man. 'She's not
playing! If she hadn't been there it would have hit the door and I
would have scored a boundary!'

'She caught you bang to rights, guv'nor,' said one of the clerks. 'You're out.'

'Not the first time you've been caught out by a girl!' roared another, to a chorus of laughter and cheers.

'All right,' admitted the batsman. 'Time permitting, we'll continue the match this afternoon.' Smiling, raking his hair back with his fingers, he moved towards Rosie. 'Good catch,' he said. 'We'll keep you on the team. My name is Jack Cameron. Is there anything I can do for you?'

You could do a lot, thought Rosie, but she did not say so.

'Are you the boss?' she asked.

'Sort of,' he replied. 'Although you wouldn't think so, the way I get treated by this lot!' The clerks, who were now back at their desks, laughed openly.

Rosie could not help smiling with them, nor could she help making a mental comparison between this office and the one she had just left. The room was bright and cheerful, with colourful pictures of Indian tea-plantations on the walls, and the clerks sat at individual desks on proper chairs. Even more extraordinary was the attitude of the boss who seemed to be on such relaxed and easy-going terms with his staff. Rosie decided that she liked young Mr Cameron and his firm.

'Is there anything I can do for you?' he repeated.

'I was looking to buy some tea,' she said.

'Tea! Well, well. The lady has come to the right place, eh, lads?' The clerks chuckled and nodded as he took Rosie by the arm and led her towards an inner office.

'This way, if you please. Jack Cameron at your service. Come into the sanctum and we'll see what we can do for you.'

Was it Rosie's imagination or did he wink at his clerks as he whisked her off?

She found herself in a small, rather untidy room which seemed unable to make up its mind whether to be an office or a store. There was a desk beneath the dusty window, plus a hat-stand and two chairs, both of which bore the weight of piles of ledgers and papers, but most of the wall-space was taken up with shelves stacked with black wooden containers. These were shaped rather like large vases and each one was labelled in gold lettering with the name of a grade of tea. In one corner there was a sink and beside this, on the wooden draining-board, stood a small gas-ring, a gleaming copper kettle and some china cups and saucers.

Jack Cameron up-ended a chair, tipping its load on to the floor. He bade her sit, perched himself on the edge of the desk and for the next ten minutes explained about tea, illustrating his words with a variety of samples. Rosie did not take in this technical talk, nor was she much concerned with the difference between Broken Grades and Leaf Grades and all the varieties of Pekoe. She was interested only in what she called ordinary tea, the sort that was in daily use in Shakespeare Street, and, in the end, she found what she wanted.

'That looks more like it,' she said, when he showed her a sample of blended tea. 'Is that the stuff they sell in the shops?'

'What shops do you mean?' he asked cautiously.

'Pearks. The Home and Colonial. Liptons,' she replied.

'Ah,' he said, 'you are talking of English common tea.'

'Common?' she asked sharply, resenting the implication.

'Nothing wrong with it,' he said hastily. 'It is just the name we use in the trade. The blend might vary in quality but this is more or less what you would buy in the High Street.'

'Then that is what I want,' she said.

'Would you like to try it?'

'If it's no trouble.'

'No trouble at all. In fact, it is a pleasure.' He smiled at her, his eyes twinkling with mischief. 'You are a jolly sight more attractive than most of the buyers I get in here.'

She felt her cheeks redden slightly and she was tempted to tell him to keep his mind on the subject of tea, but she smothered the thought and managed a little smile in return. He had a rugged, pleasant face beneath the untidy sandy-coloured hair, an open face that seemed to have no guile to conceal from the world, and his bright eyes held a perpetual gleam of amusement, as if he found life to be a nonsensical affair which had to be treated lightly.

As he filled the kettle and put it on the gas-ring he asked, in a casual tone: 'I've just realised. I don't know your name.'

She had adopted the practice of using her maiden name in her new business life, and she replied: 'Carr.' Then, as an afterthought she added firmly: 'Mrs. Mrs Carr.'

'And you own a shop, do you, Mrs Carr?'

'No. I don't own anything. Certainly not a shop.'

'But you are proposing to sell tea? That is the idea?'

'Oh, yes. My guv'nor works the markets, you see.' And, seeing his puzzled look, she explained about Mark and his barrow and the techniques of street-trading. He prompted her with questions and by the time she had finished answering the tea was ready.

'Bone china,' he said as he put a cup and saucer before her. 'It's not the only way to serve tea but it is the best, don't y'know.'

She saw that the china was thin and delicate, a long way removed from the thick mugs and cups she used at home. And, when the tea had cooled a little and she sipped it, she had to admit that the fine cup did seem to bring out the flavour.

'Well?' he asked.

'Yes,' she said, 'yes. This will do very well. How much is it?'

He smiled, perhaps at her directness. 'It comes in chests. Each chest contains a hundred and twenty pounds of tea, just over one hundredweight. I can let you have it for – say – five pounds per chest.'

In the past few months she had developed a facility for simple arithmetic and she did a quick sum in her head.

'That works out at tenpence a pound.'

'Does it?' He looked surprised.

'Too much,' she said firmly.

'Oh. Of course, if you were to order a hundred or more chests, I might be able to make a reduction.'

'A hundred chests? Give over! I don't want to drown in tea! No, I was thinking of three or four to start with. But the price is too high – there would be no profit in it.'

'Oh? What figure did you have in mind?'

'Make it four pounds ten shillings a chest,' said Rosie. 'Ninepence per pound. I can go to that. If my boss agrees I'll take four chests to start with – and if it goes well I will be back for more.' This was the part of the business, the cut and thrust of dealing, that she enjoyed most and she spoke confidently. But there was no cut and thrust on this occasion for he simply cocked his head to one side and the mischief gleamed in his eyes again. 'All right, Mrs Carr,' he said. 'It's a deal – on two conditions.'

'Oh, yes? And what might they be?'

'The first is that I incur no delivery charges. You will collect the chests from our warehouse in Shoreditch.'

'That will be easy enough.'

'The second condition is that you have lunch with me.'

Rosie, who had now overcome her initial shyness, put back her head and laughed.

'I am serious!' he protested.

'You are a cheeky devil, Mr Cameron.'

'People who don't ask don't get,' he said, 'What do you say?'

'I can't,' she replied, 'thanks all the same. I must get back and tell my guv'nor about the tea. If he agrees, I'll be here tomorrow with the money.'

'Marvellous!' he cried. 'So we'll have lunch tomorrow, right?'

'I may not come back. He might not agree the price.'

'Oh, you'll be back,' he said confidently. 'Tell your boss that at four-pound-ten a chest he is getting the snip of the century.'

He escorted her to the front door past the smiling faces of the clerks. 'I'll see you tomorrow then. Don't let me down.'

She walked to Liverpool Street and caught the tramcar which would take her back through Dalston, Stoke Newington and Stamford Hill to Tottenham. As the tram swerved and rattled along, she felt curiously lightheaded, almost as if she'd had a drink or two. The feeling had nothing to do with the motion of the tram. Her thoughts were on her morning's work and on the intriguing figure of Jack Cameron. He put her in mind of Douglas Fairbanks, whom she had taken the children to see in the film *The Three Musketeers* a few weeks after starting her job with Mark. There was little or no physical resemblance between the film star and Jack Cameron but the impudent don't-give-a-damn manner was just the same.

She thought about his offer of lunch and wondered where he would take her. Would it be somewhere posh? The idea chilled her for a moment. What on earth should she wear? More than that, what on earth had she got in the way of clothes that would do justice to the occasion?

By the time she reached her stop at Ward's Corner she had decided that she would have to find some excuse to back down. She had no desire to embarrass young Mr Cameron in public and certainly no intention of showing herself up in front of a restaurant full of well-heeled customers.

Still another thought occurred to her as she walked towards the warehouse, a thought that made her all the more determined to turn her back on Mr Cameron. She had made it plain, indeed she had emphasised the fact, that she was a married woman: if there had been any doubt on that score, there was her wedding-ring, which he must have seen. She had not volunteered the information that she was a widow, nor had he asked.

If he was the kind of man who indulged in affairs with married women, then she needed to be wary. With him, she told herself firmly, she would stick strictly to business. Which was a pity, she added, with a little secret smile as her sense of humour surfaced, for, rake or not, she liked his style.

CHAPTER SEVEN

1

Street-trading may be an open affair but its practitioners form a tightly knit, almost closed society in which there is little space for secrets and a good deal of room for gossip. Inevitably, Mark's steady, if unspectacular, rise in the markets had not gone unnoticed and there was increasing talk in the cafés and around the coffee-stalls about his skill, his sharpness, his uncanny ability to put his hand on cheap supplies.

Most of the talk was the simple admiration of one good tradesman for another, but there were those who resented his success and hinted that he was getting too big for his boots, and still others who went further and muttered that these bloody Jews were pushing them out of business. That this was patently untrue had no effect, for there was no reason in their arguments, only a bone-headed prejudice which fed on their own inability to match his success.

In these meaner areas of gossip, Rosie was found guilty by association. At best, it was said that she should know better than to work for a sheeny; at worst, that she spent most of her time at the warehouse on her back with the Jew-boy on top of her and was little better than a whore.

Perhaps because they were too busy and had little time for socialising, neither Mark nor Rosie was aware of this latent feeling, but it was there nevertheless, hissing like a slow-burning fuse.

As always, one exaggeration spawned a bigger one. When the word got out that Mark had opened a bank account, this was taken as certain proof that he was rolling in money. Day by day, the speculation increased the balance which stood to his name.

To the market traders all this was no more than gossip, the small-talk of the tea-break, but other ears were listening and taking careful note.

2

The two men had watched Mark and checked his movements for over a week. They knew which market he would go to on a particular day, what time he would get there, and roughly when he would leave. His visits to the bank were less regular, sometimes twice and sometimes three times a week, but they noted that he always went around midday. And, of course, they were well aware that he carried large sums of money about him because so many of his suppliers insisted on cash on the barrel.

The more respectable-looking of the two men had followed Mark into the bank that morning and, while ostensibly filling in a form, had observed the withdrawal of an interesting wad of banknotes. Mr Lightblow, the bank cashier, had made no comment about this for he was well used to the fact that Mark's money went out almost as quickly as it went in, but he did point out that this withdrawal left the account with a balance of less than two pounds.

'Nothing to worry about, Mr Lightblow,' Mark said cheerfully. 'It will all be back in a couple of days – and more beside.'

Mr Lightblow smiled and nodded. Despite doubts on the part of his manager, he had faith in this young man, especially since Rosie had joined him. Some instinct told the cashier that Mark had the spirit from which success is made and, though he would never have admitted this to anyone, not even the estimable Mrs Lightblow, he secretly envied him. His life offered so much more excitement than could be found in the humdrum routine of a bank clerk.

Mark left the bank with £185 tucked safely into an inside pocket. Some of the money would be needed for Rosie's purchase of tea: just how much, he was not sure, but he had figured that twenty to thirty pounds ought to cover it. In any case, he had begun to have second thoughts about the possibilities of tea and he had decided to limit the risk. The rest of the money was earmarked, partly for the settlement of an outstanding account for some sardines, amounting to thirty-five pounds, and partly for the buying of a large consignment of soap which he proposed not only to sell in the market on his own behalf but also to sell through travelling agents on a commission basis. It was to be his first modest venture into this form of selling, but he was confident of success. Soap, he reasoned, had always been good to him.

He was full of optimistic thoughts for the future as he loaded his barrow with the last of his current stock: four cases of corned beef – a line that had done very well – and some boxes filled with tins of Skipper sardines acquired from the bankrupt stock of a wholesaler. He reckoned to shift the lot at the Caledonian Market that afternoon. After that he would concentrate on the soap.

The shadows of the two men darkened the doorway of the warehouse as he loaded the last box. He looked up, expecting to see Rosie, and was about to greet her, when they pounced. Instinctively, he put up an arm to protect himself from the swinging cosh but it smashed into his wrist and he screamed with pain. He heard a muttered curse, caught a brief glimpse of a swarthy face half-covered with a scarf, and then the cosh came down on the back of his head. He stumbled like a drunken man for a moment, felt himself sliding down into a swirling grey mist which crackled with flashing sparks of light and then he pitched to the floor with no more thought for soap, sardines, or anything.

One of the men, for good measure, kicked Mark in the ribs with a hob-nailed boot: the other removed the wad of notes and some loose change from his pockets, ripped off the silver watch and chain which he wore so proudly, and then tipped the barrow over on top of him. They paused only long enough to stuff some loose tins of sardines and corned beef into two bags and then fled with the loot.

Rosie arrived five minutes later, her head full of thoughts of tea and of Jack Cameron, to find the unconscious Mark half-buried under the heavy boxes. She stifled a scream and set to work to release him. Blood was pouring from his face and arms where the sharp edges of the boxes had smashed into him and she saw that there was more blood coming from the back of his head.

She took a pillow from the bed in the alcove and put this under the nape of his neck, then brought water and a clean towel to bathe the wounds. Still he made no response: only the slow beating of his heart told her that he was alive.

Her first reaction, that this had been an accident, that Mark had tripped or slipped and brought the barrow and its contents down upon himself, now began to appear unlikely, if not impossible. His injuries, especially the ugly gash in his head, were too serious for that. She was sure now that he had been attacked and she looked around fearfully, as if the thugs might still be lurking there.

She tried once more to rouse Mark and, failing to do so, went out to seek help and raise the alarm.

3

'Concussion, a scalp wound, a fracture of the left arm, two cracked ribs and sundry cuts and bruises.'

The Matron at the Cottage Hospital recited the list of injuries with a note of accusation in her tone, as if she were blaming Mark for carelessness, for needlessly adding to the workload of the hospital.

'Can I see him?' asked Rosie.

'Are you his wife?'

'No. A friend.'

'I see.' The Matron took a moment or so to consider this. She was a thin, flat-chested woman with a face that appeared to be permanently set in a mask of irritation, and the sort of gimlet eyes which can detect a spot of dust at forty paces. 'He is not really in a fit state to see anyone. He has only just recovered consciousness. The police will be here to question him in fifteen minutes. He will require all his strength for that.'

'Just for a minute or two. Please. I won't upset him.'

A gleam of compassion appeared briefly in the Matron's eyes, re-uniting her with the human race. 'Very well. A few minutes, no more.'

She summoned a passing nurse with an imperious gesture. 'Nurse! Take this young lady to see the new patient in Nightingale Ward.'

'Yes, Matron.' The young rosy-faced nurse gave a little respectful bob as she responded to the command.

'She can see the patient for five minutes. No longer, you understand.'

'Yes, Matron.'

'Thank you,' said Rosie, but the Matron had already turned away and the words were directed to her departing back.

Nightingale Ward was small, like the rest of the hospital, and as clean as human endeavour could make it. The faint scent of carbolic hung in the air and there was an almost churchlike hush about the place which suggested that to speak in any other tone than a whisper would be a mortal sin.

Four male patients of various ages lifted their heads to look as Rosie entered with the nurse as if in the hope that she had come to call on them: a fifth slept on, obediently restraining his snores to the level of sound allowed by the authorities.

Mark, the sixth patient, was hidden behind a set of screens. It was not until Rosie touched his hand and whispered his name that he stirred and opened eyes that looked drained of life and lustre.

'How are you feeling?' she murmured, regretting the stupidity of the conventional question as soon as it had been uttered. He made an effort to smile, as though to reassure her, but the effort was clearly too painful. Instead, he nodded his bandaged head in a barely perceptible movement.

'I found the tea, Mark,' she said, desperately trying to think of some subject which would cheer him. 'A nice place, very

decent people. Good price too. We can buy it in at around
ninepence a pound. It's good stuff. I reckon we can package and
sell it at fourpence a quarter-pound. A good profit margin. I
thought if we tried it out with, say, four or five chests . . .'

Her voice trailed away, for it was clear from his expression-
less face that he was not taking in her words. She sat in silence
for a few moments and then tried again: 'Mark. What
happened?'

'I was done, Rosie,' he whispered hoarsely. 'Done over good
and proper. Two men, I think. Done me.'

'Who?'

'Never got a proper look at them.'

'Bastards! We'll find them, don't worry, and they'll get what
they deserve.'

'Cleaned me out, Rosie,' he whispered.

'What?'

'Took the lot. Just been to the bank. A hundred and
eighty-five quid. Gone. I'm finished, Rosie.'

'You are talking rubbish,' she said briskly.

'I'm skint. I owe thirty-five quid on those sardines. Where
am I going to get the wherewithal to pay that and buy new
stock?'

'We'll find the cash somehow,' she said with a cheerfulness
which she did not feel.

'No,' he said. 'I've had the markets. Shan't go back. Shan't go
back.'

She felt a sudden surge of bitterness and rage against the men
who had perpetrated this crime. It was not the money that
concerned her, or the threat of losing her job with Mark, but
the thought of what they had done not only to his body but to
his spirit. She put out a hand and touched his face gently.

'Don't talk about it now. You are not in a fit state. You
concentrate on getting better and leave me to look after things.'

'I'm wiped out,' he whispered hopelessly, and as he turned
his head away she saw tears glinting in his eyes. Her own eyes
misted over as though in sympathy.

'Is there anything you want?' she asked. 'Shall I go and see your family? Do you want them to know about this?'

He pressed her hand lightly in what she took to be an affirmative gesture and closed his eyes wearily.

'That's right,' she whispered, 'you go to sleep. Get all the rest you can and don't worry. I've tidied up the warehouse and locked up. I'll be back tomorrow.'

She bent over and kissed his cheek, noting even then that it was as rough as sandpaper.

As she began to tiptoe from the ward, a thin-faced man in the next bed hissed at her.

'Miss. Miss.'

She hesitated for a moment and then went over to him. He clutched her hand with bony fingers and she saw that his skin had the transparency and colour of butter-paper.

'Is he going to die?' he whispered, nodding his head in the direction of Mark's bed.

'I should hope not!' said Rosie firmly.

'They usually put the screens up when you are going to die,' he insisted.

Thanks, thought Rosie, thanks a million for cheering me up! Aloud she said: 'He's not going to die and neither are you.'

'I've been here three months,' he said. 'I've watched them come in and I've watched them go out. It's the screens that give the game away.' And he added, with a hint of what sounded like pride: 'I shan't be long.'

'Get away with you,' she said sternly.

'TB,' he whispered. 'They can't do nothing for it.' He took her hand again, gripping it with surprising strength. 'You are a lovely lass. Would you do me a favour?'

'What would that be?'

'Would you lift your skirt and let me see you in your drawers?'

'You dirty old sod!' she said indignantly, pulling away.

'It's the TB,' he cackled. 'It makes you randy.'

4

It was early evening when Rosie left the hospital and, as if to match her mood, a layer of sombre grey clouds had taken possession of the sky and a chill northerly wind was making mischief with the trees in nearby Woodlands Park. Tightening the collar of her coat, she made her way to Huggins's fish shop to buy four pieces of rock salmon and chips, and then turned her head for home.

The latchkey of the house in Shakespeare Street hung from a piece of twine attached to the inside of the door: all one had to do to get in was to slide a hand into a slit in the door, euphemistically called a letter-box, grasp the twine and haul up the key. As Rosie did this and slid the door open she was surprised at the abnormal silence in the house: usually she could expect to be greeted by either Van or Eddie, or to hear the sound of some argument or other between Mr and Mrs Bennett upstairs.

'I'm back!' she called.

There was no response to this and she hurried towards the warmth of the kitchen. To her relief, she found Gran and the children grouped around the kitchen table, but before she could open her mouth, they hushed her to silence. One end of the table was occupied by the wireless set that Eddie had been putting together for the past month: Eddie himself was wearing a pair of earphones and twiddling with something that looked like a piece of wire but which Rosie learned later was called a 'cat's whisker'. Screwing up his face in the effort of concentration, he was trying to find the right spot on the crystal.

As Rosie watched she was conscious of a sense of guilt, of the feeling that she had been concentrating on the business of earning a living to the neglect of her children. They did not complain, bless them, and Eddie, in particular, more mature than many boys of his age, was a sensible lad on whom she could rely in most things. All the same, difficult though it might be, she told herself that she must organise her life in a way that would make it possible for her to see more of the children.

'Got it!' said Eddie suddenly, a smile breaking through the concentration.

'Let me! Let me hear!' cried Van. He passed the earphones over and her eyes widened in wonder as she listened. 'Music!' she whispered. 'I can hear music!'

'Let me have a turn!' rasped Gran.

'Wait a minute!' Van repelled the grasping hand for a minute and then reluctantly handed the earphones on to the old lady. Reminded by the heat of the newspaper that she was still holding their supper, Rosie put the fish and chips on a flat metal tray, lit the oven, and slid the tray inside to wait until appetite triumphed over the wireless.

Gran was nodding her head, as if in time to the music, and Rosie smiled. She could almost believe all the talk about wireless being a modern miracle: it had not only kept the children's minds off the subject of supper, it had actually succeeded in coaxing a reluctant smile from Gran!

'Do you want a turn, Mum?' asked Eddie.

'I wouldn't mind, son,' she replied.

'Let me finish, let me finish,' cried Gran, waving them away. 'It's lovely, lovely!'

When Rosie eventually took possession of the earphones, the music had been replaced by a crackling upper-class voice which, as far as she could make out, was talking about the weather. It had been, said the voice, the coldest winter for twenty-five years and experts predicted that there was no immediate sign of improvement.

From this sombre subject the voice went on to announce on a new political scandal. Ramsay MacDonald, the first socialist ever to become Prime Minister, had admitted, under pressure, to accepting the gift of a Daimler car from a prominent capitalist, together with a sum of money to help with its upkeep.

Rosie just had time to hear the voice mention that King

George V would open the great British Empire Exhibition at Wembley, on St George's Day, April 23rd, when Gran reclaimed the earphones.

'What do you think, Mum?' asked Eddie.

'Did you build it all yourself, son?' she asked.

'Yes,' he answered proudly.

She ruffled his hair. 'You are a clever one, you are, no mistake.'

'Do you like it?' he asked.

'I like anything that can keep your gran quiet for ten minutes,' she said, smiling.

'They are talking!' complained Gran. 'I don't want to hear them gassing, I want the music!'

'And I want to lay the table for supper,' Rosie said firmly. 'Come on, Van, give me a hand.'

Of course, as soon as they had grouped themselves round the table and were ready to attack the fish and chips, the door opened on Mrs Bennett and they had to get up again so that she could squeeze through to the lavatory.

'Fish and chips. On a Tuesday!' she said, in a tone which suggested that she had interrupted some luxurious banquet. 'Very nice for some,' she added, implying this time that she wished that she could afford such luxuries, and went on her way without a word of apology for disturbing them.

'I tell you something,' Rosie said in a fierce whisper. 'I'm not going to put up with this much longer. We're getting out of this place – we're going to move!'

'Move!' cried Van excitedly. 'Where to?'

'I don't know yet. Somewhere better than this, that's for sure. Somewhere we can get a bit of privacy!'

'Can I have a room of my own?'

'I expect so,' Rosie said.

'You're not going to leave me behind?' asked Gran plaintively.

'I'd like to,' said Rosie, with a teasing smile, 'but I won't.'

'Nice thing to say,' Gran grumbled. 'Nice thing!'

'When will we move, Mum?' asked Eddie quietly.

Rosie remembered then what had happened to Mark, that

her prospects were by no means as bright as they had been just a few hours ago, and she answered cautiously:

'Soon. Just as soon as we can afford it.'

5

She remembered also her promise to inform Mark's family of the accident and so, leaving her own brood in front of a glowing fire, happily arguing over whose turn it was to use the earphones, she set off once again. Although she had known the address for some time and had a rough idea of the location, she had never been to Mark's home. Indeed, apart from telling her that he had a brother, a sister and a widowed mother, she knew very little about Mark's background, for it was a subject on which he was unusually reticent. In the past few months, with the business making increasing demands, he had slept at the warehouse almost every night, returning home but rarely.

She was surprised when she reached the dimly lit street to find that it was largely occupied by grim tenement blocks. The name, Flower and Dean Street, had conjured up a picture of a pleasant road lined with trees: the reality was something that looked more wretched than Shakespeare Street. Even the cold wind seemed unable to dispel the musty scent of decay and damp, overlaid with a faint smell as of rotting vegetables.

She climbed two flights of stone stairs in the shadowy interior of one of the blocks, shivering as the chill dampness struck through to her bones, and knocked tentatively at the door of Number Five. It was opened after a few moments by a tall, burly young man in shirtsleeves and braces, whom she assumed to be Mark's brother. He looked at her with a neutral expression, neither welcoming nor hostile.

'Yes?'

'Is Mrs Moss in?' she asked nervously.

'Yes,' he said uncompromisingly, and made no move to open up the doorway.

'I'd like to speak to her for a minute, if I could.'

'I'm her son. What is it about?'

'Mark. He's had an accident.'

'Mark!' He spoke the name as if it were a sneer and no hint of concern showed on his face. Turning, he called: 'Mum – it's for you.'

A small, plump, motherly woman with greying hair replaced him in the doorway, looking at Rosie with curious but friendly eyes.

'What can I do for you?' she asked. There was an accent there, a foreign accent, slight but unmistakable, that Rosie could not place.

'I've come about your son, Mark. I'm afraid he's had an accident.'

'An accident?' Mrs Moss's eyes quickened with alarm.

Rosie explained the circumstances as briefly as possible, trying not to sound too alarmist.

'Oi-yoi!' The woman shook her head and looked at the brother who was standing beside her. 'Did you hear, Bennie? Our Mark has been hurt.'

'I heard, I'm not deaf. If you want my opinion, it serves him right.'

'Bennie, Bennie – don't shame me! How can you say such a thing? Your own brother!' She turned to Rosie. 'Is it bad?'

'I spoke to one of the doctors. He said Mark is young and strong. He should be out in a few days.'

'Where is he, may I ask?'

'In the Cottage Hospital in Tottenham. Visiting hours are six-thirty to seven-thirty in the evenings and three to four on Sunday afternoons. I shall go to see him tomorrow. Is there any messages you want me to take?'

'Message? No. No offence, but what use is a message?' She looked at her son again. 'Tomorrow we go see him, Bennie.' He gave her a half-hearted shrug in reply.

'Well, that's it then,' Rosie said. 'I must go.'

'Wait, miss,' said the mother, plucking Rosie's sleeve. 'You are a friend to Mark?'

'Yes.' And to prevent this from being misinterpreted, she added: 'Well, that is, I have worked for him for the last eight or nine months.'

'I see,' the mother nodded but there was a question in her eyes. Then she said briskly, addressing her son: 'Here's a fine thing. This young lady comes all this way, in the freezing cold, to bring us news of Mark and we keep her standing on the doorstep like a bad neighbour! What must she think of us?' To Rosie, she said: 'Forgive us, my dear. To receive a shock is no excuse for bad manners. Please. Come inside. Let me get you a glass tea.'

'I ought to go,' Rosie said, wondering what a glass tea could be.

'Please. Come in – warm yourself. Please.'

'All right,' said Rosie. 'For a few minutes.'

The room in which she found herself presented a small miracle of compression. Two-thirds of the space was packed with old furniture and was obviously the living-area; a treadle sewing-machine and a wooden rack on which a dozen or more dresses were hanging took up the rest. A coal fire, banked high, sent out a glow of welcome. Despite the clutter, Rosie noticed with approval that there was a basic cleanliness and order about the place.

A young woman was bent over the sewing-machine, her fingers guiding a length of light material under the needle. As Rosie entered she stopped and looked up with a smile and Rosie saw that she was lovely. Jet-black hair, gleaming in the fire-glow, framed an oval face from which the liquid dark eyes looked out with an extraordinary expression of warmth and gentleness.

'Debbie!' said the mother sharply. 'Don't sit there. Can't you see we have a visitor? A friend from Mark! Put the kettle on, make tea!'

The girl rose and went behind a screen in one corner of the room. She was quite tall, a head taller than her mother, and she walked with the easy grace of a dancer. Mrs Moss bustled around, clearing a space near the fire, and thrust Rosie into what was clearly the best armchair. The son, Bennie, took a place at the table and, picking up a book, separated himself from these activities. Rosie could not help but wonder at the disparity between this son and the daughter, the one so uncompromising and surly, the other so gentle and welcoming. And then there is Mark, she thought: he is different again, not at all like his brother and sister. She found it strange to think that they had all sprung from the same stock.

'I don't want to put you to any trouble, Mrs Moss,' Rosie said.

'Trouble? It's no trouble.' Raising her voice, the mother called: 'Debbie. Bring the biscuits.'

Debbie emerged from behind the screen with a tray and four thick glasses, each standing in a polished holder with a handle. Tea in a glass, thought Rosie. That's a novelty. She placed all this on the table and advanced on Rosie: 'We haven't said hello. My name is Debbie.'

Her voice was low and musical: unmistakably a London voice but without the stridency of the broad cockney or any trace of her mother's accent.

Rosie introduced herself, noting as she did so a flicker of interest from Bennie.

'And Mark?' asked Debbie. 'How did it happen?'

'We are not sure,' said Rosie cautiously. 'The police . . .'

'The police!' cried Mrs Moss, interrupting her. 'Is he in trouble? The police!'

'No, no. He was attacked and robbed. Two men, he thinks, though he can't be sure. They knocked him unconscious and took all his money.'

'Money!' The comment came in a contemptuous grunt from Bennie, though he did not lift his eyes from the book.

'It could have been worse,' said Debbie.

'Worse!' moaned Mrs Moss. 'Of course it could have been worse. Also, it could have been better. If it hadn't happened it would have been better!'

She went behind the screen, perhaps to hide her tears.

An awkward silence followed. Rosie, feeling that it was time to change the subject, nodded towards the rack of dresses.

'You have a nice lot of frocks,' she said politely.

'They're not mine!' Debbie smiled. 'Mother and I make them up. We're out-workers.'

'Sweated labour,' growled Bennie.

'It's work, Bennie,' she replied in mild reproof.

Mrs Moss reappeared with a teapot and a sliced lemon and initiated Rosie into the mystery of 'glass tea'. She liked it well enough but doubted privately whether it would ever catch on in Shakespeare Street.

'So you work for our Mark,' said Mrs Moss, who seemed to have gathered herself.

'I help with the paperwork and do a bit of buying,' Rosie answered modestly. But for how much longer? she wondered.

'And for this he pays you?'

'Oh, yes. He pays me.'

'You hear that, Bennie? Our Mark is now an employer, a boss!'

'I heard,' murmured Bennie.

'And your husband?' Mrs Moss looked at Rosie's wedding-ring. 'He works also?'

'He is dead. He was killed in the war.'

'Oi-yoi,' said Mrs Moss, shaking her head in sympathy. 'The war. So many young men. But the Angel of Death doesn't care about age, isn't that so? He does not look at calendars. Did he leave you with children?'

'A boy and a girl,' Rosie answered. She was beginning to find the interrogation irksome. Pushing back her glass, she rose to her feet. 'I really must go. Thank you for the tea.'

'You came by the tram?' asked Mrs Moss.

'Yes.'

The mother turned to Bennie and her voice took on a sudden authority. 'Bennie. Put your coat on and walk the young lady to the tram-stop.'

'No, please. It isn't necessary,' protested Rosie. But Bennie was already on his feet and Mrs Moss swept aside Rosie's objections.

'Please, no arguments. Bennie will be glad to do it.' At the door, she squeezed Rosie's hand. 'Thank you for coming. It was a kindness. You are a good person, I think.'

Debbie said goodbye in her gentle fashion and added her own thanks. 'It was good of you to take the trouble. We will see you again, I hope.'

'Wait, wait!' cried Mrs Moss. She hurried into the living room and came back with two polished apples.

'For the children,' she said. 'A piece fruit.'

6

'Mark is doing well in this business of his?' asked Bennie.

They had been walking in silence since leaving the tenement flat and the sudden question took Rosie by surprise. She was puzzled by this man and his apparent hostility to his brother. How much should she tell him? How much would Mark wish him to know? She decided to play for safety.

'He makes a living,' she said.

'Is that all?'

'He works hard for what he gets,' she replied defensively. His sudden critical attitude was beginning to annoy her.

'Oh, he works. For what? Money. To make money – and after that, more money.'

'What is wrong with that?' she asked sharply.

'You also think that money is everything?'

'No. I don't. But I know this – you can't live without it!'

Two drunks, middle-aged men, staggered out of a public house on the corner, suddenly blocking their path. One of them eyed Rosie lewdly and breathed an unwelcome blend of tobacco and beer fumes into her face.

'Hello, my little darling,' he murmured.

Bennie pulled Rosie aside gently and confronted the two

men. 'On your way, mates,' he said in a quiet, firm voice. 'On your way.'

The man who had spoken lifted his head slowly and looked at Bennie, dimly taking in his bulk. 'No offence, matey, no offence.'

'None taken,' Bennie said.

'Here,' said the drunk. 'A present. It will do you good!' He thrust a paper into Bennie's hands and grasped his mate by the arm. The two of them moved off, weaving from side to side in slow crab-like fashion, chuckling together as if at some private joke.

Bennie looked down at the crumpled paper and Rosie saw him smile for the first time. It seemed, somehow, to change his whole appearance, making him altogether more human and likeable. In that moment too she detected, also for the first time, a resemblance to Mark that stamped them as brothers.

'Look' he said, 'look what he gave me.' It was a copy of the Salvation Army paper, *War Cry*.

'The Sally Ann has been at work,' she said with a smile, remembering the evenings at The Winged Horse when the lassies in their bonnets had done the rounds of the customers with copies of *War Cry* and *Young Soldier*.

The incident seemed to have lightened her companion's spirits for he said: 'Don't get me wrong about Mark. In many ways he has a good heart and he is my brother, after all. But he believes that money is the path to freedom and I don't. For such an attitude I have only contempt.'

'If you had two kids to feed and clothe, maybe you would take a different attitude,' said Rosie tersely.

'You think I am rich?'

'No. Of course not. I didn't say that.'

'You think I like to see my mother and my sister working ten hours a day or more over that machine to make a few shillings?'

'I should hope not. Perhaps if you had more respect for money they wouldn't have to.'

'Respect for money? Don't you see that it is the pursuit of wealth for its own sake, the greed for profit, that is the basic evil in this world? If I made a fortune and rescued my mother and sister from their daily toil, I should only be participating in this evil. Why? Because I could make that fortune only by exploiting others – people like them. No, we must choose a different way.'

They had reached the tram terminus now and, as they waited, he took her arm. Speaking quickly, his face animated, he went on: 'What we have to do is change society. That's the only path. We must not pursue our personal goals at the expense of others. We must work together, in a united fashion, to create a society in which all men are equal, where one man cannot have the power to exploit another. The means of production, the mines, the factories, the land must be owned in common, by all the people.'

Rosie was gripped suddenly by the memory of another place, another time, and of another young man who had said similar things to her. His eyes had burned with the same urgent gleam as, lying in the attic at The Winged Horse, he had talked of building a new world. He too had spoken as if from a book using strange words.

He had also told Rosie Carr, the little drudge, that he loved her, the first man ever to do so. And at the time she had been half in love with him. A strange sort of love, she thought wryly. He had gone from her life one morning, vowing that he would never forget her, and after that she had heard nothing. Not a word. So much for love, so much for promises!

'I met a man once who spoke just like you,' she told Bennie. 'Perhaps you have heard of him? His name was Frank Lambert.'

'Oh. Him!' His lips pursed themselves in disdain.

'You do know him!' she said eagerly. 'Where is he? What is he doing?'

'He sold out. He's in Parliament. And he is in the so-called Labour government, a junior minister. One of Ramsay MacDonald's cronies.'

Rosie had heard of Ramsay MacDonald, the Prime Minister – the first socialist to achieve that high position – indeed, she had voted for the Labour candidate in North Tottenham at the last election, not so much from conviction but because she had heard that her former employer, Mr Goldie, was publicly supporting the Tory. But the rest of what Bennie had said puzzled her.

'I thought – from what you said – that you were a what-do-you-call-it – a Labour man?'

'Never in a million years!' he said contemptuously.

'Then what are you?'

'A communist. I want to sweep away the capitalist system – not just tinker with it here and there, like your MacDonalds and your Frank Lamberts!'

Rosie did not respond. The day had been long and she was tired of the discussion, most of which was beyond her reach. To her relief, a tram rattled into view and pulled up.

'Thank you for your company,' she told Bennie politely.

'Here,' he said, 'I would like you to take this.' For a moment she thought he was going to give her the copy of *War Cry* but instead he handed her a thin pamphlet. 'Read it. It will help you to understand what must be done.'

God, she thought, it was Frank Lambert all over again! He, too, had given her a book. 'Read it, Rosie,' he had said. 'The truth is in that book.' The fool! The truth then was that she could not read or write anything but her own name. Still, she told herself with more kindness, she owed something to Frank for it was he who had pushed her to take the first steps towards learning to read and write, shaming her into it.

On the tram she looked at the pamphlet. It was called *Towards a Worker's Britain* and it had been written by someone called William Gallacher. She put it on the seat beside her, too tired to go any further, and closed her eyes.

The next thing she knew was the touch of the conductor's hand on her shoulder and his voice in her ear: 'Wake up, missus. Your stop coming up.'

As she stepped down from the tram, he called after her, waving the pamphlet: 'Here – you forgot this.'

'You keep it,' she said impishly. 'It might come in handy for wrapping up your fish and chips.'

CHAPTER EIGHT

1

Rosie woke the next morning in a mood of black depression. It was partly sheer tiredness, for the day before had been long, exhausting and filled with bewildering incident, and partly the oppressive thought that, once again, her luck had run out.

The months spent working with Mark had been the best of her life; she had looked forward to each day as if it were a holiday, a holiday in which exciting, unexpected things might happen. From the beginning Mark had treated her more as a friend and partner than as a hired hand and this sense of freedom had acted on her like wine. The days of drudgery at Mr Goldie's laundry had retreated to some distant frontier of memory, like time spent in a half-forgotten far-away country. She had felt herself growing, coming alive, heard herself talk with a confidence that she had never dreamed possible.

And with all this there had come some measure of financial relief. The regular wages, the occasional bonus, had enabled her to pay off the arrears of rent and other debts, redeem her wedding-ring, get better clothes for the children and put meat on the table at least three times a week. There was still no margin for saving but that hadn't seemed to matter. For the first time in her life she not only had a degree of security: she had an inner certainty that her life was at last on the right lines, that it could only get better. Until yesterday, the prospect had been as full of promise as a bright morning in spring.

Until yesterday.

Her mood seemed to rub off on the others. Gran whined about her aches and pains, the children quarrelled, and Rosie, snapping at them all, made it worse. And when Mr Bennett, down for his morning visit to the lavatory, pushed his way into the kitchen, Rosie flew at him, exploding the pent-up anger of years.

'Can't you knock!' she screamed. 'Haven't you got any bloody manners? Morning after morning, day after day, you come marching into my kitchen – my kitchen – without so much as a by-your-leave! I'm fed up with it, do you hear, I've had a bellyful of it!'

'I just want to get to the lavatory,' he said mildly, stunned by this unexpected assault.

'All right, all right, all right! But bloody well knock before you come in my kitchen! And since you are so fond of the lavatory, why don't you get your missus to clean it once in a while, eh? I'm sick of taking her turn as well as my own!'

'She's not well, she hasn't been up to the mark!'

'Not well!' Rosie said scornfully. 'She's a lazy bloody cow, that's what she is! A lazy bloody cow!'

'Now, look here . . .,' he began sternly, but she was in no mood to listen. Holding open the door to the yard she said imperiously:

'You want the lavatory? Right. It's out there!'

Not the brightest of men, he stood staring at her for a moment, his mind fumbling for an adequate retort, his stomach rumbling. All he could manage in the end was a feeble 'You'll hear more of this,' and an exit that he hoped would convey the full extent of his masculine indignation.

Rosie, unimpressed, slammed the door behind him.

'Cor, Mum,' said Van, her eyes wide with wonder.

'You shut your trap, my girl,' Rosie hissed, 'or you'll feel the back of my hand!' And when Van began to snivel, she shouted: 'And you can turn off the waterworks!'

'Mum,' said Eddie nervously, tentatively.

'And I don't want to hear from you either!' she snapped. 'Just leave me alone, all of you, leave me alone!'

She knew, even at the height of her anger, that she was behaving badly, unfairly, but the storm of feeling swept reason aside. The children left for school with pale, troubled faces, Gran fled to the safety of her room and Rosie, trembling and spent, lowered her face to the table and wept.

'Anything wrong, missus?' It was Mr Bennett returning from the backyard.

Rosie lifted her head, dabbed at her eyes with the back of her hand and shook her head. 'No. I'm all right,' she whispered.

'Trouble?'

She shook her head. He moved across to the other door and paused, searching once more for words. 'I know,' he said at last. 'It gets to you sometimes. Life. Sort of builds up, know what I mean? Comes a point where you can't hold it in no more. Life. It's a right old bugger.'

She looked at him through misted eyes. It was the longest speech he had ever made to her. And she saw too that this big, fat, unshaven man was not an enemy to be railed at but someone who was as much a victim of circumstances as herself. 'I'm sorry,' she muttered. 'Just now. I didn't mean . . .'

'No bones broken,' he said, 'no bones broken.'

When he had gone she released a long deep sigh, expelling the last of the anger from her body, the bitterness from her mind.

Yet the problem was still there, unresolved. What, if anything, could she do about it? She needed to talk it over with Mark but there was no way the hospital would allow her in to see him until the evening.

For the time being, at least, she was on her own.

2

The story of the assault on Mark spread quickly round the neighbourhood, gaining embellishment as it rolled from street to street, and it was not long before it came to the ears of Mr Lightblow, at the bank. By this time the tale had become overlaid with much horrific detail: it was even said that Mark lay near to death and hopes of his recovery were so slight that the police had already called in the Murder Squad from Scotland Yard.

Beneath the dark suit, the stiff collar and cravat, and the grave demeanour which Mr Lightblow put on each day as befitting a bank clerk of thirty-two who had already reached the rank of Assistant Branch Cashier, there lay a sensitive and modestly adventurous nature. Married to a sensible wife and with two sensible children to maintain, he clung to his job and his hopes of further promotion out of economic necessity, but there were times when the prospect of another thirty years in the strait-jacket of banking weighed on his spirit like a rock.

From his position behind the polished mahogany counter of the bank he felt like a prisoner looking out on the real world: he saw men no older than himself who had not only identified business opportunities but found the courage to take advantage of them. He had seen one of these young men grow very rich in the space of five years by speculating in property and at least two others who had built thriving businesses. In one instance it had been Mr Lightblow himself who had pointed a customer in the right direction and organised a small starting-loan from the bank. The result had proved satisfactory for the customer but less so for Mr Lightblow, who derived no benefit from the success of what, basically, had been his idea.

Yet it would be wrong to think of him as an unhappy man. He enjoyed his wife and family, he enjoyed his garden and the games of weekend tennis at the Palmers Green Bowls and Tennis Club, he enjoyed books. He was currently reading the latest popular success, *The Constant Nymph* by Margaret Kennedy, a book he thought far superior to the year's other best-seller, *The Green Hat*. No, he was not unhappy but, when he allowed himself to think about it, he did have this persistent feeling of dissatisfaction, particularly because he suspected that the fault lay in his own lack of courage and enterprise as much as in the closed-in nature of his job.

Perhaps because he recognised these qualities in Mark, he had, from the beginning, taken a very personal interest in the young street-trader's career and given help which was often above and beyond his duty as an Assistant Branch Cashier. So it was that, after a call on one of the bank's more important clients and finding himself in the vicinity of Culross Road, he decided to look in at the warehouse, in the hope of meeting Rosie there and getting the true story of the attack on Mark.

He found her checking the remains of the stock of corned beef and sardines in response to a request by the police for an estimate of what had been stolen. It was the first time she had seen Mr Lightblow outside the walls of the bank and, for a moment, she was apprehensive. Had he come to bring more bad news, perhaps about Mark's finances?

In his slightly solemn manner he laid these fears to rest, accepted the offer of a cup of tea and, while she was making it, sat down without ceremony on an up-ended box.

'Tell me,' he said, 'tell me – what is the truth of what happened yesterday? I've heard all sorts of rumours – none of them very encouraging, I'm bound to say.'

When Rosie had told him, he made a little clucking sound and shook his head: 'Bad, very bad. I suppose the only consolation is that it might have been worse. It is the violence that is so distressing. I blame the war, you know. For four years we encouraged our young men to kill and maim other young men. We actually taught them to be violent. Small wonder that some of them have not forgotten the lesson.'

'Were you in the army, Mr Lightblow?' she asked.

'The navy,' he replied, 'the Royal Navy. I served – in a humble capacity, you understand – I served in minesweepers for the last two years of the conflict.'

Rosie, boiling kettle in hand, peeked at him from the alcove, thinking that Mr Lightblow was quite a surprise packet. She had never imagined him as other than a bank clerk, certainly never envisioned him as a sailor, treading the deck of a rolling ship.

'That must have been dangerous,' she said.

'It had its moments,' he said. 'All the same, I'm bound to say that, from all accounts, it was better than being in the trenches.'

'Thank God, it's over,' said Rosie.

'For the time being,' he replied solemnly.

She looked at him in some alarm. 'What do you mean? You are not saying that it is all going to start up again, are you?'

'Well, let me put it this way. I don't think the war solved the problem at all – and the peace certainly hasn't. No, indeed. Personally, I don't like the look of things in Europe, I don't like them at all. You might say that all the seeds of a future conflict are present.'

'God forbid,' she said fervently.

'He could have forbidden the last war but He didn't. No doubt for reasons best known to Himself,' he said. His tone was neutral and Rosie could not tell whether he was being serious or making a joke. She brought the tea, set the cups out on another box and sat down opposite this new and unexpected Mr Lightblow.

'Well,' he said, stirring his tea, 'I suppose you will hold the fort until Mark is fit to return.'

'I should be so lucky!' she said ruefully. 'There is no fort to hold.'

'How is that?'

'Well, look around. This is all that's left. A couple of hundred tins of sardines and no more than about eighty of corned beef. That's the lot. And there's no money to buy more stock – those villains took every penny. At least, that's what Mark told me last night at the hospital. He said they'd wiped him out. Of course, he was still in a state of shock – maybe he was exaggerating.'

'No. It may well be true, I'm afraid,' Mr Lightblow said cautiously. 'In normal circumstances, what happens between the bank and its clients is confidential. But I think I could go so far as to tell you this – Mr Moss drew out a rather large amount yesterday leaving only a trifling sum in the account.'

'There's nothing left?'

'Just under two pounds. I am speaking in the strictest confidence, you understand.'

'Of course.' She sighed deeply 'There you are, then. No money in the bank, no stock to speak of, in debt for the sardines – we're finished. Done for.'

'It is not as bad as that, surely?'

'It takes money to buy stock,' she said. 'I mean, I've got the chance to buy some tea. I'm sure that would go well. But without the cash to buy it and Mark to sell it, I'm scuppered. Up the creek without a paddle.'

'I see.' Mr Lightblow sipped his tea. 'It is possible – vaguely possible – that the bank might help.'

'How do you mean?'

'A small loan. Enough to get you started again.'

Rosie's face opened in a smile. 'That would be marvellous. Better than a slap in the face with a wet kipper!'

'Don't build your hopes too high,' he warned. 'Mr Purcell, the manager, can be rather conservative – that is to say, difficult – in these matters. He does not consider street-trading to be – how shall I put it? – to be a sound business. I have heard him say as much. There are no real assets which can be taken as security, you see. And even if he is favourably inclined it will take some time – a week, perhaps, or ten days.'

'But this Mr Purcell will listen to you?' she asked anxiously.

'Possibly. We shall have to see. All I can promise is that I will do my very best.'

'That's good enough for me!' she said, her eyes bright with new hope. 'You are a real gentleman, Mr Lightblow.'

'As to that,' he said, 'there are various schools of opinion.' Again, she could not tell from his expression whether he was serious or otherwise.

'I can't wait to see Mark's face when I . . .' She checked, remembering the conversation with him at the hospital, and continued more slowly: 'There's a problem.'

'Another one?'

'Mark. Those villains have knocked the stuffing out of him. Last night he vowed that he was finished with the markets, that he would never go back.'

'People say a lot of things when they are in shock – things they don't mean.'

'Without him to do the selling, we're sunk,' she said gloomily.

'You couldn't do the selling yourself? Just until Mr Moss recovers?'

'Me? I wouldn't know where to begin!'

'I can hardly believe that. You've seen enough of the markets, I'm sure.'

'No.' She shook her head. 'It's – well – it's something special. The gift of the gab – and more. I'd be hopeless.'

'Now, now!' he said sternly, rising to his feet. 'Don't disappoint me.'

'Pardon?' She looked up at him, puzzled by this remark.

'Shall I tell you what appealed to me about you and Mr Moss? I liked your spirit. I received the impression that you were the sort of people who would not easily be defeated. Don't tell me that I was wrong.'

'But what can I do? Without Mark . . .' Her voice tailed away and she shook her head.

'He will get better. His spirits will revive. It is largely up to you. If you can prove to him that this is not the end – merely a temporary setback – he will come round, I am sure.'

'But how?' she pleaded.

'I can't advise you there. I have little or no experience in these matters. But I am sure you will think of something.' He took her hand and shook it formally. 'I must go. Good luck.'

'Thank you,' she murmured.

She watched him move away up the narrow street, a prim, erect figure, old for his years. Good luck, she thought wryly. All I've got is fisherman's luck, out in the cold with nothing in the net!

But Mr Lightblow had, after all, put a spark to the tinder. As she turned back and her eye fell on the tins of sardines and corned beef, what he had said about selling came back to her and a sudden surge of defiance quickened her blood.

Why not, Rosie, she told herself, why not? What have you got to lose? Don't stick around here feeling sorry for yourself. Make your own luck! Have a go, girl, have a go!

She began to load the goods on to the barrow, quickening the pace as her resolution stiffened and her excitement grew. Ten minutes later she was pushing the barrow out of the warehouse, on her way to the Fortune Street market.

3

Some luck, at least, was with Rosie that morning. It was a fine day, though cold, and there was no shortage of shoppers in the market. In addition, her appearance at Mark's old pitch had a certain novelty value: regular customers came in a steady stream to ask what had happened to the cheeky young man, and many of them, when they heard the story, bought something as a gesture of sympathy.

This goodwill encouraged Rosie. She had started her spiel nervously but as time passed her confidence grew and she began positively to enjoy the experience. Mark had once said that a street-trader had to be a cross between a politician and an entertainer and she now realised what he meant. There was pleasure, plus a sense of power, in being able to sway a crowd of people, to feel them respond, to hear them laugh, which she found intoxicating.

By two o'clock, after three hours, she had sold out and was on her way back to the warehouse. When she counted the takings she found that she had accumulated a total of £3 19s. She made a careful note of this in her account book, estimating that £1 14s had come from the sale of sardines and £2 5s from the corned beef.

So far, so good, she thought, as she sipped tea and nibbled a cheese roll which she had bought in the Fortune Street café. She consulted her book again and, after making a rough calculation, she worked out that the profit on the morning sales amounted to twelve shillings and twopence.

Not bad. But the warehouse was now empty except for those wretched clocks and even if she used all the takings there would not be enough to acquire new stock. Where, where, where could she raise some money? She could not wait for Mr Lightblow to come through with a loan, if he ever did. She needed to act now, at once, so that she could convince Mark that there was real hope. Above all, she wanted to make a start on selling Carmo Tea, for she felt in the depths of her being that this was an idea too precious to be lost.

And then, as she sat there pondering the problem, banging the fist of one hand into the palm of the other, an idea came to her. It was an idea so shocking in its implications that she stood suddenly upright, knocking the empty tea-mug to the floor. It shattered into a dozen pieces, as if in reproach, but she ignored it, gripped by her thoughts.

Gran's money. The twenty-one pounds which had been put aside for funeral expenses. With that, and what she had in hand, she could get some bags printed and buy four or five chests of tea! The money was there, to hand, in the back section of her purse, it was there for the taking.

She tried to reject the idea, arguing fiercely with herself. It would be stealing – but then, was it not stolen money anyway? And it would be a loan, strictly a loan, to be repaid as soon as the business was on its feet. More difficult to answer, because it went against all her deeply ingrained instincts, was the notion that she might be robbing the dead. Working-class folk looked to death for the dignity that had often been denied them in life: the ritual of burial demanded and received solemnity and respect and the cost was seldom counted. People paid their pennies into insurance companies for the whole of their working lives to ensure that they would not suffer the final dishonour of a pauper's funeral.

On the other hand, on the other hand, surely her duty was to the living? She had a family to feed, including Gran herself. If she lost her job with Mark, God alone knew where she would find another. According to the papers, there were a million and a half unemployed: Ramsay MacDonald and his Labour government had not delivered the jobs or the prosperity which had been such a feature of their election speeches. What chance would she have of getting decent work at a decent wage?

The thought of going back to cleaning other people's doorsteps, washing other people's clothes, scrubbing other people's floors, appalled her. She had put that sort of drudgery behind her, she had tasted a kind of freedom.

Finally, she convinced herself that the money would, after all, only be a loan. As soon as the business was back on its feet, or the cash came through from the bank, she would repay it. In any case, Gran was still alive and kicking, she didn't look as if she was going to die just yet, and it was plain daft not to put the funeral money to some good use.

Clutching her purse, she locked up the warehouse and went in search of Mr Milton, the printer.

4

'What can I do for you?'

Mr Milton, proprietor of A. Milton, Stationers and Printers, wiping crumbs from his drooping moustache, emerged from a back room and advanced on Rosie. His manner was belligerent, as if some important private concern had been disrupted by the intrusion of a mere customer. He wore a stained apron that had once been white, and his hands and his face, right up to the high domed forehead, were likewise splashed with ink, like bluish-black scars.

'I'd like to get some printing done,' Rosie said mildly. She had a fleeting absurd notion that she should apologise for making such a request.

'Then you've come to the right place, haven't you?' he said brusquely. 'What is it you want?'

Rosie explained about the bags and produced a sample on which she had written: CARMO TEA – THE PEOPLE'S FRIEND.

'Hmph.' Mr Milton grunted and shook his head. 'Bags!' He spoke as if bags were beneath him, as if bags were for lesser mortals and that to ask him to print bags was like asking a Constable or a Rembrandt to whitewash a wall.

'Can't you do it?' Rosie asked anxiously.

'Oh, I can do it,' said Mr Milton wearily. 'I can certainly do it. A thing like this presents no problems, no problems at all. You might call it child's play.' His tone implied that he would infinitely have preferred something that was not child's play, a job that would offer a real challenge.

Local gossip had it that Mr Milton must have something to hide since he kept himself so resolutely to himself and held intruders at bay by his spiky manner. The mystery was further compounded by the fact that he often worked late at night, behind the closed blinds of the shop: some neighbours had complained that the steady thump-thump of his Cropper Charlton printing press disturbed their sleep.

At this time the communist regime in Russia was much in the news and the latest theory maintained that Mr Milton was in league with the Bolsheviks and their comrades in Britain and that he spent those closed evenings printing clandestine leaflets which were aimed at the promotion of bloody revolution.

The reality was altogether more romantic. Alfred Milton was, quite simply, in love with words. His favourite day-dream was to imagine the shop-bell tinkling and the door opening upon the entry of some literary giant, like H. G. Wells, his favourite author. Mr Wells would then confess that he was unhappy with his present arrangements and invite Mr Milton to set and print his latest literary work.

Since Mr Wells had so far failed to appear, he was filling in the waiting-time by setting and printing a new and simplified version (revised by Mr Milton himself) of *The Moral Discourses of Epictetus*, a Stoic philosopher whom he much admired. It was his view that the world would be a far better place if the thoughts of Epictetus were more widely known.

Rosie, of course, knew nothing of this secret life but she would not have been surprised to hear it. She had lived in London long enough to know that its people had unsuspected depths, and talents which were often left fallow because of the sheer effort to keep alive.

'Can you supply the bags?' she asked. 'They must be able to hold a quarter-pound of tea.'

Mr Milton turned the sample over in his hands and grunted. Crossing to one of the crowded untidy shelves, he selected a brown paper bag and thrust it at Rosie.

'That sort of thing?'

'Yes. That would do.'

'How many?'

'Two thousand five hundred to start with.'

'When do you want them?'

'As soon as possible, please.'

'Next week?'

'No, no!' Rosie's voice signalled alarm. 'It's urgent. I wondered about – say – tomorrow?'

'Tomorrow!' Mr Milton glared at her, pale eyes glinting behind spectacles.

'Please,' she begged. 'I'd be ever so grateful.'

Mr Milton was neither too old nor too far into philosophy to ignore the charms of a pretty woman and he found Rosie's sweet air of supplication difficult to resist. Softening a little, he said gruffly: 'I'll see what I can do.'

'Thanks ever so,' she replied, smiling her gratitude.

'It will be cash,' he said sternly.

'Of course. How much?' She produced her purse as proof of good intent, but he waved it aside.

'You can pay when you collect.'

They agreed a price of twenty-two shillings and sixpence, discussed the colour and the sort of type, and concluded the transaction. When this was done, Mr Milton allowed his curiosity to show through for a moment.

'Carmo Tea?' he said thoughtfully. 'I've never heard of that brand.'

'No,' Rosie answered. 'But you will, you will!'

5

Ninety minutes later, she knocked on the door of Jack Cameron's office. It was now past five o'clock and clerks from other offices pushed past her eagerly, the light of release in their eyes.

She tried the door and it opened to reveal an uninhabited

room. The chairs were pushed neatly under the desks, the desk-tops were clear except for the inkwells, the pen-holders and an occasional file. The silence mocked her and she felt a surge of frustration. It was in her nature, both a strength and a weakness, to push forward at full speed once she had decided on a course of action, and the thought of waiting until the morrow irked her. And her disappointment had another edge, one which she would never have admitted: she had been looking forward to meeting Jack Cameron again, looking forward with an eagerness which had nothing to do with business.

Frowning, she turned back to the entrance but, as she did so, the door to the inner office clicked open. Wheeling round, she saw him standing there, in a smart raglan overcoat buttoned to the neck and a grey, wide-brimmed trilby hat, worn at a jaunty angle, looking more like a refugee from literary Bloomsbury than a trader in something so mundane as tea.

'Mrs Carr – as I live and breathe!' he said cheerfully, lifting the hat in an extravagant sweeping gesture.

She felt herself blushing and smiling at the same time as she murmured: 'I'm sorry. I didn't realise that you would be closed.'

'No, no!' He waved her apology aside. 'It is a pleasure, you know, an unexpected pleasure. I wondered what had happened when you didn't turn up this morning. I missed you.'

For some reason, this simple statement made Rosie's heart beat a little faster, or appear to do so, at least. She knew it was absurd and told herself so, but it made no difference. Gathering herself as best she could and trying not to look into those brown mischievous eyes, she said: 'I couldn't make it sooner. Something came up.'

'Better late than never. Instead of lunch, I'll take you out to dinner.'

'No!' she said quickly, a note of alarm in her voice, and added more quietly: 'Sorry. I didn't mean – I just can't. I have to visit someone in hospital.'

'In that case, I'll take you for a drink,' he said, without hesitation, crooking an arm towards her invitingly.

Really, she thought, this is all getting out of hand, you must pull yourself together, Rosie. Aloud she said resolutely: 'I haven't come to skylark around. I'm here on business – I want to buy five chests of that tea.'

'Capital!' he exclaimed. 'We'll settle it over the drinks.'

She shook her head in mock despair. 'Do you always go on like this?'

'No,' he said gravely. 'Actually I am a very quiet, reserved, studious man. Noted for it.'

'And the rest!' she said, smiling into his eyes. My God, Rosie, she thought, what the hell are you up to? You are behaving like a schoolgirl with his fellow. Pull yourself together!

'It's you,' he continued. 'You do seem to have the most extraordinary effect on me.'

'Five chests of tea!' she said firmly, producing her purse. 'I've brought the cash.'

'No sale!' he said.

'What?' She stared, wondering what he was up to now.

'No sale unless you take a drink with me.'

'That's blackmail!'

'I know. Well?'

'All right,' she said, with a show of reluctance. 'One drink.' And, for good measure, she added: 'You are a cheeky sod, do you know that?'

6

Mr Waterlow, who was still on duty, saluted Mr Cameron respectfully and then almost lost control of his face when he saw his companion. Rosie's name took shape on his lips but he changed direction just in time and murmured hoarsely:

'Good evening, madam.'

'Good evening,' she replied jauntily, giving him half a wink.

'A cab, Waterlow,' said Mr Cameron, 'if you would be so kind.'

'Yes, sir!' Mr Waterlow sent Rosie a startled glance and

darted off. Rosie made a move as though to stop him but she was too late.

'Anything wrong?' asked Mr Cameron.

'Well, I hope you are not taking me anywhere posh. I'm not dressed for it.' She was wearing a new cloche hat and a decent enough coat, bought only a month before from the Co-op Clothing Club, but beneath this she had on an old skirt and blouse which had done duty in the market.

'You look magnificent,' he said seriously and touched her arm. 'Truly.'

The taxi arrived before she could argue further. She received one more look from Mr Waterlow as he opened the door for her, a look that seemed to hold a hint of warning. Rosie responded with a smile and a cheeky 'Thanks ever so,' and they were off.

'Where are we going?' she asked as she settled back, trying to look as though riding in a cab was an everyday experience for her.

'The Ritz?' he said.

'Gawd – no!' she cried.

'My rooms?' he said cheekily.

'No, ta very much,' she declared firmly. 'I'm not just out of the egg, you know. What about a nice quiet little pub?'

'If you say so,' he said and leaned towards the driver. 'Change of direction, Driver. Take us to the Lion and Lamb in Coptic Street.'

'Right you are, guv'nor,' said the driver, implying by his tone that he wished people would make up their minds. He slowed down, crashed the heavy gear through the gate and made a left turn.

Their destination settled, Rosie relaxed and they drove on in silence for some minutes. Her companion seemed disinclined to talk but each time she stole a glance at him he smiled back, his eyes twinkling. He had contrived to edge close without appearing to press her unduly, and when the cab jolted, as it did frequently, she could feel the warmth of his thigh against her own.

'I want to collect the tea tomorrow morning first thing,' she said, thinking it best to keep to the subject of business. 'Five cases at four pounds and ten shillings each.'

'Chests,' he said, 'we call them chests.'

'Five chests, then. Where do I pick them up?'

He produced a wallet and extracted a card. 'Here. At our warehouse.'

She took the card and he watched in amusement as she counted some notes. 'I make that twenty-two pounds and ten shillings,' she said. 'Here.' As she gave him the money she felt a little stab of apprehension. Should she have ordered four chests instead of five or perhaps only three? With Gran's funeral money of £21 plus £3 19s from the sale of the corned beef and the sardines, she had a total capital of £24 19s. Payment for the tea and the bags would leave her with the slender balance of £1 6s 6d. If the sale of the tea did not come up to expectations, she would really be in queer street.

She became aware that he was talking to her. 'I wish all my customers were as businesslike as you.'

'I shall need a receipt,' she said, putting the doubts behind her.

'Give me your address and I will deliver a receipt in person,' he said, smiling again.

'Leave it at the warehouse tomorrow,' she replied tartly, as his leg bumped hers yet again.

He slid the money into his wallet. 'Good,' he said. 'Now we can put business behind us and concentrate on more pleasant things. For a start, I cannot go on calling you Mrs Carr. Give me a name, eh?'

'I think we'd better keep it as it is,' she said.

'Oh, come along. You don't strike me as the stuffy type. Look – I'll give you a lead. My friends call me Jack.'

'You can hardly call us friends. We've only known each other five minutes.'

'Five minutes, five years – what does it matter? I knew when I first saw you that we were going to be friends. First impressions and all that – they are the best, don't you think? Didn't you feel the same way?'

'Perhaps,' she said, knowing that he had spoken the truth.

At that moment, the cab slowed and pulled up outside The Lion and Lamb. 'Here we are, guv'nor,' called the driver.

'Which hospital do you have to go to later?' asked Jack.

'The Cottage Hospital in Tottenham,' she answered, a little surprised at the question.

'What time must you be there?'

'Seven o'clock.'

'Right.' He checked his watch and then addressed the cabby. 'I want you to wait and then take the young lady to Tottenham. Can you do that?'

'I was going home after this fare,' said the cabby.

'I'll make it worth your while,' said Jack.

'Righto, guv'nor,' said the cabby, with more grace this time.

'No!' Rosie protested. 'I can get a bus.'

'No arguments,' he said firmly. 'It's all arranged.'

'A waste of blooming money,' she grumbled.

'It's in a good cause,' he said. 'I shall have longer with you.' He took her hand as he spoke and, again, she felt that odd fluttering inside.

'I don't know,' she said, shaking her head, 'I don't know what to make of you, I really don't!' But she did not move her hand.

'Friends?' he said gently.

'All right,' she said, smiling at him.

'And the name?'

'Rose,' she said, 'but everyone calls me Rosie.'

He lifted her hand and brushed it with his lips. 'Pleased to make your acquaintance, Rosie,' he murmured.

What a bloody silly thing to do, she thought, but at the same time she rather liked the gesture.

CHAPTER NINE

1

The Lion and Lamb turned out to be a small, intimate place, quite unlike the rather big, noisy pubs that Rosie was used to. A log fire blazed in the fireplace of the saloon bar, rows of gleaming copper and bronze pots and pans and horse-brasses were lined up along the dark beams, prints of cartoons by Gillray hung on the smoky, mushroom-coloured walls, wooden chairs that were surprisingly comfortable stood in groups around small circular tables polished to such perfection that they winked back the light like mirrors.

A small pretty woman with shining black hair and eyes to match greeted Jack with easy familiarity as he entered. She spoke in a soft Welsh accent that reminded Rosie of Mr Llewellyn Davies, a maker of coffins, who occupied a regular corner seat at The Winged Horse each Saturday night.

'Evening, Mr Cameron. What are you doing here so early?'

'Thirst, Mrs Taffy,' said Jack. 'Driven mad by thirst.'

'We'll soon put you out of your misery then, won't we? The usual for you, I expect. And for your lady-friend?' She gave Rosie a half-appraising look followed by a warm smile, as if, by some subtle mental chemistry, she had recognised a kindred professional and approved.

'I'll just have a half of mild and bitter, thanks,' Rosie said.

'Oh, come on,' Jack protested, 'push the boat out! A gin – a port – a sherry?'

'No, I'll stick to the beer,' Rosie said.

'You let the young lady have what she wants,' said Mrs Taffy sternly. 'Sit down and I'll bring them over.'

As Jack led the way to a small alcove by the fire other

customers greeted him with a nod, a smile, a word, taking a quick look at Rosie as they did so. Summing me up, she thought, wondering if I'm Jack Cameron's latest. But despite their curiosity they seemed pleasant enough and the speculative glances did not bother her. On the contrary, she felt a little glow of pride at being seen in his company.

'They seem to know you here,' she said.

'It's my local. I have rooms in Bedford Square, just along the road. I come in two or three evenings a week.'

'A nice place,' she said, looking round and thinking that she would not mind running a pub of this sort. 'Very nice indeed.' The fragrant smell of cooking drifted towards her from somewhere behind the bar, reminding her stomach that it had taken no food except the cheese roll since breakfast.

Jack caught the scent also, or perhaps he read her thoughts, for he said immediately: 'Would you like something to eat?'

'No, no. I'm all right,' she replied.

He must have noticed a slight hesitation in her voice and rebuked her gently: 'Nonsense! You can't leave The Lion and Lamb without tasting Mrs Taffy's Cornish pasties.' And as that lady came over with the drinks he gave the order for two of her best pasties.

'Best, indeed!' she said. 'There's no best and no worst, Mr Cameron, as well you know. They are all good and wholesome.' She smiled at Rosie. 'My husband bakes them. He's the cook here. When it comes to cooking I'm useless, all fingers and thumbs. Pity his rabbit pie is not on tonight. He makes the best rabbit pie this side of Cardiff castle.'

'I can confirm that,' Jack said as Mrs Taffy departed in the direction of the kitchen.

Rosie watched him for a long moment as he lifted a pewter tankard to his lips, thinking that he was the kind of man who made friends easily and who could make himself at home in almost any company. She found herself liking him more and more. And the question, too direct by half, slipped out before she could restrain her tongue.

'Are you married?'

He laughed lightly and lowered the tankard. 'Not that I'm aware of. How about you?'

'I was. I lost him in the war.'

'Ah.' He nodded his head in sympathy. 'Children?'

'Two. A boy and a girl.' She watched his reaction, for experience had taught her that the speed with which men lost interest in an eligible widow bore a direct relationship to the number of children there were to support, but she saw no shadow in his eyes, no change in the warmth of his expression.

'That's something, at least,' he said. 'I mean, a consolation. Company. You are not alone. But it must be hard for you, Rosie – a family to support.'

'It isn't easy,' she admitted. 'It's not just the kids. I have his mother as well.' She smiled ruefully. 'And she can be a real pillock at times, a right old handful.'

'Wait until you meet my mother,' he said. 'I'd be willing to bet that your old lady is an angel with wings compared to mine.'

'One's enough,' said Rosie. 'You keep yours, I'll keep mine.'

The pasties arrived, hot and steaming, and tasting every bit as good as their fragrance had promised. They ate in silence, occasionally catching each other with a smile of appreciation.

'Another one?' he asked.

'Lord, no!' she protested. 'I couldn't. I feel as if I'd eaten two dinners as it is!' Then she added anxiously: 'How's the time?'

'You've a few minutes yet,' he said and reached across the table to lay his hand on hers. She looked round quickly but no one seemed to be looking in their direction. 'You have nice hands,' he continued.

Echoes. Echoes. How many years since the young Frank Lambert had said the same thing?

'No.' She shook her head. 'They've seen too much hard work, too much scrubbing for that.' She lifted her other hand and looked at it ruefully.

'All the better for that,' Jack said. 'Honest hands – no nonsense about them.' He paused for a moment, before going on, softly, to say: 'Well, where do we go from here, Rosie?'

'Pardon?' She looked at him with genuine surprise.

'You know what I mean.'

'I don't,' she replied, although she had now grasped his meaning.

'You don't imagine that I am going to let you move out of my life now, do you?'

'You don't know me.'

'No. But I want to. I want to know you more than I've ever wanted to know anybody. Truly. I want to know everything about you.'

And, yet again, she felt the quickening of her heart, heard singing in her head. All the same, she took her hand away and heard a voice that did not seem to belong to her say briskly: 'You don't waste much time, do you!'

'Not if I can help it. My father used to say – when you are on to a good thing, son, back it for all you are worth.'

'Makes me sound like a perishing racehorse!' She paused and added: 'You are talking a lot of codswallop, you know that, don't you?' He looked pained but she pushed on regardless: 'You don't really want to know me. I'm not your sort. We come from different sides of the tracks.'

'What the hell does that matter?'

'A lot. You'd be fed up with me in a month.'

'No, Rosie, no.'

'You would, believe me.'

'And you with me?'

'I didn't say that. We are not talking about me, we're talking about you.'

'Ah,' he said, smiling, 'that is a very revealing statement.'

'I have to go,' she said, half-rising, but he said urgently, 'Wait – give me two more minutes,' and she sat down again.

'You know your trouble, Rosie, don't you?' he said.

'No. Tell me.'

'You are a snob.'

'That's a nice thing to say!' she said angrily. 'Thank you for the compliment!'

'It's true. You have a severe case of inverted snobbery. You think never the twain shall meet because we come from different social backgrounds. I'm not your sort – you are not mine. Right?'

'Right!' she said.

'Those days are over, Rosie, over and gone. The war did for all that. We are all in the same boat now.'

'Not where I live,' she said tartly. 'We are not in your boat, not by a long chalk. People like you would stick out like a monkey on a stick down our way. The war didn't make any difference to the way *we* live. If anything it made it worse. It took our men and made it worse.' She regretted the sharpness of her tone as soon as she had spoken and she added a feeble 'Sorry. I didn't mean—'

She could read no offence on his face as he replied: 'All right. Point taken. But I still don't see why that should make any difference to you and me.'

'If you don't see, I can't explain,' she said.

'May I ask you one more question?'

She nodded. 'I suppose so.'

'Would you meet me again? For dinner, lunch – whatever?'

Her face broke into a smile. 'Don't you ever give up?'

'Answer the question, Rosie.'

'Yes,' she said, 'all right.'

'It's just as well you said that,' he said.

'Why? What do you mean?'

'I wouldn't have taken no for an answer.'

As they left The Lion and Lamb he took her arm and, before helping her into the cab, he kissed her lightly on the lips, taking her by surprise. But on the journey to the hospital she felt herself glowing with a new warmth remembering that kiss with a sense of happiness and anticipation that made her want to burst into song.

The word 'love' formed in her mind. Was she falling in love with Jack Cameron? No. The idea was ridiculous, she had only met the man twice. But the fact remained that he had made a greater impression upon her than any man she had ever met. Images of him, smiling, talking, eating, followed each other in her head, like the slides in a magic-lantern show.

The cabby, who had received a five-pound note from Jack Cameron – more than the rest of his takings for the entire day – was also in good humour and he began to whistle 'I'm Forever Blowing Bubbles'.

Rosie made it into a duet by humming the tune. By the time they reached the Cottage Hospital, they had gone through three songs and were halfway through one of Rosie's favourites, 'If You Were the Only Girl in the World'.

2

She saw at once, and with relief, that Mark's spirits had taken a turn for the better. Much of the old brightness had returned to his eyes and smiling did not seem to be such an effort.

'Don't make me laugh,' he warned. 'I tried it this afternoon when the bloke in the next bed stubbed his bare toe on the foot of the bed and it hurt me more than it hurt him.'

'You look tons better, you really do.'

'I feel it. The Doc says I ought to be able to leave in a couple of days.' He looked at her keenly, sensing something different in her manner. 'What about you, eh? You look like the first day of spring. What happened? Did you win a fortune, perhaps? Or maybe you are in love?'

'That'll be the day,' she said, putting as much scorn into her voice as she could muster. But she felt her cheeks redden under his teasing scrutiny.

'You know what they say, don't you?' he went on. 'Three things can't be hidden: coughing, poverty and love. That's what they say.'

'Give over, Mark,' she said, 'give over.' And she continued quickly, anxious to get away from this awkward subject: 'I sold the rest of the sardines and corned beef today. Sold the lot!'

'You did!'

'Don't sound so surprised! I suppose you didn't think I was capable, is that it?'

'Rosie,' he said seriously, 'I think you are capable of anything you set your mind to. Would I lie to you? No. It's the truth. Tell me more.'

She described her experience in the market, but for reasons which were obscure, even to her, she said nothing of her plan to launch Carmo Tea upon the world. Later, she would persuade herself that she had held back so as not to worry him. If she failed, it would be her failure, not his. But in her heart she knew that she had not wanted either to tell him that she had stolen – borrowed? – Gran's funeral money or to answer questions which might lead to Jack Cameron.

'Good for you, Rosie,' he said. 'If you go on at this rate you won't need me!'

'I need you out of that blooming bed and back at the market just as soon as you can make it!' she replied firmly. 'It's your business.'

'What business? I told you – I'm cleaned out.'

'I saw Mr Lightblow from the bank. He was ever so nice. He is going to see if he can get you a loan – enough to start you up again.'

'You've had a busy day,' he said. If only you knew it all, she thought, smiling inwardly. 'I've been busy also,' he continued.

'Doing what?'

'Thinking. First chance I've had to have a real think for a long time.' He leaned towards her, wincing a little. 'We have to look beyond the markets, Rosie. They're all right, they bring in a fair living, but that's not enough. Do I want to be street-trader all my life? The answer is no. I don't want to be a street-trader even in ten years. Don't misunderstand. I'm not ashamed of what I do . . .'

'I should hope not!' she interrupted.

'—but I want something better,' he concluded.

'Such as?'

'Transport, Rosie, transport!' he said, with the air of a conjuror pulling a rabbit from a hat.

'You've lost me,' she said, wrinkling her face in bewilderment.

'Listen,' he said, 'listen. What is happening to London? Are you blind you haven't noticed? It is moving, Rosie, moving outwards. They are building a new Underground line from Morden in the south to Edgware in the north. They are electrifying railway lines to the suburbs. On the roads what do you see? The motor-car. The car has already taken over. Do you know how many motor-cars there are on the roads in this country? I will tell you – thirteen million, Rosie – thirteen million motor-vehicles. And more to come. Now, you tell me – what does all this transport mean? Tell me.'

'No. You tell me,' she said, smiling at his enthusiasm.

'All right. What it means is that people won't have to live near their work any more. They can move out, to Morden, Edgware, Southgate, Croydon – a dozen places – and travel to work in London. Also, many factories and offices will open in these places – attracting more people to live there. New suburbs, even new towns, will grow like mushrooms all around the edge of London. Ask yourself what this means, Rosie. It means people. People living out there, housewives living out there. And what is the housewife going to do? You think perhaps she will get on a bus or train and come to London for her shopping? Will she come to our markets? A foolish notion! She will want to buy near her home, do you see that?'

'Yes. I do. What you are saying makes sense.'

'So what conclusion do you draw from this?'

'If they won't come to us – we must go to them?' she asked tentatively.

'Correct,' he said triumphantly. 'The nail on the head.'

With these thoughts chasing around in her mind she had to leave him, for his mother arrived at that moment flanked by Bennie and Debbie.

'Here's your family,' she said. 'I'll leave you to it.'

'You don't have to go.'

'I don't want to barge in. I'll see you tomorrow.'

Mark's mother, shaking her head, clucking her gums, met Rosie at the ward entrance and drew her aside. 'How is he?' she asked, in a low voice.

'Oh, he's well on the mend,' said Rosie cheerfully. 'He'll be out in a couple of days.'

'From such injuries he is already better?'

'Much better. Truly. You'll see for yourself.'

Mrs Moss stopped shaking her head and nodded. 'You got home safe last night?'

'Yes, thank you.'

'My Bennie – he didn't bother you?'

'Of course not.'

'I mean, with his wild opinions. He is a good boy, you understand, but he uses strange words sometimes, even I don't know what he means and I am his mother.' She sighed. 'Mark and Bennie, two sons, two apples from the same branch yet so different.'

She turned back to her daughter and Bennie. 'You wait here,' she ordered. 'First I want to speak to our Mark myself.' Bidding Rosie goodnight, she headed towards Mark's bed, clutching a small bag of grapes.

Rosie smiled at the others. 'Well, I'll leave you to it. I must go.'

'I hope we will see you again,' Debbie said.

'I hope so too,' Rosie replied politely.

Bennie said nothing but at least his big, serious face opened in a brief smile.

3

All thoughts of Jack Cameron, the sale of tea or the growing mobility of Londoners were expelled from her mind the moment she entered the house, for Eddie and Van greeted her with the news that Gran was ill and had taken to her bed.

'Is she really ill or is she just putting it on as usual?' asked Rosie suspiciously.

'She said she had a pain in her inside like as if a rat was gnawing at her vitals,' said Van, with a certain relish.

'I cooked her one of the kippers you left for our tea and she wouldn't touch it,' Eddie added.

For Gran not to wolf any food placed before her was so extraordinary an event that Rosie went pale. A savage, uncharitable thought entered her mind. It would be just like the old girl to choose this moment to turn up her bloody toes: selfish to the last, she would die just to spite Rosie, to accuse her from beyond the grave of stealing the funeral money!

Repressing this shameful thought, Rosie flew towards the stairs. Halfway up she slowed down deliberately, took off her shoes and crept to the door of Gran's bedroom. A strip of light showed through the narrow gap at the bottom but no sound came from within. Easing the door open, she peeped inside.

She hardly knew whether to laugh with relief or explode with anger at what she saw. Gran was sitting up in bed fully clothed, a thin blanket around her bony shoulders, a bottle of Gordon's Dry Gin at her lips, and a smile of utter content on her face.

'What the hell do you think you are doing?' Rosie demanded, advancing towards the bed.

The old woman looked up, startled only for a moment, and immediately composed her face into an expression of pain.

'Oh, Rosie,' she said, 'it's my innards. It's like a knife, like someone is twisting a knife in my guts.'

'And where did you get this?' Rosie demanded, snatching the half-empty bottle of gin.

'I bought it, didn't I? I had to have something for the pains.'

'Where did you get the money?'

'I saved it.'

'You're a bloody liar! Have you been on the pinch again?'

'No, Rosie, no! I swear. I saved the money!' Gran said vigorously, perhaps too vigorously, for the disbelief took firmer shape on Rosie's face. Her eyes swept the room suspiciously while the old lady followed her look with an expression of innocence.

'All right!' Rosie said. 'Where have you hidden it?'

'Hidden what? I haven't hidden anything. I don't know what you are talking about.'

But as she spoke Gran darted a little fearful give-away glance

towards the foot of the bed and Rosie pounced. Pulling up the
corner of the mattress she revealed a worn brown leather purse.

'What's this, then?'

'I don't know,' whined Gran. 'I've never seen it before.'

'I suppose it walked there of its own accord!' Rosie opened
the purse, shaking her head. It contained a two-shilling piece
and a few coppers. Anger left Rosie to be replaced by a sudden
sense of helplessness.

'Oh, Gran, Gran, what are we going to do with you?'

The old lady looked at her warily but chose a diplomatic
silence. Rosie sat on the edge of the bed. 'Now,' she continued,
'I want the truth. Where did you get this?'

'I found it. Honest, Rosie.'

'The truth, I said! I'll shake it out of you if I have to!'

'It was in the market. I went there to treat myself to a dish of
jellied eels. You know I'm partial to jellied eels.'

'Get on with it!'

'There was this woman in front of me. Talking away, nineteen to the dozen, to this bloke. The purse was lying on top of her
shopping bag. I mean, she was asking for it, wasn't she? People
didn't ought to leave their bags open and the purses on top.'

'Oh, my God,' said Rosie, 'oh, my God!'

'Nobody saw me, Rosie. I whipped the purse ever so careful
and slipped away. I took a butcher's hook a minute or two
later and she was still gassing away.'

Rosie took a deep breath. 'Look at this purse,' she said
quietly. 'Look at it! Does it look as if it belongs to a duchess? No!
It belongs to someone like me – some poor cow who is
struggling to make ends meet! And you robbed her – robbed her
blind! Oh, Gran, I could kill you for this, I could kill you!'

'People shouldn't put temptation in the way of others,' Gran
said resolutely. 'That woman has only got herself to blame.'

'How much money was there?'

'Not much.'

'How much?'

'I treated myself to a dish of pease pudding and faggots and
the gin. The rest is in the purse.'

'Did you know the woman?'

'Of course not,' said Gran scornfully. 'Never set eyes on her before. What do you take me for? I wouldn't half-inch a purse from someone I knew.'

'You'd steal from anybody,' said Rosie, her voice rising. 'You'd steal the milk from a blind man's tea and then go back for the sugar.' She got to her feet, slipped the purse into her coat pocket, and looked fiercely down on the old woman. 'This is the last time, you hear me? The last time. If you put your sticky fingers on so much as a farthing that doesn't belong to you, I'll turn you out! I mean it, Gran, don't think I don't. I'll put you out and you can fend for yourself.'

The old woman shrank back against the pillow. 'I won't do it any more, Rosie. On my mother's grave, I swear.'

Rosie moved to the door, clutching the bottle of gin. 'You'd better not,' she said softly. 'You'd better not, because I've had you up to here. Up to here!' She put a hand against her throat in illustration and went out.

A moment or two passed and then, a smile cracking her face, Gran slid a hand inside her black dress, reached down towards her withered breasts and brought out a pound note. She was smoothing it between her fingers, cackling a little, when, too late, she heard the door click open and Rosie's voice:

'You lying old bitch! Come on – hand it over!'

4

After the Cornish pastie she had eaten at The Lion and Lamb and her clash with Gran, Rosie had little appetite for food but Eddie had cooked her a kipper and carved two thick slices of bread from a fresh cottage loaf and she had not the heart to refuse. But first she poured the remainder of the gin down the sink and sent Van out to put the empty bottle in the dustbin.

As she sat at the table, trying to do justice to the supper, the children took up position on either side of her, anxious that she should enjoy every mouthful, clearly happy to have her with them.

'I spread the bread, Mum,' said Van.

'Very nice too,' replied Rosie.

'Butter. Real butter,' said Van.

'It's a lot better than that old margarine,' said Rosie. It was a measure of their improved circumstances that they could now afford the occasional half-pound of Danish butter.

'Is Gran going to be all right?' asked Eddie.

'Of course. She was only putting it on,' said Rosie.

'Does she have to live with us, Mum?' asked Van.

'She's your grandmother – your father's mother. Where else would she go?'

'She smells,' said Van, wrinkling her nose.

'Well, we can't put her out in the street, can we?' Rosie said, contradicting the threat she had made to Gran a few minutes before. She glanced at the clock on the mantelshelf. 'Time you two were in bed.'

'Oh, Mum,' Van protested, 'not yet. We've hardly seen you.'

The truth behind the words struck home and Rosie felt the familiar prickle of guilt. Once again, she had become so absorbed in the business of earning a living, in the excitement of her day-to-day work, that she had taken her children for granted. Yet what could she do? She wanted the best for them and that meant money and the security, the opportunities, that went with it.

She laid down her knife and fork. 'Come and sit by the fire,' she said, 'and we'll talk a bit.'

'You haven't finished your kipper, Mum!' said Eddie, looking hurt. 'Was it all right?'

'It was lovely, son. Really. But I've had enough.'

Rosie took the old armchair by the stove and once again they settled on either side of her. 'Listen,' she began, 'I want to explain something. I want you to understand. First, you know I love you, I love you both very much.'

'And we love you too,' cried Van.

'I know you do, darling,' said Rosie, resting a hand on the

girl's shoulder. 'What I want to say is this. I've got all sorts of plans in my head. For a start, I want to get us out of this place, into a house of our own, where we don't have to share.'

'That would be terrific, Mum!' said Eddie.

'Where? Where?' clamoured Van.

'I don't know yet. But we'll find somewhere. A nice house with an indoor lavatory and a proper bathroom.'

'Cripes!' said Eddie in awe.

'And we'll need new furniture. You will each have a bedroom to yourselves, with a wardrobe and cupboards and bookshelves – oh, everything. And perhaps we'll have a bit of garden – not a yard like here – but a real garden with grass and flowers.'

'Can we have a dog?' asked Van.

'I don't see why not,' answered Rosie. 'But all that is just the beginning. You haven't had much in your lives so far – I want things to be better for you. Education, for one thing.'

'But we go to school,' said Eddie.

'Yes. And that's good. But I want you to have the chance to get more education. Perhaps to go on to one of those colleges. It's the people with education that seem to get on in this world. And, of course, there are lots of other things – clothes, books, holidays together, lots of things.'

Van clapped her hands together in excitement and cried: 'Terrific! Terrific!'

Eddie, the practical one, said: 'All that will cost an awful lot of money, Mum.'

'That's what I'm trying to explain, son,' said Rosie. 'That's why I'm out such a lot, working so hard. I think I'm on to a good thing, I think I see a chance, a real chance. But I can't do it without your help.'

'What do you want us to do, Mum?' asked Eddie.

'First, to understand. If I am out a lot, it is not because I don't love you – it is because I am working for us all. I want you to be patient.'

'That's not helping!' Van protested. 'We want to *do* something.'

'It will help me if I know that you understand what I'm up

to,' said Rosie. 'That will be something. And I promise you – cross my heart and hope to die – that, once I've got this market business sorted out, we'll spend much more time together.'

'But, Mum, isn't there anything we can do now?' pleaded Eddie.

They had turned their eager young faces towards her, their eyes shining, and Rosie's heart went out to them in a great leap of emotion. She cradled their heads, feeling herself near to tears, thinking the thought of all mothers. How long, how much longer, will their gentle innocence last, how long before their lives are stained and changed by the world outside? Aloud she said: 'Listen, my darlings, listen. I have an idea. You can help me tomorrow. It won't hurt if you have one day off school. I've got a big job to handle and I could do with some extra hands.'

'What? What do you want us to do?' asked Van.

'You'll find out,' said Rosie, releasing her embrace. 'Now, have a good wash, clean your teeth and turn in.'

'Would you read to us a bit, Mum? You haven't read to us for ever such a long time. Please,' pleaded Van.

'You are old enough to read to yourself,' said Rosie.

'But it's much better when you do it.'

'All right,' conceded Rosie. 'Shout when you are ready and I'll come in.'

Five minutes later, she sat on a chair in the back bedroom with a copy of Oliver Twist open before her. 'Where did we get to?' she asked.

'The bit where Nancy brings Oliver to Bill Sikes,' said Van.

'And Bill Sikes loads his pocket-pistol,' added Eddie.

Rosie found the place, smoothed back the page and began to read. 'Well,' said the robber, grasping Oliver's wrist, and putting the barrel so close to his temple that they touched; at which moment the boy could not repress a start, 'if you speak a word when you're out o'doors with me, except when I speak to you, that loading will be in your head without notice. So, if you do make up your mind to speak without leave, say your prayers first.'

She read on for ten minutes or more, until she saw their eyelids flicker in the effort to keep awake. Laying the book

aside, she bent and kissed them each in turn. Van, the
demonstrative one, threw her sleepy arms around Rosie's neck.

'I love you, Mum,' she whispered.

'Yes. I dare say you do,' answered Rosie. 'And I should love
you more if you washed your neck properly when I ask you.
You could sow seeds in that neck and bring up a good crop of
cabbages come the spring.'

5

Rosie longed for her own bed but she had one more job to do
before her day was finished, a job that would not wait. She
slipped on her coat, made a quick check on Gran and the
children, and left the house, moving in the direction of an area
known locally as the Estate, a collection of streets which had
been put up by a speculative Victorian builder with an eye to a
quick profit. Born into the world as James Albert Ernest Wigg,
he had used these and other family names to christen the mean
streets from which he had made his fortune.

Thus there were Wigg Road and James Street, Albert
Crescent and Ernest Avenue: after these, his wife came into the
reckoning with Emily Road, Margaret Street and Susan Road,
and there were half a dozen other roads which were dedicated
to his children. Mr Wigg was well rewarded for his outstanding
contribution to the art of slum-building: his wealth bought him
respectability and, in due course, he became Mayor of
Tottenham, a Freeman of the City, and eventually Sir James
Wigg. Fearful that in death he might be forgotten, he had left a
sum of money in his will and a discreet direction to his widow
that a monument should be erected in his honour. With the
permission of the Borough Council a statue of the late Sir James
was erected on the patch of green opposite the Town Hall, to
which site it was enthusiastically welcomed by successive
generations of local pigeons.

Rosie was heading for a corner house in Margaret Street, a
road whose grim, crumbling houses belied the gentleness of the

name. She skirted The Fox and Hounds, a notorious local pub, avoiding a group of young louts who had gathered outside. Their voices, raised in coarse and noisy argument, followed her as, keeping to the shadows, she made her way to a house halfway down, where Margaret Street was bisected by Susan Road. The house resembled all the other houses in terms of style and decay but it had one distinguishing feature: since it occupied a corner site, the yard lay to one side rather than at the back and it covered a greater area than the others.

As Rosie knocked at the front door, a horse whinnied from a shed in the yard, as though in response. A young woman, a baby suckling at her breast, opened the door and peered outwards.

'Yes?'

'Is Mr Christmas in?'

'Who wants him?'

'Tell him it's Rosie Carr. He knows me from The Winged Horse. I play the piano there, Friday and Saturday evenings.'

The woman shuffled nearer. 'Yes. I've seen you there.' And she added suspiciously: 'What would you be wanting with my brother?'

'It's a matter of business. I think I can put a bit of work his way.'

The young woman considered this for a moment, then she shuffled away, calling as she did so: 'Tiny! You're wanted! Someone at the door.'

The man who replaced her in the doorway had not been lucky in respect of names. Having his sort of surname had meant a journey through school in which he had suffered to be called 'Father' or 'Daddy' and endured a succession of monotonous jokes. All this he had taken in good spirit for his was a gentle, simple, non-aggressive nature, until his thirteenth year when, pressed too hard by a gang of yelling school-fellows, he had flared in brief and unexpected anger and laid three of them flat on the pavement in the space of two minutes. They had paid the penalty of failing to observe that young George Christmas had shot up at a surprising rate and was developing into a muscular giant.

In the last year of the war, his comrades in uniform had

christened him Tiny, thus perpetuating his problem with names: but since they used the nickname with careful respect and some affection, he had accepted it with good grace.

He stood before Rosie now, his bulk filling the doorway, his rolled-up shirtsleeves revealing tattooed arms and swelling muscles. 'Rosie!' he said, the great face widening into a smile. 'Rosie! What brings you here?'

'I was wondering if you could help me with a bit of business in the morning,' she said.

'In the morning?' he said doubtfully. 'I've got my round in the morning.' Tiny was the local rag-and-bone man, making an uncertain living by the collection and selling of old clothes, old iron, bottles, jars and junk of all sorts. It was said that his cry of 'Rag 'n bone! Rag 'n bone!' or 'Any old iron' could carry for half a mile if the wind was in the right direction.

'It won't take long,' said Rosie. 'I've got to pick something up at Shoreditch and bring it back to our warehouse in Culross Road. You could do it in an hour with the horse and cart. An hour and a half at the most. I'll pay you – well – say, five shillings?'

'It's as good as done, Rosie,' he said, 'as good as done.' He spat briefly on one large hand and held it out to seal the bargain. 'Sorry I can't ask you inside,' he continued, lowering his voice, 'but the place is in a right two-and-eight.'

'Oh, I have to go,' said Rosie. 'See you in the morning. Eight o'clock suit you?'

'Eight on the dot,' he said.

And that, Rosie thought as she walked home, is that. All the pieces were now in place. The tea, the transport, the bags. She would do the packing with Eddie and Van to help. With any luck, she might be able to start selling the tea the following afternoon. Carmo Tea. She had the feeling – why, she could not say – that this would be the breakthrough which she had been seeking for so many years. At the same time, she felt a sort of trembling nervousness inside, like a bride at the altar. What if it should all go wrong?

She crossed her fingers for luck and slipped her hands into

her pockets. The purse stolen by Gran lay there, and as she touched it Rosie went rigid with guilt. The feel of the worn leather was hateful, she wanted to be rid of the thing quickly. On impulse she stopped by the front door of one of the houses and pushed the purse, money and all, through the letter-box. It dropped with a thud and she hurried away.

It wasn't until she got home and slid, at last, into bed that her mind went back again to Jack Cameron. And it was with images of him floating in her head that she slipped into sleep.

CHAPTER TEN

1

Tiny Christmas was better than his word. He arrived at the warehouse promptly at eight o'clock the next morning at the wheel of a dilapidated truck, a weary veteran of the war. The legend, FANY, still appeared on the bonnet, and there were traces of the Red Cross on the sides, just discernible under layers of mud. Greeting the astonished Rosie with a huge smile and a bravado toot of the horn, he explained the absence of his horse and cart.

'Shoreditch is a bit too far for my old nag. He hasn't got the legs for it. So I borrowed Tubby Wilson's lorry. Well, it's an old ambulance really.' He pointed to the lettering on the bonnet. 'First Aid Nursing Yeomanry. Seen some service, she has, but she is still in good nick. She'll do it in half the time. Less. All right with you, Rosie?'

'Fine,' answered Rosie, looking with some doubt at the truck which appeared to be heavily dependent upon a crisscross collection of rope and wire: she had the feeling that if these were removed or cut the vehicle would burst open, rather like a fat lady whose corset strings had snapped.

'Don't worry about her,' said Tiny, seeing Rosie's look. He jumped to the pavement and, to illustrate his point, gave the truck a thump which would have felled Jack Dempsey. It responded with a shudder, a rattle and a couple of squeaks but then settled back without further complaint.

'I didn't realise you could drive, Tiny,' Rosie said..

'I was in transport during the war. Picked it up there.' He looked at Van and Eddie who were surveying the truck with undisguised enthusiasm. 'Ah. Playing the wag from school, eh?'

'They're going to give me a hand,' Rosie said. 'We've got a busy day.'

'Right,' said Tiny. 'The sooner we get started the better. Rosie, you come in the cab with me. You kids hop in the back.'

'And keep your heads down until we get clear of the district,' Rosie ordered. 'We don't want you to be spotted by the Schools Inspector.'

There were moments on the journey when Rosie wondered if they would ever make it to Shoreditch. They chugged out of Tottenham in reasonable style but the old truck took an evident dislike to the steep ascent leading to Stamford Hill and slowed at such an alarming rate that cyclists, leaning forward on their pedals, overtook it with cries of derision. Tiny, outwardly calm, somehow kept the thing going and his confidence seemed to transmit itself to the truck, for it began to pick up speed and soon they were rolling along through Stoke Newington at a fair lick.

A few more minutes and Tiny pulled to a halt in New Inn Yard, outside a large, imposing warehouse building. A board beside the double doors bore the inscription: CAMERON AND SON – WAREHOUSE. The doors were open, and standing there, a welcoming smile on his face, Rosie saw Jack Cameron himself.

'A very good morning to you, Rosie,' he said, moving forward to help her down.

'I didn't expect to find you here.'

'Couldn't miss an opportunity to see you, could I?' He smiled into her eyes and she felt herself glow with pleasure. And then she became aware that the children had jumped down and were standing beside them, studying her shining face with curious looks. Blushing with embarrassment she said, with as much briskness as she could summon up: 'Well, I haven't got all day. Can we get loaded up?'

'We are all ready,' Jack said. 'The only problem is – do you think that old lorry can take the weight?'

Tiny Christmas seemed as affronted by this remark as if it had been addressed to him personally. 'You said five chests, Rosie. A hundred and twenty pounds each. That's just over five hundredweight. You can tell the gent that this old lorry as he calls it can take twice that and more!'

'I'm sorry. I beg your pardon. No offence meant,' said Jack quickly.

'None taken, guv'nor,' said Tiny, 'none taken.'

'This is Mr Christmas,' said Rosie. 'He's giving me a hand this morning.'

'Pleased to meet you, Mr Christmas,' said Jack, showing no surprise at the name. He held out a friendly hand which Tiny, after a precautionary wipe on his trousers, took in his huge fist and pumped up and down.

Jack rescued his hand. 'Right,' he said. 'If you will back the lorry up against the entrance, my chaps will lower the chests down from up there.' He pointed to an opening on the first floor over which a block and tackle hung in readiness.

While the loading was going on, Jack introduced himself to Van and Eddie and took them to inspect the warehouse. Rosie followed a few paces behind, noting once again how easily Jack got on with people: he seemed as much at ease with the children as he had been with the customers in the bar of The Lion and Lamb, talking to them without condescension, as equals. Within minutes they had lost all their initial shyness and were laughing and firing questions at him.

'Where does it all come from?' asked Eddie, looking up in awe at the towering rows of plywood chests.

'Most of this lot comes from Ceylon,' replied Jack. 'Do you know where that is?'

'Of course,' said Van scornfully. 'On the map, it is at the bottom of India.'

'Do you have to go there to buy the tea?' Eddie asked.

'No, no. I have been to take a look, of course. But there are regular auctions of tea at Mincing Lane – that's where I buy it.' He went on to explain that he was a dealer and that he sold the tea to wholesalers who, in turn, packaged and labelled it for distribution to the shops.

'I'm surprised you bothered with my piffling little order,' Rosie said.

'Ah, you never know,' Jack replied. 'What starts as a tiddler might finish up as a salmon.'

'And are you rich?' said Van.

'That's enough, Van!' Rosie said sharply.

'Oh, that's all right,' Jack said easily. 'Let me put it this way, young lady. I am neither a pauper nor a millionaire. Does that answer your question?'

'Not really,' said Van frankly.

Tiny came to the door and announced that all was ready for the return journey.

'Now,' Jack said, 'I've been giving thought to your enterprise. Have you got everything you need? Scales, for instance?'

'Scales?' said Rosie.

'For weighing up the tea.'

Rosie thumped her head in anguish. 'Oh, cripes! I forgot about scales!'

'Fear not!' said Jack. 'I will lend you scales. And two scoops. And a trolley. You will need all these things – right?'

'I'm ever so grateful.'

'I shall need more tangible evidence of your gratitude on another occasion,' he said, meeting her eyes.

She scolded herself silently as she climbed in beside Tiny: Rosie, Rosie, for God's sake stop blushing like a schoolgirl every time that man looks at you!

2

CARMO TEA – THE PEOPLE'S FRIEND!

The bags Mr Milton had supplied and printed looked very attractive, much more so than Rosie had expected. He had found a supply of cream-coloured bags, much lighter than the plain brown one he had shown her originally, and printed the label in bold blue letters.

'Stands out better,' he had explained. 'And the bags are of finer quality. No extra charge.'

Turning one of the bags over in her hands, holding it up to the light, feeling the texture of the paper, Rosie felt a current of excitement and pride prickle her blood. She remembered a moment, years before, when as a pupil at an evening class for illiterates run by the Workers' Educational Association, she had composed and written her first sentence and seen it there on the page in front of her. She had felt then as if a great shutter had opened in her mind, as if a new life, full of promise, lay before her. Something like the same sensation warmed her now as she stared at the simple paper bag and its inscription. Was this also the beginning of something big and exciting?

But there was no time now for dreams or questions. Once the chests were installed in the warehouse (she could never have managed without Tiny's willing strength) and once they were opened, Rosie realised the enormity of the task she had set herself. At the end of an hour, working flat out with Eddie and Vanessa, they had only filled about one hundred bags and used just a quarter of the tea in the first chest.

'Wait,' Rosie said, 'wait. We've got to find a better way than this or we'll never get through it in a month of Sundays.'

'It's the weighing-up, Mum,' said Eddie. 'We have to wait while you weigh it out. If we had another pair of scales we could work twice as fast.'

'Another pair of scales? Do you know where we could get them? I don't.'

They looked at each other in grim frustration for a moment and then Eddie suddenly brightened. 'We don't need them, Mum!'

'What are you talking about?'

'Tins, we need tins!' He almost shouted the words in his excitement and his eyes raked the room. Rosie watched, puzzled, as he ran to the alcove and came back bearing two round cocoa tins. His face glowed with triumph as he explained:

'Look, Mum, we clean these out. Then we put in a quarter of a pound of tea to check the level. We mark that level on the tin and hey-presto – after that we don't even need the scales. We have a quarter-pound measure.'

Rosie threw her arms around the boy and hugged him: 'Eddie, you are a blooming genius.'

'And there's another thing,' he said, easing himself out of her embrace. 'If we opened the bags first – say, fifty or a hundred at a time and stood them side by side on the bench – that would be a lot quicker too. Van could do that. Then all you and I have to do is to move along the rows of bags and fill them from the measures.'

'I've read about this sort of thing in the papers,' said Rosie. 'It is all the rage in America. They call it mass production and some other long word I can't remember.'

'Rationalisation,' said Eddie.

'How the hell do you know that?' asked Rosie in wonder, thinking, not for the first time, how quickly Eddie was growing up and how little she really knew of him.

'I read an article about it in Boy's Own Paper,' he said modestly.

3

By mid-afternoon the stacks of quarter-pound bags had reached formidable proportions. Vanessa had long since grown tired and bored by the whole operation and had been sent off to play, but Eddie and Rosie, apart from a short break for a lunch of rock salmon and chips, worked on steadily.

Then, in mid-afternoon, when they were about to start on the last chest, an extraordinary thing happened. Or rather began to happen, for at first Rosie did not see it as being anything out of the ordinary. It was quite usual for some of the local people to look in on the warehouse to see what new bargains were about to go on offer and to make a purchase; and, in this instance, a Mrs Graham and a Mrs Hughes, whom Rosie recognised as regular market customers, called to ask if she had any more of the corned beef that had been on sale the day before.

'Sorry,' Rosie said, 'it's all been sold.' The women turned to go and she added quickly: 'How about some tea? It's a new brand – Carmo. Top-grade tea. Special offer.' Then, in a flash of inspiration and without really knowing how or why the idea popped into her head, she went on: 'We've only got a limited supply – and it is in big demand. So, to be fair to everyone, we are rationing each customer to two quarter-pound packets.'

The effect of this statement on the two women was electric. It was almost possible to read the thought on their faces: if Rosie was rationing the stuff it must be good, it must be worth having.

'How much?' asked Mrs Graham, hand reaching for purse.

Rosie had done her homework here. She knew that the cheapest tea in the shops was selling at fivepence per quarter pound, rising to sixpence or even sevenpence in some places.

'Fourpence a quarter-pound bag,' she said. 'Eightpence for two.'

'I'll take two,' said Mrs Hughes and Mrs Graham echoed the order a split-second later.

'We shall be taking this lot up to the market tonight or tomorrow morning,' Rosie said as she took their money and handed over the tea. 'It will go like hot cakes. So tell your mates to come along here if they want to get in first.'

Thanking Rosie in tones which suggested that she had done them a big favour, the two women departed. As soon as they were out of sight, Rosie turned to Eddie.

'Quick. In that cupboard over there you will find a tin of black paint and a brush. Get it for me, will you, son?'

She took the plywood lid of one of the cases and, since she knew Eddie's writing to be better than her own, instructed him to paint an inscription on the thin board. When he had finished, they both stood back to admire his rough-and-ready effort.

CARMO TEA
The People's Friend
Top Quality Tea at a
Bargain Price
4d per quarter lb bag
SORRY!
Only two bags per customer

'It'll do,' said Rosie. 'Stand it outside, where people can see it.'

The effect of this rudimentary piece of advertising, coupled with some excellent unpaid missionary work by Mrs Graham and Mrs Hughes, was little short of sensational. In the next half-hour twenty customers arrived to claim and pay for their complement of two bags, and from then on the numbers rose steadily. By five o'clock there was a queue of people stretching halfway down the street and disappearing out of sight round a corner: among them, Rosie noted with amusement, were sons, daughters, and husbands of women who had already made their purchases.

At half-past eight, working under the hissing glare of a naphtha lamp, Rosie sold the last packet of tea, consoled the remaining customers with a promise that there would soon be a fresh supply, and closed the doors of the warehouse.

There were now four of them. Besides Rosie and the faithful Eddie, there were Van, who had been pressed into service once again, and Tiny Christmas who had looked in to see how they were getting on and had stayed to lend a hand. Up to this point the excitement of the hectic trading had screened them from tiredness, but now the reaction set in and they sat down, physically and mentally exhausted yet jubilant.

'Blimey,' breathed Rosie, 'that was a turn-up for the book.'

'I've never seen anything like it,' said Tiny.

'Did you see the queue!' said Van. 'It must have been half a mile long.'

'It worked,' said Rosie. 'It worked. Oh, I can't wait to tell Mark, to see his face.' She turned to Tiny. 'Thanks for your help, Tiny. I don't know what we would have done without you.'

'I enjoyed it,' he replied with a grin.

'I must pay what I owe you,' she said. 'We said five shillings – it ought to be more.'

'I've been thinking about that,' he said. 'Those empty chests. I sometimes help Tubby Wilson with his removal jobs. Those chests would come in handy for packing things. They are worth a bob each, maybe more. Let me take those and we'll call it quits.'

Rosie protested that this was not fair on him and he argued back: in the end, they compromised on a fee of half a crown plus the empty chests. During this, Eddie had been counting what remained of the paper bags.

'How many did we start with, Mum?'

'2,500.'

'There's 181 left.' He made a quick calculation on the back of a bag. 'I reckon we sold 2,319 bags of tea.'

'And we didn't go near the market,' said Rosie in amazement.

'We could have sold double that if we hadn't run out of tea,' said Eddie.

'Lucky we did,' said Rosie. 'Otherwise we would all have collapsed.' She shook her head, still warmed by the glow of triumph. 'It's a gold mine, a blooming gold mine. We've struck gold.'

'Shall we count the takings?' asked Eddie.

'No, son. That can wait till we get home. Come on. We'll get some pease pudding and faggots from Coltman's on the way back.'

4

'We sold out in about four hours. Sold the lot. Not up the market. Here – here in the warehouse. Five chests of tea, Mark. And I've worked out, after paying Jack Cameron and Tiny and other odd bits and pieces, we made fourteen pounds' clear profit.'

It was the next morning and Rosie, tired but still exhilarated, sat in the warehouse with a pale-faced Mark, who had just been discharged from hospital. He had been warned to take things easily for a few days and not to lift anything heavy, but the story of Rosie's success brought a fresh lustre to his eyes and a flush of enthusiasm to his cheeks.

'You were right, Rosie,' he said. 'We are on to a winner. If we could clear fifty chests a week we'd be clocking up a hundred and forty pounds' profit.'

'Fifty chests? That's an awful lot,' she said doubtfully.

'Why? We could sell from the warehouse like you did yesterday and I could work the markets at the same time.'

'We would need some help with the bagging up. That takes time. I can't keep the kids off school any more.'

'All right. We shall have to employ someone – maybe a couple of local women, part-time. Out of a hundred and forty pounds a week profit we can afford that.'

'It's worth a try,' she said.

'Remember what I said about getting out of the markets, Rosie?' he said. 'I meant it. And you have proved me right. Offer people something they want at a bargain price and what happens? They'll come to you and they'll queue for it. If we took warehouses like this out in the suburbs, the customers would come rolling in. Not only for tea. Last week I was talking to a geezer who has a warehouse full of sugar on his hands. Bankrupt stock. We could put that into our own bags. Carmo Sugar.'

A little tremor of fear touched Rosie for a moment. Were they going too fast, being too ambitious? She loved the warmth and intimacy of their present operation. Would this go by the board if the business grew and took on more people? She was earning a living now, a good living by past standards, with the prospect of steady improvement ahead, and that surely was enough. The concept of wealth, of being rich, was something that lay beyond her understanding: riches were for other people, people seen from a distance or portrayed in the newpapers, riding in motor-cars, wearing expensive clothes, living in big houses. A house of her own with an indoor lavatory and a bathroom, a better life for Eddie and Van – these were the frontiers of her ambitions.

She was brought back from these thoughts by Mark's voice, asking a question that she had dreaded hearing.

'How did you manage to get the tea, Rosie? Did that fellow give you credit?'

'No,' she said, feeling the colour come to her cheeks. 'I borrowed the cash.'

He laughed. 'Twenty quid or more? Who do you know with that kind of money?'

'A friend,' she lied. 'She — she lent it to me in confidence. We've got to pay her back, of course.'

'When?'

'No hurry. When we've got the cash in the kitty. That will be soon enough.'

'I still owe that thirty-five pounds on the sardines,' he said.

'We can pay the chap a fiver on account and clear the rest in a month.'

He nodded. 'Rosie,' he said softly, 'I'm grateful. I really am.'

'Come off it, Mark,' she said scornfully. 'What did I do?'

'You know and I know what you did, Rosie. And I'm here to thank you.' He produced a buff-coloured form from his pocket. 'Put your signature on this, will you?'

'What's this all about?'

'What does it look like? It's a form. I've had it a couple of weeks. We are going to register a partnership, Rosie. You and me — partners in the firm of Carmo. From now on, it's going to be fifty-fifty.'

'I can't sign this!' she protested. 'It's your business; you started it.'

'I didn't have a business left a couple of days ago. Who saved it? You did — and you are entitled,' he said firmly.

'Why are you doing this, Mark?'

'You want the truth? I'll tell you. I'm scared that one day you might run off and leave me — start up on your own. That would put me dead in stook. I couldn't compete with you.'

'Rubbish!' she said. 'What's the real reason?'

'I need you, Rosie. Together we make a great team. I can trust you, I know that you would never let me down or stick a knife in my back. We are on our way, Rosie. Don't you feel that? You must feel it. We are going places, you and me.'

He paused, his eyes shining, and fondled one of the paper bags. 'Carmo. Our own name. We have an identity — we are a firm now.'

'Mark,' she said, laughing, 'you are a lovely fella.' She signed the paper in her bold hand and then gave him a quick kiss on the cheek. As she did so, he caught her arms and looked into her eyes.

'You are the lovely one, Rosie.'

He drew her closer and would have kissed her but she pulled herself away, gently. 'No, Mark. Let's keep it the way it is. It won't work otherwise, you know that.'

The disappointment showed on his face for a moment and was almost instantly replaced by a mischievous grin. 'Too late, am I?' he asked.

'I don't know what you are talking about!' she said.

'No? When you came to see me in hospital on the second night you were lit up like a shop window at Christmas. You didn't tell me about the tea then, did you?'

'I didn't want to worry you.'

'Stuff!' he said, and added casually, 'What's this Cameron bloke like?'

'Why bring him up?' she asked defensively.

'I was just curious.'

'You know what you can do with your curiosity, don't you?' she said tartly. 'You can shove it where the monkey shoved the nuts.'

He raised his hands in a token of surrender. 'All right, all right. I give in.'

'Good,' she said. 'Now, can we get back to business? I reckon we should build up gradually. Start, say, with ten more chests of tea and see how they go.'

'Twenty,' he said. 'We've tested the market, Rosie; we can handle twenty.'

'All right, twenty. In that case you are talking about ninety pounds' stock money. We've got about forty-one pounds in hand. Where are we going to get the rest?'

'The Bank? Mr Lightblow?'

'He said it would take a week or ten days before he could let us know. Anyway, I don't hold out much hope of help from that quarter.'

'Only one thing for it, Rosie,' he said lightly. 'You must go and see your friend Mr Cameron and use your charms on him.'

'What!' She turned angrily on Mark, but there was no hint of mockery on his face.

'I'm serious, Rosie. Do his other customers pay up-front, on the nail? I'll lay all Chelsea barracks to a sentry-box that they don't. So tell him that we want twenty chests of tea – and seven days' credit.'

5

They were interrupted at this moment by a light tap at the door.

'Yes?' Rosie called.

The door opened tentatively and a rush of cold air heralded the appearance of a thin, poorly dressed woman who hovered in the entrance uncertainly, shivering with cold.

'What is it, love?' asked Rosie. 'If you are looking for tea, we are all out at the moment.'

'Rosie? Mrs Thompson?' faltered the woman.

'That's right, that's me.'

The woman looked nervously from Rosie to Mark. 'I don't want to interrupt —' she began.

Rosie got up and went over to her. She could now see the lines of distress on the woman's lean face, the moistness in her eyes. She could not have been more than forty but she looked ten or fifteen years older.

'Don't stand there in the draught. Come inside.' She kicked the door shut, took the woman's arm and led her into the comparative warmth of the warehouse.

'You look as if you could do with a cup of tea,' Rosie said, and without waiting for a reply, she added: 'Put the kettle on, Mark.'

'I wondered if I could have a word,' said the woman, glancing at Mark's retreating back as if to indicate that she wanted to see Rosie alone.

Rosie noticed the look and said: 'On second thoughts, Mark,

I'll make the tea. You take a ball of chalk for a few minutes, will you?'

Mark was used to people calling on Rosie for advice and help for she had been a popular and unpaid counsellor ever since the episode with the rats. With a resigned shrug of the shoulders he turned up his coat-collar and went out to face the weather. 'Back in fifteen minutes,' he said pointedly.

'Now, what's the trouble?' asked Rosie as she filled the kettle.

'I'm sorry to be a nuisance,' said the woman, 'but I'm at my wit's end. You are the only one I could think to come to.'

'Is it money?' asked Rosie.

Half the women who came to her were in debt to small-loan sharks: borrowing in moments of desperation, they soon found that they could not escape the embrace of these predators. The interest payments were so horrendous that they seldom got close to paying off the initial loan and since most of them had borrowed without the knowledge of their husbands they were in a sort of double jeopardy. Two months before, a woman in Wigg Road, a mother of five children, had sealed off the kitchen, put her last few pence in the meter and her head in the oven and gassed herself to death.

At the inquest it was revealed that she was in debt to two moneylenders, having borrowed from one to pay the mounting interest on a loan from another. The total amount involved was fifty pounds and in two years she had paid them over a hundred pounds in interest, without making any impact on the original loans. At the inquest, the coroner had commented in saddened tones on the tragic improvidence of the poor.

'No. It's not money,' said the woman. 'It's – well – I think you know my girl, Dora.'

'Dora?'

'You worked with her at Goldie's laundry.'

'Oh, Dora!' said Rosie. 'Dora Parks. Of course I remember. You are Mrs Parks, are you?'

'Yes.'

'Is Dora all right?'

'Well—' The woman hesitated. 'She – I mean – there has been some trouble at work – at the laundry. Dora didn't want me to say or do anything – she's – well, she's a bit frightened, doesn't want it to come out. She's only a child, she doesn't want people pointing the finger, if you know what I mean.'

'Is she in the family way? Is that it?' asked Rosie bluntly.

'No, not that, thank God. But it is almost as bad.' Now the words tumbled out as if she had been holding them back for this moment. 'I only found out about it last Friday night. She said she didn't want to go to the laundry any more, she was going to throw in the job. Said she was fed up with it. Well, I lost my rag with her. I mean, she doesn't earn a lot, but with her father out of work we need every penny. I told her she would have to stick it, that jobs don't grow on trees. Well, to cut a long story short, after a while she came out with the real reason. I tell you, it knocked the wind out of my sails. I didn't believe her at first – not until she showed me the marks. Poor kid, my poor little Dora. I don't think I've slept a wink since she told me. That's why I've come to you – to ask what you think I should do. I haven't spoken to anyone else, not even my husband. He'd commit murder if he knew. But I can't just let it go, can I? Something has to be done. Everyone says you've got a good head on your shoulders so maybe you can advise me.'

Rosie had listened with patience to this recital, trying to put together the bits and pieces of scattered information and make a coherent whole. With the outline of the squalid picture forming in her mind, she said gently: 'Mrs Parks. What exactly has happened to Dora?'

'It's – it's Mr Goldie.'

'Mr Goldie? What has he been doing?'

'Well, like I said – he's been interfering with my Dora.'

'God in heaven! Are you sure?'

'I told you, I saw the marks.'

'Marks?'

'He's been beating her. Sometimes with his hand, sometimes with a cane. It's been going on for months. She was too scared to say anything in case she lost her job. It all came to a head last

Friday. He whacked her with this cane – as a punishment for being late, he said. But then – it was the first time, according to Dora – he asked her to hold him *there*. You know what I mean.'

Rosie sat down heavily, the nausea churning in her stomach. Mr Goldie the man of many mottoes, Mr Goldie the apostle of physical and mental cleanliness! Under that unctuous manner, lurking in those sharp, birdlike eyes, there had always been something that she had instinctively disliked and distrusted but never in the wildest flights of fancy would she have come near to guessing the ugly reality.

She had seen enough of life, life in the raw, to know that the impulses of sex could drive seemingly sensible and restrained people along strange paths. From her early days as a skivvy at The Winged Horse she recalled the gentle Mr Softley whom some people had branded as an 'iron-hoof' and a 'ginger-beer' and who, when threatened with arrest for the crime of buggery, had hanged himself from a hook in the beer-cellar. He had been a good friend and she had never been able to bring herself to condemn him.

But the late Mr Softley had never preached, never adopted a high moral tone, and that, in the ultimate, was the essence of Mr Goldie's crime. He was a ranting hypocrite, a sanctimonious fraud, and it was this thought more than anything else that turned Rosie's feeling of disgust into seething anger.

'Listen,' she said. 'You swear that what you've told me is the truth?'

'On my mother's grave – I swear it.'

'You could take Dora to the police – swear out a summons for assault.'

'No!' Mrs Parks's eyes sharpened with fear. 'No. It would all come out then – I mean – it would come out in the papers. I couldn't bear that. And it would be our word against Goldie's. He's on the local Borough Council, he is an important man, those sort stick together. They'd believe him before us.'

'But he mustn't be allowed to get away with this!'

'No. That's what I think. That's why I came to you, to see what's best to be done.'

'All right!' Rosie got up. 'I think I'll go and see Mr-bloody-Goldie and find out what he has to say for himself! Are you going to come with me, to back me up?'

Mrs Parks smiled for the first time since her arrival. 'I was hoping you would say that. I couldn't have gone on my own. But I'll come with you and gladly.'

When Mark returned he found a note pinned to the wall above the sink and his face registered bewilderment and then amusement as he read it.

'Sorry, partner. Got to see a man about a dog – or it could be the other way round. After, I will go up to London to fix up the tea. Luv, Rosie.'

6

Mr Goldie's house in Lansdowne Road was big by Rosie's standards. Solid and detached, with a small, disciplined front garden, it gleamed upon the world as if in imitation of its master's polished smile: the windows gleamed, the brass knocker, letter-box and door-handle gleamed and, not to be outdone, even the black shoe-scraper had the gleam of anthracite. And when Rosie and Mrs Parks appeared, a thin woman in a coarse apron was in the act of applying hearthstone to a doorstep which seemed already to be as white as a clean handkerchief.

'Is this where Mr Goldie lives?' asked Rosie.

The woman looked up wearily, pushing a stray lock of lank, greying hair away from her forehead with the back of a chapped hand. Her dull eyes surveyed Rosie without interest.

'If you are looking for laundry work you won't get any change here,' she said. 'Go to Ernest Street and ask there.'

'No, love. We are not looking for work, we are looking for him. We've been to the laundry and he wasn't there. Is he in?'

'Well . . .' The woman hesitated and threw an apprehensive look towards the nearest window. Rosie followed the look and saw, behind the lace curtain, the vague blur of a female face.

'Never mind,' she said, 'we'll find out for ourselves.' She stepped over the wet hearthstone but, as her hand reached for the knocker, the door clicked open and a plump, pink-faced woman, whom she supposed to be Mrs Goldie, glared out. Ignoring Rosie for the moment she addressed herself in a half-injured, half-sorrowing tone to the woman in the coarse apron.

'This step won't get done if you spend your time gossiping, will it, Mrs Heslop? Do get on with it, please.'

'Yes, Mrs Goldie, mum,' muttered the woman.

Mrs Goldie now condescended to turn her attention to Rosie and Mrs Parks and her voice assumed a sharper edge. 'Am I to presume that you are unable to read? There is a notice on the front gate which clearly states that hawkers and circulars are not welcome. Kindly go away and leave my woman to get on with her work.' She retreated a step and would have closed the door except that Rosie intervened.

'We are not hawkers and we are certainly not circulars, Mrs Goldie. We're here to see your husband. Will you get him, please.'

Surprise and slight shock at the boldness of this statement showed momentarily in Mrs Goldie's pale eyes. 'My husband?'

'That's what I said,' Rosie replied firmly. 'He is not at the laundry. I was told he was at home. So – tell him we want a word.'

There followed a brief silence while Mrs Goldie contemplated Rosie and weighed the question. To be addressed with such assurance and lack of humility by a person from what she and Mr Goldie, in their Christian charity, considered to be the less-fortunate classes was a new experience for her and she took a moment or two to adjust to the situation. Then, in a gentler voice, which suggested that she had decided to overlook, if not to forgive, the bluntness of Rosie's approach, she said:

'Ah. Of course. I understand. I suppose there is some problem at the laundry. It always seems to happen when my husband is away. He can't turn his back on that place for more than an hour without something goes wrong. Well, whatever it is, it will have to wait until this afternoon. Mr Goldie will be going to the laundry then. Goodbye, and thank you for coming.'

Rosie listened to this speech with an impassive face which concealed a certain sense of amusement. It was odd how Mrs Goldie seemed to echo her husband's mannerisms of speech and attitudes, as if living with him so long had moulded her in his image. Or was it simply a case of like being drawn to like? Rosie's first instinct, after hearing Mrs Parks's story, had been to feel sorry for Mrs Goldie, to pity her for being tied to such a husband, but now she was not so certain of her feelings. In many ways, the woman appeared to be just as objectionable as the man. Did she know, perhaps, of her husband's unusual inclinations and accept them as the price to be paid for domestic peace? And, wickedly, Rosie wondered whether Mrs Goldie herself had ever been persuaded to offer up her own plump bottom for her husband's gratification.

'We have not come about the laundry, Mrs Goldie,' she said patiently. 'We want to see your husband on another matter. Now will you tell him that Rosie Thompson and Mrs Parks want to speak to him and that we won't be put off?'

Mrs Goldie's self-assurance slipped further in the face of this continued firmness. She blinked and swallowed and at last, gathering herself, she said: 'My husband is not at home.' But the lie was betrayed by her tone and by the way she avoided Rosie's keen gaze.

'In that case, we will wait,' Rosie said.

'Wait?'

'That's what I said. We'll wait until Mr Goldie comes back. And if you don't want us inside, we'll park ourselves here, on your doorstep, and stay till Doomsday if necessary.'

'You will do no such thing!' said Mrs Goldie shrilly, casting an eye up and down the street as if she were afraid that the neighbours might see this strange confrontation. And, with a final show of strength, she continued: 'If you are not off these premises in two minutes, I shall call the police.'

'Do that,' replied Rosie. 'Call the police by all means. We

don't mind the police hearing what we've got to say, do we, Mrs Parks?'

Before that good lady could answer this largely rhetorical question the quarry appeared suddenly in the doorway. 'What is it, my dear?' asked Mr Goldie, easing his wife aside.

'These two women—' she began, but he interrupted immediately.

'Why, it is Rosie – Rosie Thompson, isn't it?' The familiar benevolent smile slipped into place with automatic precision but the eyes were questioning.

'Good of you to remember me,' said Rosie. She turned to Mrs Goldie. 'He was in, after all. Isn't that surprising!' Mrs Goldie gave her what she hoped was a withering look and beat what she hoped was a dignified retreat, leaving the field to her husband.

'To what do I owe the pleasure of this visit?' asked Mr Goldie warily.

'I don't think you know Mrs Parks, do you?' Rosie said.

'No. I don't think I do.' Mr Goldie turned a speculative eye towards the other woman.

'But you know her daughter. Dora Parks. She works for you.' As she spoke, she saw the fear flash across his eyes and the muscles of his jaw tighten.

Recovering quickly, he said: 'Dora? Ah, yes. Of course. Young Dora. An excellent worker, Mrs Parks, capital.'

'We'd like to talk to you about Dora, Mr Goldie,' said Rosie. She glanced at Mrs Heslop who was standing with the hearthstone in one hand and a brush in the other, watching this doorstep drama in wide-eyed wonder. 'We can talk out here if you like, with everybody looking on, or we can talk inside. It's up to you.'

'Eh? What?' he stammered. 'Oh, yes. Of course. Come in, please, of course. If it is a matter that concerns the welfare of one of my employees, I am always willing to listen.'

'Thank you,' Rosie said, and as he stood aside to let her pass, she saw the bubbles of sweat break above his upper lip.

7

The parlour to which they were taken was a dead room, a chill room, a room that seemed never to have felt the warming, untidy presence of human beings. The harsh smell of furniture polish drifted on the cold air: the three-piece suite, clad in unrumpled cushions and immaculate white antimacassars, faced an unlit fire which, in turn, was protected by a shining brass-railed fender. A stag looked down from a painting on the wall, its eyes sad and reproachful. A picture of Stanley Baldwin, the new Prime Minister, stood solemnly on a sideboard. A clock in a mahogany case, flanked by statuettes of a shepherd and shepherdess, waited on the mantelshelf, mournfully ticking the moments away.

'Cor. It's cold in here,' Rosie said, shivering. 'What about putting a match to that fire?'

'Fire?' Mr Goldie shot a startled look at Rosie, as if the idea of a fire in this place was a sacrilege not far removed from swearing in church.

'Warm the place up a bit. That's what the fire is for, isn't it?' said Rosie cheerfully. 'Here, I'll do it.' And, while Mr Goldie looked helplessly on, she took matches from her bag, pulled back the fender and put flame to the paper, wood and coal.

'That's better,' she said as the wood began to crackle. She sank back into one of the armchairs and motioned Mrs Parks to do the same.

'Take the weight off your feet, love.'

Mr Goldie felt moved to assert himself. 'Mrs Thompson – er – Rosie. I am a busy man, I have much to do. What exactly is the purpose of your visit here?'

'I told you,' Rosie said bluntly. 'It's about young Dora Parks.'

'Yes?' he said weakly.

'As I see it,' Rosie said, 'there are three things we can do. We can settle the matter here and now. We can tell Mr Parks,

Dora's father, in which case you will certainly land up in hospital or the morgue. Or we can go to the police, in which event you'll have your name splashed all over the papers and probably land up in prison. What's it to be? You tell us.'

'I really don't know what you are talking about,' he said, but there was no conviction in his voice.

'What we are talking about is what you did to Dora. Not once – several times. What we are saying is that you are a dirty old sod, Mr Goldie. Is that plain enough, or do you want me to go on?'

'If the silly girl has been telling you tales . . .,' he began.

'Oh, she has told us all right. And she showed her mother the marks of the last beating you gave her.'

'This is ridiculous! I will admit that I have had cause to reprimand the child – she was often late and impudent – it was my duty to – to – bring her back into line.'

'Do you deny giving her a walloping and caning her?'

'Emphatically!'

Rosie looked at Mrs Parks and sighed. 'Oh dear. He wants it the hard way. No use staying here – best go to the police and lay a charge. "Indecent assault", I think they call it.' And with this she rose to her feet.

'Wait. Please. There is no – there is no need to be precipitate.' Mr Goldie's voice was hoarse with fear now and his eyes were moist.

'Well?' Rosie demanded.

'I did – I confess that I asked the girl to submit to a – to a certain discipline,' he whispered. 'It was for her own good, as I thought. And she agreed, she accepted willingly.'

Mrs Parks spoke for the first time. 'You liar, you bloody liar! You scared her into it!' She moved to him as she spoke, swinging her arm, and struck him on the cheek with all her strength. 'You bloody rotten liar!' she screamed again.

Mr Goldie sat down heavily on the sofa, his hand to his face, tears in his eyes, as the door opened and a worried Mrs Goldie looked in.

'Is everything all right, dear?' she asked tentatively.

'Yes, yes. Leave us, leave us!' he answered desperately.

'A fire!' she gasped suddenly. 'A fire in here!'

'Yes!' It was his turn to scream now. 'Get out! Get out!'

She retreated hastily, closing the door. A silence followed and then Mr Goldie spoke. He seemed somehow to have shrunk inside his clerical grey suit, and his voice was the voice of a supplicant.

'Please. Don't go to the police. It would – it would ruin me. I'll make restitution, I'll do anything you say. It won't help to ruin me, will it? I'd have to sell the laundry – your friends would lose their jobs. Please, Rosie. I've worked hard all my life – don't make me lose everything because – because I was weak. Please.' He held out his hands and she had the feeling that in a moment he might even go down on his knees.

'You are pathetic!' she said, in disgust. 'Pull yourself together and I'll tell you what you must do.'

'Yes, yes, of course. Anything.'

'First, you will write out a full confession, admitting what you did to Dora. I'll keep it – and no one else will see or know about it, providing you behave yourself in future. But if you do anything like this again, I'll take the confession straight to the police and shop you. You understand?'

'Yes,' he said humbly.

'Dora won't be coming back to the laundry. That's your fault, not hers. No reason why she should suffer for your sins. What do you pay her in wages?'

'A pound a week.'

'Right. Before we go, you will give Mrs Parks twenty-six pounds. Six months' wages for Dora.'

'Twenty-six pounds!' he said in a startled voice.

'Make it fifty-two, if you like,' said Rosie. 'A year's pay. Yes, that might be fairer all round.'

'I'll give her the six months' money as you suggest,' he whispered.

'I thought you might,' said Rosie grimly, and added: 'I see from the local paper that you are going to be the next Mayor.'

He looked up at her, his eyes quick with fear, wondering what was coming next.

'Don't worry,' she said. 'We won't split on you. But when

you are riding around in that big car with the gold chain on your neck, don't cut it up too proud, will you? Remember that notice you used to hang up in the laundry? Humility is the first rung on the ladder of happiness. Or some such bloody rubbish.'

They left him fifteen minutes later, slumped on the sofa, staring into the fire. In Rosie's bag there was a letter in a sealed envelope and Mrs Parks's purse was richer by twenty-six pounds, more money than she had ever seen, let alone owned, in her entire life.

'What will you do with that letter?' she asked Rosie.

'The letter? Oh, I shall burn it.'

'Burn it?'

'Yes. I don't want the bloody thing. I shall put it on the fire as soon as I get a chance. But Goldie won't know that, will he, eh, because we won't tell him. So the old bugger can go on sweating.'

They smiled broadly at each other and walked on in silence for a few yards.

'You ought to have some of this money, you know,' said Mrs Parks.

'Keep it,' said Rosie. 'It belongs to you and Dora. Tell you what you can do. You can treat me to a tuppenny piece of cod and a pennorth of chips. Then I must dash off up to the City to fix up some more of that tea.'

And, suddenly, the thought of seeing Jack Cameron again lightened her step.

CHAPTER ELEVEN

1

For a few moments, as she hovered between sleeping and waking, between night and day, Rosie lay still, aware of an extraordinary feeling of tranquillity. It seemed in those moments as if she were floating in a sweet, rose-coloured, rose-scented space, cocooned in a comforting silence: there was no tension in her limbs and in her mind no motion except the thought that life was good, that it held no hint of threat. She clung to the sensation of calm which seemed to embrace her whole being, longing for it to continue, telling herself that this must be true happiness.

Then Jack, still asleep, stirred and moved beside her. His hand fell lightly on her breast and the real world began to hammer in her head.

She was in his rooms and in his bed and she realised, with a sort of wonder, that she was naked under the single crumpled sheet which half-covered them. Only once in her whole life had she gone to bed without a nightgown. Another man, Russell Whitby, in another place, at another time, had undressed her and carried her to his bed but that had been almost an accident, an evening's adventure, never since repeated. With Tommo, who had been her husband, she had taken care always to put on her nightwear before removing her underclothes so that he should not see her naked body.

This strange modesty was not peculiar to Rosie: the women in the market could be coarse and loose-tongued but, in their code, fully to expose oneself to a man, even to a husband, was at best an act of daring, at worst a sign of wantonness. It was on a par with the wisdom, handed on to their daughters by successive generations of women, that the act of sex had to be endured rather than enjoyed, that sex was the price a woman had to pay for the respectability of a wedding-ring. It had been like that between Rosie and Tommo, a bargain sealed and faithfully maintained; for her, a duty to be performed, not always without some pleasure, but a duty nevertheless.

Yet this morning, in spite of all, she felt no hint of shame, only a sense of release, of contentment, together with surprise at her own boldness. Perhaps, she thought, this is what love, real love, is about: to embrace gladly, without shame, to give and to receive happiness and pleasure so fully that there are no secret places of the heart or the body.

For she was in no doubt now that she loved Jack Cameron as she had loved no one else. Since Tommo's death she had been out for the occasional evening with perhaps half a dozen young men, but she had found no spark there and, on her initiative, these contacts had gone no further. Indeed, she had begun to wonder if the lack lay in her own nature, to wonder if the barrier was created by an indifference to sex – or a fear of it, perhaps – which, as she grew older, seemed to take stronger hold.

Before Jack, she had been to bed with only two men, Russell Whitby and Tommo, and she had loved neither of them. For Tommo she had felt, and still felt, a deep fondness which had its foundations in compassion: a spell in prison and the war had combined to wreck the flamboyant, devil-may-care man she had once known and he had leaned on Rosie as a crippled man leans on a stick. He had need of her and she had given of herself willingly. But she knew in her heart that, if he had come back from the trenches, her marriage would have taken on the shape of a life-sentence.

With Russell Whitby, it had simply been a thing of the moment. She had met him at a time when she was under stress, at her most vulnerable; and, because he was kind and gentle, she had gone to his bed with an eagerness that had surprised them both. The events that followed this uncharacteristic lowering of her guard had, at first, been disastrous. Rosie discovered not only that she was pregnant but that Whitby, with careless timing, had been killed in a riding accident. Forced to give up her job, she would have been destitute had it not been for the kindness of friends.

All that was past, water under the bridge. In the event, she had come out with a bonus in the shape of a fine son. And now, at least, the days of grinding poverty seemed to be behind them, her son and her daughter were safe. Or almost safe, she told herself reprovingly, for she was too practical to believe that the corner had been turned for all time.

Still, the last few months had registered an extraordinary uplift in their fortunes, making reality of what had once seemed to be impossible dreams. The days had sped past so quickly that time itself had become an extraordinary blur. Winter had given way reluctantly to spring and spring had moved without murmur into a golden summer but she had scarcely noticed. It was as if someone had blown a whistle and, like a train that had been held up at a wayside station, her life was screaming along the tracks as though determined to make up for all the lost and wasted time.

The business was thriving. They were now selling around one hundred chests of Carmo Tea each week, together with salmon, tinned milk, corned beef, soap, sugar, margarine, baked beans and other lines. The markets had become a thing of the recent past and they had opened five covered warehouse-type stores in the outer suburbs of London, operating under the name of Carmo Cut-Price Bazaars, where the goods were sold, market-style, by auctioneers called 'pitchers', using the same kind of vigorous patter as the street-traders. Mark and Rosie had plans to open still more of these Bazaars and, most ambitious of all, to turn the Edgware site into a proper store, with counters and assistants and a full range of foodstuffs.

'Good morning, Rosie.'

She abandoned her thoughts and, turning, saw that Jack was awake, his eyes smiling at her.

'Good morning to you,' she said and kissed him lightly on the lips. 'Would you like me to make a pot of tea?'

'Not yet.' His hand slid from her breast down past the smoothness of her stomach and gentle fingers eased her legs apart.

'Oh, Jack!' she whispered, and moved towards him. A few minutes later, breaking from a long kiss, he looked into her eyes and said huskily:

'Kneel across me, Rosie.'

'What?'

'Kneel across me. Quickly!'

She did not fully understand what he meant but raised herself and knelt across his loins. He lay beneath her, a film of sweat on his forehead, and even as he thrust upwards to meet and enter her, she could not hold back the impish thought that flashed like a bird across her mind.

The girls in the market, the women in Shakespeare Street, would not have been at all surprised to learn that she had been to bed with a man, but the suggestion that, without benefit of nightdress, she should have sex with him in this unheard-of position would have astonished and shocked them.

2

'Love you, Rosie,' he said, reaching across the breakfast table to touch her hand.

'Do you?' she asked, half teasing, half in earnest. She was still glowing with happiness but her mind had rejoined the workaday world.

'Oh, come on!' he said, reprovingly. 'Can you doubt it now? It was good, wasn't it?'

'It was better than good – it was wonderful.'

'There you are, then.'

'I think you think you love me,' she answered calmly. 'I know I love you.'

'Oh, Rosie! Bless you for that. But I do love you. Cross my heart! I adore you.'

'All right, Jack – let us leave it at that.'

'What must I do to convince you? Tell me.'

It was on the tip of her tongue to say that he could have mentioned marriage, a word that had not passed his lips in relation to her. Part of her felt hurt that he had not done so: her plain upbringing had taught her, rightly or wrongly, that this was one of the proofs of love and his failure had etched a question-mark on her mind. But she held back the words and simply said: 'It doesn't matter.'

He glanced solemnly at her, as if he had read the thought, then his face opened in the boyish, mischievous smile that she could not resist and he said: 'Come back to bed and I will give you a practical demonstration.'

'Bed!' she answered, returning the smile. 'Is that all you can think of?'

'It has taken me nine months to get you here. I have a lot of time to make up!'

'If you think I am going to get undressed again, you have another think coming,' she said briskly.

'I'll undress you,' he said, half-rising.

'Give over!' she said. 'I've work to go to, even if you haven't.'

He sank back in his chair and ran a hand over his sandy-coloured hair. 'Work! It will be the ruin of you, Rosie, my darling. It is an over-valued occupation, best left to other people.'

'I like work,' she said.

He pointed a butter-knife at her. 'Ah. That is a dangerous flaw in an otherwise admirable character. You must take yourself in hand.'

'I must stop listening to this rubbish and take myself off,' she said, rising from the table.

At the door he held her close and whispered, 'Thank you, Rosie, thank you for coming.' He kissed her and, as she felt the tightness of his body under the silk dressing-gown, the desire began to surge anew in her own flesh and she had to force herself to break away.

'I must go,' she said.

'When will you come again?'

'God knows,' she replied lightly. 'God knows and He won't tell.'

'I'm serious. When will you come?'

'I don't know, truly. It isn't easy, dear. I have to think of the kids. And there is Gran.'

A tremor of guilt throbbed briefly in her head as she thought of the children. She had lied to them, making the excuse (which seemed feeble now) that she had to go to Luton to check on the possibility of setting up a new Carmo Cut-Price Bazaar and would have to stay the night. She had told the same story to Mrs Archibald and asked her to look in to see that Eddie, Van and Gran were all right, but whereas the children had accepted her explanation with confidence and even a little excitement, she had the feeling that Mrs Archibald had not believed a word of it.

'Could you organise a weekend, Rosie?' he asked.

'A weekend?'

'I'd like to show Paris to you and you to Paris. We could take the boat-train on a Friday and get the one back on Monday. That would give us three nights and two days together. Will you do it?'

'You are crazy!' Her heart pounded with excitement at the idea but her mind told her that such an adventure would be almost impossibly difficult to arrange.

'It would do you good,' he insisted. 'You need a break. Please.'

'I'll think about it, darling,' she said, putting a hand to his face. 'And now I really must go.'

A mild summer morning greeted her as she stepped outside, a friendly south-west breeze fanned the green leaves of the London plane trees which lined the square. There had been some rain in the night and, filling her lungs with the cool resin-scented air, she walked down Bayley Street towards Tottenham Court Road and the bus-stop. In the past two or three weeks the sheer pace and pressure of work had begun to weary even her sturdy constitution but this morning all the tiredness seemed to have slipped away so that she felt as though she was glowing with health, strong and invigorated.

Well, Rosie, she told herself, you have burnt your bridges now, you really have thrown your bonnet over the windmill. For months she had held Jack Cameron at bay, fighting her own nature and inclination and his persistence, knowing all the time that she was falling more in love with him each day. She loved his humour, his quicksilver mind, his easy way with people, even his casual attitude to life, though she did not quite approve of that. Above all, she had never known a man who could stir and arouse her as he did, reawakening in her body urges that had lain almost dormant for years, dispelling any notion that, for her, sex was a lost cause. Even as she fended off his advances she had understood how desperately she wanted him to make love to her: at night, alone in her bed, she would find herself trembling for him, feel the tell-tale welcoming dampness between her restless thighs.

Why, then, had she held out for so long? It was partly a sheer question of time, for between the needs of the family and the exciting growth of the business she had little enough of that, and partly the caution that her experience with Russell Whitby had imprinted on her mind. And another factor was Jack Cameron himself. She could not quite pinpoint her uncertainty: it was simply that, behind the boyish impudence that attracted her so much, she sensed a sort of immaturity.

In one sense, life had come too easily to him, he had never had to struggle for a crust in the back streets, never known what it was like to be hungry. Yet, on the other hand, he had been a pilot in the Royal Flying Corps during the war and, although he would not talk about his experiences and she was careful not to press him, she knew that he must have seen death at close quarters many times, felt its wings brush his own shoulders.

Perhaps this, after all, explained why he liked to live from day to day, without heed for the future, as if he were fearful that tomorrow some dark hand might snatch it all away. Perhaps it also explained why, despite his protestations of love, he had never mentioned marriage: to make such a life-long commitment, to take on board such a responsibility, was simply not in his nature.

So, she thought cheerfully, I shall just have to take him as he is, warts and all. There was no going back now, no way would she give up this newly discovered happiness. She would accept Jack on his own terms, enjoy him while she could. It was her own life to lead as she wished and, as long as she hurt no one in the process, she was content.

Rosie paused at a news-stand which was displaying two placards: HOBBS BREAKS GRACE RECORD and MINERS EMBARGO MOVEMENT OF COAL. She bought a *Daily Sketch* which carried a picture on the front page of the Prince of Wales playing golf in a daringly patterned Fair Isle pullover. The caption read: PRINCE INTRODUCES NEW FASHION.

Flicking through the paper as she sat on the 29 bus bound for South Tottenham, she noticed an illustrated advertisement for ladies' underwear and realised, with a little secretive smile, that she had left her nightdress in Jack's rooms. It was a new one, in the peach-coloured artificial silk known as celanese, rather low-cut at the bosom and, unlike her usual ankle-length cotton or flannel nightgowns, the skirt only just reached below her knees.

She had bought it at Burgess's Store in the High Street for the enormous sum of two shillings and elevenpence and she had blushed as she handed over the money, partly because of the extravagance and partly because she was sure that the assistant knew that she was buying this sensuous garment for some illicit purpose.

What a waste of hard-earned money, she thought. Jack never even gave me a chance to wear the bloody thing!

3

'What kept you?' asked Mark, with some irritation.

'Why? What time is it?' answered Rosie.

'Almost nine o'clock. We arranged to meet Mr Lightblow here at half-past eight. He has been waiting almost half an hour.'

'Oh, God, I'm sorry. I clean forgot.' She advanced on Mr Lightblow who was sitting calmly on an upturned box at the far end of the warehouse. 'I'm sorry, Mr Lightblow. I overslept. I'm sorry.' This explanation did not quite square with the truth but she felt that it was near enough for comfort.

'That's quite all right, Rosie,' he replied courteously. 'The way you have been working, it would not have surprised me had you slept in all day!'

'Can we make a start then?' said Mark sharply.

Rosie gave him a quick glance. He was normally an equable man who, whatever the pressures, kept his temper on a tight rein and seldom showed displeasure or irritation, but in the past weeks she had noticed that he had become increasingly irritable and impatient. Was the rapidly growing workload getting too much, even for him?

The door opened and Tiny Christmas appeared, his bulk sending a huge shadow across the room. He had been taken on the payroll some five months before and given the job of delivering supplies to the Bazaars in a secondhand Dennis van specially acquired for the purpose.

'I'm just going to run this load to Edgware,' he said, a cheerful smile creasing his craggy face.

Once again, the sharpness edged Mark's voice. 'All right, Tiny – get on with it, get on with it! I want you back here no later than twelve o'clock to take those cases to Mitcham, so don't hang about!'

Tiny's smile disappeared and a look of bewilderment shaded his brown eyes. He looked at Mark, rather in the manner of a big, uneasy schoolboy, wondering what he had done to deserve both the tone and the nature of this implied criticism.

Rosie's eyes sent a rebuke in Mark's direction, then she turned quickly to the big man in the doorway and said gently: 'All right, Tiny. Get back as soon as you can, eh?'

'Of course I will, Rosie. I mean, I'm not going to hang about, am I? I know I got the Mitcham and Chingford runs to do.' Reassured by her words, he gave her a little wink and then the door closed behind him. This was followed by a short, tetchy silence, until Mr Lightblow coughed and said: 'Well, I'll begin if you don't mind.'

He glance down at a manila file which was lying on his lap

and extracted a sheet of notes. He studied this for a moment or two, as if to refresh his memory.

Rosie, still glowing inside, thought of Jack. He was probably dressing now, taking his leisurely time as always: he seldom got to his office in Mincing Lane before ten a.m. and she had often scolded him about this slackness, insisting that he was wasting the best part of the day. What a happy-go-lucky devil he is, she thought, smiling. She remembered an evening when he had stopped at a flower-seller near the Mansion House and bought her the astonished woman's entire stock. Too embarrassed to go home laden with so many flowers, Rosie had made a detour and put most of them on various graves in the local cemetery.

Then there was the time when he had sent her that extraordinary telegram. She had opened it, in the presence of Eddie and Van, trembling inwardly, for in Shakespeare Street telegrams were rare and usually brought bad news. But this one was unsigned and carried the strange message: RUTH, CHAPTER ONE, VERSE SIXTEEN. STOP.

Rosie knew at once that the telegram must have come from Jack and tried to pass it off, but the children, their curiosity aroused, would have none of it, and Eddie brought out his Bible. As he read out the verses he had looked more and more puzzled.

'Intreat me not to leave thee or to return from following after thee: for whither thou goest, I will go; and where thou lodgest, I will lodge: thy people shall be my people, and thy God my God.'

'What does it mean, Mum?' Van had asked.

'Oh, it is some silly joke,' she had replied unconvincingly. 'I bet a woman sixpence that those words came from the Song of Solomon.'

'You lost your bet!'

'Yes. I will have to pay out.'

'Fancy sending a telegram,' Eddie had said scornfully. 'I mean, that must have cost her more than she was going to win.'

Oh, what a fool you are, Jack Cameron, what a fool, she thought. And you must be daft yourself, Rosie, to take up with such a character. Why couldn't you fall in love with a nice, steady man of your own kind? But you don't want a nice, steady man, she told herself. You want Jack Cameron, you love him, and you are stuck with that!

'Are you with us, Rosie?'

Rosie came out of her reverie with a start, and saw that Mr Lightblow was looking at her under raised eyebrows, no doubt wondering why she was sitting there with a dreamlike smile on her face.

'Oh, yes,' she lied. 'Carry on.'

'I was making the point that you urgently need to get in a first-class book-keeper. That implies no criticism of you, Rosie, none at all. You have done very well. But with all the expansion that has been going on – and with the new projects you have in mind – well, frankly, it will soon get beyond you. There are other problems too. For example, you have made no tax returns to the Inland Revenue.'

'Do we have to?' asked Rosie in some alarm.

'Well, I rather think they will expect it,' said Mr Lightblow. 'It is a legal obligation, you know. The Inland Revenue do not take kindly to people or firms who do not fulfil their obligations. Sooner or later they will catch up with you – and you might possibly face a large bill for arrears of tax and a fine into the bargain.'

This ominous statement seemed to knock the irritation out of Mark and it certainly ended Rosie's daydreaming. They looked at each other in dismay.

'There is another question,' continued Mr Lightblow calmly. 'Quite apart from the profits of your partnership, there is also the matter of income tax on your personal salaries.'

'Salaries?' echoed Rosie.

'Wages, if you prefer. I see that you are now drawing ten pounds each per week.'

'I was thinking of putting it up to fifteen pounds,' said Mark. The remark surprised Rosie, for she was more than happy with what she had been getting. Out of her ten pounds she was saving five pounds each week against a rainy day and with the balance to spend she felt like a rich woman. Still, she said nothing.

'It is a great deal,' said Mr Lightblow, mentally comparing

this large sum with his own salary at the City Bank. 'But that must be your decision. There will be personal income tax to pay, of course. Not a great deal, but some.' He paused for a moment. 'Now, if we turn to your future plans, it is clear that you cannot finance them out of earnings. You will need financial support – from banks, building societies and so forth.'

'We can manage on our own,' said Mark.

'With respect, I don't think so,' said Mr Lightblow. 'Let me put it this way. In the past year you have made substantial advances, there can be no denying that. But, in my estimate, you have almost reached the perimeter of what you can achieve out of your own resources.'

'All right. What do you propose?' asked Rosie.

'Well, I have said that you need a trained book-keeper but, on reflection, I believe that you require a little more than that. You ought to look around for someone who could act in the capacity of finance manager.'

'A stranger in here to look after the cash?' said Mark, with a touch of scorn. 'No, thank you. This we do not need.'

'Wait, Mark, wait,' Rosie said. 'Let him finish. He has always given us good advice in the past.'

'The days when you could keep your accounts in penny notebooks, and carry your working capital around in your pockets, are over,' Mr Lightblow went on. 'You are a business now and you must be set up and behave as such in a proper and legal fashion. Everything you do must be subjected to strict financial scrutiny. At the moment, for instance, you are renting the premises for your Bazaars. Is that wise? Real estate, property, is a developing asset. You should consider whether it would be to your advantage to buy – on mortgage. Let me give you another example. Take this new store you are planning to open. You will not be able to stock it entirely from your usual lines of surplus goods. You will need a far wider range and for those you will have to arrange a line of credit with established manufacturers and food suppliers. Well, you simply cannot go along to them with a fist full of cash. They will require to know with whom they are dealing, they will want bank references, they will want to be sure that you can meet your liabilities. Do you understand?'

'It sounds very complicated,' sighed Rosie, who was beginning to wish that they could stay as they were, making a decent living without too many problems.

'It isn't really,' said Mr Lightblow and, picking up her thought, he continued: 'You cannot stay as you are, you cannot stand still. And I'm sure that you do not wish to go back.'

He leaned forward and a gleam of enthusiasm glowed in his eyes. 'Mark. Rosie. I've watched you over these past months. You have done wonders together. I believe that you have special gifts. But you must use those gifts to the best advantage – in buying, selling, identifying market opportunities and so forth. I believe, I genuinely believe, that you are on the verge of a major breakthrough. In two, three, perhaps five years, who knows what you might not achieve? Do you know how many branches Sainsbury's have opened since nineteen-nineteen? Over thirty – and they are planning a dozen more in the next year. Why shouldn't you do the same?'

Rosie looked at Mr Lightblow in astonishment. How could he speak of Sainsbury's and their tiny operation in the same breath? The name Sainsbury was a household word, their shops were everywhere, the quality of their food was legendary. What on earth had happened to Mr Lightblow's normal caution?

'Blimey, Mr Lightblow,' she said, 'have a bit of sense. We are not Sainsbury's, nowhere near.'

'But we could be!' said Mark, catching Mr Lightblow's enthusiasm. 'Why not? They had to start somewhere, didn't they?'

He got up and began to pace the room, carving spaces in the air with his hands.

'You are right, Mr Lightblow. We can't stand still. On the other hand, can we develop if we continue like a bunch of bloody amateurs? The answer is no. Negative. I know how to buy, what to buy and how to sell. So does Rosie. But what do we know about books and banks and building societies and all that financial fangle-dangle? Next to nothing. We could write all we know about that on the back of a penny stamp and still have enough room for the Ten Commandments! Yes, you are right, you are right, you are a hundred times right! We've come about as far as we can on our own. We need help, like you said. Am I ashamed to admit such a thing? No, I am not. I admit it!'

'That is the point I came to put to you,' said Mr Lightblow. 'I am delighted that you have taken it so well. Now, I have written a list of things you must put in hand without delay.' He consulted his notes. 'Incorporation of a limited company. The name of a suitable solicitor for same. Employment of a book-keeper, and draft advertisement for same . . .'

'Wait,' interrupted Mark. 'Rosie hasn't said what she thinks of all this.'

'I'll go along with whatever you decide, Mark,' she replied. 'I'll certainly be glad to load the book-keeping on to someone else's shoulders. It is becoming a nightmare.'

'Good!' said Mark briskly. 'Now, Mr Lightblow, you said that we really needed someone who was more than a book-keeper. Right?'

'That is my view.'

'How about you?'

'Me?' Mr Lightblow's voice squeaked and, for a moment, he looked as if someone had stunned him with a mallet.

'You are just the ticket. We know you, you are not a stranger. We trust you and that is half the battle. And we are going to grow, as fast as we can, make no bones about that. This means we shall be on a good thing – you too if you come in with us.'

'But I have my job at the bank!' protested Mr Lightblow.

'So? What does that pay you – a fortune, perhaps? What do you make – six quid a week, three hundred a year?'

'Well . . .,' muttered Mr Lightblow, embarrassed by this blunt and rather personal question. In truth, Mark had somewhat over-estimated his circumstances, for as an assistant cashier, one peg up from the rank of clerk, his annual salary amounted to £120.

'Mark!' said Rosie reprovingly. 'Don't bully the man. He has a family to think of. You are asking him to give up a good, regular job.'

'A good, regular job!' cried Mark, getting into his stride. 'A good, regular job!' He turned to Mr Lightblow. 'And what will you finish with? A job as a manager paying maybe five hundred or six hundred pounds a year? A lifetime behind a counter, watching other people make money, counting other men's profits?'

'Mr Lightblow – take no notice!' said Rosie, terrified lest the man should take offence and walk out. But the man in question did not seem to hear her warning: he was staring at Mark as if he had just seen a vision.

'Take a gamble, Mr Lightblow,' Mark continued, his voice rising. 'Come in with us. All right, you want we should make you an offer? Good. Here it comes – provided Rosie agrees. You come in on the same wage as us – fifteen pounds a week. And we'll give you ten per cent of the business, five per cent from me, five per cent from Rosie. Is that a fair offer or isn't it?'

'It's more than generous,' said Mr Lightblow, who was doing lightning calculations in his head.

'Well?' demanded Mark.

'Give the man time to think!' protested Rosie.

Mr Lightblow looked from one to the other and licked his upper lip. This, after all, was the opportunity he had dreamed about. Did he have the courage to take it? And the money! More than ten times his present income. It took him only a few seconds to decide. Holding a hand out towards Mark, he said: 'I accept. With thanks.'

'Marvellous!' said Mark, grasping the hand and pumping it up and down. 'Bloody marvellous!'

Rescuing his hand, Mr Lightblow looked towards Rosie. 'It is all right with you, Rosie?'

'All right!' She went across and kissed him on the forehead. 'Welcome! You've taken a load off my mind, I can tell you!'

'When can you start?' asked Mark.

'I shall have to give notice at the bank. I believe the rule is two weeks.' He glanced at his watch. 'Which reminds me – I'd better get back there.' He picked up his file and rose from the box. 'I'll let you know as soon as possible.'

'The bank won't give you any trouble?' asked Rosie.

'Oh, I should not imagine that there will be any difficulty there. For one thing, they will be anxious to keep the account – our account – I should imagine.' He paused and shook his head. 'But how Mrs Lightblow will respond – ah – that is quite another matter. She tends, shall we say, to be rather on the conservative side where our affairs are concerned. Still, that is my problem, isn't that so? I know that I shall enjoy working with you. I need a new challenge and I am grateful to you both for the opportunity.'

As he moved to the door, Mark stopped him. 'Mr Lightblow.'

'Yes?'

'What's your first name? We can't go on calling you "mister".'

Mr Lightblow shifted from one foot to the other in some embarrassment. 'Well, you see, I come from a large family. Actually, I am the seventh son. My father was something of a student of Roman history and he read somewhere that a seventh son was thought to be lucky. With this in mind, he gave me a Roman name.'

'What?' asked Mark, mystified by this explanation.

'Septimus,' said Mr Lightblow gravely.

'Septimus!' said Mark incredulously.

'I know,' said Mr Lightblow. 'It is a little hard to swallow.' He smiled. 'So, as soon as I reached an age, I arranged for my friends to call me Jim.'

'Jim. Thank God for that!' Rosie said, with a sigh of relief.

'Welcome aboard, Jim,' said Mark.

4

'Excuse me, madam, would this belong to you by any chance?'

Rosie turned and gasped as she saw Jack Cameron standing in the doorway with an absurd grin on his face, holding her nightdress out at arm's length, tweaking it gently so that the flimsy material seemed to be dancing in the sunlight.

'Jack! You fool!' She ran across, snatched the nightdress from his hands and, crumpling it into an untidy ball, stuffed it hastily into her handbag.

'I thought you might need it,' he said lightly.

'You are crazy, absolutely crazy!' She shook her head and laughed.

'Is that all the thanks I get?' He reached out and tried to take her in his arms but she dodged away.

'For God's sake, Jack! Not here!'

'Why not?'

'The door's open – anyone might come in!'

'I don't care if you don't. Anyway, what is an open door between friends? Hey, presto!' He closed the door with a flourish and turned back to her. 'I had to see you, Rosie.'

'You saw me a couple of hours ago,' she said, more gently.

'Two hours? Is that all? It feels like weeks, months, years. I love you, Rosie.'

'What am I going to do with you?' she asked, going to him. As they kissed, she heard echoes of the warmth and excitement of the night before murmur in her mind, felt her body respond to him yet again. She broke away breathlessly and, as she did so, there came a knock at the door.

'There. I told you!' she hissed. Patting her hair, conscious that her cheeks were burning, she opened the door. The face of the girl standing there was immediately familiar but, for a moment, she could not put a name to it.

'Yes?' she asked.

'I'm Mark's sister. Debbie.'

'Of course, of course. Sorry,' Rosie said. She hesitated aware of Jack's presence behind her, then gathering herself she added: 'Come in, Debbie. I'm afraid you have just missed Mark. He has gone out to Chingford to look at some new premises.'

'Oh.' The disappointment showed on the girl's face as she stepped inside. 'Do you know when he will be back?'

'Not until late afternoon,' answered Rosie. 'Oh, let me

introduce you. Mr Cameron – Debbie Moss, Mark's sister.'

Jack smiled and held out a hand. 'How do you do, Miss Moss? Delighted to meet you.'

'Thank you,' Debbie said, taking his hand.

'Mr Cameron is one of our suppliers,' Rosie said quickly, by way of explanation of Jack's presence alone with her behind closed doors, but her voice faltered a little as she spoke.

'Not just a supplier. A friend also, I hope,' said Jack mockingly.

'Of course.' Rosie flashed him a fierce warning glance, then turned to Debbie. 'Is there anything I can do?'

'No, I don't think so, thanks all the same. I won't keep you.'

'A cup of tea?'

'No, thank you. I must get back.'

Once again, Rosie was struck by the gentle beauty of the girl and, perhaps most of all, by her air of calm repose. She radiated a kind of stillness which suggested a quiet and peaceful spirit: perversely, it was precisely this quality which made her beauty all the more striking and caused eyes to turn her way when she entered a room.

'Will you excuse us for a minute, Jack?' Rosie said. She drew Debbie to the far side of the warehouse, to the area Mark had once used as sleeping quarters. He had graduated to a small rented apartment nearby and the space, equipped with a table, two chairs and a cabinet, was now used as a somewhat inadequate office.

'Please don't mind me asking,' Rosie whispered, 'but are you sure everything is all right? It's just that Mark has not been himself these past few days. Nothing serious, you understand, only that he has been a bit on the irritable side. That's not like him, so naturally I wondered . . .'

The girl's dark lambent eyes held Rosie's for a moment and then she replied: 'It is Bennie. Our brother. You met him, I think.'

'Yes, of course.' A mental picture of the big, surly young man, so critical of Mark and so different from him, surfaced briefly in her mind.

'He has left home. It is breaking my mother's heart. First Mark, now Bennie.'

'But children do leave home when they grow older. It's only natural. We all have to break away some time,' said Rosie, remembering how she had been forced out at the age of thirteen by her Uncle Bob and sent to The Winged Horse to work as a skivvy.

'I know. But it is hard for Mother to understand. She came from Poland when she was fourteen, you see. In some ways, she is still a stranger in a strange new land. The family is all she has.'

'She has you. And the boys will come to see her, surely.'

'That is the trouble. We have not seen or heard from Bennie since he left. That is over two weeks. And Mark is so busy, we are lucky if we see him once a month. Oh, he is good and kind, he leaves money and food, but that isn't everything, is it? He came last Saturday, the first time in weeks, and when my mother scolded him he flew at her and they quarrelled. I came to ask him to come soon, to make peace. I can't bear to see our mother as she is now, breaking up inside.'

Rosie nodded. 'Would you like me to have a word with Mark about it?'

A look of alarm disturbed the calm of Debbie's face as she said quickly: 'No, please. He would be offended to hear that I'd been discussing the family problems. I spoke only because I know that you are a friend. Just say that I called and would he get in touch.'

'If that's what you want. Of course. I won't say anything more than that.' Rosie paused. 'Have you no idea where your brother Bennie has gone?'

'No. He just packed some things and left a note to say we should not worry and that he would get in touch. But so far – nothing, not a word. We think it must be something to do with the Party.'

'The Party?'

'Bennie is a communist. It is his whole life. A religion. A church. He would not move unless the Party agreed.'

'People do strange things when they are young. He will probably grow out of it.'

'I don't think so. Not Bennie. He wants to change the whole world and he is sure that he has found the only way to do it.'

'The world could do with a bit of changing,' Rosie said.

'I agree. But how? Whose way is correct? I don't understand politics.' Debbie touched Rosie's hand. 'I must go. Thank you for listening.'

'Any time,' Rosie said. 'There's one thing you can be happy about. Mark is doing well – the business, I mean.'

'That's good. I am glad for him.' They moved back to where Jack was waiting and Debbie said quietly: 'Goodbye, Mr Cameron. I am glad to have met you.'

'I have to go too,' said Jack, glancing at his watch. 'Duty calls. Perhaps I can drop you somewhere, Miss Moss? I have my car outside.'

'No, really. I can get the tram,' Debbie protested.

'Are you going home – to Bethnal Green?' asked Rosie.

'Yes.'

'Then that's perfect. Jack – Mr Cameron – has to go to the City. It is in the same direction.'

'If it is no trouble,' said Debbie.

'My pleasure,' said Jack. He took Rosie's hand and pressed it. 'See you again – very soon.' His eyes sent her a warmer message.

Rosie watched them go, waving as the Morris Cowley pulled away. Then she saw Van running towards her.

'Blimey, this must be visitors' day!' she said as she held out her arms and hugged the girl.

'Mum, Mum!' cried Van, struggling free. 'Come quick. Gran has had an accident.'

'An accident? Is it bad?'

'I think she's dead,' said Van and began to sob, the tears flooding her face.

CHAPTER TWELVE

1

Life has a well-established and disconcerting habit of mocking fiction. It has a talent for the incredible situation and, with the death of Grannie Thompson, it exercised that talent in full measure, coming up with an ending for this strident magpie of a woman which, while entirely apt and appropriate, was almost unbelievable. It was the subject of gossip in Shakespeare Street and its surrounding taverns for many months and heavily embroidered versions of the event passed into local folklore.

When she learned the circumstances, Rosie, who was hardly a superstitious woman by nature, could not entirely suppress a feeling of guilt, a feeling that fate had given with one hand and taken back with the other. She had been allowed to give and receive a sort of illicit pleasure in Jack's bed and now she had to pay the price. Nor could she resist the thought that the timing was in keeping with Gran's character: it was just like the old lady to choose to die on the one night when Rosie had gone out to an assignation, so that, from beyond the grave, she might haunt her daughter-in-law with the thought that she had selfishly and immorally neglected her family duties.

It turned out that Gran, after the children had taken themselves off to school, had decided to pay a visit to the Fortune Street market. Whether she had gone there with an intention to steal could not be established but, however it was, when an opportunity came along she could not resist the temptation. As before, a woman shopper had left her purse on top of some supplies in her shopping-bag and, in a flash, it found its way into Gran's grasping hand.

Unfortunately for her, only a few seconds passed before the

woman noticed her loss and noticed also that the old lady who, a moment before, had been waiting beside her at the stall, was now moving away, having purchased nothing.

Her suspicions aroused, she set off in pursuit, calling: 'Here, Here, you – wait! Wait!'

Gran, hearing this, had increased her speed as best she could, whereupon the woman, raising her voice, shouted: 'Stop her! Stop thief! Stop her!'

In a panic, and growing breathless, Gran paused for a moment near the public-bar entrance of The Winged Horse. Unfortunately, draymen were delivering fresh supplies of barrelled beer to the pub and the trap doors in the pavement, giving access to the cellar, were wide open. As her infuriated and screaming victim came rushing across the road towards her, Gran took a step back, lost her footing and fell into the cellar, landing on some kegs of beer at such an angle and with such brutal force that she broke her back.

She had been rushed to the Prince of Wales Hospital but, not surprisingly, was found to be dead on arrival. Later, at the inevitable inquest, the potman who had gone to her aid described how Gran had fashioned her own wry epitaph.

As he lifted her head she had opened her eyes, and taking note of the kegs of beer nearby, murmured: 'I knew the bloody drink would get me in the end.' He swore that she smiled as she spoke.

2

The old lady would have been proud of her funeral. Rosie gave her all that she had asked for and more: a splendid oak coffin with gleaming brass handles, a hearse drawn by two black-plumed horses followed by two carriages, and at Tottenham cemetery a simple headstone with the inscription: RIP MARIA THOMPSON – 1846–1925.

As she had predicted, there was no shortage of people

prepared to support a good funeral. Most of the residents of Shakespeare Street, casual acquaintances from the public bars she had frequented, men and women who had not found a good word for her while she lived, all turned up to salute if not to mourn the passing of this legendary character.

Even the local constable, PC Dykes, who had suffered assault at Gran's hands on three occasions, put in a respectful appearance, although there were those who commented that he had come only to make sure that the old lady really was dead and to see her buried safely, out of harm's way.

The Reverend Turnbull, vicar of St Ann's, had never seen Gran or, indeed, most of the congregation at the funeral service, but he rose to the occasion with an eloquence which drew tears from many of those present. He made no mention of the way she had lived or of the manner of her dying, for death, it seems, had washed all Gran's sins away: he hailed her as a wife and mother who, with great fortitude, had risen above poverty and hardship, a selfless example to all. He left them in no doubt that the old lady would enter heaven in triumph and, though she might not get to sit exactly at the right hand of Jesus, she would be pretty close.

Van cried theatrically, Eddie sat in thoughtful silence, Rosie remained dry-eyed and unconvinced, mourning Gran in her own way. She had been a selfish, thieving old woman and no words from the pulpit could alter that: on the other hand, life had not given her too much of a chance. Like so many others, she had been a victim of circumstances and of her own nature and, if a balance had to be struck, there was this to be said for her: she had never allowed the harshness of life to smother her. She had fought back, tooth and claw, like a wildcat and she had gone out as she had lived, undefeated and indomitable.

And, at the very end, as her coffin was being lowered into the grave, great claps of thunder burst from the black clouds above, followed by a firework display of lightning and rain so fierce that the mourners were soaked in seconds. Looking up, it occurred to Rosie that Gran, as usual, was having the last word.

Suspecting that there would be a good turn-out, Rosie had

booked the local Co-operative Hall for the wake that traditionally followed the burial. She laid on what she hoped might be an ample supply of the obligatory funeral-meats – ham, tongue and brisket of beef – together with bowls of salad, rolls and butter, sausage rolls, cakes, jellies and pineapple chunks. A large barrel of beer stood on a trestle in one corner and on a table nearby she had set out bottles of port, gin, lemonade and ginger beer. In a tiny kitchen adjoining the hall, tea was available for those few who preferred it. Rosie, assisted by Tiny Christmas, Mrs Archibald and the children, had prepared and set up the feast earlier that morning.

Mrs Archibald had commented that there was enough food and drink in the hall to satisfy a regiment of Grenadier Guards but, like Rosie, she had underestimated the appetites of the mourners. The party began at three p.m. with all the whispered solemnity proper to such an occasion, but gradually, as throats were moistened and collars loosened, the damp clothes were forgotten, the voices grew louder, the comments bolder, the eating and drinking faster. By five p.m. the food had disappeared, the bottles were almost empty and the barrel showed signs of running dry.

'Blimey,' said Mrs Archibald, 'you would think that they'd never seen a square meal before.'

'A lot of them haven't,' said Rosie, 'not for a long time, any road.'

Donal Ryan, who could recognise a good wake when he saw one, insisted on making a speech, calling drunkenly for order and clapping his hands as he mounted a chair.

'Oh, give over, Donal!' cried Nell, Rosie's friend from her days in the laundry.

'No, no! Wait!' he said, swaying dangerously. 'I don't think we should allow the occasion to pass without rendering our thanks to Rosie.'

This brought cries of assent and some applause, and thus encouraged he continued: 'You have done the old lady proud, Rosie, you have done her proud, and I defy anyone to contradict me on that score. I have seen a few send-offs in my time and this tops the lot. It will be long remembered, long remembered. Our heartfelt sympathy goes out to you and your family in your deep sorrow and sad loss. But the old lady had a fair trot and you looked after her to the end with loving care. And in the days to come, you will have your memories to look over, Rosie. As we say back home – memory is the only friend that grief can call its own. So, as you face the future . . .'

Intoxicated by the beer and his own words, Donal's eyes were becoming moist and his gestures more and more theatrical. Unimpressed by this maudlin performance, Nell pulled him down with her big hands and pointed him firmly towards the door.

'All right!' she said. 'All right! That's quite enough of that guff! Time you were on your way. Time we were all on our way.'

The level of noise fell like a slow curtain as the mourners, mindful once again of the nature of the occasion, filed past Rosie murmuring condolences and thanks. When they had gone, she prepared to clean up the chaos of crockery and glasses left behind, but Nell, backed by Mrs Archibald, intervened once again.

'Oh, no, you don't! Leave this lot. Mrs A and me will do the clearing up.'

'We'll clear up,' echoed Mrs Archibald.

Rosie began to protest but Nell overruled her. 'You heard me, you haven't got cloth ears! On your way. I'll look in on you over the weekend.'

'It's good of you,' Rosie said.

'Stuff!' said Nell. 'Now get your skates on and go, before we change our minds.'

Thankful to be released, Rosie turned to Van and Eddie. 'Wait here for a minute. I'm just going to the office to settle the bill for the hall.'

3

The Secretary, a grey-haired, stern-faced woman who reminded Rosie of the Miss Jones who had once taught her to read, looked up in some irritation.

'What is it?'

'Oh, I'm sorry,' said Rosie, backing off. 'I didn't realise you were busy.' She glanced apologetically at a young man in a shiny blue serge suit who was sitting opposite the Secretary. He had the brown, healthy-looking face of a man who worked outdoors, a pleasant smile, and kindly blue eyes which he turned upon her now.

'It's all right, Mrs Carr. I can wait a minute. It is Mrs Carr, isn't it?' His voice had a gentle country cadence which was unfamiliar to her.

'Yes, that's right,' said Rosie in some confusion, wondering how on earth he could know her name.

'You have been pointed out to me,' he said, reading her unspoken question. He looked at her keenly as if he were making some sort of assessment.

'I see,' said Rosie, more confused than ever. She turned to the Secretary. 'I came to settle for the hire of the hall. You said it would be thirty shillings, including the use of the crockery and glasses. I paid ten shillings deposit – here's the rest.'

'Any breakages?' said the Secretary, taking the proffered pound note.

'A few,' answered Rosie. 'I'll call in tomorrow or the day after and you can let me know the damage.' As she spoke she was aware that the man in the blue serge suit was still studying her.

'I'd prefer that you settle now,' the Secretary said brusquely.

'They are still clearing up. I shan't know what breakages there are until they've finished and I am not waiting around for that.' She met the Secretary's steely eye with a look of her own and added tartly: 'Don't worry. I'm not going to run away!'

'I should hope not!' said the Secretary. 'Very well, Mrs Thompson. Tomorrow or the day after.'

The young man in the blue serge suit pursued Rosie out to the narrow corridor. 'Mrs Carr – excuse me!' As he came up to her, he held out a calloused hand.

'The name is Colson, Ken Colson. Councillor Colson, actually. I've been anxious to meet you for some time, Mrs Carr.'

'It is Mrs Thompson, actually,' she said.

'Oh, I'm sorry.'

'It's all right. Most people still call me Carr. What can I do for you?'

'You are quite a local personality, you know. Everyone knows how you fought the Council bureaucrats when we had the rat invasion. And I know you have helped a lot of people in other ways.'

'I haven't done anything to write home about,' she replied awkwardly. She edged away, anxious to go, but he took her arm.

'Look, I'm sorry. This is hardly the time for me to intrude. But I wonder if I might call on you in the near future – just for a chat, you understand.'

'What for?' she said bluntly.

'Well, I'll explain when I see you,' he replied. 'But just let me leave a thought with you. A question, really. Would you be interested in contesting the Harringay Ward in next April's elections for the Borough Council?'

'Me?' She looked at him in genuine astonishment.

'We are looking for a good candidate to put up against Morton Goldie. Do you know him?'

The use of the first name threw Rosie for a moment and then, like a trap door snapping shut, it came to her. Goldie! Our Mr Goldie – the one and only Mr Goldie. Oh, yes, she thought, I know him better than you think! Aloud, she said: 'I worked in his laundry once.'

'Good!' he said, smiling as if this information had cheered him. 'Good! Will you think about it?'

'I'll think about it,' said Rosie, 'but it won't do any good. I can't see myself sitting on any Council.'

'I'd have said the same thing about myself a couple of years back,' he said. 'But I took the plunge and I'm there now. Anyway, don't give me an answer yet. I'll call round some time. Will that be all right?'

'Yes, fine,' said Rosie, still thinking about Mr Goldie. It was odd how the man kept coming into her life. She had half a mind to take up Mr Colson's offer just for the pleasure of seeing the face of her ex-boss when she confronted him.

'By the way, you are Labour, I take it?' said Mr Colson casually.

'Me? I don't know what I am,' she replied truthfully.

'How did you vote at the last election?'

'I don't know. Labour, I suppose. Yes – it was Labour.'

'Fair enough,' he said, 'fair enough. You live in Shakespeare Street, I believe. What's the number?'

'It's fifty-five. But we shan't be there much longer.'

'Oh, you are not moving away, I hope?'

'No, we shan't be going too far,' she said.

4

'There we are, then,' Rosie said. 'What do you think?'

Eddie looked at the house with all the gravity befitting the man of the family: Van clapped her hands and exploded with delight.

'Oh, Mum, Mum – it's lovely! It's beautiful!'

'What do you think, Eddie?' asked Rosie.

'It looks very nice on the outside,' replied Eddie carefully.

Rosie smiled. She had brought the children to Number Two Napier Avenue straight from the wake in the hope that it would take their minds off the events of the day, but she now realised that her concern had been misplaced. Young people are resilient and practical: their minds do not linger on death for long. For them, Gran was already a receding memory: in many ways, her passing was more of a release for the children than it was for Rosie herself. The days of the old lady's petty tyrannies were over.

There was release for them all in another sense. Rosie had deliberately delayed making a move from the cramped conditions at Shakespeare Street because of Gran. She could not put words to what she felt but, in blunt truth, she was ashamed of the old lady who in the past few months had grown increasingly dirty, cantankerous and foul-mouthed. She had not wanted to carry this burden with her to a new house, to have Van and Eddie exposed to the questioning looks of neighbours or the taunts of their children.

Napier Avenue was only a few minutes' walk from Shakespeare Street, but to Rosie it seemed to be in a different world. Chestnut trees shaded the pavements and the tiny front gardens were bright with patches of green lawn, roses, snapdragon, pansies, daisies, and a dozen other flowers to which she could not put a name. The garden of Number Two was a little overgrown, but the beds were bursting with bloom, and a rambling rose, heavy with little pink flowers, clung to the wall near the front door, scenting the air.

'That will be a job for you two,' said Rosie. 'I shall look to you to keep the garden tidy.'

'Are we going to take it, Mum?' asked Van excitedly.

'It depends if you like what you see inside. It is your decision.' She took the keys she had collected from Coolings, the estate agents, out of her purse and opened the front door. 'Right. It's all yours.'

They raced past her, their feet sending up echoes from the naked floorboards, their cries ringing through the empty house. Rosie made her way to the kitchen and through the back door into the garden beyond. It was small, no more than twice the size of the strip at the front, but it was surrounded by other, similar gardens and, despite the frontiers of fencing, gave an impression of space, of freedom.

An elderly apple tree, laden with green fruit, spread its

branches across the bottom of the garden, standing sentinel over a worn rustic bench. The physical and mental strain of the funeral had now begun to catch up with her and, stepping across the damp grass, she sat down thankfully.

The retreating storm had left behind a pure blue sky and a kindly sun: the air, fresh and clean, perfumed with honeysuckle, caressed her skin and filled her lungs, inviting her to relax, invoking a drowsiness which was hard to resist. She loosened the throat of her black dress, closed her eyes and thought, not of Jack Cameron, but of Tommo.

I've done it, Tommo, I think I've done it. I've kept my promise. I have a job now that pays well and we are getting out of Shakespeare Street. Do you remember Napier Avenue? Well, you won't believe this, but we are going to move there. I've found a nice house, nothing grand or special, but it has a garden back and front, a climbing rose and an apple tree. And, best of all, it has an indoor lavatory and a bathroom. Imagine! A proper bathroom, all our own, nobody to share it, nobody to push their way through the kitchen to get to the lavatory.

The kids will each have a room and they'll have carpets on the floor and bookshelves and patterned curtains at the windows. Eddie and your little Van are fine, Tommo, you couldn't wish for two better children. Eddie is the serious one, quiet and thoughtful, good with his hands and not afraid of hard work. Van is different, bright and full of imagination, always dreaming dreams, forever making a drama out of the simplest things. I think you would like them, Tommo, I am sure you would love them. I know that without Eddie and Van I would be lost, nothing would have been worth while.

Your mother has gone, Tommo. I've never lied to you and I would be lying now if I said that I was truly sorry. Well, I don't have to explain to you, you know what she was like. But I did my best for her and I gave her a good send-off. End of a chapter, isn't that what they say? Me? I'm all right, Tommo. A bit tired and I'm not getting any younger. But, by and large, I'm happy. I can look ahead now, you see, there's some kind of future, I don't have to worry where the next penny is going to come from.

Marriage? Not yet, if ever. I've found a fellow and I think I am in love with him. No, that's not right. I know I'm in love with him and I'm pretty sure he feels the same. But he is from the other side of the tracks, Tommo, and over there they don't think as we do. At any rate, he doesn't. He lives for the moment, he doesn't want to be tied down. I suppose that is what happens to you when you have never had to worry about money. Just my luck to fall for someone like him, but there doesn't seem to be much I can do about it. Yes, I suppose I would marry him if he asked me but I don't think that he is likely to do that. In any case, I couldn't be sure that it would work out, I've grown to like my independence.

I'll tell you something, Tommo, something that will give you a good laugh. I met a young fellow this afternoon, seemed a nice enough chap, who asked me if I would stand for the local Council! Can you imagine it? Me sitting up at the Town Hall with all those toffs? Councillor Rosie Carr! What a turn-up for the book that would be! I am not sure that . . .

'Mum! Mum!'

She opened her eyes as the children came running from the house, their excitement exploding over her.

'Mum, please, we must take it!' cried Van. 'I simply must live here, I must!'

'Can we afford it, Mum?' asked Eddie.

'I want the upstairs front room!' said Van. 'I bag the upstairs front bedroom.'

'It's got a bathroom, Mum, and an indoor lav,' said Eddie.

'And a parlour, a proper parlour!' added Van.

'We won't have enough furniture to fill this place,' said Eddie.

'Don't sit here, Mum – come and look!' cried Van, pulling Rosie by the hand.

'Wait! Wait!' said Rosie, laughing. 'Give me a chance. Now, sit here by me and listen.' As they sat on either side of her, eager eyes searching her face as though awaiting a verdict, she drew them closer.

'You like the place?' she asked.

'Oh, yes, yes. It's marvellous!' said Van.

'If we can afford it . . .,' said Eddie cautiously.

'The rent is twenty-eight shillings a week,' said Rosie. 'I think we can just about manage that, so don't worry your head on that score. If you are happy, we'll take it.'

'But you haven't seen it!' said Eddie.

'Oh, yes, I have. A few days ago. I decided then that if you liked it, we'd move in.'

'Mum, Mum – I love you,' said Van, hugging her.

'We'll have to go steady to begin with,' Rosie warned. 'I spent most of what was saved on Gran's funeral. We can afford to buy linoleum and curtains and some bits of furniture but not everything. We'll have to get the rest as we go along.'

'When can we move?' asked Van.

'In about a week, I should think.'

'I can't wait to leave Shakespeare Street,' said Van. 'I hate it there.'

'Now, watch it, Van!' said Rosie sternly. 'Don't get above yourself. Shakespeare Street has been good to us.'

'I can't help it,' Van insisted. 'I hate it.'

Before they left, Rosie took one more look at the bathroom. The brass taps were dull, rings of grime stained the enamel of the bath, but she was not in the mood to dwell on such minor imperfections. There was nothing wrong that elbow grease could not put right.

What stirred her emotions was the thought that, for the first time in her life, she had a bathroom of her own, a real indoor bathroom. It was one more step forward, a dream come true, a moment she would never forget.

She stood there for a long time and when the children, growing impatient, came to find her, she was weeping.

5

As Rosie made her way to the warehouse the next morning she found herself looking back on the events of the past few days with a certain rueful wonder. So much had happened: the sudden, exciting flowering of her relationship with Jack, the equally sudden death of Gran, the funeral, the decision to move house. All this on top of the pressures of the business had, for the moment, left her feeling as if she had used up all emotion and had no more left to give. She longed now for a period of peace in which to gather herself.

The expansion of the business had made it necessary to rent an adjoining warehouse where two girls were employed to weigh and pack tea, sugar and other loose commodities into the distinctive Carmo bags. Both girls, who were sisters, came hurrying towards Rosie as she took out the keys and opened up.

They presented a picturesque contrast in styles. Elsie, the younger, followed the latest fashions from pictures in the newspapers, and from the cinema, and copied them as best she could within her limited means. Much to the disgust of her elders and the admiration of her peers, she wore her hair in an Eton crop, plucked her eyebrows, painted her lips cupid-bow style and wore dresses that reached only to her knees. It was whispered that when she went to a pub or a dancehall she smoked cigarettes through a long elegant holder.

Elsie was bright, cheeky and hard-working, and Rosie defended her against all comers, taking the view that the girl was entitled to have her fling while she could. If her dress and attitude shocked some of the older women, so much the better: they could do with a shaking-up. She had seen girls like Elsie before – Lily Hoddle was one example – girls who flashed across the scene with all the brightness of butterflies, only to be sucked down inexorably into the drab routine of everyday life, knee-deep in children and up to their elbows in drudgery.

Before that happened, Elsie had a right to make her brief statement, to enjoy her youth and beauty.

The other girl, Betty, had looks of a different order: if she had a role-model, which was doubtful, it was nearer to Mary Pickford than to film vamps like Pola Negri or Theda Bara. Her light brown hair fell to just above her shoulders and was held in place by two bows of blue ribbon, she wore just a trace of make-up, and her skirt discreetly masked most of her shapely legs.

'Morning, missus!' cried Elsie cheerfully.

'Sorry if we're late,' said Betty.

'You are here, that's the main thing,' Rosie replied.

'We didn't expect you to come in today – what with the funeral and everything,' Elsie said.

Rosie could not think of a decent answer to this so she fell back on words that had been honed into a cliché over the centuries and mumbled: 'Life has to go on, isn't that what they say?'

'We saw a terrible commotion in Margaret Street as we came along,' said Elsie as she and her sister put on their white working overalls.

'Oh? What was that?' asked Rosie without too much interest.

'At number nineteen. The broker's men were there, chucking Mrs Hodge and her five kids into the street.'

'Into the street?' Frowning, Rosie turned on the girl and repeated: 'Into the street? What for?'

'I don't know. They say she is miles behind with the rent. You should have heard her – she was screaming and scratching them as they carried out her stuff. They had to call old Dykes, the copper, to hold her.'

'And the poor kids were yelling and crying fit to bust,' added Betty.

'I'm not surprised,' Rosie said grimly. 'What's going to happen to them?'

'God knows,' said Elsie, without emotion. 'Mrs Holloway next door took in the two youngest kids but the others are sitting there on the pavement with their mother, refusing to budge.'

'I expect they'll end up in the workhouse, poor things,' said Betty. 'I mean, there's nowhere else for them to go, is there?'

'All right, all right,' Rosie said sharply. 'That's enough. Make a start on that new batch of tea – and don't dawdle over it.'

She worked on in silence for a few minutes, checking a consignment of tinned fruit which Tiny had to deliver to one of the Bazaars, but her mind kept going back to the conversation and the plight of Mrs Hodge. She had passed the time of day with the woman but beyond that she scarcely knew her. It was common knowledge that she had been deserted by her seaman husband and did charring jobs in a hopeless effort to make ends meet.

Even so, it was a long time since a family had actually been put out on the street for non-payment of rent or other debts. Since the war people had become less willing to stand idly by while their neighbours were cast out and, correspondingly, landlords were liable to think twice before invoking the law. But the real incentive was fear: people paid their rent even before they bought food because homelessness was often a greater threat than hunger.

The last instance that Rosie could recall had occurred in Shakespeare Street itself some two years before, when an elderly couple had been evicted. The proceedings in that case had been handled swiftly and almost secretly, so that the pair were installed in separate segregated wards in the workhouse before their neighbours realised what had happened.

A mental picture of the destitute family continued to plague her mind and, after a few minutes, Rosie put down her papers and told the sisters that she was going out.

'Where are you going, missus?' asked Elsie.

'Ask no questions and you will hear no lies,' answered Rosie tartly. 'If Mr Moss should get back before I do, tell him I'm out on business.'

6

She found Mrs Hodge sitting on a kitchen chair on the pavement outside Number Nineteen Margaret Street, surrounded by pieces of worn furniture, two ramshackle bedsteads with stained mattresses, a pile of old clothes and some battered pots and pans. She was a grey-faced sagging woman with features which gave hint of a vanished beauty: her eyes bore the look of someone who had reached the end of the line. Three ragged and unwashed children, ranging in age from five to twelve, sat around her, two of them looking at their mother with frightened eyes while the third, the oldest, glared boldly at the world, his eyes blazing with hatred.

The little group of sympathetic neighbours made way expectantly as Rosie approached, murmuring greeting. One of the group addressed Mrs Hodge: 'Here, lovey, here's Rosie Carr. She'll know what to do.'

To Rosie's surprise, she saw Ken Colson, the man she had met at the Co-operative Hall, squatting down by Mrs Hodge, talking to her in low, comforting tones. He straightened up and smiled as Rosie appeared.

'Good morning, Mrs Carr.'

'It doesn't look like a very good morning to me,' said Rosie sharply.

She felt a tiny surge of guilt as her eyes took in the pathetic ring of belongings: she thought of her own changed circumstances, of Napier Avenue with its apple tree and rambler rose, of the indoor bathroom and her plans to buy curtains, carpets, new furniture. And she remembered also that, not so long ago, she had come within days of being turned into the street herself. All right, all right, she told herself sternly, people should pay their rent, they should not expect to live for nothing: but there had to be a better way than this, there had to be. The children were not responsible for their father's desertion or their mother's poverty – yet what chance would they have? If there was a God why was he so selective – giving so much to some and so little to others?

'I've told Mrs Hodge that she can camp out in the Labour Rooms for a couple of nights,' said Mr Colson. 'Just while we see what better we can do, you understand.'

Rosie nodded and gave the young man a quick appreciative glance. She was accustomed to people murmuring empty words of sympathy: he, at least, was trying to give practical help.

She turned to Mrs Hodge. 'Who is your landlord, love?'

'What?' The woman gave her a blank look.

'Your landlord. Who do you pay rent to?'

Mrs Hodge still gave no sign of understanding; the shock seemed to have robbed her of speech. A neighbour edged forward with the answer: 'She's the same as me. We pay to Coolings. They're the agents. God alone knows who the bloody landlord is!'

'Whoever he is, he ought to be shot!' put in another woman. 'The houses are a bloody disgrace. He hasn't spent a penny on them in years.'

'I'm afraid to slam the door in case the place falls down!' added the first woman.

'You want to see the damp?' asked a third neighbour. 'I'll show you if you like. The walls are green with damp. And they have just put the rent up by two bob a week.'

Rosie turned to Ken Colson. 'I'm going up to Coolings. I want to try and find out who is behind this. Can you get them to your Labour Rooms?'

'As soon as I can organise some transport,' he replied.

'Do you know the warehouse in Culross Road?' He nodded. 'Go up there and ask for Tiny Christmas. Tell him I sent you and tell him to get the van down here double quick. He'll help you move the stuff. But hurry, or you will miss him.'

'I'm on my way,' he said and went off at a run.

Police Constable Dykes, who had been hovering on the edge of the little crowd, now stepped forward. He addressed Rosie as if in her he recognised some natural authority.

'She can't stay here, Rosie,' he said awkwardly. 'Obstructing the footpath and all that.'

'Oh, give over, can't you?' she replied. 'Give the poor cow a chance.'

'Just doing my job,' he muttered.

'Yes, I know,' she said witheringly. 'A great job it is too, putting a woman and five kids on to the street. What's the matter – have you run out of tea-leaves? No housebreakers or bag-snatchers to chase?'

'Rosie—' he protested.

'Don't "Rosie" me! I tell you what you can do, Mr Dykes. Go and find that bloody landlord – and charge him with taking money under false pretences.'

An appreciative murmur rose from the crowd and, glad of the diversion, Dykes turned on the group of women, his voice heavy with authority: 'All right, all right – that's enough, that's enough. Break it up! You are unlawfully causing an obstruction!'

Encouraged by the sound of his own voice and by the shuffling response of the weaker characters in the crowd, he spoke to Rosie with greater firmness. 'They can't stay here and that's that. The Guardians have been notified – they will be taken care of.'

'In the workhouse?' said Rosie scornfully.

'No! No!' Mrs Hodge found her voice and screamed the words, clutching one of the children to her.

'Look,' said Rosie, in a more conciliatory tone, 'look, Mr Dykes. Councillor what's-his-name – Colson – Councillor Colson is going to take them to the Labour Rooms. He's gone to get transport, he'll be back in half an hour – less.'

Mr Dykes considered this for a moment and then nodded gravely. 'Very well. I'll give it half an hour.'

'Good. Many thanks.'

He hesitated and then spread his hands in a gesture of apology. 'It's not a job we like doing, Rosie.'

'I know.' She smiled at him, thinking that he wasn't a bad man as coppers go. It could not be easy being a policeman, always standing in the firing line, always doing other people's dirty work.

She turned to one of the women who had spoken earlier: 'Right – I'm away to try and pin down this bloody landlord. You look after her until Mr Colson gets here with the van.'

And dropping a hand on Mrs Hodge's shoulder she murmured: 'Don't give up, lovey. You've got mates – friends. Don't give up.'

7

Mr Edwin Cooling, of Cooling & Cooling, Estate Agents, was one of the few people who called Rosie by her married name.

'Good morning, good morning, Mrs Thompson,' he said eagerly. 'Sit down, do. Take a seat, please.' He put his head to one side and smiled. A small, spare man of about thirty, his jet-black brilliantined hair, bright restless eyes and that curious habit of crooking his head put Rosie in mind of a blackbird. 'You've come about Napier Avenue, I assume?'

It has to be said that Mr Cooling did not normally deal with small rented properties himself, preferring to leave such details to his clerk. But he was a shrewd man who kept his eyes open and his ear to the ground and he had been monitoring the steady growth of Rosie's business for some months. The name Carmo had begun to crop up in conversation at the local Conservative Club and his friend, Mr Lightblow, of the City Bank, had told him that the enterprise was well worth watching. Indeed, Mr Lightblow, knowing of Rosie's desire to move, had recommended that she call on Mr Cooling. Thus his interest in Rosie was conditioned more by hope of future prospects than by any thought of the small commission he would receive for renting Number Two Napier Avenue.

'I'd like to take the house,' Rosie said.

'Capital, capital. It is a very attractive little property, I knew you would see that at once. When would you like to move in?'

'As soon as possible. Next week?'

'Why not, why not? The house is empty. No problem, no problem at all.'

He produced a standard rental form and began to fill it in, the pen scratching over the surface. While he was so occupied, Rosie said casually: 'By the way, Mr Cooling, you wouldn't happen to know who owns Number Nineteen Margaret Street, would you?'

The pen stopped scratching as he looked up at her. 'Margaret Street? You would not be interested in that sort of property, would you?' He spoke with a distaste that was genuine, for his connection with slum landlords lay heavy on his conscience and, one by one, as he could afford it, he was discarding them and their business.

'No, no. Not me,' said Rosie, without faltering. 'A fellow I met in the way of business. He is interested in buying these old places and doing them up.'

'There are a great many houses that require doing up in Margaret Street. But why on earth anyone should be interested is beyond me.'

'This fellow makes a business of it. Buys the houses cheap, does them up and then either sells them at a profit or lets them out at a higher rent. He seems to do very well.' She was surprised at how easily she embellished the original lie.

'I see.' Mr Cooling looked at her doubtfully. 'I can't envisage such an investment paying off in this neighbourhood.'

'Still, I did promise that I'd find out,' Rosie persisted.

'Well, I can tell you this. Number Nineteen is one of a block of ten houses in Margaret Street that are owned by – by my clients. I doubt if they would be interested in selling just one of them.'

'Clients?'

'A local property company.'

'Who is the boss?'

'I don't think I can divulge that,' said Mr Cooling. 'Such matters are confidential.'

'You could tell me the name of the company, couldn't you? No harm in that, surely.'

'Why?' Mr Cooling sounded suspicious. 'Your – er – business friend can always deal through me.'

'Of course. No question about that. But he will probably be interested in all ten houses. And he'll have to know what firm he is buying from, even if he does go through you, isn't that right?'

'I suppose so.' Mr Cooling sighed, torn between the possibility of a sale and loyalty to his clients. 'You may tell him that the company is called AMG Property Developments (1922) Ltd.'

She repeated the name and added: 'Don't they have an address?'

'They can be contacted through this office.'

'Isn't there a law about companies? Don't they have to be registered?' asked Rosie, recalling something Mr Lightblow had once told her.

'That is correct,' said Mr Cooling uneasily, regretting that he had allowed the discussion to go so far. He was beginning to understand why Mr Lightblow held this young woman in such high regard: behind the smile and the engaging manner there was a shrewd mind, no doubt of that.

'So all I have to do is go to the place where they register business companies and look up the names of the directors of AMG Property Developments?'

'The register is open for inspection by the public – yes.'

'Well, then, Mr Cooling,' she said, smiling, 'why don't you be a good chap and save me the time and the trouble?'

'What do you mean?' he asked weakly, aware only too well that he had painted himself into a corner.

'Tell me the names and addresses. I mean, if I can go and find them out anyway, what's the harm?'

He looked at her and made a mental vow that he would never again allow himself to underestimate an attractive woman. Shaking his head, he drew a thin file from a drawer of the desk. Still, he hesitated.

'Why are you interested in this company, Mrs Thompson? What are your real reasons?'

'Does it matter? I mean, you've told me enough. I can easily find out the rest.'

'Yes,' he said, uncertainly. He laid the file on the desk between them and stood up. 'I am afraid I can go no further. It – er – would be unprofessional for me to name names. Would you excuse me.' At the door he paused and added, with unusual emphasis: 'I shall only be a couple of minutes.'

The file was in Rosie's hands almost before the door closed. The first few documents carried long lists of houses in the locality, the vast majority of which she knew to be slums. She hadn't time to count but there were well over two hundred.

Turning over she found a sheet of paper that made her heart thump with excitement. There were three directors of AMG Property Developments (1922) Ltd, and each of them had given the first letter of his surname to make up the name of the company. She took out a notebook and listed them, one by one, her lips tightening as she did so.

Ralph Atkins, Esq., of 4 Gentleman's Row, Enfield, Middlesex.

William Edward Morgan, of The Laurels, Windsor Avenue, Winchmore Hill.

Morton Albert Arthur Goldie, of 29 Lansdowne Road, Tottenham, N.17.

8

In the Labour Rooms an hour later, Rosie, still inwardly seething with anger and excitement, put a proposal to Mrs Hodge.

'Listen. How about this? We were going to move out of Shakespeare Street in a week. Well, we'll speed it up and go the day after tomorrow. You can stay here for a couple of nights and then move into our old rooms. I'll fix it with the landlord, no need to worry on that score.'

'But, Rosie, how will I pay the rent?'

'You are going to come and work for me. At the warehouse – packing and odd jobs. I'll pay you thirty shillings a week.'

'Rosie, I couldn't . . .'

'Of course you could! You'll be doing us a favour. We need an extra hand.'

'Oh, dear God – I don't know what to say!' Mrs Hodge looked up at Rosie, her eyes moist with tears.

'Don't say anything. Here.' Rosie took a half-crown from her purse. 'Take this and get some grub inside those kids.' She smiled, seeing the fear go from the eyes of the youngest children: only the boy remained unmoved, the expression of bitter hatred still etched on his thin, dirty face.

Rosie drew Ken Colson aside and showed him the notes she had taken in Cooling's office. He whistled between his teeth as he read the names.

'My bloody oath, Rosie, are you sure?'

'Positive.'

'This is dynamite, dynamite. Morgan is the Mayor. And Goldie – Mr Morton-bloody-Goldie – the respectable church-warden – a slum landlord, no less!'

'I'm going round to see him,' Rosie said. 'I'm not letting him get away with this.'

'No, Rosie, no!' he said urgently. 'Don't put them on their guard. We'll keep this up our sleeves and spring it on them at the right moment.'

'I don't know what you are talking about,' she said bluntly.

'Your first lesson in political tactics, Rosie,' he replied with a smile. 'Goldie is only one man. The Mayor is only one man. Sure, we want to expose them. But that is not enough. We need to get rid of their whole rotten gang, to sweep them out of office at the next local elections. And this bit of information will help us do just that, don't you see?'

'I'm not sure,' she said doubtfully.

'You've done a lot for the people round here. They look up to you, and rightly so. But there is a limit to what one person can do alone. We have to change the conditions that make it possible for men like Goldie to make money out of other people's misery. We have to change a system that makes it possible for a woman with five kids to be thrown on the street. It is not enough to expose a couple of slum landlords – we must get rid of the slums themselves. To do this, we must win political power – at the ballot-box. One person can't do that, Rosie. An organisation is needed, a party. Thousands of people working together for the same cause.'

He spoke quietly but there was a passionate edge to his voice that brought back a memory of an attic at The Winged Horse, years ago, when the young Frank Lambert had spoken to her in much the same way. Yet though she recognised the sense of what he was saying, she found the rhetoric irritating. To her, a problem was not something to be shelved, or saved up until later, or mixed up with words like "political tactics".

'Maybe you're right,' she said, reluctantly. 'It's time things were changed, that's for certain. But I don't like the idea of letting Goldie off the hook.'

'We shan't do that,' he said. 'I promise. Trust me. We'll nail him, don't worry – but at the right moment. And you can be the hammer. Stand against him at the election, Rosie. What do you say?'

'I was going to say no,' she said, 'until this morning, but seeing that poor cow on the pavement with her kids and her bits and pieces – I don't know – it made me bloody angry. If standing against Goldie will help – well, I'll have a go. But it stops there. I don't know about your politics and your parties, I'm not sure I want to. Getting rid of Goldie – that is straightforward. That I understand.'

'Rosie,' he cried, 'you are a natural! And I'll tell you this for nothing! You'll crucify him, you'll beat him out of sight!'

'As to that,' she said calmly, 'I've learned not to count my chickens before they come out of the eggs.'

CHAPTER THIRTEEN

1

It is only a half-hour journey from North London to Victoria Station but at the end of those thirty minutes Rosie felt as though she had arrived in a strange and bewildering new land, inhabited by strange and bewildering people.

Day excursions with the children to Southend-on-Sea, usually on public holidays, had provided her only previous experience of rail travel and on those occasions the trains were always crowded with cockneys like herself, homely people who spoke her language. But now, all around her, pushing towards the boat train, were people in splendid suits or equally splendid hats and dresses, chattering away in what the cockneys described as cut-glass accents. Many of them were trailed by uniformed chauffeurs in peaked caps and shiny black leggings, sweating under the weight of trunks and cases: porters, trolleys piled high with baggage, cut swathes through the crowd as they headed towards the platform.

Oh, God, Rosie thought, what am I doing among this lot? And how the devil will I find Jack in this scramble? Clutching the new case containing the clothes she had bought for this special weekend, she pushed in behind one of the bustling porters and followed in his wake.

'Rosie!'

Relief flooded over her as she saw Jack standing by a noticeboard inscribed with the words: BOAT TRAIN: DOVER – PARIS. DEPARTURE 10 A.M. He came towards her with a big easy smile on his face and kissed her boldly on the lips.

'You made it, darling,' he said, relieving her of the case.

'Just about,' she said ruefully.

'You should have let me pick you up.'

'No, it was all right. Tiny gave me a lift here in the van.' Having Jack pick her up was something she had taken pains to avoid. The sight of her going off, case in hand, with him, would have fuelled the neighbours' appetite for gossip for weeks.

'You look tremendous, Rosie,' he said.

'Hmph!' she declared. 'I feel like a rag doll up against this lot!' She nodded by way of example towards two handsome women, dressed with stunning elegance, who were just going through the barrier.

'They can't hold a candle to you, my lovely,' he said. 'Come on. I've claimed our seats.'

He checked the tickets with the collector and led the way down the platform to a Pullman coach, where a respectful attendant took Rosie's case and saw them to their places in the plush interior. Stone me, thought Rosie, how the rich live! This was more like travelling in an expensive drawing room than a railway carriage.

'Jack,' she whispered, 'this must be costing a fortune!'

'It's only money,' he said lightly. He took out a silver hip-flask and offered it to her. 'Would you like a snort of brandy?'

'Lord, no!' she replied. 'It's a bit early in the day for brandy.'

'We're on holiday,' he said, and lifted the flask to his lips. Then, as he screwed back the top, he added: 'Do you know what I'd like to do now?'

'What?'

'Make love to you.'

'It's a bit early in the day for that too!' she said, laughing and smoothing the skirt of her new navy-blue suit.

'It's never too early,' he protested, taking her hand.

'Are we supposed to be married?' she asked.

'I've booked us as Mr and Mrs Cameron, yes. You don't mind, do you?'

'Not really. Only if we are supposed to be married, you'd better be careful. Married couples don't sit around holding hands.'

'They do if they are on honeymoon, lovely.'

'Oh.' She laughed again. 'Is that what this weekend is all about?'

'It's not a million miles from the truth, is it, after all? It will be a sort of honeymoon.'

'You are a cheeky sod, Jack Cameron,' she said, looking into his face and thinking how handsome he was.

An elderly woman with a severe, haughty expression came through at that moment and was shown to a seat opposite. Her clothes and manner put Rosie in mind of the pictures of Queen Mary that appeared regularly in the papers, but this lady's expression was infinitely less kindly. She was accompanied by a plainly dressed young woman whose humbler demeanour indicated that she was either a maid or a paid companion or both. The mistress sat bolt upright in her seat, her back rigid as a ramrod, and fixed Jack, and then Rosie, with an uncompromising stare. Rosie was tempted to snap at the woman, to ask her whom she thought she was staring at, but she crushed the idea. Jack, on the other hand, turned on the charm that came so naturally to him.

'Good morning. It is a beautiful day, isn't it?'

The woman, reassured perhaps by his accent or his smile, allowed her face to relax a little.

'Beautiful,' she agreed. She turned to her companion who sat with her head slightly bowed as if in acknowledgement of the fact that she was travelling in superior company. 'Did you bring the lozenges, Walters?'

'Yes, Mrs Summerfield,' the girl replied, reaching for her bag.

'It is all right, girl! I don't want them now. Just so long as you remembered,' said the woman with a touch of irritation. She gave Jack a glimmer of a smile. 'Frost's Lozenges. I find them invaluable against seasickness – against all kinds of sickness in fact.'

Rosie thought it remarkable that such a woman should admit to any sort of weakness but she restrained herself once more.

'One cannot be too careful,' said Jack politely, taking out a cigarette case. 'Would you mind if I had a gasper?'

'If you must,' said the woman sternly. Don't ask me if I mind, thought Rosie.

'Would you care to . . .?' asked Jack holding the case towards Mrs Summerfield.

'I don't, thank you. I disapprove of women smoking. In my view, it is unfeminine. I hope your wife does not indulge.' She laid a peculiar emphasis on the word *wife* as if she were awarding Rosie this status with some doubt.

'No, oh, no,' Jack said. 'You have never smoked, have you, my love.' It was a statement, not a question.

I'm not having any more of this, Rosie told herself, irritated by the undercurrent of patronage. Aloud, she said blithely, with a determination to shock: 'As a matter of fact, I have smoked an odd fag, here and there. I quite like the occasional fag.'

In truth, she had not touched a cigarette since she was fourteen, when an attempt to smoke a Wild Woodbine had made her physically sick, but the lie served its purpose. Mrs Summerfield stared grimly at Rosie who stared boldly back and, in the end, it was the older woman who broke off the engagement.

'My magazine, Walters,' she commanded, turning to the maid. A copy of *The Lady* was produced and, with a final glare at Rosie, she settled in behind it. Rosie gave the maid a smile and a wink and received a nervous smile in return.

'Walters?' Rosie said. 'Did I hear your name was Walters?'

'Yes, that's right.' The young woman spoke in little more than a whisper and gave a nervous glance in the direction of her mistress. *The Lady* responded with a rustle.

'I knew a family called Walters who lived in Emily Road, Tottenham. Wouldn't be any connection, I suppose?'

'I don't think so. My family came from Colchester, in Essex.'

'Ah,' Rosie said cheerfully. 'Nice place, Essex. I've been to Southend on a day-excursion a few times with the kids. I love the air there. You can smell the what-do-you-call-it – the ozone – even from the train.' She felt Jack's foot pressing on her own as if in warning and she turned to him. 'Anything wrong?'

'No, no,' he muttered.

'What were you treading on my foot for then?'

'Let us take a stroll down the train,' he said hastily.

Outside in the corridor he asked, with a frown: 'What was all that about, Rosie?'

'What?'

'All that chat about taking the kids to Southend. And the rest of it.'

'It was the truth. Why? Did I sound too common? Are you afraid that I might have shown you up?'

'No. You know me better than that. It was the young woman. You embarrassed her by chatting away like that in front of her mistress.'

Rosie considered this for a moment. 'I suppose you're right,' she admitted. 'I laid it on deliberately because that old woman got up my nose with her high-and-mighty ways. And you didn't help.'

'What did I do?' he protested.

'When she asked if your wife smoked you should have told her to mind her own bloody business!'

'Rosie, darling, don't be so prickly! You can't go around taking offence at every remark.'

'I can't help it. It makes my blood boil when people behave as if they own the earth. I mean, the way she spoke to that girl – you heard her. She treats her like dirt – speaks to her as if she is a skivvy. Well, I've been a skivvy and I know what it is like. That's why I'm prickly, as you call it.'

'Let's forget it, darling.'

'All right. But there's one other thing, Jack.' She pulled him round and looked into his face. 'Don't ever ask me to pretend to be something that I'm not. I'm Rosie Carr, plain Rosie Carr, take it or leave it. I'm not ashamed of where I came from, what I've been or who I am.'

'You are certainly not plain, Rosie,' he said gently, touching her cheek. 'And I wouldn't want you to pretend to be anything or to change one little bit.'

'I'm not much good to you, am I?' she said guiltily. 'Forever opening my big mouth and putting my foot in it.'

'You are the best thing that ever happened to me, Rosie.'

'I love you so much, Jack,' she said. 'That's the trouble.'

'Of course you do,' he replied, taking her in his arms. 'I am a very lovable person.'

2

From that moment, the weekend took a distinct turn for the worse. The train was held up outside Dover, without explanation, for over an hour and the Channel crossing proved to be uncomfortably rough, especially to an unseasoned traveller like Rosie. Jack, who was unaffected by the choppy sea, told her blandly that seasickness was really only a state of mind and that she should force herself to concentrate on other things.

'Go away, Jack,' she croaked, 'go away before I kill you!'

Death did indeed enter her mind more than once on the sea journey, not for Jack but for herself. The constant nausea seemed to affect her whole body, creating a state of mind in which she felt that dying would be a welcome release from this heaving misery. It was with the relief of a survivor that she stepped ashore at Calais, too shattered and exhausted to take in the fact that for the first time in her life she was in a foreign land.

On the train, Jack pressed her to take champagne and slowly, very slowly, she felt herself returning to the living world.

'How do you feel now?' he asked.

'As if I've been under a steamroller,' she replied. 'My God, Jack, I never want to go through that again.'

'It often happens first time, Rosie. I heaved my heart out first trip. But you get used to it – it gets better.'

'It couldn't get any worse!' she said tartly. And then, suddenly conscious of her appearance, she added: 'I must look a terrible sight.'

'A bit grey around the gills,' he admitted, smiling.

'Sorry,' she said, touching his hand. 'Not a very romantic start to the weekend, is it?'

'Don't worry. We'll put in a strong finish,' he said. 'Now, why don't you go along to the Ladies' Room and tidy yourself up? You'll feel better.'

On the way to the toilet, Rosie was surprised to be stopped by Mrs Summerfield. 'I fear you had a bad crossing, my dear,' she said sympathetically.

'Not very good,' answered Rosie.

'I know how it is. I saw that you were suffering but I did not interfere. With seasickness one wishes only to be left alone. It really is the most debilitating thing. When I first experienced it, I just felt as though I wanted to die.'

'I'm glad I'm not the only one to feel that,' said Rosie.

Fumbling in her handbag, Mrs Summerfield brought out a small bottle. 'Take these, my dear. For the journey home. Frost's Lozenges. I have found them an invaluable protection against seasickness. Take two an hour before sailing – just let them dissolve in the mouth.'

'But you'll need them yourself,' Rosie protested.

'I have an ample supply. Please.'

'It's awfully kind of you.'

'Not at all. I hope they help.'

Mrs Summerfield smiled and moved on, leaving Rosie to feel a mixture of guilt and bewilderment. What strange people the rich were! On the one hand, able to perform such acts of thoughtfulness and yet, on the other, capable of treating their servants as if they were creatures from a lesser planet! She was reminded of Mr Goldie who drove his workers to the point of exhaustion yet brought them ice-creams and cakes. There is something, she reflected, a special quality that they all seem to have in common: assurance, self-confidence, an unshakeable belief in their own position and authority. Mrs Summerfield certainly had all this: she had seen it in Russell Whitby all those years ago and, in his own lighthearted way, Jack Cameron appeared to be free of any hint of self-doubt. Was this what a prosperous background, a privileged upbringing, a special education could do to, and for, a person?

The weather, so full of promise at Victoria, now turned sour, greeting them at the Gare du Nord in Paris with a brooding ashen sky and drizzling rain.

'Blimey, Jack,' said Rosie, 'we would have done better to stay in London!'

'It will get better,' he said, without too much conviction.

With many of the other English passengers, Jack and Rosie stood in line for one of the infrequent cabs only to discover that the French had little regard for such niceties: no sooner did a cab appear than one of the natives, pre-empting the queue, ran towards it waving and shouting and took possession.

'Don't they know about queues over here?' Rosie demanded angrily.

'The French have a proper sense of the priorities,' he answered philosophically. 'They will queue for a seat in a restaurant but not much else.'

'Two can play at that bloody game!' she said, and, when the next cab hove into view, she broke into a run and beat a screaming Frenchman to it by a short head. He responded to this defeat with a torrent of angry words and tried to jostle her away from the door. Rosie had not the least idea what he was saying but the purport was clear enough and she replied in kind.

'You shove me again, mate, and I'll lay you flat on your arse!'

The Frenchman paused and looked at her for the first time. In an instant, like a curtain rising, the darkness disappeared from his face to be replaced by an appreciative smile. He gave her a small graceful bow and said: 'Je vous demande pardon, madame.' He waved a hand towards the cab: 'Servez-vous!'

'Thank you,' she said, smiling in return, thinking that what she had been told about the charm of the French was turning out to be true. Jack arrived with the bags at that moment and the Frenchman, tearing his eyes from Rosie's face with some reluctance, looked at him and gave a sigh of envy. 'Félicitations, monsieur.'

'What did he say?' asked Rosie, as they settled in the cab.

'He was offering me congratulations,' Jack said.

'What for?'

'Because he thinks that you are beautiful and I am lucky.'

'He should have his eyesight tested,' she said. But the incident had revived her spirits and she smiled.

3

For reasons that she could not define, Rosie had been dreading the moment of arrival at the hotel, the moment when Jack had to register her as Mrs Cameron. It was as if, at this point, the lie, the subterfuge, would be made public and manifest. She was still sensitive about their illicit relationship, still guiltily aware that if it became public knowledge she would be branded as a loose woman and that the odium might do harm to her children.

In the event, she need not have concerned herself. Madame Nicoud, the large, full-bosomed, comfortable woman who ran the Hôtel de Varenne, not only greeted Jack as if he were the prodigal son returned but gave Rosie a reassuring smile which held no hint of suspicion or mockery. As Jack registered, Madame Nicoud chattered away to him in French, nodding towards Rosie with obvious approval.

'She says that you are very beautiful,' explained Jack.

Rosie felt the sudden thrust of jealousy, an emotion of which she had little previous experience. Was she being compared to other girls Jack had brought to Paris for a weekend? She put the thought away for later examination and thanked Madame Nicoud.

'It's rather too damp to go out tonight and I expect you are tired, so I've ordered dinner in the suite. Is that all right with you, darling?' said Jack, putting an arm round her shoulders.

'Yes, yes. That's fine,' she stammered.

An asthmatic porter wheezed his way upstairs clutching the luggage with Jack and Rosie following.

'What's a suite?' whispered Rosie.

He smiled. 'A set of rooms. You'll see, darling. Actually, we've got the only suite in the house. It is a sort of honeymoon suite.'

'It's a lovely hotel,' she said, more for something to say than anything else.

'Small but very exclusive,' said Jack. 'It belongs to Madame Nicoud, the lady we saw downstairs. She runs it very well.'

'You've been here before then?'

'Oh, yes. Several times. Never stay anywhere else.'

'And do you always have the – the honeymoon suite?'

He laughed. 'Not always. It is in great demand.'

As the porter fumbled with the key, two ladies emerged from a room opposite. One of them had close-cropped hair and wore a tweed costume with a collar and tie; the other had on a yellow woollen dress and looked so small and blonde and fluffy that she put Rosie in mind of an Easter chick.

'Good evening,' said the taller one politely and gave Rosie a speculative look as she guided her companion towards the stairs.

'They are on their second honeymoon,' Jack whispered. 'Or maybe the third.'

'What?' she asked, puzzled.

'I've seen them here before. They are lovers.'

'Are you pulling my leg?'

'No. Oh, Rosie, what an innocent you are. They are lesbians. You know what a lesbian is, don't you?'

'Of course,' she said stoutly.

'Nothing wrong with that,' he said breezily. 'Wouldn't do for everyone to be the same, would it? Variety is the spice and all that. Makes for the gaiety of nations.'

This is a different world, thought Rosie, and I *am* a bloody innocent. She had heard of men who had affairs with other men and, years ago, she had actually known one, the kindly Mr Softley, who had encouraged her to play the piano; but such people were a rare phenomenon in working-class Tottenham, where they were derided as pansies or queens and driven away by the force of intolerance. And despite all her years of experience working at The Winged Horse, she had never heard of women who slept together, never before heard that strange word *lesbian*. The idea made her shiver a little: she could not imagine any circumstances in which she could love or be loved by another woman, certainly not in that way.

Jack did not allow Rosie to dwell on these thoughts for long. He tipped the waiter, closed the door and, snatching her up in his arms, carried her through to the bedroom and dropped her on to the biggest bed she had ever seen.

'Jack, you idiot!' she cried.

'Oh, God in heaven, Rosie, you are beautiful!' he whispered and began to rain kisses on her lips, her cheeks, her forehead. His tongue teased her ears and she went tense with pleasure.

'The waiter, Jack. You said they would bring dinner here,' she murmured, breaking free for a moment.

'In an hour. I told them, not for an hour.' He kissed her again and as his hand fell on her breast she felt the excitement rising in her flesh, a spark quickening to a flame.

'Wait, Jack,' she urged, 'wait. I don't want to mess up my new costume.'

She stood up and he tried to unfasten her skirt while she slipped off the jacket and her white lace-trimmed blouse. He fumbled badly and she said: 'Let me do it, darling.' She took off the skirt, folded the suit neatly, and then removed her suspender belt and stockings. When she turned back to the bed, Jack was pulling off his shirt.

'My turn now,' she whispered and, surprised by her own boldness, she began to unbuckle his belt.

4

It is like a honeymoon, thought Rosie, or at least what the romantic side of her nature had always imagined a honeymoon to be. She and Jack were forever touching each other, holding hands, sending signals with their eyes, and making love as if there was to be no tomorrow. She was constantly aware of him, her mind and body filled to overflowing with warmth and tenderness. And, to set the seal on it all, Paris, dear Paris, atoning for yesterday's waywardness, blessed the lovers with blue skies and mellow sunshine.

With all the quivering excitement of a child on its first holiday, she drank in the sights and sounds of this new city. Hand in hand, they walked through the narrow streets of whitewashed houses in Montmartre to the Place du Tertre and watched the artists painting Parisian scenes from beneath the shelter of coloured umbrellas.

She lingered by one artist who had on display pictures of the square itself. 'Oh, Jack, these are beautiful!'

'Rubbish, Rosie. They paint them for tourists. The same scene over and over again. Picture-postcard stuff.'

'But I like them,' she protested and opened her purse, a movement which brought the artist to his feet as quickly as if she had pressed a spring.

'Put that away,' said Jack. 'If you want one, you shall have one.'

He took her to a restaurant, where they sat in the open air, and watched in amusement as she ate her way through the bread and butter and the dish of radishes which were placed before them.

'You won't have any room for the lunch if you go on eating that bread.'

'I thought this was the lunch,' she replied.

'Lord, no. That will come in a minute.'

She buttered another chunk of bread and smiled. 'I don't care. This is the best bread and butter I have ever tasted. I could eat it all day.'

There was a note of something almost like envy in his voice as he took her hand. 'I think that is what I love most about you, Rosie, my darling. You are so uncomplicated, such a straightforward and uncomplicated person.'

'And you are not?'

'I wish to God I were.'

She met his eyes, shaken for a moment by his tone. 'Jack,

dear, I've never thought of you as – well – as complicated. You are always smiling, always on top of the world.'

'Laugh, clown, laugh,' he said, with a shrug.

'What is that supposed to mean?'

'A joke, darling. Forget it. Hey, look at that woman over there.'

He directed her attention to the pavement where an old woman was making her way through the midday crowd with an enormous collection of multicoloured balloons which bobbed and weaved over her head, straining at their strings as if they were desperate to be free.

Rosie turned and looked and smiled, but her mind stayed on their conversation. It seemed to her as if Jack had dropped some invisible guard: the easy, happy-go-lucky manner had slipped for a moment to reveal a wistfulness, even a sadness, that puzzled her, and, not for the first time, she thought how little she really knew of this man who was her lover and whom she loved so much.

A woman came to sit at a nearby table with two children, a boy and a girl, who were not much different in terms of age from Van and Eddie, and their appearance sent her thoughts in a different direction. She had confided her secret to Nell, her friend, and arranged for her to move into the house in Napier Avenue for the weekend to keep an eye on the children. With Van and Eddie she had been more circumspect, telling them only that she had to go to Paris on business, a statement that had drawn as much excitement from them as if they had been making the trip themselves. One day, my darlings, she thought, one day I shall bring you here to this wonderful place.

With Mark, it had not been so easy. Although she had never told him about her affair with Jack in so many words, he had guessed the truth of it long ago and, when she announced that she was taking the weekend off to go to Paris, he took it for granted that she was going with her lover. To this he raised no objection, but they were busy with plans to open the new store and he felt that it was wrong for Rosie to spend virtually four days away at such a critical time. In the end, Mr Lightblow who, in a few weeks, had become an influential figure in the business, persuaded Mark that Rosie would be all the better for a break and the matter was settled. Thoughtful as ever, Mr Lightblow had also helped her get a passport and a supply of French currency.

'When do the shops close?' she asked suddenly.

'Oh, not for hours yet,' said Jack. 'Why?'

'I must buy some presents for the children. And for Nell and Mark – and Mr Lightblow.'

'Is that all?' he asked drily. 'Are you sure you haven't forgotten anyone?'

'Jack – I can't go home empty-handed, can I?'

'I suppose not, darling.' He took her hand again and smiled into her eyes. 'I tell you what I suggest. After lunch, we will go back to the hotel for a siesta and then I'll take you to the shops.'

'A siesta? What's that?'

'A sleep. A little snooze. On the Continent a lot of people take a siesta after lunch.'

'I see,' she said, keeping her face straight. 'You mean, we'll go back to the hotel and go to bed.'

'That's the general idea. Any objection?'

'No. But I bet we won't do much sleeping.' And she added, wickedly: 'I've had my clothes off so often since we got here, I wonder if it's worth putting them on.'

'Rosie, darling,' he said, 'you have a thought there. Hang on to it.'

5

By the time Sunday evening arrived, they had tramped the length of the Champs-Elysées, been to Notre-Dame, the Eiffel Tower and the Folies Bergère, sat on the steps of the Sacré Coeur church eating ice-cream, and cruised over the waters of the Seine at the rail of a gaily painted paddle-steamer. In between, they had contrived to make love by night and day, their mutual passion for each other seemingly insatiable, their enjoyment so complete and perfect that Rosie felt as if she were living in a dream.

On that last evening, Jack took her to a little restaurant on the Rue St Augustine where some of the tables were set in alcoves, discreetly screened from the sight of other customers. After the waiter had served another round of coffee and cognac and pulled the curtain, Jack turned and took Rosie in his arms.

'I love you, darling Rosie,' he whispered. 'I adore you. You know that, don't you?'

'Of course, of course.'

'This has been the best weekend of my life.'

'Mine too.'

Releasing her, he took a small blue leather box from his pocket and placed it on the table. 'For you,' he said.

'What is it?'

'Open and see.'

A ring nestled against the blue velvet of the interior, the light glistening on the violet-coloured stone with which it was set. Rosie closed her eyes, robbed of words, overwhelmed with happiness. When she opened them again, Jack was slipping the ring on to the second finger of her right hand. She leaned across and kissed him.

'Oh, Jack, dear, it is so beautiful.'

'A souvenir of the weekend. Something to remember me by,' he said lightly.

'I don't need a ring to remind me of you,' she said gently and even as she spoke she fought down a tiny quiver of disappointment. Had she expected, hoped, that the ring would have more significance? 'But it's lovely – I've never had anything like this,' she added, 'never.'

'It's an amethyst,' he said. 'There's a legend that an amethyst will protect the wearer against drunkenness – did you know that?'

'I hope it works,' she said, smiling. 'This is my second brandy and your third – on top of all that wine!'

'Who's counting?' he said. 'This is a celebration.' He lifted his glass and chimed it against hers. 'Thank you, Rosie, thank you for everything.'

She kissed his cheek in reply and a little loving silence fell between them, as if they had run out of words adequate to express their happiness. Then, for no reason, except perhaps that the wine had relaxed her, a thought came unbidden into her head and tumbled, without pause, on to her tongue.

'Tell me about you, Jack.'

He looked at her in surprise and laughed. 'What is there to tell? You know all that is worth knowing.'

'I don't, darling,' she argued. 'I know that you are Jack Cameron and that you run a tea business. You've told me other bits and pieces but not all that much.' His face told her that she had wandered into forbidden territory and she added hastily: 'It's because I love you, only that. I want to know everything about you. Your family, friends – all that. Everything.'

'For example?' he said, tersely.

Why did she persist? She knew at once that she should have changed the subject, gone on to something else, but some devil of obstinacy drove her on.

'Well,' she said weakly, feeling around for the words. 'Well – I mean – like – well, we see each other – what? – once a week, sometimes not even that. What do you do with the rest of your free time? I mean – you know what I do – I've got the business and a family, they keep my hands full. But what do you do?' She paused and added placatingly: 'I'm not being nosy, darling. It's just – well – that I would like to be able to picture you when we are not together, don't you see? Imagine what you are doing.'

'Oh,' he said, with a cold smile, 'there is no mystery. I spend all my spare time with other women.'

'Oh, Jack,' she cried in distress, 'I didn't mean that.'

'Then what did you mean?'

She was near to tears as she replied: 'What I said. I mean, we're supposed to be in love—'

'Supposed to be?'

'All right. We are in love. And when two people are in love – I mean, truly in love – isn't it natural that they should want to know everything about each other?'

'It may be natural,' he said, 'but it is also fatal.'

'What? I don't understand.' She looked at him blankly.

'Rosie,' he said, more gently, 'why can't you accept what we have? Isn't it enough? Love doesn't give one person freehold rights in another. It doesn't give a right of possession. We have the right to offer only so much as we wish, no more. I have seen relationships, marriages ruined because one partner demanded to know too much about the other. That isn't love – it is tyranny.'

The amethyst winked at her as she twisted the ring on her finger, thinking over his words. Then, lifting her head and looking him in the eyes, she asked: 'Is that why you never got married?'

He met the question squarely. 'I never married, darling, because marriage is a futile attempt to achieve the impossible. It tries to impose permanence on a relationship which, by its very nature, is in a constant state of change. You marry today and in five, ten years, you wake up and find that you are sleeping with someone who has changed out of all recognition. Of course, you have changed also. So each partner is tied, not to the person they married but to someone else. Suppose you don't like the new person you see? How do you escape? By that time you are probably hemmed in with children, debts, possessions. No, it doesn't make sense.'

He leaned over and touched the amethyst with the tip of a finger. 'Love is an intoxication, Rosie. It confuses the brain. When you are in love you are in no fit condition to make decisions, especially if they are going to affect your whole life. But people do it all the time – and with disastrous results.'

That's it, then, Rosie, she thought. You have been well and truly put in your place. She had told herself a dozen times that Jack was not the marrying kind but she had never quite dispelled the hope that she might be wrong. Now, at least, he had nailed down the question once and for all. Aloud, she said: 'If everybody thought like you, the parsons would be out of work. No one would get married.'

'Very few people think alike, Rosie, and even fewer think as I do. The world is full of idiots fighting to get to the altar. So don't worry – the human race will survive.'

'At least you are honest about it,' she said.

'Honest? Honesty?' He laughed. 'I am not sure what that is. It is all relative. What may be honest to me would probably be condemned as the height of immorality by your parsons.'

He took her hands in his and kissed her gently on the lips. 'What it amounts to is this, my darling. I'm as incapable of looking into the future as you are. Who knows how things will turn out? In the mean time, the gods have been very generous and brought us together. Well, I'm not going to argue with higher authority. I am delighted – and properly grateful. So – no more questions, eh? No more debate. Let's just carry out their orders and enjoy each other. What do you say?'

'You could talk the corner off a round table, that is what I say, Jack Cameron.'

'It's the drink,' he said. 'I don't think that damned amethyst is working.'

'Do we have to sit here?' asked Rosie gently.

'No. What do you have in mind?'

'I can think of better ways to enjoy each other,' she said shamelessly. 'Let's go back to the hotel.'

CHAPTER FOURTEEN

1

Back in England and the familiar territory of North London, Rosie had hardly put a foot inside the house in Napier Avenue before she found herself plunged into a sea of troubles. It seemed that as far as she was concerned, at least, fate had an inflexible rule: whatever pleasure it allowed her to enjoy had to be paid for later, in full and with interest.

She learned, first of all, that in her brief absence in Paris, Van had managed to contract conjunctivitis, a mild disease of the eyes, and Dr James, summoned by Nell, had ordered that she be kept in bed in semi-darkness for a day or so. Since Van seemed to be quite well in other respects and since her favourite pursuit of reading was denied her, she had become bored and petulant and was demanding constant attention.

Then again, heavy rain over the weekend had seized upon a flaw in the roof and found its way through the joists and the ceiling of the upper front bedroom. Nell had coped as best she could with buckets and bowls and had persuaded Mr Kipling, the local jobbing builder, to give up his Sunday morning to repair the tiles, but the damage had been done. A bulging stain disfigured the ceiling, the rank smell of dampness pervaded the house and the mattress and bedclothes were still drying out on the line in the garden.

Rosie was not superstitious by nature but in the past she had observed that unexpected events, good or bad, tended to come in threes. Many years before, her mother had sternly maintained that if you met one Hottentot, you were sure to meet two more; if you found a sixpence, you could expect to enjoy two further bits of luck; and one piece of bad news would have two others treading on its heels. She was only mildly surprised, therefore, when Nell announced that a man who claimed to be Rosie's cousin had turned up unannounced on the Saturday evening and asked for a bed for the night.

'A cousin?' asked Rosie, puzzled.

'He said his name was Harry Daines. Reckoned he'd been in Canada.'

'Oh, my God!' breathed Rosie, shivering as she remembered that terrible day when her Uncle Bob had told her that he was going to Canada with his three sons, Harry, Albert and Ron. She had been a child of thirteen at the time, with no known relatives other than her uncle and cousins; and, terrified at the prospect of being alone, she had begged him to take her along. His angry shouted reply still jarred her memory: 'I'm not a pair of bloody braces. I can't hold you up as well as everyone else. I've fixed you a good job. You're an ungrateful little cow!' And so she had gone to The Winged Horse pub, carrying her few possessions in a brown paper bag, to live in and work as a skivvy.

Harry, she remembered, was the oldest of the three boys, and she had never liked him. Like his younger brother, Ron, he had been pressed from the same ugly mould as his father. Only Albert, the middle one of the three, had shown her occasional moments of kindness.

'Did you let him in?' Rosie asked.

'Not bloody likely,' Nell replied. 'I mean, he could have been lying, couldn't he? Is he your cousin?'

'I think so,' said Rosie, still stunned by this echo from the past. 'But I haven't seen him for nearly twenty years.'

'Well, you'll be seeing him again soon. He's coming back this evening.'

'Did he say what he wanted?'

'No. And I didn't ask. If you want the honest truth, I didn't take to him. He may be your cousin——'

'Don't worry, Nell. If he's anything like he was – if he hasn't changed – I shan't take to him either.' Rosie paused and sighed, thinking that, after Paris, she had come back to earth with a vengeance. 'I'm sorry, Nell. You've had a rotten weekend. I turn my back for a couple of days and all this happens.'

'It's all in a day's work,' Nell said cheerfully.

'I'm ever so grateful.'

'Forget it! Listen, I've been thinking. You are going to have your hands full for the next few days, with Van and the business and everything. Would you like me to stay for a while?'

'Would you? Could you?' Rosie asked eagerly, clutching at this lifeline.

'Why not? To tell you the truth, I like the company. I get fed up listening to my own voice back in those two rooms. My old mum was a miserable old bitch but at least she was there.' Nell was another member of the legion of war widows and she had been completely alone since the death of her mother some eighteen months before. A massive, cheerful woman, her father had been a bricklayer and it was said, though not to her face, that instead of conceiving her in the normal way he had fashioned her out of a load of spare bricks. She had been fired by Mr Goldie for what he saw as impertinence and she regarded as simply standing up for herself, and since then she had scratched a living as a charwoman. More recently she had helped Rosie at the warehouse on those occasions when there had been an urgent need for more hands.

'That's settled, then,' said Rosie. 'Now I must go up and see Van.'

'She's in the back room,' said Nell. 'I moved her in there until the front room dries out.'

Eddie, kind, gentle Eddie, was sitting with Van, reading aloud from *Little Women*. Van, clearly determined to make the most of her illness, hugged Rosie dramatically, as if she had been away for a year: Eddie, more reticent, allowed himself to be embraced, but his eyes told his mother that he was happy to have her home.

'Did you bring us a present?' Van demanded.

'Oh,' said Rosie, 'is that all you can think of?'

'You promised to bring us something,' said Van.

'And suppose I said that I forgot? Suppose I said that them that ask don't get?'

'Oh, Mum!' Van protested.

'All right.' Rosie opened her bag and brought out the gifts – a wristwatch for Eddie, a slender gold bracelet for Van. Attached to the bracelet was a tiny gold charm, a model of the Eiffel Tower.

'A watch!' Even Eddie could not contain his pleasure. 'My first watch!' He strapped it on his wrist and announced proudly that it was seven-thirty p.m.

'Is it real gold, Mum?' asked Van, twirling the bracelet on her wrist.

'Does it matter?' asked Rosie.

'No. It's lovely – beautiful – terrific. But if anyone asks me—'

'If anyone asks, you can tell them that it is nine-carat gold.'

'Gold! Real gold!' cried Van. 'I feel like a princess.'

'Mum,' said Eddie suddenly, 'I'm just going out. I won't be long.'

'Wait!' said Rosie. 'Where are you going?'

'Back in ten minutes,' he called, already halfway down the stairs. A moment later the front door slammed behind him.

'Well, that's a fine thing,' Rosie said with a wry smile. 'I just get in and he goes out.'

'I expect he's gone to show Pearl his new watch,' said Van smugly.

'Pearl? Who is Pearl?'

'Pearl Relton. She lives next door but one. She is Eddie's big romance. He is deeply and passionately in love with her.'

'How long has this been going on?'

'He met her the week we moved here. I don't know what he sees in her. She is terribly conceited – carries on as if she was a film star or something.' Van paused and shrugged. 'Still, I expect he'll get over it.'

My God, thought Rosie, they are growing up so fast! Too fast. Eddie, at thirteen, already hanging his hat up to a girl! It was probably just a childish crush but that didn't alter the fact that he was now in his teens and, in a few years, would be a young man. She felt a sudden chill of fear: boys of Eddie's age needed a man around, a father or a father-figure. Would he feel able to turn to her later on, to tell her his problems? And would she be adequate to the task?

Then there was Van. Still a child at eleven but the childishness was slipping away with each month that passed. There was no doubt that she would be a beautiful young woman and that, in turn, would bring its own problems.

Was she being selfish, putting her own happiness before their needs? Did she owe it to the children to marry some good, decent, reliable man who could help her see them through the difficult growing-up years? And then the thought of Jack Cameron made her heart beat faster and her flesh glow with warmth and she knew with certainty that she could never bring herself to give him up.

Shaking her head, she turned to Van. 'All right, young lady. Let me have a look at you.'

'It's conjunctivitis,' Van said, almost as if she were proud of her ailment.

'I know,' Rosie said. The girl's eyes, usually so full of eager brightness, were red-rimmed and without lustre.

'Will I go blind?' asked Van in a matter-of-fact way.

'What are you saying!' cried Rosie, deeply shocked. 'Blindness isn't a joking matter!'

'I wasn't joking,' said Van, now well into one of her roles. 'Only I read this story, you see. It was called "Hope for Tomorrow", and it was all about this girl who went blind but she was so brave and courageous and everything. If it did happen to me, I would be like her. You wouldn't have to worry. You would be proud of me.'

Rosie, near to tears, hugged the girl. 'You fool, you little fool. You frighten me when you talk like that. And anyway I'm proud of you now, don't you know that?'

A heavy rat-a-tat-tat from the knocker on the front door interrupted them, and Rosie, moving downstairs, braced herself for an unwelcome meeting with her long-lost cousin.

2

The man at the door looked like a complete stranger: had they met in the street she would have passed him by without any flicker of recognition. He had been fifteen when she had last seen him, but now the thin rangy boy had swollen into a big, paunchy, coarse-faced man: dark calculating eyes gleamed at her, yellowing teeth showed briefly below a clipped moustache as he summoned up a smile.

'Rosie?'

'Yes,' she said, uncertainly.

'Harry. Harry Daines. You remember me?' He thrust out a hand and she shook it reluctantly.

'Yes. Of course.' And she added limply: 'I wouldn't have recognised you. You've changed.'

'I would have known you anywhere,' he said. 'You look great – just great.' There was no trace of the former cockney in his speech; the accent reminded Rosie of the way she had heard American soldiers speak during the war.

Still at a loss as to what to say or do, she dredged up a question. 'How did you know where to find me?'

'Oh, that wasn't so hard. I asked at The Winged Horse and the lady there sent me to Shakespeare Street. I got this address from one of your old neighbours.' He made a sound in his throat, rather like the rattle of old bones in a bag, which she took to be a chuckle.

'I see,' she said mechanically. She felt uncomfortable in the presence of this figure from the past. He was an unwelcome intrusion, someone whom she had disliked then and disliked on sight now. Was it her imagination or could she detect the smell of rottenness about him, like the dank odour of decay in an old neglected house?

'I just had to look you up, Rosie, find out how you were. Blood's thicker than water, eh?' he drawled.

The thought filled her with revulsion and, finding her wits at last, she said sharply: 'Is it? That's not what you or your father said when you pushed off to Canada and left me to fend for myself!'

He looked pained by this assault. 'Gee, Rosie, you can't hold that against me. I had no say in the matter, I was just a kid.'

'So was I. I was thirteen.'

'It was a long time ago, Rosie.'

'Yes,' she said bitterly. 'A long time. And none of you bothered to write in all those years. Not even a card to ask whether I was alive or dead! Well, now you've come back. What do you want?'

Once again the hurt came into his eyes, like a dog who has been kicked. 'I told you. I just came to look you up and say hello for old times' sake. That's all. But if I'm not welcome—'

He moved as if to turn away and she checked him with a sigh. 'I suppose you had better come in. I'll make a cup of tea.' He turned back quickly, smiling, and she added bluntly: 'But that's all. There's no bed here for you.'

'OK, OK. I've got lodgings,' he answered.

'Just so long as we understand each other,' she said, standing aside for him to pass. As he moved to the kitchen she whispered to Nell who had been standing in the passage: 'I don't want the kids to meet him, Nell. When Eddie comes back, keep him out of the way.'

'Right,' said Nell. 'And if you want me, just shout.'

'Don't worry. I've got his measure,' answered Rosie grimly.

3

'Ah,' said Harry Daines, as Rosie put a cup of tea and a wedge of Nell's home-made fruitcake in front of him. 'A cup of good old English tea. They don't make it like we do back in Canada. It's coffee most of the time out there.' He took an appreciative sip and nodded. 'Great!'

She was not in the mood for small-talk and she said directly: 'Why have you come back?'

'Missed the old country,' he answered. 'Never did settle in Canada. All right for some, I guess, but I always reckoned on coming home.'

'What about the others? Your father and your two brothers?' She could not bring herself to put a name to her Uncle Bob, any more than she could address this stranger who sat before her as Harry.

'Dad died. Three years back. Caught pneumonia and never got over it. Albert joined the Canadian army in the early days of the war – he was killed in France in nineteen-seventeen.'

For her uncle she felt nothing, no joy or regret at his passing, only a neutral acceptance of the fact, but Albert's death did register and she thought of him with sadness. He had been the best of the bunch, the only one who had sensed her unhappiness in those early days and done his best to cheer her. Why did the good ones always have to go first?

'And your other brother?' Again, she could not speak the name.

'Don't ask me about Ron!' he said disdainfully. 'He's in Vancouver making a fortune from real estate.'

'Real estate?'

'Land. Buying and selling land and property. He struck lucky. Married a Canadian girl whose father has money coming out of his ears. And, of course, he doesn't want to know about me. As far as he's concerned, I don't exist!'

There was a whine of self-pity in his voice that stirred Rosie's contempt. 'Why would he behave like that?' she asked.

'Like I said, he's riding high. I'm not good enough for him. When I went to him for help, he showed me the door. My own brother!'

'What sort of help?'

'Well, I'll be frank with you. I had a bit of bad luck, you see, Rosie. I had a steady job in Hamilton, driving a delivery truck for a wholesale grocer. One day I stopped off for a bite to eat and someone stole the truck and the load. The police said it was a put-up job and accused me. Accused me of stealing my own truck! Of course, they couldn't prove anything, but I was fired. And a thing like that hangs round your neck – I couldn't find other work. That's the gospel truth.'

'And how did you raise the money to pay your fare home?'

'My dear brother,' he sneered. 'Ron. He wouldn't give me money to get started again, but he wanted to see the back of me so he bought me a one-way ticket. Steerage,' he added bitterly.

Rosie nodded, wondering about the truth of the story and what had been left out. It made her the more determined to have nothing further to do with this man who was certainly a liar and probably a crook.

'I hear you are doing well, Rosie,' he said.

'And who told you that?' she asked sharply.

'Everybody I asked. As soon as I mentioned your name they all said how well you were doing. Shops and bazaars, they said. You are in business with some yid, is that right?'

'What did you say?' she asked coldly.

'Your partner. He's a Jew-boy.' He saw the look in her eyes and added hastily: 'Mind you, I've nothing against them. The Jews, I mean. Can't blame them for being sharp businessmen. Where there are Jews you'll find money, eh?'

'You go down the East End you'll find plenty of poor Jews,' she said.

'Of course. Like I said, I've nothing against them.' He paused and crumbed a piece of the cake in his fingers. 'Rosie, I don't suppose you—'

'No!' she said sharply.

'I was going to ask—'

'You were going to ask for either money or a job. The answer in both cases is no.'

'I'm a good driver. I can drive a truck.'

'I said no. We already have a driver,' she said, and rose from the table. 'Now, I think you had better go!'

'You haven't given me much of a welcome!' he said harshly.

'What did you expect – banners in the street and the band of the Grenadier Guards?'

'I expected more than a cup of tea and a slice of bloody cake!'

'I'm sorry you've been disappointed!' she said. 'But I owe you nothing – and that is precisely what you will get here. Nothing!'

'We took you in when your mother died! You didn't have two farthings to rub together. We took you in and gave you a good home.' The fawning manner had gone now and he snarled at her, the viciousness etched on his reddening face.

'You are a liar! It was your mother who took me in – Aunt May. She killed herself drudging for you lot. And when she died, it wasn't a home any more – not for me. I was the unpaid skivvy. You never lifted a finger for me.'

'You are an ungrateful bitch!' he shouted.

'That's what your father said,' she answered. 'He was a pig of a man and you take after him.'

He struck out then, suddenly and viciously, a stinging backhanded blow across the mouth that made her cry out with pain. 'That's what you should have got years ago, that and more!' he said between clenched teeth.

The door opened at that moment and Nell stood there, holding in one large hand the sturdy copper-stick which they used on wash-days to stir the clothes as they boiled up in the copper. She hurled herself at Harry Daines, the stick held high, and Rosie screamed: 'No, Nell, no!'

The stick halted within an inch of his skull and he backed off quickly. Nell followed up, prodding him until he stood cowering before her, his back pressed against the dresser.

'Say the word, Rosie,' said Nell, 'and I'll flatten the bastard!'

'Let him go, Nell,' said Rosie wearily. 'He's not worth it.' Her bottom lip had cracked open and she dabbed at the blood with a handkerchief.

'You shouldn't let him get away with it,' said Nell, pressing the stick into the softness of the man's guts.

Gasping and sweating, he looked at her fearfully. 'I didn't mean it. I didn't mean to hurt her. I lost my head.'

'You'll lose more than that if I have my way, you rotten tripehound!' Nell said. Lowering the stick, she brought her knee up sharply and buried it in his crotch. The breath seemed to expel itself from his body in one great rush of painful sound and, bent double, he rocked from side to side in agony.

'That was just a taster,' Nell said. 'There's more where that came from. Now – out! Out!'

Stumbling across the kitchen, one hand clutched between his legs, he gave Nell a last look, half-bewildered, half-malevolent, his eyes watering, and staggered out. She followed and propelled him to the front door and out into the street.

'If I see your ugly mug around here again,' she warned, 'I'll skin you alive and feed your rotten carcass to the pigs. Though I doubt if they would eat it.'

4

It seemed that there was to be no respite for Rosie that evening, for, half an hour after the unceremonious departure of Harry Daines, Mark arrived, looking grim.

'God!' he said, staring at Rosie's swollen lip and bruised cheek. 'Did you get into a fight with a Frenchman?'

'It's my fault, Mr Moss,' said Nell quickly. 'I pushed open the door a bit sharpish, just as Rosie was coming through the other way, and caught her a nasty whack on the face. That's me – my second name is Clumsy.'

This unlikely explanation had been concocted between Rosie and Nell to avoid any need to mention the earlier incident, and Mark, who clearly had other matters on his mind, accepted it without question.

'Can I have a word, Rosie?' he asked. He glanced at Nell and added: 'On business.'

'Come through to the front room,' she answered, with a hint of pride. The front room was the first parlour she had ever possessed: it had been furnished with a sofa and armchairs, a polished table, a large hearthrug, and a sideboard. A new clock in a wooden case occupied the centre of the mantelshelf flanked by a china shepherd and shepherdess, a vase of freshly picked flowers stood on the table, and a new wireless set held pride of place on the sideboard.

'Nice, Rosie,' said Mark approvingly, seeing all this for the first time. 'You've done it well.'

'It will be all right when it's paid for,' she said, with a smile. 'I bought the furniture on the never-never. I'm paying it off at a pound a week.' The thought of the picture Jack had bought her came into mind and she decided then and there that she would hang it on the wall above the fireplace.

'I'm glad you are back, Rosie,' said Mark, settling in an armchair. 'I've got a spot of trouble. You'll have to take over for a few days while I sort it out.'

'What sort of trouble?'

'It's Bennie. You remember him, my brother?' She nodded and he went on: 'I don't suppose you've seen the newspapers?'

'I haven't had a chance.'

'Well, he has been arrested.'

'Oh, my God!' she said. 'What for?'

'It's complicated. You remember he left home, disappeared? It turns out he went to Moscow, to attend a special school or course for communists. He was there for about a month. When he came back he went to work for the Communist Party as some kind of industrial organiser. Well, last week the police raided the communist headquarters at King Street, in Covent Garden, and arrested twelve of the leading members. Bennie was one of them.'

Rosie stared at Mark, trying to take in what he had said. 'But they can't arrest a man just for going to Moscow, can they?' she asked.

'No, no. You don't understand. He is being charged with incitement to mutiny. The police reckon that they found documents and letters which prove that the communists were trying to organise strikes in the armed forces – trying to persuade soldiers and sailors to disobey orders.'

'Why would they want to do that?'

'A good question. And the answer? The answer is I don't know. But you've heard Bennie talk. He believes a revolution is just around the corner. So, when the balloon goes up, he wants the troops to be on his side. Yes, I know it is a crazy notion. It is also against the law, which is more serious.'

'What can you do?'

'Get him a good lawyer for one thing. The best I can afford.'

'If I can help . . .,' she began.

'No. This is a family business. Whatever he's done or not done, Bennie is my brother. You can help best by looking after the business.'

He produced papers and brought her up to date with the stock position and the progress of the new store at Edgware, which was due to open in two weeks. As he talked, she found herself studying this man whose friendship and trust had transformed her life, thinking how little he had changed in the past two years. His enthusiasm was undimmed, his appetite for work as prodigious as ever: he led from the front, throwing himself into the breach whenever a crisis loomed up, inspiring their growing band of workers by energy and example.

He spent little on his own needs or pleasures; indeed, he never seemed to think of himself, and much of what he earned went to support his mother and sister. Six months ago he had moved them from the tenement in Flower and Dean Street into a decent house in Foulden Road, Stoke Newington. Now, without question or hesitation, he was preparing to help a brother from whom, over the years, he had received nothing but bitter criticism.

Yes, she thought, you could go a long way and search for a month of Sundays to find a better friend. She loved Jack Cameron with a passion that both disturbed and delighted her, but, in many ways, her feelings for Mark had deeper roots. Was it, perhaps, because sex had never been allowed to colour their relationship?

He handed over the last of the documents and rose to go. As he reached the door, he paused and turned, shifting awkwardly from one foot to the other. She was surprised to see a tinge of red in the cheeks of his square, rugged face.

'Oh, there's one other thing,' he said, trying, without success, to bring the words out casually. 'I almost forgot. I've taken on a new girl for the Edgware store. She will be assistant to Tom Conway, the manager.'

'Does she know the business?'

'Well, actually, I stole her from Jack Cohen,' he said, with an impish smile. 'She has been in charge, more or less, of his Bargain Centre at Sutton. Oh, yes, she knows the score.'

'Has Tom Conway met her?'

'I took her to see him on Saturday. The girl will be an asset – those were his words. She made a good impression.'

'Then that's all right,' said Rosie. 'I'll run the rule over her myself tomorrow. What's her name?'

'Irene Green.' The flush on his face was unmistakable now but he looked at her defiantly as if daring her to probe further.

Irene Green, she thought. So that's the way the wind blows – you've found yourself a girl! She kept the thought silent and said instead: 'How is Conway making out?'

Mark made a small sucking noise and shook his head. 'I am not sure. He's a nice enough fellow but – I don't know – I have the feeling that there is a weakness there. He lets things get on top of him. We shall have to watch out.'

'You think we made a mistake in picking him?'

He shrugged. 'Too late to change now. Let's wait and see.'

'All right.' She kissed him lightly on the cheek. 'Thanks for letting me take a break, Mark.'

'I'm sorry, I should have asked,' he said. 'How was Paris?'

'Marvellous!' she replied, her eyes shining. 'It was – it was – oh, I can't explain, Mark – just wonderful.'

'That's a good answer,' he said, smiling. 'What you can't say I can read in your face. But don't get too carried away, will you – we have a business to run. You know the saying – love, like butter, is better with bread.'

'Mark, you don't have to remind me about the business,' she said, half-reproachfully.

He put a hand on her arm. 'I know. I was joking. To see you happy is better than a banquet, believe me. All the same, to speak frankly, I worry about you and this man of yours. I don't want to see you hurt, Rosie. Excuse me for saying this. I speak from the heart, sincerely. Just tell me it is none of my business and I will shut my mouth.'

'No,' she said. 'Between us there is nothing that can't be said. But don't worry about me, Mark, I know what I am doing.'

'Good. So now the subject is closed,' he said, pressing her arm. 'As my mother would say – enjoy, enjoy!'

'How is your mother?' she asked.

'Well, she is not happy. She worries about Bennie – who can blame her? I worry myself.'

'Your sister, Debbie, she is with her?'

'Debbie?' Mark sighed. 'Oh, yes. She is around. But there is another cause for concern.'

'What do you mean?'

'It is hard to say. At one time, she hardly left the house. Now she is out two or three evenings a week. But she won't say where she goes. Ask her a question and she just says that she has been with friends. I think maybe she is in love. Sometimes I see the same springtime look on her face as I see on yours.'

'Am I so obvious?' Rosie asked, smiling.

'I always know when you've been seeing Jack Cameron. You come back shining like a chandelier.'

'I'll try and control myself in future,' Rosie said. And at the front door, she added: 'Good luck with Bennie. I hope it all works out.'

'A little luck would be welcome,' he said solemnly. 'For luck, I will leave the door on the latch all night.'

CHAPTER FIFTEEN

1

For the next ten days Rosie had little time to think of anything but the problems of the new store. At odd, unexpected moments a picture of Jack floated into her mind and her heart ached with a longing to be with him again, but there was no time, no time. She knew that with the opening of this first Carmo store they were launched on their greatest gamble: there were times when she shivered with fear at the thought of the risks they were taking. If the project failed they could be wiped out.

In line with Mr Lightblow's policy, they had bought the freehold of the property for four thousand pounds. All this money had been borrowed, with fifteen hundred coming from the bank as a cash payment and the remaining two thousand five hundred in the form of a mortgage from the Woolwich Equitable Building Society. Fitting out the store had called for another hundred and twenty pounds, and stocking the shelves and counters with the wide range of goods needed to meet customer demand had absorbed more cash. To many wholesalers, Carmo was an unknown entity and some, though not all, had either refused credit or insisted on an initial deposit. It had taken all Mr Lightblow's skill, ingenuity and persuasive powers to raise the necessary money and, even so, they faced large interest payments on these loans.

'We are in for £4992,' said Mr Lightblow in his precise way, as they walked round the store, checking the stock and fitments.

'Oh, my God!' said Rosie breathlessly.

'Don't worry,' he said lightly.

'Don't worry! With that lot hanging over our heads!'

'You'll make it work, Rosie. I have the greatest confidence in you and Mark.'

'I'm glad someone has!' said Rosie fervently.

Tom Conway, the manager, came out of the stock room at this moment, followed by a girl in a blue wrap-around overall.

'Ah, Mrs Carr,' he said, 'I'd like you to meet Irene – Irene Green. She has just joined the team.'

'Hello,' said Rosie, holding out a hand. 'Welcome to the firm.'

'Thank you,' said the girl, taking the hand in a firm, purposeful grip. She was a good three inches taller than Rosie, handsome rather than pretty, with dark bobbed hair and bright expressive eyes. Rosie could see at once why Miss Green had caught Mark's interest for, apart from her looks, there was about her an air of composure, of quiet confidence, as of someone who was in command of herself and the job. Mr Lightblow had told Rosie that the girl was twenty-five but she carried herself with the authority of someone who was ten years older.

'How is everything going?' Rosie asked.

'Oh, the usual last-minute hold-ups and snags, but nothing we can't handle,' Irene said. She had a deep musical voice which added to the overall impression of self-reliance.

She moved on, and Conway began at once to catalogue some of the problems they faced, going into them in excessive detail. Listening to him, Rosie had to control a rising feeling of irritation. He was a man of about thirty with a ruggedly handsome face which invited trust: it had been this and his experience as an assistant manager at the local branch of Sainsbury's, the big firm of food retailers, which had prompted Mark and Rosie to hire him. Closer acquaintance had planted seeds of doubt in their minds. The trustworthy look concealed an uncertainty which was the last thing they needed at this crucial time: he had already shown himself to be a man for whom a decision represented a major crisis and whose response to a problem was panic. With this man in charge of the new venture Rosie began to feel that they were flying into the future on one wing.

As he embroidered his list of complaints, they moved around the store, arriving eventually at the room which had been set aside for the use of the staff. The tangy smell of fresh paint floated on the air, a gleaming new desk was backed against the window, a young girl sat at a table nearby pecking at a typewriter.

'What's this?' Rosie asked sharply.

'My office, Mrs Carr,' said Conway. 'I felt that I needed a place near the shop floor, so to speak.' There was a touch of embarrassment in his voice.

Rosie turned to Mr Lightblow. 'Did you authorise this?'

'No,' he replied. 'It is a surprise to me.'

She turned back to Conway. 'What about the staff? This was supposed to be their rest room. Where are they supposed to take their breaks?'

'There is a room in the basement, Mrs Carr. It is quite adequate.'

'Basement!' Her voice rose in anger. 'Basement! You mean the cellar, don't you? The staff are supposed to muck it in the cellar while you lord it up here! Office indeed! Your place is out there, with the customers, not sitting on your arse behind a bloody desk!'

'There is a great deal of paperwork, Mrs Carr,' he stammered.

'In this store,' she said grimly, 'the customers come first, the staff second, and your bloody paperwork comes a long way behind!' She knew for certain at this moment that their doubts had been justified. With Tom Conway as manager, they were on a collision course for disaster, and on the heels of this thought came the decision. With some surprise, she heard herself say:

'How much are we paying you, Mr Conway?'

'I don't understand—'

'It's quite simple. How much are we paying you?'

Alarm showed in his face. 'Of course, if you wish, I can turn this into a staff room . . .,' he began.

'Too late for that now,' she said. 'You've missed the bus. What are his wages, Jim?'

'Three pounds a week,' said Mr Lightblow.

'Have you got twelve pounds on you?' she asked.

'I think so.' He brought out a wallet and counted the notes into her hand. Conway watched, his full lips trembling.

'There you are, Mr Conway,' Rosie said. 'One month's money. You are fired. Nothing personal. You are a decent fellow but I don't think you are quite what we were looking for. Sorry.'

'You can't do this!' he protested.

'I'm doing it!' she said 'I've done it. Just leave quietly. If you want a reference for your next job, Mr Lightblow will give you one.'

The rattle of the typewriter had stopped, the girl was looking from Rosie to Conway with wide eyes. Conway's lips moved but the only sound that came out was an indistinct murmur: his face seemed to crumble, his eyes grew moist, then, stumbling slightly, he took a trilby hat and a brown raincoat from a hook on the door and went out. At the door he turned to give Rosie a look that was half-bewildered, half-frightened, a look that flooded her with guilt.

She sat down abruptly, her hands trembling as she rested them on the surface of the new desk. In the past, she had known what it was like to fear the power of an employer, she had known the terror that came with the loss of a job: now, in some mysterious way, the power had passed to her. It was as if she had crossed a great divide and the idea filled her with disquiet. She was appalled by this revelation of a ruthlessness in her character which she had never before recognised or known to exist, and her immediate impulse was to hurry after Tom Conway and call him back.

Instead, she turned to the girl and, making a deliberate effort to keep her voice calm, said: 'What's your name?'

'Elsie Lewis, ma'am.'

'All right, Elsie. Go and find Miss Green and tell her I want a word with her. Then go out and get yourself a cup of tea.'

'Very good, ma'am,' said the girl.

The word 'ma'am' echoed in Rosie's mind, reviving memories of the countless times she herself had been forced to use it, and she said gently: 'You don't have to call me "ma'am", Elsie. "Mrs Carr" will do – right?'

'Yes, ma'am – Mrs Carr.' The girl scuttled out of the door, as if escaping from the presence of a demon.

Rosie sighed and looked at Mr Lightblow. 'All right. Don't stand there like an empty glass waiting to be filled. You think I've done the wrong thing, don't you?'

'Your decision does present us with certain problems. We haven't got a manager – and we open in four days.'

'I don't know what got into me,' said Rosie. 'It just built up inside. The way he nattered on about the problems. And this room was the last straw. If we want to attract good staff and keep them, we have to pay them well and treat them well.'

'You don't have to convince me,' said Mr Lightblow with a smile.

'Better no manager than a bad one,' Rosie said. 'That man would have been a disaster.'

'You don't have to convince me,' he said again.

'So you think I did the right thing?' she asked, willing him to give the reassurance she craved.

'Let me put it this way,' he said cheerfully. 'I couldn't have done it, I wouldn't have done it. But yes, on the whole, I think your instinct was right and that you acted wisely. He would have had to go sooner or later – better that it should be sooner.'

There was a tap at the door and Irene Green appeared. 'You wanted to speak to me, Mrs Carr?'

'Yes,' Rosie said. 'Come in.' The girl moved towards the desk and she continued: 'Mr Conway has left us. I know you've had experience of running a store. Do you think you could take over as Acting Manager until I've had a chance to talk things over with Mr Moss?'

The face remained impassive but the eyes brightened as Irene replied: 'I think so, Mrs Carr.'

'Good,' said Rosie. 'Then that's agreed. Of course, we'll be around to give you all the help you need. Mr Moss will be back tomorrow.'

'Thank you, Mrs Carr. Now, if you will excuse me, I have to

check a delivery of tinned fruit.' She moved calmly to the door and went out.

'Well,' Rosie said, as the door closed, 'she didn't seem too surprised.'

'She's been doing most of the work anyway,' said Mr Lightblow.

'Now you tell me,' said Rosie.

'People are your department,' he said. 'I just look after the books.'

She stood up. 'That's the first time I've ever fired anyone. It isn't a very nice feeling.'

'We are all learning fast, Rosie,' he said enigmatically.

Rosie stayed on at the store, doing what she could to help, but by mid-afternoon she began to feel like one of the boxes of tinned milk which Mark had bought in at a bargain price and which were stamped with the legend: SURPLUS TO REQUIRE-MENTS. Released from the flabby hand of Mr Conway, Irene Green slipped easily into her new role, dealing with the problems that had baffled him with an easy, impressive authority. Rosie looked for a flaw but in vain: the calm self-assurance remained undimmed.

At midday, for instance, the four new sales assistants came in for a sort of rehearsal and, as Rosie watched Irene put them through their paces, she realised that this girl was a natural manager. One of the new intake was a man of about forty-five with years of experience on the fresh food side of retailing and his first reaction was one of barely concealed resentment at finding this young woman in charge. Irene seemed to sense this immediately and, within the hour, by a combination of flattery and firmness, she had won him over.

She seemed aware that she was under Rosie's scrutiny for, from time to time, she looked up and their eyes met. For the most part these silent exchanges were straightforward enough but there were moments when Rosie felt as if the girl was quietly taking her measure.

Eventually she put on her hat and coat and took Irene aside. 'You don't need me here. I'll only get under your feet. I've got plenty of work I can get on with, so I'll leave you to it.'

'Very well, Mrs Carr.'

'Four days to go,' said Rosie. 'It's getting close.'

'We'll be ready,' Irene said.

'Yes.' Rosie spoke briskly, feeling a need to assert her authority. 'I want everything to be right on the day. No slip-ups.'

She took one last look round as she reached the door and could not resist a small surge of pride at the neat, well-stocked shelves, the gleaming scales and meat-slicing machine, the new cash-desk, the assistants in their white overalls embroidered with the title CARMO.

She remembered the time – it seemed so long ago now – when Mark had been attacked and robbed and it looked as if the fledgling business was about to founder. She had gambled everything then, including Gran's funeral money, on Carmo Tea and, by some miracle, the gamble had come off. The stakes were much higher now, too high to think of with any comfort.

They had done everything they could think of to ensure success, they had planned and worked to the point of exhaustion. Now all they could hope for was a little of the luck that had carried them through the earlier crisis.

As she moved into the street, Rosie crossed two fingers on each hand, willing the luck to come.

2

Was it luck that, instead of a long journey on two or three buses, she should find Tiny Christmas and the van parked outside the store and that he should offer to run her back to Tottenham? Was it luck that decided him to depart from his usual route and go via Wood Green and so pass the Wood Green Empire, the old music-hall where the billboards announced that Nellie Wallace, the 'Essence of Eccentricity', and Randolph Sutton were appearing?

Mark was to assert later that luck played no part, that it was a flash of sheer inspiration from Rosie that did the trick. Equally, Rosie would not allow the element of luck to be ruled out, insisting that if Tiny had not been there and if she had gone by bus, the idea would never have entered her head in the first place. And, as she pointed out, there was the little business of the defective elastic. How could that be explained except in terms of luck?

Whatever the truth of the matter, Rosie, bubbling over with excitement at the boldness of the idea which had formed in her mind, burst into the house and announced to Nell and the children that they were going to the first performance at the Empire that evening. There was some initial doubt as to whether she should take Van but the conjunctivitis had more or less cleared up and Rosie decided that the boost to the girl's morale would more than compensate for any risk.

'What's on, Mum? Who's on the bill?' she asked excitedly.

'You'll see,' Rosie said and bundled them out of the house, promising that they could have a fish-and-chip supper on the way home.

It was some time since she had visited the Empire and, on the last occasion, she had sat in the gallery looking down on the vast, glittering stage and on the incredible Gracie Fields singing her heart out in a show called *Mr Tower of London*. Tonight she decided to indulge the family and bought four tickets for the fauteuils, in the centre and only five rows back from the footlights.

Glancing round she could not help but notice that the old Empire was beginning to show signs of age: the seats were shabby and worn, the gold paint on the cherubs above the stage had all but flaked away, giving them a forlorn, deserted look. A sharp, pervasive scent like that of oranges hung around the auditorium, which was only half-filled. It is true, then, she thought sadly, it is true what the papers say: the moving pictures and the wireless are killing the music-hall.

But as soon as the house darkened and the curtains parted it became clear that the performers had not heard these pessimistic reports or, if they had, were determined to prove them much exaggerated. Within minutes they had formed a partnership with the audience, who clearly regarded them not as lofty artistes but as friends, the sort of people that they could invite to their homes, with whom they could share a pot of tea.

Wandini the magician and his plump girl assistant, who seemed to have been poured into her gold tights, were greeted with coarse but not hostile ribaldry. The Arturo Troupe, a team of seven slightly middle-aged acrobats, were given similar treatment: there were groans and catcalls when the lady member of the group twice failed to vault to the top of the human pyramid formed by her partners and a rousing ironic cheer rang out when, at the third attempt, she made an unsteady landing. Molly Noonan, a soprano singer who appeared clad in emerald green, hushed them to silence with her winsome beauty and the ballads, sad and boisterous, of her native land. Van slipped her hand into Rosie's as the girl finished with the song 'Mother Macree' and, looking round, Rosie saw that she was weeping.

These and other acts were but a prelude to the two artistes heading the bill and whom most people had paid to see. Randolph Sutton, youthful-looking and dapper, tantalised them with his dry humour and delighted them with his sentimental songs: when he began to sing 'On Mother Kelly's Doorstep' the audience roared its approval and joined him in a noisy rendering of the chorus. And Nellie Wallace, outrageous, ugly, with her high-button boots, tartan skirt and worn grey jacket topped by a preposterously feathered Glengarry hat, rounded it all off with raucous sketches and suggestive songs which carried just the right amount of shock to make the audience cheer her daring and go home happy.

It had all been rather like a bloody good party, thought Rosie as they edged their way towards the street: a bit of aggravation, a lot of noise and laughter and some meaty, down-to-earth entertainment. And it had done her some good: for an hour or so she had forgotten the business and almost forgotten her longing to see Jack.

Van, deeply impressed, assumed her dramatic voice and announced: 'That's what I'm going to do when I'm older. Go on the stage.'

'Go on the stage? You!' said Eddie scornfully.

'I shall be an actress,' Van insisted. 'On the stage and in films. Like Mary Pickford.'

Yes, you might well do that, Rosie thought wryly. You spend half your time acting now. She smiled and put her arm round the girl. 'Right,' she said briskly. 'I want you to go home with Nell. On the way, you can get fish-and-chips at Huggins's.'

'What about you?'

'I've got to see a man about a dog. I shan't be long. Put my fish in the oven till I get back.' She reached into her purse and gave Nell a shilling. 'There you are, Nell. Four twopenny bits of cod and four pennyworth of chips.'

She watched them move off and then made her way towards the narrow alley that led to the stage door. As she did so, she saw a man moving away, a man who seemed so familiar that she ran up to him crying out in surprise and delight: 'Jack! Jack!'

The man, a stranger, turned a puzzled face towards her and her heart seemed to fall like a stone. 'Sorry,' she mumbled foolishly. 'I mistook you for someone else.'

'It's all right, lady,' he smiled. 'No bones broken.'

She stopped in the semi-darkness of the entrance to the alley and leaned against the rough brick wall, overcome by a sudden surge of loneliness and longing. Oh, Jack, Jack, where are you, what are you doing, why haven't you been in touch with me? It seemed to her at this moment that their relationship was without hope. She knew that the brief, beautiful interludes of being together were not enough for her, that she could not much longer bear the agony of the long absences, the silences, the separations that stretched between them like some vast grassless plain. If he loved her, if he truly loved her, would he not feel the same? How could he be satisfied with the little they had now when it was possible to have so much more?

In a burst of anger and frustration she banged the wall with a clenched fist and, as she did so, she felt something snap and give at her waist. The anger dissolved as quickly as it had appeared and her sense of the ridiculous surfaced in a smile. The elastic in her knickers had broken and she could already feel them sliding over her thighs!

'This is what you get for feeling sorry for yourself, my girl,' she murmured, and made a tentative step forward. The offending underwear, part of the batch of clothes she bought for the Paris trip, responded by slithering to her knees.

Only one thing for it, she thought, and glanced round to see if anyone was about. Then she did a quick shimmy, shaking the knickers to her ankles, stepped clear and snatched them up.

3

'I'd like to see Miss Nellie Wallace, please.'

The elderly stage-door keeper, without raising his head from the *Daily Sketch*, answered her with a grunt. 'No visitors between the shows.'

If she needed further proof that luck was on her side it was provided in the next second, when she realised that she had seen the old man before, in the saloon bar of The Winged Horse. Another flash of memory brought forth his name and she said boldly: 'Oh, come on, Mr Cornforth. You are not going to turn away an old friend, are you?'

He looked up in surprise, the steel-rimmed glasses sliding to the tip of his nose. 'Rosie! Rosie Carr! What are you doing here?' She was pleased to hear a real welcome in his voice.

She waited as Wandini's assistant, wearing a mackintosh over her stage costume and carrying a large jug of beer, pushed past her and headed for the narrow stairs. Rosie saw, with a sense of shock, that the plump girl she had seen on stage was, in reality, a woman well into her middle years.

'That's Mrs Wandini,' said the stage-door keeper. 'Well, that's the stage name. It's really Wainwright.'

'I saw her in the show,' Rosie said. 'She looked a lot younger.'

'It's the lights. She won't see forty-five again and her old man has turned fifty. Poor devils – they don't get a lot of bookings these days. They've just about had it, I reckon.' He clucked his gums as a token of sympathy and continued more briskly: 'You want to see Miss Wallace, you said. What for?'

'A matter of business,' replied Rosie.

'I see.' He dabbed at a grey moustache, the ends of which were stained yellow by nicotine, and studied her for a moment. Then, realising that he would get no more from her, he said: 'Pity you gave up playing at the pub. We miss you.'

'I miss it myself,' said Rosie. 'But I've got other things to do now.' She took out a half-crown and put it down before him. 'Next time you are in The Winged Horse, have a couple on me, Mr Cornforth.'

'Well, I'm much obliged, I'm sure, Rosie,' he said. He spat on the coin and slipped it into his pocket. 'Miss Wallace, eh? On a matter of business. It is more than my life is worth but I'll see what I can do, for old time's sake.'

She followed him along a musty corridor and up a spiral iron stairway. The sad signs of neglect were more evident here than in the theatre itself; tattered posters, proclaiming former glories, were peeling from the cracked plastered walls as though in shame, the air swam with the reek of damp and decay.

'Ah, yes,' said Mr Cornforth, as though he had reached her thoughts, 'I can remember when this place was a palace, a real palace. Now look at it. Nobody cares any more, that's the be-all and end-all of it.'

He tapped at the first door in the upper corridor. 'Miss Wallace?'

'What is it?' Rosie's heart sank as she heard the note of irritation in the familiar voice.

'Visitor to see you.' He opened the door quickly, pushed Rosie inside and left her. She stood there, listening to his footsteps hurrying towards the stairway, wishing that she had never embarked on this foolish enterprise.

Her eyes took in the room, the like of which she had never seen before. A huge mirror, framed with lights, reflected her image, pots of cream and tubes of make-up stood in military order on the long fitted dressing-table. A chipped sink with stained brass taps occupied one corner and on a rail along one wall hung the costumes, a good dozen of them, including the tartan skirt and the Glengarry hat.

Then a curtain swished across a small alcove and Nellie Wallace, the great Nellie Wallace, appeared, buttoning on a long gown. She still wore her stage make-up but, once again, the footlights had proved to be deceptive for, in real life, she looked younger and certainly less ugly.

'Look,' she said sharply. 'I don't see visitors between shows. You'll have to come back later.' The broad accent that she adopted for her act had all but disappeared.

'It won't take a moment, Miss Wallace,' Rosie stammered.

'That's what they all say. Now, off you go and let me have a few minutes' rest.'

Suddenly, Rosie's nose twitched and she felt an uncontroll-able urge to sneeze. She thrust a hand into a pocket and exploded into her handkerchief; at least, she thought it was a handkerchief until she heard Miss Wallace's shrill laugh and, looking down, she saw that she was holding the errant knickers.

'Oh, my God,' she murmured. Thrusting them back into her pocket, she added weakly: 'The elastic snapped. I had to take them off.'

'Is that why you've come? To borrow a pair of drawers?' The other woman's face twitched with humour.

'No, no. It's a matter of business.'

The ice had been broken now and Miss Wallace motioned her to a chair. 'Sit down and tell me about it, girl. But don't take all night, I've got another show to do.'

Gaining confidence, Rosie told her of the plan for the new shop. 'We've had Bazaars before – we've still got some – but this is our first shop. We've sunk nearly all our money into it. We want to start with a bang, make people sit up and take notice. Would you – would you be free next Monday at about ten o'clock to do a sort of official opening?' She added hastily: 'We would pay you, of course.'

'How much?' asked Miss Wallace promptly.

'I don't know. I've never done anything like this before. Whatever is customary. I mean – would, say, five pounds and expenses be right?'

'Hmph. You are a mug at this game. Twenty-five pounds would be nearer the mark, girl.'

The figure rocked Rosie for a moment. Then she thought, why not? We are in for almost five thousand pounds already, a few more quid won't make all that much difference. And if she draws the crowds, it will be worth it.

'All right. That will be fine. Twenty-five pounds.'

'And expenses.'

'And expenses.'

'Good,' Miss Wallace said. 'I'll take ten pounds now and the balance when I've done the job.'

Blushing, Rosie fumbled in her purse. 'I haven't got ten pounds on me. I can manage – let me see – I can manage five pounds.'

'I see.' Miss Wallace gave her a hard, level look. 'Well, I'll take you on trust. Now, give me the details.'

4

Twenty minutes later, Rosie rang the bell at the door of Mr Milton's darkened shop. She waited impatiently until she heard the old printer's shuffling footsteps and heard him call: 'Who is it?'

'Rosie Carr, Mr Milton.'

'Wait a minute.' He fumbled with bolts, the door opened and he stood there, still wearing an ink-stained apron. 'What is it now?'

'I've got an urgent job, Mr Milton.'

'With you everything is urgent!' he grumbled. But since the day when he had printed the first batch of Carmo Tea bags, Rosie had become too substantial a customer to turn away and he opened the door wider, inviting her to enter.

'I want some posters,' she said. 'And I must have them by Saturday at the latest.'

Their relationship had now reached the point where he could use her first name and, with a sigh, he said: 'Rosie, Rosie. Always in a sweaty haste. When will you realise that time is too precious to spend on the run? It is necessary to stop sometimes, to pause, to give the mind a chance to extend itself.'

'You are a fine one to talk, Mr Milton. I notice that you are still working.'

'It's a little private project,' he replied uneasily. Was it her imagination or had a faint blush appeared on his thin pale cheeks?

'Anyway, this is what I want.' She took a pencil and wrote a rough outline.

MISS NELLIE WALLACE
Famous star of Music Hall
will open the new
CARMO CUT-PRICE STORE
at 84 High Road, Edgware
at 10 a.m. on Monday, 18th October
EVERYONE INVITED
Special offer for One Week Only.
A quarter pound of our popular
Carmo Tea to every customer
spending 2/- or more.

Mr Milton studied the draft carefully but impassively. 'You will leave the lay-out to me?'

'Of course.'

'How many?'

'Say two hundred and fifty. By Saturday.'

'By Saturday,' he said gravely. As she moved to the door, he added: 'Wait. You are on the run again.'

'My supper is in the oven, and it will be ruined if I don't hurry.'

'I have something for you, Rosie. I won't keep you a minute.'
He disappeared into the back room and came back with a slim
volume. 'Here. Take this. And try to find time to read it.'

'That's lovely. Thank you.' She glanced at the title: *The Moral
Discourses of Epictetus. Edited by Alfred J. Milton.*

'You wrote this!' she said in awe.

'No, no. I simply edited the text. Epictetus was a philosopher,
Rosie, a very wise man.'

'He had a funny name.'

'It didn't seem so to him. He was a Greek, you see. And a
remarkable person. He began as a slave and ended as one of the
great teachers. Take a little time, Rosie, and study his words.'

'I promise,' she said. 'Now, I must fly.'

'What are you chasing, Rosie – a fortune?'

The words set her back for a moment and then, shaking her
head, she said: 'No, Mr Milton. I honestly don't think I want a
fortune. I wouldn't know what to do with it. All I want – all I
want for myself and my kids – is to have a decent life. I want
them to have a good education, I want there to be enough bread
and meat on the table, I don't want to be forever worrying
where the next penny is coming from.'

'A reasonable ambition,' he said. 'And other people's
children?'

Again the question surprised her. 'I want the same for them,
of course.'

'Good,' he said. 'You already have a fortune, Rosie. Your
children. Better than money in the bank. They hold the future
in their hands. Bring them up to love peace and respect wisdom,
Rosie.'

5

It has to be said that Mr Milton's words did not stay with Rosie
for long. She was too excited by the success of her evening's
work: her imagination danced ahead, filling her mind with

pictures of the crowds that would be drawn to the new store, of Nellie Wallace cutting a tape at the door to the cheers of the multitude. And this was only the beginning! After Edgware they would turn their existing Bazaars into proper shops, build new and bigger stores. Her earlier fears forgotten for the moment, she felt as if she wanted to burst into song, to dance a jig on the pavement.

It was this state of euphoria, plus the appearance of a taxi, a rare event in that area, that brought on another attack of impulse. The idea that she would go and see Jack flashed into her head and, acting on it without thought, she waved the taxi down and directed the driver to take her to Number Seventeen Bedford Square.

Her excitement did not last. She had scarcely settled back in the seat when the doubts began to assail her. Would he be there? And if he were, would he be happy to see her? Would he regard her unexpected arrival as an intrusion?

Another voice argued against these doubts. After all, he had told her more than once, and especially in Paris, that he loved her. If this were true – and what reason had she to think otherwise? – he would be longing to see her. She pictured him opening the door, the surprise on his face turning to delight.

Still the uncertainty remained and she toyed with the idea of telling the cabby to turn round and take her home. But the need to see him, just to see him, was too strong in her and, in the end, she worked out a plan. She would tell Jack that she could not stay, that was impossible: she had called simply to invite him to the opening of the new store on Monday. She would have one quick drink with him, they would kiss lightly, not too passionately, and she would depart. Perhaps they would arrange another evening, even another weekend, when they could be together.

In this resolve, she asked the cabby to wait and went upstairs to Jack's apartment. Relieved to see a sliver of light showing under the door, she rang the bell and waited, her heart drumming with anticipation. The door opened after a few moments, not on Jack, but on a total stranger, a young man, whose face opened in a leer of pleasure as he surveyed her. From within the apartment she heard the sound of male voices, of laughter that had a drunken edge to it.

'What can I do for you, beautiful?' said the young man. The voice was thick and uncertain and he swayed slightly as he spoke.

Appalled now by her own stupidity in coming without notice she drew back. 'I wanted – I came to see Mr Cameron. But it doesn't matter. I'll – I'll call another time,' she said weakly.

He lurched forward and took her arm. 'No. Don't go, beautiful. He's here. Come in.'

'No.' She tried to shake herself free but he held her fast. 'It isn't important.'

He lurched nearer, breathing a mixture of tobacco and whisky fumes into her face. 'Wait,' he said. 'You are – you are – you must be – Debbie!' He repeated the name in triumph. 'Debbie! His friend Debbie. Right? Am I right?'

It was as if he had punched her in the stomach. She stared at him for a moment, too stunned to speak, then, pulling loose, she ran for the stairs. Halfway down the first flight she heard Jack call her name.

'Rosie! Rosie!'

She hurried on, but he came clattering down after her, still calling. Her hand was on the handle of the front door, she had it half-open, when he caught up with her. He pressed the door shut and put his back against it.

'Rosie, darling. Why didn't you tell me you were coming?'

'Who is Debbie, Jack?' She felt as if she were standing outside herself, listening like an eavesdropper to her own voice.

'Debbie?'

'The man who answered the door – your friend – he called me Debbie.'

'He is drunk, Rosie. I'm having a little party – friends from the Royal Flying Corps.' He giggled. 'We're all a little bit tight.'

'I'll leave you to it, then,' she said evenly.

He drew her forward and kissed her lips. She held herself rigid, giving nothing; he tried to part her lips with his tongue, his hand slid over her thigh, and she felt him harden against her skirt. Absurdly, then she remembered that her knickers were in her handbag, that she was naked under her slip, and this thought, together with his insistent touch, brought a quiver of response from her flesh.

'No!' Angered by her own weakness, she forced herself free with such force that his head crashed against the door, although he seemed not to notice.

'Come upstairs, Rosie,' he urged.

'With that lot?' she said contemptuously.

'Don't worry about them.' He advanced upon her again. 'I've missed you, darling.'

'Have you? I haven't noticed that you made any effort to get in touch.'

'I was going to. Truly.' He tried to kiss her but she turned her head. 'I want you, Rosie, I want you.'

'You'll have to want then, won't you?' she said sharply. 'I must go.'

'Why did you come in the first place?' he asked sulkily.

'If you don't know, I'm not going to tell you. Let me pass, please.'

He seized her wrist and pulled her forward so that their faces were almost touching. 'Don't play games with me, Rosie!'

'Jack,' she said, 'you are drunk. Don't do anything you will regret later.'

His face took on the look of a small disappointed boy. He released her wrist and stepped aside. 'All right,' he said, spitting out the words. 'Bloody well go! And don't bother to come back!'

'Don't concern yourself, Jack. I won't,' she said quietly.

She forced herself to walk to the waiting taxi, holding her head up, sealing her lips tight to keep back the tears. As she gave the cabby instructions to take her to Napier Avenue, Tottenham, Jack came running from the house and rapped on the window. She was tempted to ignore him but, in the end, she wound the window down.

'Yes?' she asked coolly.

'Rosie,' he stammered, 'I'm sorry. You are right – I am drunk. It was the whisky talking. Will you come tomorrow evening? I shall be here alone. Please. Will you come?'

She studied him for a moment, thinking that, in many ways, he was a child; and with the thought there came a sudden surge of tenderness. Even so, she would not commit herself.

'I'll think about it,' she said.

6

'Where did you get to?' asked Nell. 'I was worried.'

'I had to see someone on business,' Rosie answered shortly.

'Your fish and chips are in the oven. But they won't be much cop – they are all dried up.'

'I don't want them. Where are the children?'

'In bed, of course.'

'That's where I'll go, I think.'

'Rosie – is anything wrong?' Nell asked.

'No. What should be wrong?'

'You have a face as long as a wet weekend.'

'I'm tired, that's all. I'll see you in the morning.'

'The water is hot. Would you like to have a bath? That might perk you up.'

'Yes. A good idea. I'll leave you to lock up and put the lights out. Goodnight, Nell.'

'Goodnight, Rosie. And thanks for the outing. It was a lovely show. Randolph Sutton has always been one of my favourites.'

Randolph Sutton, Nellie Wallace, the show, thought Rosie, as she dragged herself to the bathroom. All that seemed to have happened long ago, in some distant happy past. She remembered her earlier excitement and pleasure and shook her head, as if to dislodge the memory. None of it was important now.

The warm water soothed her flesh but it could do nothing for her mind, in which one name beat a constant tattoo. Debbie. Debbie. Debbie.

Why should Jack's friend have called her by that name? Was

it just a drunken mistake, a mix-up of names, or had he genuinely thought that she was someone else, a girl called Debbie?

She could think of only one Debbie, Mark's sister. It was unlikely, almost impossible, that Jack should know her: she could not recall that they had ever met. Why should they have done? They lived in different worlds. But the thought would not go away and she sat up suddenly, the water splashing around her, as her mind fastened like a trap on the memory of one morning at the warehouse when Jack had brought back the nightdress she had left in his rooms.

Yes, of course! Debbie had turned up shortly after Jack's arrival! Rosie had introduced them and, more than that, she had persuaded Jack to give the girl a lift back home. Had that been the beginning of something, had they been meeting since then?

What was it Mark had told her only a few days before? There had been a change in Debbie, he had said, she was going out two or three evenings each week and would not say where. Oh, dear God, she thought, it all fits, it is all beginning to come together.

And yet, remembering the sweet and gentle girl, with her dark beauty, Rosie could not believe that she would launch herself into an affair with a man like Jack. On the other hand, why not, why not? Hadn't she done exactly that herself? Nor was she alone. Jack, with his handsome looks and buccaneering charm, must have turned the hearts of a regiment of women.

She lay back, crushed by a feeling of utter desolation. It was over, then, it was over. She would see Jack no more. If he wanted he could have Debbie but there was no way that he could have her also. She had been prepared to take Jack on his own terms but there were limits beyond which pride would not let her go.

But why didn't she hate him now, why didn't she explode with anger and jealousy? Why did she feel only this emptiness, this terrifying emptiness, as if all purpose had gone from her life? In her anguish, she cried his name aloud and Nell, passing the door, stopped to ask in an anxious tone: 'Rosie, are you all right?'

'Yes, Nell. I'm fine,' she lied.

As she listened to Nell's receding footsteps, her eye fell on the amethyst ring that Jack had bought her in Paris. It had been on her finger day and night since he had placed it there. The memory of Paris came flooding back to her and in her head she heard the echo of his voice, murmuring words of love.

The tears came then, splashing down her cheeks to fall on to her breasts.

CHAPTER SIXTEEN

1

By morning, after an almost sleepless and wholly restless night, Rosie's thoughts, like a wayward compass, had swung in another direction. Unable to face the possibility of life without Jack, she told herself now that she had been wrong to jump to conclusions, to place such importance on a name. In all probability, the drunken friend had got it all wrong. And, after all, Jack had always been honest with her, he had never made any promises. The doubts would not go but she tucked them away into a corner of her mind and built herself a small, frail platform of hope.

When she came down to the kitchen to get breakfast she found that Nell had beaten her to it. The table was set, the smell of frying bacon hung in the air, and the children were already in their places. Moreover, they had a guest. Tiny Christmas sat between Eddie and Van, happily engaged with a huge plateful of bacon, eggs, tomato and fried bread.

He lumbered awkwardly to his feet as Rosie entered and Nell said quickly: 'Tiny has come to give you a lift to Edgware. The idiot didn't have any breakfast, so I've given him some. I hope you don't mind?'

'Of course not.'

'That bloody sister of his thinks a man can keep going on dripping toast,' Nell said scornfully.

'You are more than welcome, Tiny,' Rosie said.

'Thanks, Rosie,' he muttered and, as he resumed his seat, he threw a grateful glance in Nell's direction.

'You shouldn't be doing all this, Nell,' Rosie protested.

'Rubbish. I'm not here to sit on my arse, am I?' said the big woman briskly. She gave Rosie a keen look. 'Did you have a good night? Sleep well?'

'Yes. No complaints,' Rosie answered, avoiding Nell's eyes. The thought of Jack was there, like an ache in her flesh, and she wondered wearily how she would get through the long hours that divided morning from evening.

'Sit down and I'll get your breakfast,' Nell ordered.

'I'm – I'm not hungry, Nell. A cup of tea will do.'

'You didn't eat supper last night,' said Nell firmly. 'You must get something inside you. Sit down.' She looked accusingly at Van and added: 'Van – don't bolt your food. It won't run away.'

Eddie pushed his chair back and stood up. He looked like a young adult in his long grey flannels and the blue blazer with the Grammar School crest on the breast pocket. 'I must go,' he said, running a speculative hand over his chin.

'He has started shaving,' said Van.

'I have to!' he answered, blushing. 'I can't go around with whiskers, can I?'

'Whiskers! Is that what you call that fluff on your chin?' she taunted. 'I bet you are shaving just to impress Pearl Relton.'

'Shut up, Van!' he shouted.

'It's true!' she said. 'I've seen you together, all lovey-dovey.'

'If you don't shut up . . .,' he threatened.

'That's enough!' Rosie heard herself scream. 'Enough! Enough! Shut up the pair of you and get off to school!' Then, feeling the astonished silence and seeing the shock on their faces, she added weakly: 'I can't stand your bickering. I've got a headache.'

They went meekly out and Tiny, embarrassed, went also, muttering his thanks and adding that he needed to check the engine of the van. When he had left, Nell said quietly: 'Rosie – whatever it is that is worrying you, there is no need to take it out on the kids.'

Rosie nodded wearily. 'I know. I'm sorry. It was their yelling – it went through me.'

Nell put bacon and an egg before her, but she pushed it away.

'No, Nell, please. I couldn't.' She got up from the table quickly, feeling the nausea retch in her stomach.

'You are overdoing it, girl,' Nell said. 'Stay at home and I'll get the doctor.'

'I don't need a doctor.'

'You need someone or something. What is it, love? Are you having trouble with your bloke?'

'I must go,' Rosie said. 'I shall be late back. Don't wait up.'

2

Ken Colson came hurrying towards her as she left the house. 'Rosie, I'm glad I caught you. Could I have a quick word?'

She forced a pale smile. 'Of course. What is it, Ken?'

It was now some three months since she had been accepted into membership of the local Labour Party and she had grown to know and like this courteous, softly spoken man. He had an earthiness about him, a natural dignity and a plain commonsense way of speaking to which she could relate easily and she suspected that this was not unconnected with his occupation. Together with a brother, he ran a small garden centre on a plot of land near Downhills Park, raising and selling plants, shrubs and vegetables.

To Rosie, gardening was like a foreign country and Ken had given up evenings and the odd Sunday morning to help her lick the overgrown garden at Napier Avenue into shape. She had seen then that he had the same firm but gentle way with plants as with people.

'Have you heard about Goldie?' he asked eagerly.

'No.'

'He has resigned from the Council! Resigned!' The jubilation rang in his voice like a bell.

'Resigned! What for?'

'They are putting it out that he has resigned on health grounds. But it's a big cover-up, Rosie. The word is that he was pulled in by the police for kerb-crawling. He was caught trying to pick up young girls near the Manor House pub. The big guns at the Town Hall went into action and it was agreed to hush it up if he gave up his seat on the Council.'

'Poor devil,' she said. She felt a sudden rush of pity for the man, the old enemy, who had been brought down by his own weakness.

'Don't waste your sympathy on him, Rosie,' said Ken tersely. 'The man is a bloody hypocrite! Preaching and praying against sin by day and chasing after young skirt by night! It's not the first time either. I heard a rumour that he has been too free with his hands with the girls up at his laundry—'

A brief, painful remembrance of her scene with Goldie over Dora Parks flashed across Rosie's mind and she cut in sharply. 'Rumour is a bad messenger, Ken, it is best ignored. As for Goldie, he probably deserves all that he has coming to him. All the same, you have to wonder what drives a man like that to do such things.'

'I suppose so,' he admitted. 'Anyway, forget Goldie. The point is that there will be a by-election for his seat in the next few weeks. You have to stand, Rosie.'

'Oh, Ken, I don't think I could do it now.'

'But you must, Rosie,' he insisted. 'You must. We are banking on you. Look, I'll call round this evening and we'll talk over the campaign.'

'No,' she said quickly. 'Not tonight. I – I'm busy.' Tonight, she thought, tonight is for Jack.

'All right. How about Sunday morning? I've got some cuttings for the garden – I'll bring them over.'

'Sunday morning,' she said.

'Councillor Rosie Carr,' he said, smiling. 'It has a very nice ring to it – what do you say?'

'I told you once before that you shouldn't count your chickens before they come out of their shells,' she said.

3

When she arrived at the Edgware store, she found Mark and Irene Green working together, putting price-labels on a range of canned foods. She heard them laughing and talking like lovers, their heads together, and she felt a wholly unreasonable stab of jealousy. What right had other people to be happy?

Mark turned to greet her and checked in mock horror, throwing up his hands. 'Rosie – you look like death warmed over! What happened?'

'I had a bad night. A bit of toothache,' she lied and, changing the subject quickly, she drew him aside and asked: 'What's the news of Bennie?'

'Bennie!' he said. 'You tell me a cure for stubbornness and I'll tell you about our Bennie. He is out on bail, which is something at least. But will he have a lawyer? The answer is no, a hundred times no. That crazy brother of mine declares that he will defend himself, would you believe it? It's true. He says that he will use the courtroom as a platform from which he, the great orator, will expose the evils of capitalism, imperialism, militarism and half a dozen other isms I can't remember. Bennie, I tell him, for this they will give you ten years. And what is his reply? It will be for a good cause – this is his reply.'

'Is there nothing you can do?'

'Oh, yes,' he said scornfully. 'There is something. I could treat my dear brother like a treasure and bury him underground with loving care.'

'How is your mother taking it?' Rosie asked, then added the name that still jangled in her head. 'And Debbie?' She tensed, waiting for his reply.

'More trouble,' he said, shaking his head. 'I challenged her last night and she confessed. She is meeting this goy—' He checked hastily. 'Excuse the expression, Rosie. I mean a non-Jew, a gentile. She tells me also that she is in love with him.

For myself, I don't mind. She is over twenty-one, she must live her own life. But if Mother heard of this, it would break her heart. The last straw. First Bennie, then Debbie.'

Oh, my God, thought Rosie, feeling her heart turn to stone. It is true, it is true. And then the anger flared, a tense inner anger, that made her curse the stupidity that had led her into this morass. She knew then that there could be no waiting for the evening, that she had to see Jack at once. There would be no peace until she heard the truth from his own lips.

'Are you sure you are all right, Rosie?'

She saw that he was staring at her, his eyes wide with concern, and she said quickly: 'Yes. I'll get back to the warehouse, I think. You seem to have things well under control here.' She was surprised at the calmness in her voice.

'I had a bit of a shock when I heard that you had fired Conway,' he said. 'But you did the right thing. That girl Irene has more gumption in her little finger than he had in his entire body.'

'Yes,' said Rosie, 'she seems to know what she is doing.' She added: 'I did something else last night. I hope you approve.' She told him of the deal with Nellie Wallace and of the posters Mr Milton was printing. Mark's face broadened in a smile.

'Rosie,' he said enthusiastically, 'Rosie, you are a genius!' This is a stroke of pure genius! Nellie Wallace! She will stop the traffic. People will be lining up round the block!'

'We ought to put the posters up on Sunday morning,' she said. 'And I'll let the press know.' As an afterthought, she told him about Mr Goldie's fall from grace and of the possibility that she might contest the by-election. 'Would you mind?' she asked.

'It's not for me to mind, Rosie,' he said. 'This is a decision for you. But let me make two points. First, you will make a good councillor. We need people like you to come forward. Second, to take the selfish view, it won't hurt our business to have a director who is also a councillor, a leading person in the community.'

'I'm not sure whether I will do it yet,' she said. 'And if I do stand, I may not get elected.'

'You will do it,' he said confidently. 'And you will win by a landslide. Everybody respects and loves you, Rosie.'

Oh no, you are wrong there, she thought. Not everybody.

4

'I'm afraid Mr Cameron is not here, Mrs Carr,' said the clerk respectfully.

'Have you any idea where he is?' asked Rosie.

'He is probably at home.'

'I see.' She had not been to the office for some time and there was a deserted look about the place that puzzled her. The pictures of tea-plantations had been stripped from the walls and, apart from the desk and chair being used by the solitary remaining clerk, the furniture was stacked in neat piles near the door.

'What's happened?' she said. 'Are you moving?'

'Yes,' said the clerk. 'I thought you would have heard. There was an item about it in the financial pages of *The Times* this morning.' He picked up a folded newspaper from the desk and handed it to her. A small paragraph had been ringed in red ink.

Cameron and Son, of Mincing Lane, tea importers and blenders, which was founded in 1827, has been acquired by Dominic and Porter. We understand that the latter firm will henceforth trade under the name of Dominic, Porter and Cameron.

'I don't understand,' said Rosie. 'What does it mean?'

The clerk shrugged. 'I don't know, Mrs Carr. Mr Cameron simply told us that the firm was to be merged with Dominic and Porter. They are one of the biggest companies in the business.'

'What about you and the other clerks?'

He made a wry face. 'I'm the lucky one. Mr Cameron paid the others off last week. I have to clear up the odds and ends here, and on Monday I start with the new firm. I'm not looking forward to it exactly,' he added confidentially. 'Mr Cameron was a good boss. A bit too free and easy, some might say, but I enjoyed working here. The new place won't seem the same, won't have the same atmosphere. Still, beggars can't be choosers, as they say.'

'He told you last week?'

'Yes. Last Friday.'

She shook her head, scarcely able to believe what she was hearing. All this must have been in Jack's mind while they were in Paris and he had said not a word.

'Is Mr Cameron moving to the new firm?'

'I don't know, Mrs Carr. He did not say. But I imagine that you will get your supplies without interruption. You are a valued customer now, you know.' He smiled. 'I was here that first morning you came. We were playing desk-cricket as I remember. Much has changed since then. Judging by the size of your orders, your business has made remarkable progress.'

'Yes. Thank you.' She wished the clerk luck and went downstairs, where she found Mr Waterlow on duty at the front entrance.

'You found a bit of a change up there, eh, Rosie?' he said, lifting his top-hat in greeting.

'I'll say,' she said. 'I never even knew it was happening. Did you know about it?'

'It's been on the cards for some time,' he replied. 'In my job, you can't help picking up the odd trifle of news. And people have been saying for some time that Mr Cameron was heading for trouble, that the business was going downhill. Well, you can't be surprised, can you? He is a happy-go-lucky sort of chap and he spends money as if there is going to be no tomorrow. I liked him, mind you. A decent, generous sort of chap.'

'Are you telling me that he is broke, that he has gone bust?'

'Well, of course, I don't know all the details,' said Mr Waterlow carefully, 'but I think that statement is not too far off the mark.'

'Would you do me a favour?' she asked suddenly. 'Would you get me a taxi?'

'No sooner said than done,' he said.

The thought occurred to her that she was making a habit of

riding in taxis and spending a small fortune on them but she dismissed it quickly to concentrate her mind on this new and dramatic development in her relationship with Jack. With Debbie forgotten, for the moment at least, Rosie felt a sort of guilt, as if she had let him down, failed him at a time when he most needed support. She thought of Paris and of the times before Paris, searching her mind for clues that she might have picked up: there had been that brief moment in the restaurant when she had detected an undercurrent of sadness under his bantering manner and, later, their conversation about marriage. Had he been trying to tell her then that marriage was out of the question, not because of some strange principle, but because he was ruined financially?

You fool, Jack, you fool, she thought. Why didn't you tell me?

5

Rain was falling from a threatening sky as she arrived in Bedford Square and the gutters were already awash with muddy water. It took Rosie only a few moments to pay off the cab, but even so her hair and clothes were half-drenched by the time she had run to the shelter of the doorway.

Once again, as she hurried up the stairs, she felt the pinch of doubt. Had she done the right thing in coming? Would he be in? Should she have waited until the evening?

He opened the door almost immediately after her ring and her heart quickened with joy. Her first impulse was to throw herself into his arms but there was a stiffness in his manner that held her back.

'Rosie, this is a surprise!' He stood facing her as if uncertain what to do.

'Are you going to keep me standing here?' she asked, smiling.

'No. Sorry. Come in.' He stood aside for her to enter, making no attempt to kiss or embrace her. 'Oh, you are wet. Let me get a towel,' he said. There was an awkwardness about him that puzzled her and the crazy switchback of her emotions took another downward turn.

As she dabbed carefully at her hair, he said: 'What brings you here?' It was as if he were talking to a stranger.

'I was passing—' she began and then rejected the lie. 'As a matter of fact, I have just come from your office.'

'Ah.' He nodded. 'Would you like some coffee – tea?'

'Damn coffee!' she said sharply, tossing the towel on to a chair. 'Jack, why didn't you say something? Why the hell didn't you tell me?'

'There was no point.'

'I might have been able to help.'

'Nobody could have helped. It has gone beyond that.'

'I don't understand. We went to Paris. You spent money like water. And all the time this – this thing was hanging over you.'

'Paris was a sort of last fling, Rosie.' He smiled for the first time and added: 'And it was worth every penny.'

'Is it true? Are you broke, Jack?'

'Not quite. I shall come out with two or three thousand pounds. Enough to keep me in booze for a few months.'

'Jack, don't joke. You know it makes no difference to me, you know that, don't you?'

'Yes, I know.' He went to her then and gave her a light kiss. 'You are a good 'un, Rosie.' He moved away at once as if wary of closer contact and added quickly, lightly: 'Sorry about last night. I'd been drinking. It was a farewell party.'

'Farewell?'

'To Cameron and Son. My business career.' He turned away, rubbed some condensation from the window with a clenched fist, and stood staring down at the wet street.

She watched him, longing to cross the chill distance between them but overcome by a feeling of hopelessness. After a moment, she said: 'What will you do now?' His only answer was to lift his shoulders in a shrug and the forlorn gesture twisted her heart. 'Jack, for God's sake, I love you. Don't shut me out!' More gently she added: 'All right. Not now. I understand. I'll come this evening, like you said.'

'No!' The word came out like a bullet as he turned back to her, then his tone softened as he added weakly: 'I – I was going to send you a telegram telling you not to come.'

Their eyes locked across the room. She nodded and heard herself say: 'I see.'

'I am going away.'

Again she said: 'I see.'

'Some friends of mine are running a flying-circus in America. I'm going to join them. I'm a damn sight better at flying than I am at selling tea.'

There was a long silence and then she heard herself say: 'So. This is the finish. It's all over.' She added bitterly: 'All that talk in Paris about love, about how much you loved me. That was a lie, was it?'

'No, Rosie, no.' He came to her and tried to take her hands but she turned angrily away. 'I loved you then, Rosie, and I love you now. But I'm – oh, I don't know – I don't think that I am capable of your kind of love. That's true of most men, we cannot sustain love as women do. We haven't the depth of feeling or, if we have, it isn't durable. You take love seriously – we don't. That's true of me, at least. We would not last together, you and I.' He smiled ruefully: 'I'm the original playboy of the Western world, you are one of the world's workers. I'd drive you crazy in a year.'

'And Debbie?' she said savagely, swinging round. 'What about Debbie?'

She had expected to shake him but he took the attack in his stride. 'Ah, Debbie. What about her?'

'Have you been carrying on with her? Have you?'

'Carrying on? If by that you mean have I been seeing her, the answer is yes.'

'Sleeping with her?'

'As often as possible.'

She hit him then with all the force of her pent-up feelings, her open hand stinging his face, and spat out the word: 'Bastard! Bastard!' She would have struck again but he seized her wrist and looked into her angry eyes with a sad, half-mocking smile.

'That's not fair, Rosie darling.'

'Fair!' she shouted.

'I never gave you any pledges, did I?'

'You said you loved me!'

'So? Does that make it exclusive – does loving someone mean that you must shut out everyone else?'

'Do you love her?'

'I suppose I do. Not in quite the same way as I love you, but, yes – I do. I don't suppose you can understand that.'

'No, I can't.'

'Rosie, I love women, I love the company of women. I told you once, I could no more tie myself to one woman than I could harness myself to a coal-wagon and pull it through the streets.'

'And what about Debbie? Never mind me, never mind my feelings. What about her feelings? She is in love with you, don't you know that?'

He sighed. 'I told her what I told you. But she is like all women, they hear but they won't listen. Instead of enjoying love, they turn it into an obsession. If a man tells a woman that he loves her but adds that he believes in neither marriage nor any other permanent arrangement she doesn't believe him. She simply smiles her secret smile, convinced that with her it will all be different. And when she fails to change the man, what does she do? She blames him, hurls abuse at his head and accuses the poor devil of breaking her heart! It isn't really fair, Rosie. I may be a bastard as you said, but I don't make a habit of lying.'

'You didn't tell me about Debbie,' she said. 'That was a sort of lie.'

'Why should I have told you? I have never given you the right to select my friends or to order my time.'

'All these fine words,' she said quietly. 'They don't really mean anything, do they? The truth is – you wanted me, and Debbie too, I suppose, for one thing and one thing only. Bed. All the talk of love was rubbish, so much rubbish.'

'No,' he said, 'that's where you are wrong. Some men can pick a woman up in a bar or on the street and go to bed with her that same night. An act of mechanical sex, a business transaction, no exchange of feeling. For me, that is impossible. I have no taste for one-night stands. Truly. I need to know and like the woman, to feel affection at least, if not love. When I said I loved you, Rosie, it was the truth.' He paused, smiled, and took her hands in his. 'As for sex, it wasn't so bad, was it? You are not complaining, are you?'

She made no attempt to break free. Shaking her head, she whispered: 'You are a bastard, Jack Cameron. God help any woman who falls in love with you.'

'Any woman who falls in love with me, my darling, can be assured of a good time. It may be short, but it will be sweet.'

'Don't get too cocky, Jack. Some good woman will nail you yet.' She smiled and pulled away. 'When are you leaving?'

'Tomorrow. I have to go and face my dear mamma, which will be painful in the extreme.'

'Tomorrow? But you were going to send me a telegram telling me not to come this evening. Does that mean you intended to go without seeing me – without a word?'

'I thought it might be better. I hate goodbyes – they are not my style.'

'Well,' she said, with an effort at brightness, 'it's goodbye now.'

'I suppose it is,' he said.

'Good luck, then,' she said.

She turned towards the door but he reached out and took her arm. 'You can't go like that, Rosie.' He pulled her gently forward, their eyes met and suddenly, dropping her handbag, she pressed herself to him and found his lips. As always, but perhaps now more than ever before, she felt her body quicken under his touch and the longing leap in her like a rekindled flame.

'I'm still free this evening,' he whispered.

She forced herself back and shook her head.

'Now,' he said. 'Stay now. Just for an hour.'

Breathless, she pulled away. 'Stop it, Jack, for God's sake,' she said. 'Don't make it harder than it is.'

He stooped to pick up her bag. 'Here. Cheers, Rosie. I'll see you around some time.'

'Not if I see you first,' she said.

6

The driving rain had stopped but a chill wind was busy among
the trees in the square, stripping the copper-coloured leaves
from the branches and piling them up into small wet drifts.
Rosie walked briskly, drawing the cold fresh air into her lungs,
surprised at her own inner calm. She felt neither happiness nor
unhappiness, only a certain sense of relief that the turmoil was
over, that she could now get on with the business of living her
own life again. It was as if this last meeting with Jack had
snapped the chain of emotion and brought her back to reality.

There had been a kind of beautiful madness in her love for
him, a madness so intense that it had threatened to unbalance
and overwhelm her: now the fever had passed and, purged of
bitterness and anger, she felt as though she had regained
command of her feelings. There were no regrets: the weekend
in Paris alone had been worth whatever price she had paid.
Perhaps she would never love another man as she had loved him
and the feeling would always be there, a secret memory to warm
her heart and mind in the years to come. But she had a rein on
that feeling now and already, so soon, there was a distance
between herself and Jack as if he existed only in the past and
had no place in the present or the future: as if to confirm this,
she slid the amethyst ring from her finger and put it into her
purse.

Reality came into even sharper focus when she boarded a No.
29 bus in Tottenham Court Road and made her way upstairs. As
she settled in her seat she began to turn her mind to the tasks
ahead. Check the stocks for the new shop. See a contact about a
supply of surplus condensed milk. Check with Mr Milton about
the posters. Go to see Nellie Wallace again just to make
sure that she understood the arrangements for the opening.
Check that there were enough packets of Carmo Tea to meet the

expected demand. Look into the question of new stair carpet for Napier Avenue. Pay a deposit on the new Raleigh bicycles she planned to buy Eddie and Van for Christmas. Make sure that Eddie's model had dropped handlebars.

'Hi, there, Rosie – how are you?'

She looked up to see the elderly conductor smiling down at her. He was one of her new friends, an active trade unionist and a leading member of her local Labour Party.

She returned the smile. 'Oh, I'm up and down like Tower Bridge, Charlie. Can't complain.'

'No point in complaining, is there?' he said cheerfully. 'Where do you want to go, Rosie?'

'Green Lanes. The Salisbury pub.'

He took the money, punched out a ticket and, as he handed it to her, he lowered his voice to a confidential whisper: 'Did you hear about Morton Goldie?'

'I heard that he'd resigned from the Council.'

'No, no. Worse than that. He's done for himself. Put his head in the gas-oven.'

'Oh, dear God!' She put a hand to her forehead, appalled by this news.

'Yes, it's terrible,' said the conductor. 'I mean, I never had much time for the old sod, but you wouldn't wish that on your worst enemy, would you?'

She shook her head, trying to wipe from her mind a sudden picture of the sharp-eyed, dapper Mr Goldie bringing round the ice-creams on that hot summer day at the laundry, exhorting the girls to eat them before they melted. It was hard to remember that she had once hated this strange, sad man.

'Are you going to stand for Council, Rosie?' asked Charlie.

'I'm not sure,' she said. 'Ken Colson keeps on to me about it. The trouble is – I don't know anything about politics.'

'Of course you do,' he said scornfully. 'It's about getting rid of the slums, giving the kids some decent schooling, getting people a decent wage so that they don't have to go hungry, getting rid of rickets – that's what it is all about in Tottenham, Rosie, and nobody knows more about it than you.'

'Maybe,' she said doubtfully. 'I understand those things. But when they start talking about socialism, I'm lost. I don't know what it means.'

He left her to collect some fares and when he returned he pressed a small tattered piece of paper into her hand. 'I don't know much about what they call socialism either, Rosie. The Labour Party, the Independent Labour Party, the Socialist Party of Great Britain, the Communist Party – there are more varieties than I've had hot dinners. When you get a minute, read that bit of paper. I copied it out years ago and I've carried it with me ever since. It's a quotation from a man called Thomas Jefferson that I found in a pamphlet written by Keir Hardie, the Labour leader.'

'Keir Hardie!' exclaimed Rosie. 'I met him, I met him! I had to go to Parliament – oh, years ago – to see someone and he came up and spoke to me.'

In her mind she saw again the solemn-faced bearded man with the twinkling eyes and the cloth cap who looked so out of place among the other sober-suited MPs. The memory was bitter-sweet for on that day she had been sitting on the terrace at tea with Russell Whitby and, that same evening, in his rooms they had made love. It was her first time and it had been good but she had paid a certain price for, shortly afterwards, she found herself pregnant with Eddie. Would she ever be able to tell the boy – she should tell him – that his real father was not the dead Tommo but the dead Russell Whitby?

She heard the conductor, cutting through her thoughts, an edge of excitement in his voice: 'You met Keir Hardie! He spoke to you? What did he say?'

'Nothing much really. The man I was with was from the government side, a Tory. And Mr Hardie came up and smiled at me and said: "You are a bonnie wee lassie but you are in awful bad company!" Something like that. He was joking, of course.'

'He was a great man,' said Charlie reverently, 'a great man. Sea-green and incorruptible, as they say.' He paused and added; 'Anyway, read that, Rosie. Keir Hardie wrote that if you based your approach to life on those words, you would not go far wrong. Use them as a yardstick, he said. Measure the people you meet and how they behave against them. When you are faced

with a proposal in Council or anywhere else, judge its merits or
faults against those words. It may not work all the time but I
reckon it will see you through.'

'But don't you want it, Charlie?'

'No. I know it by heart. Besides, I'm coming to the end of the
road. I retire in three months and I'm going down to Cornwall
to live with my son.'

She smiled up into the wise, kindly eyes and the
weather-beaten face. Charlie, Mr Milton, Ken Colson, the late
Mr Softley and so many others – what unrecognised wisdom
there was to be found among ordinary people! 'Thanks, Charlie
– and good luck,' she said.

'You're welcome,' he said.

As she walked away from the bus stop in Harringay, Rosie
suddenly caught a glimpse of herself reflected in a shop window.
The morning rain had played havoc with her hair and she
realised that something would have to be done if she was to look
halfway decent for the grand opening of the new store. There
would be no time to have it done unless she acted now and,
following this impulse, she hurried towards Christine's, which
proclaimed itself to be an exclusive salon for ladies, specialising
in the most modern styles.

She paused for a moment to study the photographs in the
window display and the thought came to her that she would
make a change. Why not? She had thick rich hair, she always
thought of it as one of her best features, and a year ago, when
she found that she could afford a visit to the hairdresser, she had
been persuaded to model it on the style made popular by
Florence Boyfield, the musical-comedy star. Jack had expressed
his delight at the result and, mainly to please him, she had kept
the same style. Perhaps this was another reason why she should
make a change.

By a stroke of luck there was no one waiting, and Christine, a
willowy young lady who smelled heavily of perfume and whose
hair was cut in the fashionable Eton crop, ushered Rosie to a
chair with coos of welcome. But when she saw her reflection in
the mirror and, behind that, the reflection of Christine's crop,
Rosie altered her mind.

'I just want it tidied up,' she said. 'A shampoo and set.'

'You don't feel that you'd like a change?' asked Christine.

'Thank you, no,' Rosie said.

After all, she thought, you've changed quite a lot in the past two or three years. Changed inside. That is what matters – not altering your appearance. She knew that she had grown in confidence, she was more sure of herself: she had been bruised by love, she had known setbacks and disappointments but she had come through. And the future, no longer haunted by fear, stretched ahead of her, filled with challenge and excitement.

While she waited for her hair to dry she took out the much-used piece of paper that Charlie had given to her. The words had been copied in neat, copper-plate handwriting and here and there the ink had faded but after two or three readings she managed to piece it together.

Christine had switched on the radio and, in the background, Jack Payne and his orchestra were playing 'The Londonderry Air'. The wistful, haunting tune seemed somehow to provide a counterpoint to the sturdy optimistic lines on the paper. She read:

From the original draft for the American
Declaration of Independence by Thomas
Jefferson (quoted by Keir Hardie)

We hold these truths to be sacred and undeniable; that all men are created equal and independent, that from that equal creation they derive rights inherent and inalienable, among which are the preservation of life, and liberty, and the pursuit of happiness.

She said the words to herself silently. They sounded good, they made her feel good. She liked the bit about all men being created equal and independent and she liked especially the phrase 'pursuit of happiness'. That's right, she thought, that's right. Every human being has the right to be happy. What is the point of life without happiness?

You were a wise man, Mr Jefferson, she told herself and she folded the paper carefully and put it in her purse.

EPILOGUE

Almost two years later, in the early days of summer, Rosie found herself in Woodlands Park, in her special place beneath the shade of the plane trees with their fresh green leaves. So much, so much had happened since that day when Jack had gone out of her life.

She thought of him less often these days but the memory of their times together still lay within her and, at moments, that memory would sharpen like a pain. No one had – or could – replace him, although her friendship with Ken Colson had developed to a point of constant companionship. Together they organised the Tottenham Works Committee which had arranged support for the abortive General Strike and they were regarded now as two of the emerging leaders of the local movement. Rosie was a councillor, having swept to victory, as predicted, by a massive majority. She still found it a nerve-racking experience to address the Council or to speak from a platform to a public meeting, but she was improving all the time. There had been hints, no more, that she should stand as candidate for Parliament at the next General Election.

Carmo Ltd had gone from strength to strength and was still growing at an exhilarating pace. The first shop at Edgware had opened to sensational crowds and equally sensational business, providing a model for others. Since then they had opened stores in Chingford, Morden, Lewisham, Finchley, Fulham and Acton and a dozen more were in the pipeline. Their success had attracted several offers for the firm, all of which had been refused; nevertheless, these were signs of a growing respect for Carmo in financial and business circles. The days of the markets and the barrows were behind them, remembered with nostalgic affection but gone never to return.

There had been disasters too, as well as triumphs, like a fire that had destroyed a new Carmo store at Croydon and an attempt to set up a division to retail clothes which had been a spectacular failure and cost them dear. But at least from this experiment they had learned a valuable lesson – to stick to the type of business they knew and understood.

Inevitably, their personal lives had been marked by both setbacks and changes. Harry Daines, her unwelcome cousin from Canada, had been caught in the act of robbery with violence and was serving a sentence of three years with hard labour. Bennie, Mark's brother, had also spent time in prison, six months for incitement to mutiny; he had emerged a more convinced communist than ever and was now a full-time secretary for a left-wing trade-union organisation called the Minority Movement.

Debbie, his sister, on the rebound from Jack Cameron's defection, had married a wealthy German garment manufacturer and gone to live in Frankfurt. Their mother now lived with Mark, a frail, bewildered woman who looked old beyond her years. In a few weeks Mark himself was due to marry Irene Green, and had booked the Stoke Newington Town Hall for a grand reception. The formidable Irene was now a director of Carmo, with overall responsibility for management of the stores.

Then there was Jim, the surprising Mr Lightblow, who had changed out of all recognition since his solemn days as a bank cashier. He had shed his sombre image and, although he still provided the financial acumen and thrust that drove the business forward, he had emerged as a bit of a blade, a man who liked a day at the races, the modern theatre (in particular, the much-abused plays of the young Noël Coward), and meals in expensive restaurants. He had just bought himself a new Austin Seven motor-car, with a roof that rolled back.

Nell, who now worked full-time for Rosie, had become one of the family and was more of a friend and confidante than a housekeeper. She and Tiny Christmas, who was now Transport Manager of Carmo, with a fleet of ten trucks and drivers and three cars under his command, were said to be courting. They were a well-matched couple in size and temperament but, so far at least, Nell had resisted the pull of marriage.

'He's all right, one of the best,' she had confided to Rosie, 'but he'll keep. Men are like whisky, they get better as they get older.'

As the thoughts and memories tumbled through her mind, Rosie left the park and headed for home. Tonight was a special occasion, for she was taking Van and Eddie to London to the New Gallery Cinema to see Al Jolson in the first talking picture, *The Jazz Singer*.

Talking pictures, she thought. This is a new age, the world is moving so fast, it is hard to keep up. It is almost ten years since Tommo died, killed in Flanders. What will the next ten years be like – what will they bring?

As she moved through the familiar streets she saw around her the same semi-slums that she had known since childhood. One tenement block was being pulled down to make way for new council housing but otherwise little had changed. A group of children with the white peaky faces of city dwellers were playing a game of 'Release', chasing and yelling at each other. On the fringes, watching, Rosie saw a young girl who bore the unmistakable signs of rickets and she rebuked herself sternly:

'Don't you get complacent, Rosie Carr. All right, you've come through the worst. But don't ever forget what the worst is like. There's a lot of fighting and working to do yet. Life, liberty, the pursuit of happiness aren't just words on a bit of paper, and they are not just for you and your children. They are for everyone and don't you ever forget that, my girl!'